THE WARNING

Smoke drew Max to the altar piled with statues, toys and candles they had passed on the way up. Spilled candles ignited cigarette packs, money and plastic, starting a dozen small fires. Max took a step toward the altar, stopped, suddenly chilled.

The altar's Kali statue moved. Blue skin shimmering in the flickering light, skull necklace swinging, skirt of severed arms exposing her thighs, the statue side-stepped through the clutter of baby and animal dolls dressed in homemade patchwork clothing. With each step, the statue grew, until it stood as tall as Max atop the altar. Looking down on Max, Kali smiled, flicked her tongue out at him. In her eyes, Max saw the sign on the wall he had touched.

The cracked wall behind the altar burst apart. A tall, naked, muscular black man pushed through the wreckage, a body under each arm. The ruined eyes and chest hole of the corpse the stranger carried under one arm declared its undead loyalty to Rithisak. The twitching, bleeding Asian man under the stranger's other arm wailed and pleaded in the Khmer tongue Max had heard earlier in the evening. He did not need a translator to understand the dying man's plea.

Max brought the shotgun up. The Beast screamed. Max fired twice, peppering the walls and altar with shot. The Kali figure twirled, hissed, eyes blazing. The tall man, his body untouched by the pellet spray, threw the corpses down at Kali's feet, distracting her.

"You are at a crossroads," the man said, embracing Kali from behind as she scooped out Rithisak's compound from the corpse's eyes and chest hole and consumed it. "Choose carefully."

THE BEAST THAT WAS MAX

Gerard Houarner

LEISURE BOOKS NEW YORK CITY

For Dave Barnett,
who believed and took a chance. . . .

A LEISURE BOOK®

June 2001

Published by

Dorchester Publishing Co., Inc.
276 Fifth Avenue
New York, NY 10001

ISBN 0-8439-4881-7

The name "Leisure Books" and the stylized "L" with design are trademarks of Dorchester Publishing Co., Inc.

Printed in the United States of America.

Visit us on the web at www.dorchesterpub.com.

THE BEAST THAT WAS MAX

Part One

To Dance Like Mist in Moonlight

When Max pulled up to the corner of Lisbon Place and South Moshulu Parkway, Lee came out of the building entrance alone. That was not part of the plan. Max took a deep breath, fought through the sluggishness of a sated predator, and raised himself to his killer's edge.

The Beast within him rumbled, its suspicion dulled by the evening's pleasure. Still drunk on blood and pain, the Beast rolled over Max's memories of their fresh excesses and barely acknowledged Max's alarm or its cause.

Max put the Lincoln Town Car in neutral, turned off the headlights, and stepped out into the brisk early-April air. He put his hand on the Ruger in the back holster under his old French surplus motorcycle duster and scanned for an ambush. A half-dozen eight- to twelve-year-olds played under a set of lit ground-floor windows. Locals hurried past, burdened with bags or focused on their destination, taking no notice of him or Lee. Spiced meat and pizza scented the breeze. Latin and hip-hop music melted into the rhythm of passing cars and buses, children's voices, TV commercials. Ordinary stimuli, he decided.

The roofline and darkened building windows drew Max's attention, along with the cars parked along the street, then the buildings to either side and across the wide avenue, where they were obscured by gloom and budding trees. Lee waved, as if to distract him. Max's heart beat quicker, and the Beast pricked its inner ears. The avenue provided long lines of sight, but neither Max nor the Beast caught the sense of watchers behind cars or trees targeting them. The Beast resumed its slumber. Sensitive to the terror of prey, Max felt something was going wrong, that he was slipping into danger. But there was no sense of another predator's focus. At least, not yet.

Without a clear target for his suspicion, Max let his hand fall from the gun. He drifted toward the trunk, checked the curb and roadbed for blood. The seals were good. And, of course, there were no stifled moans or cries for help coming from under the hood.

Lee held both hands open and out as he closed the distance between them. Max nodded his head, acknowledging Lee picking up on his discomfort. Lee's weathered face, surprising Max with the age folded into its terrain, brightened at Max's acceptance. The man's army fatigue jacket flapped in a gust, showing the slight paunch covered by a skull T-shirt and the unbelted waist of a pair of black jeans. No weapons showed.

Before Lee could speak, Max leaned back on the Lincoln, pressed his hands against the cool metal, and asked, "Where is she?"

"Change of plans," Lee said, joining Max in leaning up against the car. "We have to pick her up."

"I have my own plans. I need to get her done, then dump the bodies."

Lee jumped off the Lincoln, glanced at the trunk, paced three steps back and forth in front of Max. "Dump the bodies? What bodies? What do you mean, get her done?"

Max went to the back, checked for anyone nearby, opened the trunk. A stench rose out of the car.

Lee stared, coughed. "Damn, Max. You were going to put her in there?"

"Of course. After I killed her. I was going to have her get in the back with you, behind the front passenger seat. We were going to take a ride on the Saw Mill River Parkway. I was going to reach across and put a round in her head when we got off on the Tuckahoe exit. You were going to help me get rid of the bodies."

Lee closed the trunk for Max. "But you're not supposed to kill her. And you're sure as hell not supposed to do that shit to her," he said, waving a hand at the back of the car. "What the hell, are you having a South America flashback or something? We're not in Guatemala anymore. You're supposed to take her to Omari's safe house and protect her."

Max froze. The Beast hissed. "What?"

"Weren't you briefed? Aw, fuck," Lee said, stamping his foot and shoving his hands into the jacket side pockets. "They set me up. They didn't want to tell you themselves, so they put me up to do it. Goddamn, I hate when they do that shit."

"I'm not a guard."

"Yeah, I noticed. But you're all they have left." He

stopped in front of Max. "The FBI's being a bitch over the World Trade Center thing, and the Russian mob's acting like they know how to fix and launch the missiles they stole. The President's in town for an international summit, so there go the best of the locals. The NSA is going through an identity crisis trying to find a new Great Satan, so it's best not to attract their attention right now. The best security team available is a couple of freelancers in town catching Broadway shows, and the pick of third-world embassy guards."

"You do it."

"With my schedule? You see I'm working as a runner. The regular guy got popped. All we found in his car were a pair of eyes and a heart on the front seat. And a shitload of blood. Figured the organs and blood belonged to him, since that kind of action isn't in his profile. Just what we need in the middle of all this: a goddam human sacrifice." Lee glanced at the trunk and waved exhaust fumes away. "I have another hand-off tonight, then an Air Force flight out of Plattsburgh. Got an insertion into Bosnia, though I'm not sure if I'm supposed to bury bodies or dig them up."

Max watched a dented delivery van go by on the other side of the Grand Concourse. "I'm not baby-sitting meat," he said, trying to catch telltale antennae sticking out from the undercarriage.

"Yeah, well, I'm not the one to talk to. Come on, let's dump the shit in the trunk and get going." Lee headed for the passenger side of the Town Car. "Hey, I don't mean to get personal, but is this guy the girl's boyfriend, or are you, like, switch-hitting these days? Should I worry about turning my back on you?" Lee's smirk showed teeth like thorns, sharp enough to pierce.

Max closed his eyes. The Beast rose to challenge Lee's taunt, but Max assuaged its rage with memories of work performed with the operative in the hidden arenas of Southeast Asia, South America, Eastern Europe during the Warsaw Pact days. Blood spatter and screams filled his head. The Beast remembered, growled, slinked back to its nest of pain.

Max sympathized with the Beast's caution. He preferred working alone, keeping as little contact as possible with the people who contracted his services. But tactical and political imperatives sometimes demanded partnerships. Almost always, he felt more endangered by the people he worked with than by the opposition, precisely because of the kind of chaos unfolding around him. Often, driven by the Beast or by his own judgment, he had eliminated his team members along with targets because they had provoked his inner demon, or simply to ensure his own survival. Lee, in his prime as good as any Max had ever witnessed, reminded Max of himself. Calm in the face of obstacles, he passed no judgments on assignments and never let personal preferences, agendas, or desires interfere with the work. He was consistent, a rock limited only by the frailty of his human body, and the darkness writhing in the crevices of his face. He trusted Lee more than anyone else involved in their kind of work.

Which did not prevent him from scanning the street one last time when he opened his eyes, got up from the car, and slowly walked to the driver's-side door.

"He belongs to the twins," Max said, at last answering Lee's good-natured taunt.

"Looks like he died a happy man."

"But I don't think he was happy to die."

"Still cleaning up after them?" Lee asked, trying the handle on his side of the car. It was locked. He gave Max a quizzical look, picked up on his countersurveillance routine, and joined Max in studying the vicinity.

The area still felt secure. Max let himself be drawn to the children play-fighting, dancing, showing each other moves learned from video games and TV wrestlers. He envied their boundless energy, the innocence cocooning the darkness within them. He had always had an abundance of the first, though during the past decade the Beast had provided him, through its madness and abandon, with more of the prowess he had taken for granted in his younger days.

Innocence was foreign to him. He had lived another kind of life when he was their age. Now, when the Beast was not pacing in the cage of his mind, he wondered what it would have been like to be innocent, to be as vulnerable, and as ignorant of vulnerability, as children, his targets, or his victims.

Max hesitated before opening his door, let his gaze linger on Lee. In contrast to the youngsters, he looked even older than Max remembered. The reality saddened Max. The darkness Lee harbored was wearing him out. The killing and torture and agony he had witnessed, the atrocities he had performed, clouded his eyes, haunted his expressions. Time itself, as if in punishment, had slowed him, dulled his senses, sapped his strength. The shreds of his youthful innocence still ran through him, but instead of infusing him with vigor and charm, the vestiges of his early life served only to expose his fragility. He was no longer in his prime.

Max caught himself. Of course, time had worn him down, as well. The hard, fast current of years had run through them both, ripping youth and its blessings from their grasp. Time was part of the bond Max shared with Lee. With it had come the trust built on shared hunts and kills. The other part of the bond, for Max, was the piece of himself he saw in Lee, the man he might have been without the Beast. He saw that man on the other side of the Lincoln: weak, flawed, crippled by the conflict between needs and appetites.

The bond, he was certain, ran both ways. Lee also looked at him as the model of a man he might have been: a stronger man, if only his gifts and appetites were as terrible and voracious as Max's, if only his human needs did not war with his dark nature. Not even Lee knew about the Beast. For Lee, Max's strength, talents, and hungers were unusual, but mortal. Max understood that his image to Lee was a man who carried himself with the self-reliance of a pure predator. Max, and even the Beast, found cruel gratification in their role as the occasional companion Lee shared a kill with, admired, envied. Hated.

It was the Beast within him that separated Max from Lee, and from everyone else in the world except, perhaps, for the twins. The Beast filled Max with power, obliterating the desire, space, and interest to build stronger connections with his surroundings. Power protected him from time's ravages, made him feel he belonged to something greater than the meat of his body. The Beast was the vision of order and meaning in his existence; the luck protecting him from the consequences of his acts, contracted and personal; the comfort, cold and savage, in the lonely midnight hours between his hunger's satiation and the roaring, all-consuming madness of his appetite.

Pity for Lee and his thorn-tooth smile touched Max. He could never be what Max was. Their masters had chosen well by sending Lee with news of plan changes and foolish assignments. Another messenger might have had to answer to the Beast for the night's deceptions.

The Beast stirred, a jealous companion disturbed by soft sympathy. Its howl sent a shiver through Max, and whetted cruelty's keen edge. Max savored the advantage of his strange legacy. Sympathy evaporated. His mind turned back to Lee's question. He gave Lee a slight smile, showing him more than thorns.

"They're my nieces." Max opened the driver's-side door and got back inside. Best to keep moving, he decided, until he escaped the twisted prank of having to protect instead of kill. Even worse, guard a woman.

"Adopted nieces, Max," Lee shouted through the car window. "Makes all the difference." He tapped the glass.

Max let him in. "Not to me."

Lee gave Max a wink and a leer as he settled into the passenger seat. Over the years, Lee had witnessed Max and the Beast at play. Whether he watched for sadistic, masochistic, or other reasons, Max had never quite understood. But Lee always proved sensitive enough to his own frailties to know to never join in the game. And even though he showed interest in the twins, Max made certain he saw the result of their lovemaking and understood they were a Beast of their own. For all of Lee's talk, Max was sure his comrade knew he would not last ten minutes with the twins. If he pursued them on his own, Max could not, would not, save him. But the talking was cheap enough.

Lee checked the glove compartment for the secured .45 and clips, glanced at the mirrors and the dashboard deck with the readouts from the car's antisurveillance instruments. "To me, it would."

Max glanced at him as he pulled out onto the Grand Concourse service road.

Lee waved a hand. "But you're not me, I know. Fine. I'll help you with the bodies, no problem, but let's make it fast. We're running late, and we can't leave the pickup exposed too long. As a matter of fact, why don't you let the Blood of Killers handle this crap? They worship you, and they love cleaning up this kind of shit."

"I do my own sanitation. Just like I do my own killing. No guard duty."

"I said that when I heard they picked you. He's not the type, I said, unless you want her dead. But you see how it is."

Stopped at a light, Max picked up the car phone. "This is impossible," he said, punching in the number and securing the scrambled satellite signal.

"Yes," said the unfamiliar male voice on the other end of the line.

"Mr. Johnson, or Mr. Tung," Max said. Though the names were his own invention for his two main, anonymous contacts, the operator knew his identity through voice recognition and embedded signal codes. Calling up Max's file, the operator could see which government representatives normally dealt with him.

"Who the hell are they?" Lee asked.

"They are not available at this time."

"The men you call Mr. Happy and Mr. Smiley," Max

17

said to Lee, who rolled his eyes. The light changed. Max followed the traffic flow onto the Saw Mill River Parkway. He spoke into the phone: "Who is available?"

"I can handle your call."

"Who are you?"

"The person handling your call."

The Beast roused itself, bureaucratic insolence catching its interest. In Max's mind, a young, clean-shaven clerk had his head smashed into a screen, a mouse jammed into his mouth, and a keyboard shoved up his ass. "Why am I on this job?"

Clicking keys followed a moment's dead air. "As far as I can see, you aren't. The rendezvous is south of your position, but you're heading north."

"Unavoidable business."

"We are your business."

The Beast roared. Max's grip on the steering wheel tightened. "Do you really know my business? Would you like to find out?"

Lee tapped his thigh. "Max . . ."

The voice on the line wavered. "You were not briefed."

"Not for this."

"Briefing you is not my job—"

"Pulling guard duty isn't mine. I want to speak to someone in charge."

"I—I'm sorry, sir, but there is no one available. And there is no time. You have an operative with you. Let him—"

"Did somebody forget who I am?" Max shouted. "What I do? Do you seriously expect me to carry this assignment out?" Max gunned the gas, weaved through the traffic. The Beast surged through his heart, chased blood through arteries until life's flow burned under his skin.

"You are more than what we use you for," the voice said, finding resolve as electronic beeps accentuated manic key tapping. "You are whatever we need you to be, for whatever we must use you for." It was as if Mr. Johnson had gotten on the phone to admonish him. Max wondered if the operator had reached his normal contact through his computer terminal, and if Mr. Johnson was furiously scripting appropriate responses to the operator's screen.

"None of this makes sense. How come I didn't get to pick my team?"

"There is none. You're solo. The way you like it."

"You people aren't even following your own security protocols. If this is a defensive operation, how can I work without a team?"

"There's a bigger picture, Max. You're used to a role, which you perform to an exceptional degree. But there's a lot going on right now, and everybody has to pitch in."

Max took a deep breath, curbed the Beast, brought the Lincoln down to the speed limit. He focused on the assignment flaws. "What am I supposed to do, not sleep? Who gets the food? Who patrols the perimeter? What if there's an emergency with the target? Security breaches in the setup?"

"We didn't think you slept." Someone laughed in the background.

"Put Mr. Johnson on."

"He's not here."

"Who's coaching you?"

"Is that the problem you're taking up satellite time to resolve?"

"What I want to resolve is an inappropriate allocation

of resources. What I want to point out is that you're sending a killer to protect a target, with no backup or planning or coordination. What I'm telling you is that I feel like you're setting me up, and if you don't tell your superior what the hell's going on and get me off this assignment I'll personally kill the fucking bitch you want me to protect, and then I'll gut the bastards who were going to pick her up, and then I'll send the bunch back to you through the mail in three-by-five envelopes. Postage fucking due." He raised the phone to smash it against the dashboard. The Beast pushed him to sideswipe a passing car and send it crashing into the guardrail.

"Fucking clerks are taking over the world," Lee muttered, looking out the passenger window. "No wonder it's all going to hell." He met Max's gaze, winked. "Don't let them bully you, Max. But don't let them make you do something stupid, either."

The voice on the line settled into a cool, professional tone. "We realize your briefing has been inadequate. However, we know you are flexible enough to adapt to new situations. In addition, you have not been left entirely without resources. The safe house is fully supplied and equipped with electronic security, and the area will be monitored by local agencies for unusual activity. We can divert local assets to you if an emergency arises. And, because of the unusual circumstances, we have just been authorized to convert your assigned safe house to Nowhere House status. That should satisfy all of your concerns. You will not need a team because you will not be found, and there is a low probability of engagement with opposition forces during transport to and from the safe house."

A chill passed through Max. The Beast stopped short.

The Nowhere House was well beyond the wetwork world in which Max traveled. "Who is this woman? Who is after her?"

"It doesn't matter who she is," the voice said, toning down the strained formality of its speech. It was as if Max was communicating with several people at the same time, and he wondered if the man on the other end of the line was somehow channeling various officials and representatives assigned to deal with Max. Or perhaps he was simply mad. "The people after her are amateurs. It's the people she's going to who are important and require reassurance. They know you, even like you and your peculiar talent. They feel their property will be safe in your hands. More important, your presence raises her value. Getting the best to escort her is a sign of her importance, a badge of honor."

The Beast recovered from its momentary surprise and resumed pressuring Max to kill. "I can't do this."

"What's so hard?"

"I've never done what you're asking. I've never had to protect anyone except myself." And the twins, he thought. But they were different. They meant something to him.

"You're an assassin, you know how you would kill her. Anticipate. Though, as I said, it's almost certain you won't see action."

"So I'm wasting my time. The hell with this. You do it."

"If you don't pick up this assignment, you will die."

"You'd terminate our contract over this woman?"

"She is part of a plan. So are you. Changes require consequences. Reparations. Adjustments. Your defiance can serve the plan and sustain the value of what is being done, but only if you are punished."

"You wouldn't dare."

"Why not? Would you dare betray us?"

Max strained to contain the Beast. He wiped the sweat beading on his forehead. The hand holding the phone shook slightly. "She must be a hell of a woman."

"What is your mission status?"

Max grunted as if struck in the gut. "Operational."

"Check your contact for time limitations."

Before Max could reply, the connection was severed. He put the phone back in its cradle.

"Nice job of pulling a briefing out of those assholes," Lee said.

"Thanks," Max said, with more of the Beast's grumble than his own voice.

"So I guess you're not going to tell me shit, either."

"They said I had to check with you about time limitations."

"Let me make a call. Maybe we can buy some wiggle room." Lee took the phone, punched in numbers, spoke in low tones, listened, glanced at Max, cocked an eyebrow, checked his watch, hung up. "Damn. I was hoping to sneak over to City Island and pick up crab legs to go before my next drop. But I really do have to get this Fordham divinity student out of the city before the papal meat boys cut off a few of his heretical parts. Looks like my dinner goes the way of your passengers in the trunk. We're cleared to delay your pickup, but I hope you're not thinking of digging really deep graves."

"No digging."

Lee waited a moment, studying Max as if to gauge his

mood, then pressed on. "Goddamn awesome rating a No-where House deployment, though. Better write down any-thing you want to remember that happened to you over the past forty-eight hours."

"I thought it was twelve."

"You believe government specs? I hung out for a week-end with a team one time before they went inside. Saw them a week later during a Tibetan incursion and they took a shot at me."

Max went over the events of the past week and found nothing worth saving. "There's nothing I need to remem-ber."

"Well, don't forget the protocol and write yourself in-structions on what you have to do once you leave the place, or you're going to be wandering around the South Bronx wondering what the fuck you're supposed to do with your new girlfriend."

"I know what I should to do with her."

"Easy, big fella. You're on company time."

Max pressed the accelerator, wove the Lincoln through the close traffic on the Saw Mill's winding roadway. Horns blared and high beams flashed in his rearview mirror. The Beast was disappointed over the failure of the other driv-ers' nerves. They exited at Tuckahoe, drove through quiet, tree-lined village streets with Colonials, split-levels, and the occasional overblown Tudor or small manor set on neatly trimmed lots. A stand of trees blotted out the lights of the surrounding neighborhood. Max slowed. Another house appeared, tucked among the trees. Max turned onto the gravel driveway, switched off the lights, let the car crawl toward a single lightbulb shining over a side door to a run-down, three-story Victorian. A realtor's weathered

For Sale sign and a construction company's renovation announcement were nailed over a faded movie production poster pasted to the door. Max popped the inside trunk release, cracked the door open.

A dog's barking drifted faintly through the surrounding woods. Cold air stung his lungs as Max got out and took a deep breath of suburban air. He picked out the blood scents of a cat's and an owl's kill, the chemical bites of fertilizer and cleansers, an intoxicating burst of the season's first, fresh growth.

He joined Lee at the back of the Lincoln, raised the hood, grabbed one end of a man's ravaged, naked corpse. Blood and shit stench mingled with the twins' sweet and musky markings, and with the smell of multiple orgasms spilled by all three. Max gritted his teeth, and was puzzled by the touch of jealousy. The Beast yipped with glee. Lee whistled, took hold of the feet, and stumbled along Max as they headed toward a hole in the ground beyond the door.

"Not for nothing, Max, but what's wrong with the traditional incinerator dust-off or swamp dump?"

"At five tomorrow morning, a cement truck is going to pour a foundation in that pit for a house extension. The people buying the property require blood sacrifices to sanctify the ground on which they plan to hold future services. They've done favors for me in the past. This is the least I could do."

"Some housewarming gift."

Two sets of their shadows stretched over the hole: a faint set from the car's inside light left on by Max's open door, and a darker pair set at an angle from the house. They threw the body into the ground and went back for

24

the woman. Max bundled her in the plastic lining the trunk, taking care that none of the blood or gore dribbled out. As they approached the pit again, the body fell out of Lee's hands. He flailed about, trying to hold on to the slick package, but managed only to grab the woman's head by her blond curls. The thin shreds of skin holding the body together snapped and the torso landed with a crackle of gravel. Max scrambled to close off the open end of the package while Lee watched, the head hanging at his side from his fist. As Max crouched, his gaze met the woman's blank stare. The Beast's low rumble of satisfaction vibrated through Max. He smiled into her frozen expression of pain and terror, remembering for the Beast all he had done to shape her final rictus. He scooped up the woman's body before he lost himself in thoughts of the last twists and twitches of her flesh. The wind whistling through budding branches reminded him of the whimper of her dying breath. He threw the body into the hole and headed back to the car.

"You're dripping," he said, pointing to the head's ragged wound.

"Yeah, wouldn't want to ruin the property values for Satanists." Lee went down on one knee and rested the head on the ground, atop the blood droppings. He studied the woman's face, moving the head slightly up and down and from side to side, letting the bulb shed its glow over her face.

Max picked the shovel and flashlight from the trunk, returned, studied the ground for drippings. He gingerly picked up loose loads of stained dirt and gravel and threw them into the hole.

"You know, I've seen things like this all my life," Lee

25

said, staring at the woman. "All over the world. Men, women, kids, animals, some shit nobody could ever figure out what the hell they were supposed to be. Seen others and watched you do the work, and done my own share of it."

Max policed the area around Lee until he was satisfied there was nothing left except for the head. He put the flash beam on Lee for a moment. The Beast sensed weakness as the night bore down on Lee, framing his weary face. He moved the beam to the woman before the urge to kill overcame him. Her eyes seemed to follow him in the play of light and shadow as Lee continued to pivot the head around.

"So what. Come on, I thought you were in a hurry to get back."

"Was she good?" Lee held the head up to his face, peered into her eyes. "Did she give you a thrill?"

"Yes."

"But she didn't want to go like this."

"No."

"You didn't care."

"No."

"You just wanted what you wanted, because you wanted to, and that was it."

"Yes. Same as you. Same as always. What's your point?"

"And it was worth it. No matter how messy or what a pain in the ass it was to clean up after, it's always worth it. It always is."

Max shut off the flashlight, let the blade sink into gravel and dirt with a metallic clink. He knew what was coming, had heard the kind of talk before, in asylums and hospitals, jungle encampments, basements, tunnels, and caves. It was a moment humans seemed to find inescapable, even if the remorse they presented was only a pretense to fool themselves into believing they had feelings of sorrow and regret where there were none, and preserve their place among others and in the world.

"Do you think there's any forgiveness for this?" Lee asked, not taking his gaze away from the woman as he presented her head to Max.

"What's to forgive."

"The pain. The terror."

"Isn't that what life's about?"

Lee brought her head back to level with his. "I don't know, is it?" Her head swung away from him with the momentum of his arm motion. "I think there's more than just pain and terror."

"Yes, there's always appetite."

"Yours?"

"Yes."

"What about hers?" Again, he held her head high, swinging it slightly back and forth.

Max watched the pattern of blood dripping on the ground. He thought the drops formed a rough arrow pointing to him. "Mine was stronger."

"Don't you ever wonder if there's more than that? The game, the killing, the appetite?"

"Like what?"

"Don't you ever feel like you're not human?"

"All the time."

"Do you miss feeling human?"

The head rotated in Lee's grip to face Max. The house light fell against the folds and grooves in her face, exaggerating with shadows the expression locked in her flesh. Her eyes, which Max thought had been looking down, now seemed to rotate under the lacerated brow and glare at him through a hanging eyebrow and loose strands of golden hair.

"What is there to miss?" Max answered through the Beast's mad roar as it rose in outrage to answer the challenge of the dead. "It's better being the hunter than the prey. To feel human is to be prey." He put a hand to his holster, loosened his gun, put his finger on the trigger. The Beast urged him to aim, to put a bullet in the man's head. Its raging voice was louder than the crack of the gunshot Max anticipated. It was louder than a cannon barrage falling short of its target, and threatened to carry him away on winds more terrible than those raised by a stray bombing run laying down arc light on the wrong position.

"You've never been hunted?"

Max raised the Ruger, pointed it at Lee. "No."

Lee smiled, looked to Max. He grinned at the gun. "Shit. You're going to love this job."

Max shifted, fired. The bullet smashed into the dead woman's head. The head jumped in Lee's steady grip, bone and gore spraying from the back of the skull. Blond hair bounced with newfound life. The Beast screamed in frustration at Lee's survival, then roared in triumph as it relived the consummation of her death. But its joy exhausted itself in another moment as it dry-humped memory, and its passion blew away like dust.

"That'll wake the neighbors."

"The trees won't tell." He knew the stand would act as a sound barrier, and he doubted anyone beyond the trees in the village of Tuckahoe knew or remembered what gunfire was like, or would believe it resounding dimly in their haven.

The Beast rattled in his head, demanding hot, wet satisfaction. Max's hunger rose in response, as if he had never touched the woman, never heard her screams, not done the things he had done over the past few hours before meeting Lee.

"Had you going there, didn't I?" Lee asked, getting up and dumping the head in the hole. "Thought I got the fever, didn't you? Broken old man, shaking with the guilts?" Lee's high-pitched laughter drifted to the stars.

Max threw the shovel at him. "You clean the mess up." He put the gun back in the holster, started back to the Lincoln.

"Do you want me to lay some dirt over the bodies so they don't look so obvious?" Lee called back, shovel scraping against gravel.

"Don't bother, the contractor is expecting them. He has a permit to start at dawn, so no one should stumble across them."

Lee carefully looked the ground over, tossed the shovel in the pit, then walked to the house door. He looked at the movie poster and said, "I remember this piece of made-for-TV shit when it came out. They wouldn't know a psycho killer if he bit them in the ass. And I sure as hell felt like biting them after watching that crap." Laughing again, he unscrewed the bulb and threw it toward the grave. "Let the dead rest in peace," he said, sliding into the passenger seat.

Max backed out of driveway, checked the woods on both sides with a small night-vision scope. A car rounded a corner, sped past, leaving a crescendo from Beethoven's

Second Symphony reverberating in its wake.

Max waited until it was gone, turned on the headlights, and headed back toward the city. The Beast would not rest. It roamed the emptiness he created for it in his mind, scraped the walls of the body he kept calm and in control. He did not give the Beast the reins of his self, as he had done in times past, as he did when he hunted. He focused on the mission, on maintaining discipline. He almost let himself smile as he thought of how pleased the latest of his martial teachers, the old Chan woman, would be if she could sense his discipline now. How much greater would her pride be, he wondered, if she knew the nature and powers of the monster that lived inside him? Would she try to kill him, as other masters had done, when they discovered what he truly was? Would he have to kill her when she came for him?

He pulled up behind a black Lexus parked in front of the Buddhist Temple on Albany Crescent off the Deegan. Lee stepped out, went to the car, spoke to the driver. The doors of the Temple cracked opened, revealing a flash of saffron. A group of men and women walked out, mostly Asian, laughing and talking. Lee stood, scanned the buildings and roofline, glanced at Max. Max got out and walked into the group, joined in their laughter as they drifted to the Lexus. Max identified the gathering's leaders as Khmer, immigrant survivors of the Cambodian killing fields.

A whiff of sweet incense accompanied subtle drumming spilling out of the Temple. A huddle of bald, painted heads gathered in the dark slit of the Temple door's opening. By manner, color, and spirit, Max knew them as foreign monks dragged from their isolation to reluctantly play a role in the game being played. The Beast's growl gave sympathetic accompaniment to their desperate, hungry eyes fixed on the Lexus. Max thought it was not the car, nor the superficial Western wealth of the surrounding city, that challenged the discipline of their faith. They were not a threat to the exchange, Max thought, only some its victims. Unlike the immigrants, Max was not certain they would survive.

Lee opened the back door. A woman poured out, graceful, sure, resigned. Max and the Beast catalogued her attributes. Asian but not easily sorted into one of the modern nationalities, as if a primal root of the current subtle genetic divisions had survived millennia of tribalization. Short and slim, dressed in black: beaded slippers, Capri pants, quilted silk jacket with red brocade. Her hair was a jasmine-scented waterfall of midnight oil drawn from the world's heart. Her face was a pale reflection of another world, her lips an oracle, her eyes pits deeper and more deathly than the grave in which he had just dumped two bodies and nearly a third.

Her gaze caught his. She stopped short. Lee bumped into her from behind, shook his head in irritation, became distracted by a young immigrant's insistent whispering. The woman looked Max up and down.

A warning, born from the Beast's instinct, shivered through Max. She smiled.

Vertigo swept Max up in a spinning vortex. Heart pumping madly, stomach lurching, a cold sweat breaking over his skin, Max sank into a slight crouch and let training take over. Through the assault, he checked for gas, a drug-tipped dart, the fading touch from contact poison.

Before he found the source of the attack, the world

31

shifted again and he was lost in a sensory flurry. Perspectives merged and warped until Picasso images of people's faces filled his vision, and the exact same inane snatches of conversation punctuated by empty laughter sounded from different directions, out of synch. Max floated above his body, over the street. The Beast scrambled to hang on to him.

The world settled, but was different. It took a moment for Max to recognize himself standing as the Temple crowd bumped into him, flowed around him, puzzled, disturbed. He viewed himself with curious detachment. He should have shaved that morning, or perhaps his dark beard and close-cropped, black hair stood out more under the garish street light among the clutch of innocents. A breeze picked at his duster, and he noticed his waist was thicker than he thought it should be. His black jeans were dusty, and he automatically reached down to brush himself off.

Touched a firm, round thigh in Capri pants.

From a distance, he heard the Beast roar in protest. And arousal.

He found himself in the body of the woman he was supposed to protect. New feelings crept in a quiet current though his awareness: cold nipples eager for sharper sensation; a hunger between the legs needing to receive rather than deliver passion's stroke; a hollowness in the belly yearning to be filled by a seed's blossoming. Life mingled with the death he always carried close to his heart. He glimpsed a blinding moment of what he was accustomed to snuffing out, and felt himself drowning in its glory. His impulse to kill rose like a plume of fire, and he aimed its power at the tide rising to consume him. But though his rage burned and his appetite demanded fulfilling, there was no killing to be done. His tools—the Beast, his body—did not answer his call.

A woman's laughter washed over him like rain.

Max looked out through alien eyes and searched the real, for something true to use as a weapon.

He stared at himself, reaching for contact with his flesh and the Beast. The remoteness of his own face shocked him, but the plainness of his visage drew him out of his instinctive madness. It was as if another mind, with another set of values, suffused his thoughts, calmed him, showed him a new way to perceive the world.

He studied his face. He was used to seeing it close-up in mirrors as he sometimes applied cosmetics and appliances to preserve the anonymity of his work, or brushed his teeth, or stared at the blood that had been sprayed back at him during the course of his pleasures. His hands—his true hands—fluttered by his sides, thick fingers moving restlessly with the speed and delicacy of a concert pianist. He looked lost. Steps from himself, he felt helpless.

Like a distant shadow, the Beast rose to the vulnerability it sensed across the fading channel of their bond. A shimmering black aura surrounded Max's form, as if the woman possessed special lenses that could pick out the Beast like infrared gun sights sensing body heat. The Beast shaped his true lips into the beginnings of a sneer. But another shade flew across the face, looked out at Max in the woman's body. Smiled.

And in the body in which he found himself, another spirit, ancient, obsessed, flickered like the reflection of something unreal caught in a mirror. Its presence stunned

Max, knocking him off balance as he struggled for control in an alien environment.

She carried her own Beast, though it did not boil with passions as his own did. Rather, it was a piece of something that had once touched her, leaving an imprint like an obscene cave drawing that influenced thought, shaped emotion, fired up drives. Poisoned the well in which her young soul had resided. Tainted the vision through which she perceived the world. Tangled the infant web of power, full of dance and music invoking water and fire, that had been cultivated within her when she was young.

And in the imprint was the residue of power, like a layer of fine, fallen hairs and dead skin. The power was grave cold and resonated with cries of pain and despair. As if answering Max's struggle to understand, a voice rose out of the depths of the woman's memory. Foreign thoughts intruded on his own, weaving understanding from his confusion.

It was the sliver of a victim's spirit left behind in the body, too small to live on its own or exercise control, surviving on the grief of its host. It was the heart of the woman's Beast. Ghost hands swiped at him, phantom teeth snapped. Angry at being murdered, the thing reached out to him because he was alive, because he could still breathe perfumed air and taste spiced meat.

Images of his fresh kill enraged the shade as it recognized him as a murderer, a victimizer. But in the spirit's partial state it was powerless to seek retribution. Its glacial hate, inexorable and endless, bore down on him, sending a shiver of fear and excitement through Max. Immune to his own and even the Beast's rage, its appetite for what it had lost fed on Max's awareness and grew stronger.

The Beast That Was Max

It was as if the soul of one of Max's victims had returned to share the journey of its fate with him. But he had no hand in the cause of this spirit's pain. He was not the murderer of its original house of flesh. The thing did not care. Like the Beast, like Max, it was appetite, and though it did not hunt as Max and the Beast did, it was as capable of rage and destruction if its hunger was not appeased.

Max wondered what pursuing and consuming such a power might be like. Even without the Beast at his call, he wished the full spirit had resided within her, and not as the corrupting reflection of a ghost caught in meat.

But without the Beast's reassuring savagery or the comforting rhythms of his own body, Max's confidence wavered. Separated from his tools and weapons, was he still a hunter, a killer? As whatever he was, a spirit, a soul, a wisp of imagination, could he still find a way to kill a thing accustomed to such an existence?

The woman's voice rose again, offering ways for him to handle the spirit. What he was being offered, he realized, were paths to becoming someone else and forgetting who he truly was.

The hollow, mocking roar of the Beast, itself a memory, offered another way to escape.

Before Max could feel the chill of fear over losing himself to the vengeful spirit, the woman, or in his own killing fury, he was torn out of his exile. The world spun as he landed back in his own body, as if pulled home by an elastic band's tension. A hurricane of sensations and emotions ripped through him, and for a moment he blacked out, overwhelmed by the force of the change. But only for a moment. The Beast rose from unknown depths to envelop him in its strength. His body fit like an old, comfortable coat, and responded willingly, though with a hint of sluggishness, to his will. He was Max again, stumbling, dizzy, skin cold and prickly, but a single weapon once again. One force, out of nature, with a single, insatiable appetite.

The Beast whined in confusion, but quickly snapped with joy, eager to welcome its familiar. Heart racing, Max embraced the monster. The darkness within deepened. People in the Temple group eyed him suspiciously.

"Mani Kalliyan Chea," Lee said, bringing the woman to Max. Closer to Max, Lee whispered, "Straighten out, buddy. You're looking like shit and you're freaking everybody out."

She tilted her head to the side, met his gaze, and gave him the same smile she had given him when he was in her body. The Beast reared, ready to pounce on the challenge. But then it hesitated in its routine headlong pursuit of prey, recognizing something in her. So did Max. Together, they felt the same rush of surprise and excitement in encountering a fellow traveler. Not since Paris, when the twins had captivated him during one of their murderous hungers, had he felt the same conflict between desire, dread, and rage. But the twins had been children, evoking a previously undiscovered and overruling instinct for protection. Seeing himself in them, he had not wanted their young years to be lived like his, alone and unprotected on unforgiving streets.

She was not a child. What she provoked did not fit the assignment parameters. Appetites collided. He did not know whether to kill her or fuck her.

And there was the hint of her inside him: an impression of her sinuous body pressed into the walls of his mind; a warmth permeating his senses, like a lover's body heat smoldering in the bed long after they are gone. Max understood who had smiled at him from his own body.

"This is your guardian angel, Max," Lee said to her as they followed the press of crowd toward the Lincoln.

The Lexus drove off with a squeal of rubber, as if the driver was eager to escape his passenger's presence.

"How did it feel?" Mani said, hips and shoulders swaying, watching him with the barest turn of her head. The sound of her voice resonated in his mind. A part of him was reluctant to let her go. The Beast hissed at the rival connection that had suddenly taken root in Max.

"Like death," he answered.

"And yet you live. Life is a strange paradox, is it not?" She laughed as Lee opened the Lincoln's back door and let her in.

Her body, the kaleidoscopic assault of memories and sensations, the separation from himself, returned in a play of shadows running through his mind. He shook his head to clear it. Something stuck in his mind, a feeling he had never experienced before. Not the web of her power or the remnants of an ancient spirit, but the hint of yet another thread of life and power inside her. Max tried to tease the memory from a mix of images and emotions.

The Temple group surged on, except for one young Asian man who thrust his chest out in front of Max, distracting him. "If anything happens to her, we will hunt you down," he said, with intensity surprising for his youth and stature. A grief-stricken expression crossed his face when he saw Lee close the door behind Mani.

"You won't like what you find," Max said. The boy ran away, tears streaming down his face, before Max could snatch him and break his neck. The Beast howled, frustrated once again. But the Beast's anger did not trouble Max as much as the sense that the boy had been so focused on Mani and whatever ruined emotions lay between them that he had blinded himself to the danger of the rage his provocation had raised.

Max remembered the monks peeking out from the Temple, his own near-loss of self. The woman's power ran deep into those she chose to target. Subtle, brutal, seductive, she had more than one way of conquering. Having survived her direct tests of his strength, he had no intention of falling under her sexual or emotional spell.

Max went to the driver's side and entered the car while Lee covered the area. As soon as he was inside, he turned to the woman and said, "I should kill you for what you did."

"Some add to life, others take away from it," she answered, settling into the backseat. She drew her legs up under her and hugged herself.

"Which do you do?"

"I take away from death."

"Why did you do that thing to me?" Max asked, wanting even more to ask how she had managed the transposition he had just experienced. But what drove him was the need to establish his territory, to warn her off, kill the bond between them she seemed to want to establish. Demanding explanations of how she did what she did only invited and prolonged unwanted contact.

The Beast paced restlessly, crying to vent its lust. She lingered inside him like a perfume. To Max's shock, the Beast seemed to calm down just a bit from his body's memory of her habitation.

Lee dropped into the passenger seat, slammed the door shut, slapped the dashboard twice with impatience. "Do what?" he asked, checking his watch.

"To warn you," Mani said. "And teach you that you cannot always pursue what you want by force, so we may both live to see this episode to its end."

"Are you getting yourself in trouble with her already, Max? Damn, man, just relax, okay? We're going to Mott Haven—149th Street. Take the Deegan to Third Ave. Omari's picked up a city-owned place down there. He leased that nice little factory he had in Brooklyn to a floating club called Painfreak. You ever hear of it?"

Max let the question slide over him.

"Thought you had. They burned the place down the last time the club came to town, that's why I figured you'd know them. I bet Omari's having an orgasm with that upgrade to Nowhere House status. I've been recommending him for higher-level operations status for years. Glad to see he's one of us, now. He deserves everything that's coming to him, the son of a bitch." Lee cackled. "He don't know what he's in for, do he? Fucker should waive his fee for the privilege of having Nowhere House vibe to soak into his walls. You know *his* usual customers. They'll come running once words gets out. It'll be even better than when you do your personal business in one of his places so he can get all that bad spirit and ghost vibe to sell. You never actually met him, right?"

"We never had the pleasure."

"I bet. He does know how to stay out of the line of fire. Until now. But what are friends for, right, Max? Gotta love the guy." Lee turned to the woman. "That's an unusual name you have there, Ms. Kalliyan. You Cambodian?"

"More than you can imagine."

Max pulled out, followed Crescent as it led him away from the highway but closer to its entrance. "What are you?"

"The past trapped in the present to buy the future."

"Whatever," Lee said, giving Max a warning glance and shaking his head.

Max thought he would have to be as vigilant against her as he had to be against her enemies, and his nature.

They rode in silence until the turnoff for the Cross Bronx loomed. The Beast's hunger, sharpened by the stimulation of odd occurrences and provocations, dug into Max with manic pawing. Every shift in the seat from Lee, each glance from Mani, inspired a fresh shiver of suspicion, a new source of threat. Cars coming too close made his hand twitch for a gun. Max meditated, breathing deep, relaxing muscles and thoughts. He fought for a grip on reality, sifting through the Beast's paranoia and his own demanding appetites to discover the real danger lurking on the borders of his awareness.

As if inspired by the dance of headlights and the beat of tires on the road, Lee suddenly broke into a sour bluesy drawl: "I ain't eighteen, but I'm still on a bullet; got my finger on the trigger and I'm gonna pull it." His laughter pitched higher, and he rocked back and forth in his seat. "Oh man," he said at last, sobering, "I need a fucking vacation. Right after this trip to Europe. They're giving me a choice between Angola and Iraqi weapons inspection after this next assignment, but hell no; I need to get away from crazy motherfuckers like you. All this huggermugger, macho intimidating shit is wearing me out. I'm gonna make myself a promise not to kill anything for a week.

See how long I last. Last time it was two weeks in the Yucatán. I think the tequila helped. But I think you two are going to click. Yeah, he hasn't popped you yet, Mani, so I'm thinking you're going to last the night."

"I think so, too," she said.

"I think we're being followed." The words flew out of Max's mouth before he knew he had spoken, propelled by instincts feeding on his experience, Mani's presence and powers, and his memories of being inside her. He let out a long breath as the tension drained from him. Knowing the situation meant he could control it. The Beast relaxed, anticipating prey.

"Bullshit." Lee checked his side-view mirror. "How can you tell one headlight from another?"

"He's right." She looked out the back window at the steel-cradled roadways sweeping around and above them, at the Alexander Hamilton Bridge connecting the Bronx to Manhattan. "Coming in from the West Side. I feel them, too. They know I'm moving, which direction I'm going in. They've picked up my trail."

Lee twisted around to face Mani. "What the hell are you talking about? Who knows you're out in the open?"

"My enemy."

"Come on, lady, cut the crap."

"My captor and former lover—now my enemy because I escaped him."

"Great. Always good to get the full briefing, right, Max? And how is this mook tracking you? You were supposed to be clean at the pick up."

"He's àp thmòp, a sorcerer with roots still in my spirit. He knows I'm in this city because he feels my anticipation of freedom. But it was my display with you, Max, that

41

allowed him to pinpoint me. I am sorry. I acted impulsively, from my hunger. I felt you as a kindred being, and the loneliness . . . my appetite . . ." She put a hand to her forehead and shook her head. "I should have contained myself. Now he knows something of you, as well as my interest in you. He will be jealous, and even more angry at my betrayal."

Lee continued to stare at her for a moment, then settled in his seat. "Right. Max, are we having a psychotic moment or something?"

"She's right about someone coming after us. Don't you trust my instincts after all this time?" At the prospect of bloodshed, the Beast tested Max's control. Sensing potential for a feast, it allowed the flow of Max's controlled breathing to calm it.

Mani sat forward, put a hand over the back of Max's seat. Her fingertips brushed his shoulder. "Your teacher has brought you far along the path of chi kung breathing exercises. The monster in your head responds well. I barely escaped when I was inside you."

"How did you know I was taught by a woman?"

"I was inside you. I know all the women who have touched you."

"Then you know what happens to most of the women I meet."

Mani drew back her hand. "I know what you do to those you desire."

Images from the night's hunt blossomed in the darkness of his mind: a breast stained with blood, a thigh cut to the bone, a dangling eye peering into a place within him Max could not see. "Then don't taunt me."

She sat back, closed her eyes. "I'm not. I can teach you

things. More, much more than I already have."

Lee waved his hands in the air between them. "Excuse me, girls. Can we get back to this supposed tail? How many are with this old boyfriend of yours? What are they driving? What kind of firepower are they carrying? Are they professional, or is this just a family thing?"

Mani shook her head. "I don't know. More than one car, I'm sure, though I don't know what kind. Rithisak's family must be with him—"

"Aha! At last, a name."

"—and many of them worked for Pol Pot's regime, so you may consider them professional."

Lee struck Max's biceps once with the back of his hand. "We probably know them; shit, we worked with enough of the bastards. I can see why the higher-ups weren't too concerned about them. They were pretty good against un-armed civilians, but the Vietnamese sure kicked their asses in a hurry."

"What is Rithisak's power over you?" Max asked, his hands becoming cold at the thought of a repetition of the body exchange. "What did you mean when you said his roots are still inside you?"

Mani slumped in the backseat. "He found me in the countryside, a child, survivor of a village destroyed by beisac, the souls of the murdered risen from hell to con-sume the food of the living," she said, her voice faint, shaky.

"Ghosts?" Lee asked. "How about a Khmer Rouge ex-ecution squad. Or were the Vietnamese dropping napalm left behind during the collapse and withdrawal by that time?"

"My father told the villagers to leave food out as an

offering to the beisac. But it was a hard year and there was nothing to spare. Because my people kept the village apart from the larger world, there were no neighbors to go to for help. And misfortune had been so long between visits that many did not believe they would suffer. My father tried to appease the beisac himself, but his pitiful offerings only angered them. They came. Or they angered the Khmer Rouge by filling their minds with lies about my village. Or they gazed into the souls of Khmer Rouge soldiers and drove them mad with reflections of their own hellish rage. Or maybe my people just ran into some bad luck after a thousand years of peace. However your Western minds want to interpret what happened.

"I saw my mother and father die. My brothers and sisters, friends, even the ox, and the dog, and the pigs. My jacket and pants were still soaked in their blood when Rithisak found me. The screams, I can still hear them today. . . ."

"Why did this sorcerer want you?" Max asked.

"Rithisak was drawn to my village by the plague of beisac. He was studying the ways of those spirits to harness their power. He found my trail, tracked and found me, eager to discover how I had escaped alive. I showed him how I made my spirit small, too small for anyone to notice. It was how my father, the village *kru*, the shaman, taught me to escape the Khmer Rouge—to become like a thing without a soul, rock or deadwood, so no one would think to shoot me because I already seemed dead. My father chose to try to protect the village rather than escape. The others who knew the trick were too frightened by the spirits to remember its casting. They were used to avoiding mortal soldiers, modern machines, not demons. Since I lived with my father's magic, I was used to the terror of rageful spirits."

"Yeah, I can see why you get along so well with Max," Lee said.

Mani ignored him. "Rithisak was impressed by my trick, and fascinated by the tracks the beisac left on my soul as they sniffed and prodded the dead thing I'd become. He offered his protection. I was a young girl with no place in the world. The blood, the screams . . . I'd never been alone before." Mani's hand slid across the window as she looked out at the passing buildings. "I've never been alone." She shook her head. "I had to go with him. But I also felt his power, and I knew he wanted mine. He was hungry, like the beisac. I believed myself clever enough to steal his secrets before he could take mine, and make him my servant. With him by my side, I felt I could go out into the world and survive. I played the tricks a girl thinks will turn the heads of older men. I tried to seduce him.

"He let me believe I was gaining power over him. I exposed my desire, fished for his power. But I discovered he had surrendered nothing of himself to me. I had no hold on him. His desires, his appetites were well protected, and there I was, naked to him in my raw hunger with no place to hide. Nothing more than a small, foolish spirit. I needed him, the pulse of his strength and the calm of his presence, like a poppy addict needs the pipe. I seduced myself. Traded freedom for the illusion of safety. He sank his roots into me, and over time he grew stronger from the pleasure he took from me, and from his use of me as a tool in games with rivals, the government, and drug lords. You've already experienced one of the tricks I learned from him." She straightened, sat up, and shifted her body. The air in the car thickened, the curves of her presence called, tempted, invited.

"Is it getting hot in here?" Lee asked, then turned to Mani, face flushed. "Listen, when I get back and you get settled wherever they're going to put you, you want to get together?"

Max fought with the Beast, found himself losing control. "If you want to live through the night, stop that."

"That was another," she said, relaxing.

Max cracked the window open and turned on the vent fan. The twins also stoked the sexual appetite of their prey before the kill. They had never turned the tactic on him, and after the brush with Mani, he knew he could never control himself or the Beast if they ever toyed with him in similar fashion. He counted both the twins and himself fortunate that they handled their powers responsibly. "Is that how you escaped him?" he asked finally.

"I couldn't seduce him before he showed me how to use my body. He was not so stupid as to teach me skills against which he had no defense."

"Then how did you escape?"

Lee broke in. "Who cares? Are you actually buying any of this bullshit?"

"The only way to find out about who is chasing us is to find out what she believes about him."

Lee thrust his finger at the road ahead. "Let's just get to Omari's, set up the Nowhere House, and let Rithisak wander the South Bronx looking for her."

"He will find me," Mani said with certainty.

Max checked his watch again. "There's still time."

Lee looked out the window at Yankee Stadium passing

by. "You thinking of setting up an ambush? Why not just race them to the house."

"We might have to face them anyway. If they can track her outside the Nowhere House, they could wait in the neighborhood until we go out to deliver her to the next pickup." The Beast screamed. "Besides, I'm interested in blood. . . ."

Mani shifted again in the backseat, stretching her arms and back. Max caught her in the rearview mirror staring, lips parted, at the back of his head.

Lee waved a thumb in her direction. "What about her safety? Shouldn't we call for backup?"

"She won't be in danger." The Beast's cry was a steady siren in his head.

"No, unless we both get killed."

They looked at each other. Lee laughed. Max smiled.

The smile evaporated when he glanced at Mani. Blank spaces in her story teased him. Balancing himself between the control of his breathing and the Beast's rage, he said, "The question. You never answered it. How did you get away? What weaknesses did you exploit?"

"His pride."

"Shit, I get kicked in my pride every day," Lee said, reaching under the seat and pulling out a gun bag. "You have more than this in the glove compartment, I hope," he said to Max, pulling out a Remington auto shotgun.

"The trunk, under the panels. We need specifics, Mani."

"He believes he's invulnerable."

"Trust me, that's a good thing if you keep getting kicked in your pride," Lee said, loading shells into the Remington.

"Every year I've been with him, he's grown stronger. His enemies fall, his influence grows. Even in defeat, he finds ways to win. Whether it's a curse whose consequence he turns back on its sender, or a ruined drug deal he gives up to government officials for favors, or a weapons shipment he loses to an enemy of his enemy, he always wins."

A grudging admiration for Rithisak's skills and good fortune grew in Max. He was a challenge, a test of Max's own skills. He would be fine prey.

He caught Mani's gaze in the mirror, read the eagerness to please him in her expression. And something else. A prickling sensation rose along the back of his neck.

"*Is* he invulnerable?" he asked.

A smile flickered across her face. A light glimmered in her eyes. "No."

"How did you use this pride of his?"

"I submitted, gave him what he wanted. I showed him what my father taught me, and served him in every plot he wove. I became his favorite tool."

Lee chuckled. "You sucked his dick until it was dry, I'm betting. I hate to tell you that's not what we had in mind."

"In working for him I worked with the men he dealt with, his allies and enemies. I chose among them, offering what they wanted. Me. Magic. Money. Treasures. And as my skill in seduction grew, I discovered Rithisak's true pleasures—how much young ginger and how many dried chilies to put in his dishes, what song relaxes him, which dance he prefers to see before he drifts away to sleep and dream. One night I danced and sang him to sleep, and then I stole the Sacred Sword he himself stole during the Lon Nol coup d'état, a thing one of my Cambodian benefactors wanted. I took film canisters of Cambodian massacres another desired, and records of drug transport routes, bank accounts, and Western dealers. These things bought me safe passage to the West, a new identity, and money.

"I just arrived in this country, but it's no different than the one I left. They pass me along, from one to another, eager to use me. They pretend to be strong, but I see their weaknesses. The monks' desire for sacred wisdom is as bright as their robes. The Japanese businessmen's lust for competitive advantages sticks out in their pants like raised canes. The refugees, with their wail for justice, are like children crying at the breast of their dead mother. They're blind to everything except what they want. They're not as subtle or guarded as Rithisak, but their hunger is just like his. Just like the beisac. It was different in my village, in the time long ago before the dead came with their craving for our food."

As her words rolled over him, Max caught a glimpse of his own vulnerability in Mani's abandonment of Rithisak. What would happen if he lost his own tool, the heart of his personal empire, the Beast? Mani had already shown him, whether she meant to or not. The Beast barked a protest, as honest as raw appetite. Max preferred not to dwell on the possibility, no matter how unlikely.

"Chilies and ginger?" Lee said. "Guess he didn't want a whole hell of a lot." He hesitated as he put the last shell in the shotgun, and a stunned expression crossed his face. He glanced at Max, twitching an eyebrow as a signal. "I can see why this guy is coming after you so heavy, you being his main moneymaker. Must be tough, having people wanting something out of you all the time." He placed the shotgun upright in a custom caddy between the two front seats, opened the glove compartment, took out the gun, and began to inspect it. "Hey, you'll have to excuse me for being so fucking stupid, but I can't figure out how if he had his claws into you on this deep spiritual level," he said, half mumbling, sliding out the clip and chambered round and studying the firing mechanism with fierce intensity, "and you couldn't break out of this hard-on jones for the guy for all these years, what changed? I mean, you're telling us about this slick plan of yours to get away, but how did you get him out of your system to walk out in the first place? Was it a Tina Turner thing—did he abuse you until you broke? Did you invent an antidote for his voodoo on you?" He put the clip back in the gun, chambered a round, turned around in his seat, and aimed at her head. "Or are you still hooked on him? Is this all some kind of game you assholes are running on our bosses, where Max and I are supposed to take a fall?"

Mani closed her eyes and arched her back, exposing her throat. The curves of her body shifted again, calling.

Her erotic vulnerability drew Max's gaze from the road. He soothed the Beast with his breathing, and wished he could do the same for himself.

Lee frowned, pursed his lips. He thrust the gun in her direction. "If you really wanted to get away from him, you could've killed the son of a bitch. It would've saved all of us a lot of trouble."

Mani was silent.

"Max?" Lee asked. "How much of this miscommunication crap we've been getting is bureaucratic bullshit, and how much of it is a plan to fuck us?"

The edge to Lee's voice brought Max into focus. He followed his partner's reasoning with his own intimate knowledge of their charge. He knew from the moment he met Mani that at the end of her seductive lure lay a killer.

The village massacre had left little for Rithisak to teach her about slaughter, and it was in fact her murderous self he found most enticing. Killing for her freedom would not have been a problem for Mani. The source of her entrapment lay elsewhere.

Though he could not quite bring himself to believe in spirits and ghosts, the reality of his own Beast and the twins' powers, and Mani's mind-switch trick, let his instincts overcome doubt for the moment. The beisac had tainted her, leaving the residue of a hateful thing resonating within her. But there was a hunger inside her that did not belong to the beisac.

The death of her childhood world had left her empty. Her savior Rithisak filled it. Her need for that fulfillment was as strong and real as it was the day she became small and let the village's blood spill over her. If the roots of Rithisak's worldly power remained in her, the roots of her emotional stability were still sunk deep in him.

If she could have escaped or killed him, she would have done it long ago. She had found another way to free herself.

"She can leave him because his roots are still in her," Max said. "She has a part of him with her." The blinding glimpse of the life in her came back to him. He blinked, eyes stinging. From the glare of oncoming headlights, he was certain.

"Yes," Mani said. Her voice was a breeze lost in bare branches. In the shadows of the backseat, she was so small she was almost invisible. No wonder the Khmer Rouge, or the beisac, had missed her.

But the Beast had her fixed. Max knew exactly where she was, what she was.

51

"I remember," Max said. "All the things I felt and saw in you, I remember. You gave him what he wanted. You were afraid he was going to kill you after he got it, weren't you? That's why you held out, spent so much time away from him doing his work, finding other ways to be useful to him. But in the end, when you realized you could use his need to your advantage, you gave in. That's when you went ahead with your escape plan. And that's why he wants you so badly. Why you could bargain for your freedom. You're carrying his baby."

Lee smirked. "Bingo, we have a winner," he said. "Fuck pride and all that shit."

"I taught him about life, to want a child," Mani said vehemently. Her legs and arms whipped around as she sat up and filled the backseat with her anger. "Before me, he knew nothing of the living world. It was always the dead he wanted, the dead he could control. He tracked me after the massacre because he thought he'd find something in a survivor to dominate the beisac. I showed him what I knew, but it was not enough. My father's way was life; that's the way I was born into. That's what I had to offer. But he corrupted me, turned me into what I am."

"The beisac changed you before he found you," Max said, dismissing her justifications with a wave of his hand. "Now you're getting what you need from your bond with his child."

"It's not the same," Mani said, collapsing into a corner like a broken spider drawn in on itself. "I still feel so alone. . . ."

"The child is enough to fill your emptiness and let you run. You can live without Rithisak, as long as you keep his child with you." Max glanced at Mani in the rearview mirror. In her excitement, she had lost her self-control and her scent filled the car. He smelled a boy. "But Rithisak's son is *his* future, *his* legacy, and he can't let that go. That's the real reason he's coming after you."

"A son," Mani said, looking down at her belly and rubbing it. "Less than a month old, and already you know. I wish you could've been the father."

"I don't want a child any more than you do. But you needed one, for your freedom. Are you going to make him your tool, as Rithisak made you his?"

Mani frowned. Her eyes blazed, and rage colored her face. The hunger of the dead reached out for him, tried to snatch him as it had in the street and pull him into her. But this time he was not distracted by her allure. He felt the cold of the grave creep through his flesh, the tug of bony fingers on his heart. His own rage answered, and the Beast's. Their joint roar filled Max's mind and broke her grasp on him. Her eyes widened, her lips parted. As the cry carried on, she shuddered, looked away, and put a hand up between them.

"I wanted the baby, too," she said, a tremor in her voice. "But not for Rithisak to use like me. I wanted one on my terms, to serve the living, as my father did, and as he wanted me to do. I need him, yes. I may not be able to let him go if he chooses to leave me when his time comes. But by then there may be someone else to fill me." She turned back to Max, gave him the slightest of smiles. "Or if not, the boy may care more for his mother than for the world's mysteries and dangers." She widened her smile, allowing a thin line of teeth to show.

"Damn, I must be getting old," Lee said, pushing Mani with his free hand back into the seat. "I almost missed *her* having an angle. I really do need a fucking vacation."

The Beast volunteered to toss her out of the moving car. Max held its reins tight, using its energy to fuel his racing thoughts. Lee's comment about the show of respect and honor in having someone important escort her came back to him. She was a trophy, being passed through various circles of power in a kind of ceremony. Max's superiors respected her power and what she was turning over to them. They were appeasing her with a ritual show of their strength. And at the same time, they were displaying their contempt for Rithisak. Without his favored weapon, wandering out of his Asian jungle element and into a Western urban sprawl, no one believed he had a chance to take her back. They were taunting him. And more.

They were luring Rithisak into a trap, using Mani and the child, and Max, to kill him. And once Rithisak was dead, the people Max worked for could use Mani as another weapon in their wars, controlling her through the child who had allowed her to escape Rithisak in the first place. But as Mani had shown, she had talents against which his superiors had no defense. A dangerous game was unfolding, with players holding different views of reality, conflicting sets of rules and objectives. And at the heart of it all, an unborn child grew in a mother's belly, its potential for power and control already claimed by three parties.

For once, he had a window on the machinations behind his assignment. He found no comfort in the view. Mani and his superiors were getting both more and less than what they had bargained for, which suited Max as long as he was not in immediate danger. He did not care if Mani had placed herself and her baby into circumstances worse than Rithisak's service. He had killed enough of her type for his pleasure; guilt had never been his burden to bear. If he had met her under different circumstances, she and her child would have known a great deal more pain before dying. But if his superiors had underestimated Mani, then they might have done the same with Rithisak.

It was no wonder neither he nor Lee had been fully briefed. The more he knew about the situation, the less certain and stable it became.

Max gripped the wheel of the Lincoln tight as he took the Willis Avenue exit off the Deegan. People not getting what they bargained for were not his problem. Surviving the night was.

Lee directed them away from the Mitchell Houses, across Bruckner Boulevard and under the ramp to the Triboro Bridge. They skirted freight rails and empty lots until they found a short, lonely, warehouse-lined block that ended on the water. Riker's Island prison lights, small and hard, shined in the distance. There was no one on the surrounding streets, and the windows were dark. Metal trash bins were clustered under a recessed loading dock, its rolling security door shut and locked. Across the street, the rickety frame of a fire escape stair clung to a six-story factory building like the skeleton of an extinct dinosaur to a mountainside. The breeze off the water gently herded paper and cardboard from one side of the street to the other.

Max glanced at Lee, who confirmed the place was clear with a nod of the head. Max opened the window, shot the two streetlights out with the Ruger as they cruised to the dead end. He popped the trunk open and released the front hood, then stepped out. Lee directed Mani out with the shotgun in one hand, the .45 in the other.

Max walked around and put a hand over the .45 in Lee's hand. "I don't think she's a threat."

Lee lowered his weapons. "Sorry. For a minute there I forgot who the hell we're supposed to be protecting." He went to the trunk and began unpacking weapons. "Damn, you've even got mines in here," he said, with a slight hush of awe.

"You have to arm them," Max said.

"No shit."

Max sidled up against Mani, who leaned back against the car. The dim light from the car's ceiling lamp spilled out the side window to carve her hips and narrow waist out of the night. She raised a hand to her head, accidentally bumping Max's arm. Heat prickled his skin beneath where she had touched his duster. He grunted, acknowledging her attempt to entice him.

"How can he hurt us?" he asked, poking her shoulder roughly with his index finger, trying to intimidate her. Muscle yielded only slightly.

"The same way I can. Magic."

"We're not going to start the mumbo jumbo again, are we?" Lee called out from the rear. "How about the real stuff. You wouldn't be holding out on us again, would you?" He stepped out, brought a flashlight beam to bear on her face. "Does this old boyfriend have any surprise backers? Professional reserves? Maybe someone inside our operations looking to make his bones on us?"

"No. He doesn't do things the way you people do. He only works with people he knows, or controls." Mani lowered her head, shivered. "He's catching up to us. Two,

56

three, maybe four cars. There don't seem to be many people."

Her frown sent a warning ripple through Max. Things were happening even she could not predict, and she had been Rithisak's agent for years. "Lee," Max said, holding out a hand to cut the beam off. "Set the mines up, then pick your high ground. Make sure you have an escape route. Take a headset, channel three. I'll do the remote crossfire and take the grenades."

Lee turned the off flashlight, glanced over his shoulder as a truck rumbled by on the avenue, walked up to Max. "I feel like I'm putting up a coffee shop for Mormons in Utah. Now our tail is up to four cars and just a few guys. It doesn't add up. You really believe he's tracking her through this spirit mumbo jumbo?"

"If you don't trust my instincts, trust the things you've seen with me that you can't explain."

"Yeah, sure, we've been through weird shit." Lee pointed the flashlight at Mani's face. "But she's been yanking our chain all night. You don't think she's still setting us up? You trust her?"

"No, to both."

"Then are we doing the right thing, trying to ambush her old man? Maybe she'll tip him off."

Max leaned into Lee. "Would it matter if she did?"

Lee hesitated, then laughed. "Damn, you really don't give a shit."

"At worst, how much of a problem can the opposition be?" Max took the flashlight and swept it like a pointer at the open end of the street.

Lee backed away. "Right. A bunch of half-assed guerrillas lost in the big city. Cheap mercs and street guns, at best. No special equipment. Like knocking off neighborhood wanna-be hoods."

Mani's manipulations and Lee's doubts had awakened the Beast's appetite. Keeping the Beast under control was wearing out his resolve. The unexpected mission changes only heightened his frustration. He did not want to admit to Lee how badly he needed the release of a fight, the familiar routine of killing. The Beast had to be fed again, tonight. And Max required death's reassurance to calm him in the face of so many lies, so much uncertainty, and the maddening potential of even more changes. If he did not get his ration of blood, he could not guarantee Mani surviving the shelter of his protection. He could not even promise to keep his patience with Lee.

Max turned away from Lee, who went back to the trunk. Mani brightened with Max's attention.

"Where do you want me?" Mani asked, looking at the garbage bins.

"In front of the trunk."

She snapped her head around to stare at him. "I thought you were supposed to protect me."

"Is Rithisak out to kill you?"

"No."

"Then you'll be perfectly safe out in the open. Is he the only one protected against your little mind trick?"

She nodded.

"Then he'll come after you himself and use his people to protect him. This is a small space, so you should have line of sight on them. You distract as many as you can while Lee and I close the killing box. If you're lying, you'll have no one to blame but yourself."

She held her stare on him a moment longer, gave him

a thin smile, shook her head, and looked at the ground. "This isn't what was promised to me. What would happen if I made a call to your superiors and told them what you were doing?"

"I'd cut your hand off." He waited for her reaction. She gave him none. "If you got through, I'd explain the complexity of our situation. I'd mention the fact that you and Rithisak possessed either the technology or ability to penetrate Nowhere House security. Since our safe house might be compromised, I'd point out that I had no choice but to make a preemptive strike against possible pursuers, using those measures you possessed to our advantage. You'd then have to explain and demonstrate your abilities to my employers. There would be tests. Examinations. A delay, I'm sure, in delivering your money and final living arrangements. If they found something that interested them, the delay might be lengthy. In the end, if none of these explanations proved satisfactory, I'd point out that I'm an assassin. I kill people, for pleasure and for money. Whether or not you survive, my employers received the services specified in my original contract with them. I killed for them.

"That is, if I gave a big enough of a fuck to explain myself to anyone."

Mani's gaze took in the street, the walls around them, the tractor-trailer rumbling past on the avenue. "I see. And what happens when you start shooting and blowing things up? My abilities don't work against bullets, or shrapnel."

"Jump into the trunk, close it." He led her by the arm to the back of the Lincoln. Lee backed away, dropped a bag with rope, a machete handle, and a gun muzzle sticking out, and trotted out into the street and both curbs, lay-

59

ing out a pattern of a dozen mines, letting their weight pin the loose cardboard and paper trash he used to cover them. Max took a bag of smoke and flash grenades, the .45 and shotgun Lee had left behind, an Uzi, two short tripod- and swivel-mounted guns with radio antennae, a bag of extra clips, and the bag of surveillance equipment. As an after-thought, he took out the tire iron and jammed it into the ammo bag. He locked down the weapon lockers so the trunk appeared normal once more, and showed Mani the trunk light switch, radio beacon, and cell phone compartment, and the inside hood lock.

"What if I want to shoot back?" she asked.

"You wouldn't want to do that," Max said. "I don't think you're used to combat shooting, and the plating this car does have won't stop armor-piercing rounds."

Lee returned, slipped on a climbing harness over his jeans and jacket, and put on a communication headset. As Max took out a set from the surveillance bag, Lee adjusted dials until they were able to hear each other over the ear-piece. Lee picked up the bag and headed for the fire es-cape. "Don't do anything I'd do," he said with a mocking wave as he left them.

Max pushed down the headset mike away from his mouth, took the two swivel-mounted guns, and motioned for Mani to follow him. "How did you do that trick?"

Mani pointed to her head, then to his, and back to hers. She laughed at his nod. "Why do you want to know? Do you think you can learn it?"

"If you can get inside me, maybe someone else can." Max set up one of the guns between garbage bins, bracing it against metal walls.

"Rithisak taught me how, but you don't need to worry

about his skill, unless you're easily seduced by men."

Her leg was warm against his back as he secured the clip and cleared the antenna on the gun. He stood, rubbing against her thigh, hip, breast. She grinned and leaned into him. The Beast wanted to use the muzzle of the other gun as a cock, and for a moment Max's hand shook with the desire to add his own cock to the Beast's cruel punishment. He pushed her away, crossed the street, quickly dropped the gun by a drainpipe, wedging one of the tripod legs between the pipe and the wall.

A car passed. Max started. He was sweating from the exertion of controlling himself. A cold, hard ball of nausea was working its way from stomach to throat. He headed back to the car, where the rest of his gear and Mani waited. He stopped by his equipment, wondered why he didn't go ahead, end it, fuck her, kill her, fuck her again, throw her in the trunk and drive back to Tuckahoe, with Lee in the trunk if he tried to stop her, and the men on the other end of the encrypted phone line, if they objected.

She waited, leaning back on the lip of the trunk, arms stretched above her head, fingers spread, tips pressed against the inside trunk hood. The arc of her body across the opening was a bowstring waiting for its arrow, a line daring to be crossed, a question without answer, a bottomless void demanding to be filled. The scent of her sweat caught at him, sharp as a hook. The embodiment of appetite, he realized. Like him and the Beast within him, destructive, dancing on the boundary between fulfillment and self-destruction. She was giving in to her need even if it meant a return to Rithisak's service.

Despite having fought her off, he still felt vulnerable to her, almost like prey. He was sure if Lee could know all that had gone on, he would have considered the feeling kinky, and encouraged him to surrender to his hunter. Shreds of their intimacy clung to his thoughts. Her voice, her need, echoed in his head, reinforcing the Beast's raving cry for her. And a part of him reared with jealous rage at the idea of Rithisak's importance for her. He wanted to be the sole object of her appetite, the center of her life.

The most frightening aspect she had awakened, or planted, in him wanted to protect her and the baby she carried. As strong as his drives to protect the twins and kill everybody else, this mewling newborn desire spun images of a human baby that inspired him to care and provide for it, teach it all he knew, and replace Rithisak as its father.

The Beast tore the ghost desires apart and fed on the carcass of kindness and caring.

"You're not scared of Rithisak," Mani said.

Max slung the bags over his shoulders.

"You want to know how I can enter you, and men like you? Because I understand the elements which make us."

The Beast screamed as Max took up the guns. He drew comfort from the cold steel in his hands. Through the fog of his rage, he found the outline of a sewer manhole near the street intersection.

"I'm water," she whispered, drawing him closer so he could hear. After he took a step in her direction, she said, "Rithisak is like you. Fire."

"You're drawn to fire." He fumbled with the tire iron. The Beast wanted him to swing for her head.

"But I'm not strong enough to put it out."

"You wouldn't survive my fire."

Mani laughed, brought a leg up, and hugged her knee

to her stomach. Her body broke the spell it had woven. The Beast did not care and brought Max a step closer, and another, until his crotch was jammed against her raised foot. His cock was as hard and unyielding as her heel. Her left shoulder dipped, and then her right, as she swayed from side to side between the car and Max. Her hips rolled. Pressure increased, decreased, on his cock. He smelled the stale, sweat-ripe air from the long plane ride from Asia in her hair, the incense mingled with jungle blossoms lingering on her skin, and the musty leavings of a man's sex rising from between her legs. Rithisak's scent. The Beast leapt to attack a rival's presence, and Max let his inner rage chase the lost trail of an old territorial marking. He was not supposed to kill her. He did not want to kill her.

She closed her eyes and put her head back, but the gesture was the closing of a door, not surrender. After drawing him in, she was shutting him out.

He put his free hand over her knee, passed the tire iron through her hair. Fueled by her denial and his hunger, the Beast lost Rithisak's trail and screamed itself into a storm sweeping back on a bloody path to Mani. But like the faint wail of a horn in the fog warning him away from dangerous shores, a woman's voice rose out of the storm to tell him there were other things Mani had to give him, other appetites she could fulfill. The Beast rejected the offer with a shriek that made Max's metal-filled hand shake. Her voice grew louder, clearer, becoming a siren song luring the Beast from its death focus on Mani. The voice tuned itself first to Max's thoughts, and then, settling into a deeper resonance with truth, to the Beast's roar.

A promise of flesh and blood took shape in Max's mind. Just out of reach, the shape teased the senses, becoming a salt-sharp taste not quite on his tongue, a smell lost between jungle-rot stench and the perfume of riotous growth, a touch warmer than spurting blood and colder than dead flesh. A yearning took hold of him, as if the promise had already been fulfilled, leaving his body and spirit aching with the vague memory of an appetite's satiation. It was as if he had consumed dream food that, when he awakened, could only leave him hungrier than when he had gone to sleep. It was an appetite he had never experienced before, like an addiction to a substance tailored to provoke but never quite satisfy his needs.

The Beast's hunger slid its focus from Mani to something less defined: the memory of a feast that never happened. Mani's voice and the false memories counterbalanced the Beast's insatiable drive, keeping Max in a state of hunger and not-hunger. What he seemed to want did not appear available. Appetite chased itself in an endless loop. Mani had given him the tool to help her survive his company, a light to keep his own darkness at bay.

The tool was an illusion. Max had no more wish to embrace the light than he had to hold the life he discovered Mani carried. Succumbing to distraction was an unknown thing for him, counter to the darkness and destructive nature he found more comforting. Change was not the kind of dangerous territory he was driven to explore.

For the first time he could remember, he had a choice of whether or not to rape and kill—if in fact his hesitation was his choice, and not another of Mani's mind tricks. The sensation was not pleasant. In control of himself, he missed the headlong rush of the Beast's tumultuous currents, the raw sensation of meat and blood and orgasm.

He did not choose, but he did not throw away the choices. Meager though it was, he held on to the power. It was convenient, for the moment, in keeping the Beast in check and fulfilling the mission.

Mani's touch had broadened his existence in a way he had experienced before only with Kueur and Alioune. Max fought against the realization's deadening stun. He did not want the twins to have to share their unique place in his life.

Moving to a rhythm he did not hear, Mani pushed her foot into his groin as her arms arced through the air in wider circles. His hand dropped from her knee. He took the pain shooting up from between his legs, let it tickle the Beast to see if it could be provoked. Mani's influence strained but did not break. He stepped back, letting the tire-iron hand fall to his side.

She danced away from the car, taking small, silent, delicate steps, spinning slowly in a half-crouch. She leaned forward, then arched back, hands carving shapes in the air, fingers plucking invisible strings. Her head turned in slight degrees, against the flow of her body, as if she followed a ghost's flight with her heart as her body took her on a living path. A faint luminescence emanated from her skin. Max turned to check the avenue, wondering if a new targeting technology was being applied. When he looked back, her dance had taken her a quarter of the way around the car. She glowed like a cloud-shrouded moon, the outline of her body blurred by both the dead-end street's darkness and the soft, hazy, pale white light emanating from her body. Her eyelids fluttered as if she looked out at him through a trance. The glow and the sheen of sweat on her face made her look like smooth, living stone.

"Do you like my dance?" she asked. "Rithisak did. Though not my stories. Not even my favorite. My father always told it before guiding me into the vision depths of some true part of the world. And my mother repeated it often after teaching me a step in one of the great dances she knew. Before she died. Her version was true to my father's, but longer and richer in detail, just like her dances elaborated on my father's visions."

Max heard the crackle of fire in her voice, and the crashing of waves. He shook his head to clear the noise and focus on her words. Time slowed, beating to the rhythm of her telling. The world contracted to the circle of Mani's performance, which moved with the hallucinogenic deliberateness of a bas-relief carving making its way across the stone face of its realm. He could not look away from her eyes.

"This is what my parents told me: Once gods clothed in water and fire danced over the world. Wherever their feet touched the ground, life bloomed. Every creature and plant we see, each spirit haunting the spaces between life and death, was born from a moment's kiss between the divine and the earthly. The imprint of their steps formed valleys and mountains, which wept with the beauty of the gods' sacred dance. From the earth's tears rivers great and small were born, and from the earth's sighs grew clouds and winds and song that are earth's memory of the gods' touch. In the wake of the gods' most perfect gestures, stars glittered. From the brightness of gods' eyes as they followed the vision of their dance, the sun was born. And in their hearts, where dwelled the sadness of what was to come, the moon was created and nurtured like a flawless pearl.

"The gods danced with the grace of flowing water, the

passion of burning flames. What they made illuminated the world so that no shadow could hold secrets, no truth could be hidden. But in time, when every land was marked by their passage and the world was done, the gods grew weary and had to rest, to dream new visions and prepare themselves for the next dance of creation. They surrendered themselves to sleep, and where they slept became secret places, shrouded in the mysteries of birth and death, becoming and ending.

"As the gods knew in their sad hearts, what they made could not rest. What they made grew strong in the wilderness of their absence. What grew in their wake dreamed its own dreams, danced its own steps, sang its own songs. And as the gods slept, the life that was their legacy wondered over their own creation, worshiped the mysteries that veiled the gods, explored, experimented, envied. They forged machines and built empires, harnessed elemental powers and let loose appetite. Daring to follow in the dance of the gods, prying into the secret places where gods slept, they sought to leave their mark on the world as the gods once did. The dreams of gods were stolen. Shadows grew. Truths were lost. Nightmares erupted.

"Those whom the gods created tried to shape the world as the gods had, but all that filled their vision was their own image. Now, we poor children who still follow in the footsteps of the gods are lost in a land echoing with power we can never hold. We dance in mist and moonlight instead of with water and fire. We seek to bring life and beauty to the world, but sow only death and chaos."

Mani came to a stop in front of the open trunk. She straightened out of her final broken-body posture, rising from a wide-based crouch and backward camber, lowering

arms held out akimbo, aligning twisted joints, adjusting
the sharp curve of her neck. Her glow faded with the reverberating music of her voice. The spell of her dance
dissipated, bringing the wider world back into focus. Concrete and brick loomed on either side of Max. The city's
pulse sounded from steel and machinery, the bone and
flesh of the city: a nearby subway tunnel and the elevated
highway not far off, from cables and pipes under the street,
and barges slipping quietly past on the East River. Electricity hummed. The weapons Max carried grew hot
through the bags, as if struck by a fever to discharge.

The Beast growled, sensing Max's wandering focus.
Max shook his head to clear away the confusion of returning to the real world after Mani's tale.

Mani resumed her position sitting on the Lincoln's rear.
"Do you like my story? Your people have made a world
you think you can control, made yourselves gods. But like
the gods, you can't control the thing you made any more
than you can control the things that made you."

"I thought you knew I don't make anything," Max said.
"I kill." He turned to go to his station, then looked over
his shoulder at her. "I agree with Rithisak. Your stories
are fucked."

"Fire never likes the sound of water," Mani said, voice
thick with a hunger as strong as the Beast's. "Fire prefers
making steam out of water."

Max used the space she had granted him from the
Beast's appetite to read the signals he was receiving from
her. She was drawn to fire. Destruction. Rithisak, and him.
He understood that she was driven to replace her shaman
protector with another agent of fire. With Max.

A curious pride rose in Max, as if his simple deduction

were an enormous accomplishment. And then he realized that, in the face of his own and the Beast's instincts, bothering to reason out his prey's irrelevant behaviors was an unheard-of feat.

He wondered if this was what humans were supposed to do, and what anyone did with the results.

Before moving out, Max asked, "Do you want to see your old lover die?" He waited for another sign to rise out of the depths of her need, as interested in his reaction as he was in hers.

"I want him to leave me in peace."

"Death is peaceful." Max sensed a weakness. His predatory instinct leapt. He saw ways to wound and kill with words, subtle as a poisoned bite.

"Yes, I think it is," she said, bowing her head, words drifting off.

Max tried to see where his questions had taken her. He thought of the besiac snuffling over her as a child, searching for life as she hid in death. His imagination touched on what ate at her from within, the fear beneath her hunger. Words formed in his mind, a thrust closer to her heart. Anticipating her convulsion of pain, he opened his mouth to speak.

Lee's voice crackled over the headset. "Max?"

He looked up into the dark latticework of the fire escape where Lee had hidden himself, a spider in a web of firing lines.

"He's here," Mani said, then moaned, giving Max and the Beast the pain they wanted from her.

A car drove by. Survival took precedence. Max raced to the manhole, pried it open with the crowbar. The squeaking of brakes announced the car's stopping out of sight. Max hung the bags on the rungs, climbed down, careful to pull the duster after him. Another car passed. Doors opened and slammed shut. Voices spoke: quick, sharp bursts of sound with little pitch variation, and a drop at the end of a phrase. Khmer. Someone hushed.

Something tugged at Max's attention over the Beast's rising cry for blood. There were far more footsteps than voices. Silent men lurking out of sight. Professionals, perhaps. Or something else. It was hard to pick up the scent with the wind blowing off the river.

Another car stopped before crossing the intersection. More silent men left the vehicle. Max climbed down the service tunnel, slid the cover back in place, dug a flex-eye out and poked it through the hole. A fourth car entered the intersection, turned into the dead end, and stopped at the corner, headlights on bright. Blinded, Max brought the flex-eye down, took out a heat scope, and squeezed the periscope through the narrow cover holes. Heat signatures showed up along the building walls on either side of the street, but the center was empty.

"Lee," Max whispered into the headset's mike, "anyone coming at you?"

"Nope, I've got the high ground. Two squads of four on the flanks, small arms. The idiots keep checking the roofline, didn't bother sending people up. Another dozen coming up the middle. They got nothing as far as I can see, but they look weird. I feel like I'm looking at a Village People audition. Locals, not Asian. The moron in the car has them lit up like the Rockefeller Christmas tree. I hate to think we had anything to do with training these assholes."

70

"Up the middle?" Max checked the scope again. "I don't have anything there."

"Better clean your glasses. They're right on top of you."

Max brought the heat-sensing scope down and listened to the footsteps tapping overhead. The Beast grumbled, uncertain, as if it had been robbed of its quarry. The taste of blood was in the air, but none had been spilled yet. "Something's wrong."

"Relax, Max. They're walking right into the killing box."

"Anything on the river?"

After a pause, Lee answered, "Are you kidding? What do you think this is, a James Bond flick? You expecting fucking hovercrafts or something?"

"Nothing in the air?"

"Outside of La Guardia takeoffs and landings, no. Would you—"

Max picked up the Uzi and carefully hung the ammo bag over his shoulder. "Lee?"

"Those assholes coming down the middle, I don't know—"

"What's happening with Mani?" Max knew Mani was probing the men approaching her, provoking them with her sexuality while searching for the way into their minds.

"She's cool, just looking the guys over like she wants to give them all a blow job. But Max, check out these locals. I mean, there's a couple of them that's dressed like cops down there, and a Con Ed repairman with a goofy hard hat still on, and a few street kids, and some geeks in suits, Max. I mean, Long Island commuter types. And women. One of them's pregnant. What the fuck is that?"

The Beast was cold in Max's belly, cautious in his head.

71

His heart raced, not with fear but with excitement. Twice in one night, he was being threatened with the unknown. The challenge was invigorating.

Lee spoke up. "This one guy, I swear, looks like our missing runner."

"I thought you said you found his eyes and heart in his car."

"Yeah, well, it's hard to see with the light at his back, but it doesn't look like he has eyes. None of these guys coming down the middle of the street do, as far as I can tell. And I'm thinking that blotch is the hole somebody dug in his chest to get his heart out."

"You didn't take anything to wire yourself up for the fight, did you, Lee?"

"South America was a long time ago, Max, and I ain't a kid anymore. I'm telling you this shit is crazy."

"Now who's having a psychotic moment," Max grumbled.

"Pop up for a peek. They're past your position."

Max pushed the manhole up with his shoulder until he could see a sliver of the street. He took in the men creeping along the side walls, and the backs of the group heading down the street directly at Mani. The flankers maintained their spacing and were focused on the car and building windows. Two men from each file aimed their weapons at higher ground, but the others' guns also pointing high betrayed their outdated training: They were not ready for street-level attack. The men avoided looking at Mani whenever her attention turned to them. The points were almost on the auto gun placements.

The group advancing along the middle ground was packed too tightly. Stumbling, staggering, bumping into one another as if drunk, distracted, or oblivious to each other's company, they bore down on Mani as one unit. Without weapons, they did not pose even an accidental threat. Max considered the possibility they had been drugged by Rithisak and were being used to draw fire.

Except the car's high beams illuminated the holes and slashes at the back of their clothes.

Blood tainted the air. The Beast rose to the memory of atrocities committed on the dead, hungered at the fresh possibilities.

A point flanker stared at the loading dock gun.

Mani whirled around, looked at the fire escape, and shouted, "I can't do anything with them." Fear cracked her voice, and Max caught a glimpse of how she must have looked after the beisac passed through her village.

Lee shot the flanker fumbling with his weapon to shoot out the auto gun's control mechanism. The flanking files froze. A voice shouted in Khmer from the car. Lee shot the other point man as, following Mani's gaze, he pointed at the fire escape. Rithisak's men fired at the roofline and fire escape, sending down a spray of brick fragments and cement dust and drainpipe fragments. Lee cursed in Max's ear. The narrow alley caught the burst of weapons fire and amplified it until it seemed a roaring, fire-sparking dragon had risen from the river in a surreal imitation of a cheap, man-in-rubber-suit monster movie.

Mani ducked into the Lincoln's trunk and slammed the hood down.

"Max?" Lee said, voice strained. "A little fucking support here?"

Max grunted to keep himself from laughing at his comrade's nervousness. Their enemies were shooting blind and didn't even have the presence of mind to fire up a flare. The Beast roared in his head, deepening the gunfire's resonance inside him. It was eager to kill, and pressured him to join the battle. But the Beast's joyful rage did not touch Max's heart. Detached from instincts and self by Mani's power and his unwanted role in her life, Max watched the firefight a few moments longer. The atmosphere of unreality seeped into his thoughts. If he couldn't fuck Mani, why should he save her or her unborn pup? Why did he have to kill for her?

A part of him wanted her to die, along with everyone else aboveground. A part of him wanted to walk out onto a field of dead bodies and disappear into a world where neither the dead nor the living could touch him. But the part that wanted this wish granted did not belong to him. It was a piece of Mani left behind in him.

He laughed at last at the absurd wish, broke through the space Mani had created between him and the Beast, and embraced his instincts. The Beast tore into his mind, filtering the world through its blood hunger. Max stepped farther down into the manhole, letting the cover slam shut over his head. The triggers for the autoguns and mines fell into his hands when he searched for them in the bags. He set off the weapons simultaneously.

The autoguns sprayed their clips of whizzing rounds in a sweeping arc that passed overhead like a horde of hornets. Popping mines punctuated screams of the dying. The Beast's laughter rang in his ears.

Alarms blared. Sirens wailed in the distance. The stench of smoke and blood and feces spilled through the cover's holes into the tunnel, teasing Max, the Beast. Time collapsed into a desperate ball, and Max understood that anyone caught in its final implosion had the task of explaining what had happened on the street to officials. As he had already told Mani, he did not explain himself to others. The Beast's rage surged through him in a tide of eager destruction.

The guns and mines exhausted themselves in seconds, though the din echoed for a while longer in the alley above, the tunnels below, and in his head. Max pushed the cover up just enough to peek and survey the damage. All the men along the walls were down. Moaning and twitching bodies announced that they were not all dead. Only two from the center group had fallen, legs cut to pieces by the crossfire. They still crawled forward on broken arms. The rest had gathered around the Lincoln. Some were trying to pry open the rear hood with their bare fingers, while others beat at the Lincoln's armor. The squeak and scrape of flesh against the car, the pounding of fists on metal added an arrhythmic baseline to the music of pain Max had composed. Dancing to the music, a head jerked as if slapped, a torso convulsed, hips and knees shattered, each marking a suppressed-muzzle hit by Lee shooting from his aerie. The Beast sent razor cuts of envy along Max's nerves.

"They're not going down," Max said.

"No fucking shit," Lee shouted, making Max wince.

A side window shattered on the Lincoln, and someone crawled into the backseat to break through to the trunk. The same Khmer voice shouted once again from the intersection.

Max threw the manhole cover away, ducked back down when small-arms fire from the headlight car kicked up tar and pinged off metal. The Beast snapped in reply, straining for action. Max grabbed a flash and a concussion grenade from one of the bags, tossed them both at the headlight car, picked two smoke grenades and threw them after the first pair. Explosions shook the ground, and smoke roiled in the night. Concussive shocks sounded through the flesh of his hands stuck over his ears. The roadbed trembled, and a fine rain of debris stung his face as he looked up at the circle of sky above him. Max's legs and arms tingled with restless energy as the Beast gathered itself for more direct participation in the killing.

Max held the Uzi over his head, street level, and fired a burst, replaced the clip, and stood up. The Beast sang. A single high beam still gleamed like a miracle through billowing clouds of smoke. Max emptied a clip, reloaded, and emptied another. The light vanished. Someone gurgled. The Beast sighed with satisfaction. Strings of Khmer, French, and English curses laced the night.

"That was really fucking helpful, Max," Lee screamed. "Now I can't see shit."

Max put his last clip in and waited, flat on the ground on his belly, for a target to separate itself from the dissipating smoke, car, smoldering fires, street corners. "Use your night scope."

"Those assholes around your car ain't showing up clear on it."

Because they were cold. Because they were dead. Because Rithisak's power filled and moved them, and like an electrical or magnetic field, warped their immediate surroundings.

Max passed the back of his hand across his forehead, wiping away sweat, figuratively pushing Mani's memory back into the Beast's hungry jaws.

Doors slammed shut. Rubber tires squealed. A car drove past, and someone laid down a barrage of covering fire into the smoke. Another car started and rumbled off. The ball of desperate time shrank around Max.

Max turned back to the Lincoln. Bodies seethed over the car like a blanket of grubs seeking food. He took out the .45 and the shotgun, left the rest of the equipment and weapons in the bags hanging from the manhole rungs, and charged the car. The Beast ran with him, for him, carrying him to slaughter's feast. Max murdered through the dissipating smoke.

Lee cursed in his ear. From the heavy breathing and shadowy movement on the fire escape, Max thought he might be rappelling down to the street. Between his own and the Beast's excitement, Max tried to clear a corner of his mind to remember Lee, so he would not kill his ally in the throes of a blood rage. Something grabbed his ankle. One of the broken bodies from the center group lay on the ground, peppered by shrapnel and bullet holes, and hung on to him with both hands. A face, pale broken bone sticking through shredded skin, tracked him with sightless eyeholes stuffed with leaves, twigs, wrappers, and can snap tops, like a dying flower seeking out the sun. Max kicked, then went down on one knee and smashed the corpse's arms and hands with the butts of his weapons until pulped bones and flesh slid away from his ankle. Luminescent, viscous white liquid spilled from the dead man's wounds and from the newspaper-filled hole in his chest. Cinnamon scent mingled with the stench of smoke, burnt powder, and sewer-strong filth and decay. The fluid ran like sap from a tree. Tiny seeds and dried, crushed vegetation peppered the substance. For a moment, jungle memories camouflaged the Beast in another time's desperate firefight. Max grunted as he shrugged off another unwanted memory, unsure if it was his own or Mani's. He stood, sidestepped the other corpse reaching for him, broke into a sprint, and hit the car in a bellowing rage.

Shotgun blasts rocked the layer of figures piled against the hood scrabbling for a way to pry it open. No one turned around to fight him or defend himself or herself against his fire. Max brought the gun to bear against the nearest head, a businessman's neatly styled skull, and pulled the trigger. Flesh and bone sprayed across the others and onto the rear window. The body stump of the man's corpse continued to flail against the Lincoln's reinforced trunk. Max fired again, blasting a hole through the man's back and sending his tie flapping over his shoulder. And again, up his ass. The body cracked and broke apart, twitching limbs sliding to the street in streams of glowing white lava, hands grasping at bumpers and tires and shoes. Using the shotgun and the .45, Max destroyed a police officer, two street adolescents, and a woman with a small shopping bag still hooked through her arm, shattering the dead bodies in a hail of ammunition. He laughed at the human wreckage, and the Beast devoured the carnage.

But before the broken bodies touched the earth, the Beast was howling in frustration. As with Mani, it was trying again to feed on what was not. Already dead, the men and women Max tore apart with his guns did not scream in terror and agony. They did not bleed hot life. Pain, the Beast's sustenance, had already drained away. The Beast's rage slipped and slid over the mortal destruction, claws raking over its own belly, teeth closing on its tail and snapping at illusions and ghosts.

Their hearts were gone; their eyes were blind to their doom.

The wail of sirens grew louder.

Max's weapons clicked, empty. He dropped them, drew the Ruger, but the small-caliber rounds did little damage. Failure whipped his killing frenzy. He pulled and shoved the dead aside, calling on the Beast to give him its spirit claws and fangs. He cursed himself for not bringing a machete or strapping on a Bowie.

Max found himself between the car and Rithisak's servants. Regaining their balance, the dead threw themselves at the car once again, tearing at his duster, clothes, hair, flesh. They pushed him back with their weight, crushed him against the cold Lincoln. The com headset slipped off. Plastic and metal crackled underfoot.

The Beast shook off its disappointment, welcoming the opportunity to rend flesh. Its power flowed in a tidal flood through him, sweeping away nagging little thoughts about Lee and Mani. He punched and kicked until he had space to maneuver, then reached for his closest enemy, a utility repairman still wearing his hard hat. Hands closed around the dead man's head, Max snapped the neck. The repairman clawed at his face, as if it were easier to get to Mani through muscle and bone rather than metal. Max drove his thumbs into the mud-and-glass-fragment-filled eye sockets. The corpse shuddered, its arms losing strength. But Max still fell back against the Lincoln from the weight of his attackers. Others closed in: A woman in a suit and trench coat slammed her backpack repeatedly against his shoulder instead of the car, while another woman, pregnant, worked at his ribs with her bare fists.

A hole in the body's chest, stuffed up with crumpled

magazine pages and rags, drew Max's attention. Releasing the skull, Max shifted his attack and tore away the blockage, reached into the chest cavity even as the utility worker tried to bite at Max's face. Max bobbed, ducked, dug deeper, immersing his hand in cool, thick, sticky liquid. Perforated entrails curled around his fingers; organs slithered against his skin. He squeezed his hand into a fist, crushing rotten tissue and muscle. Pulled out vines and strands of soaked newspaper and coat hanger wire. The corpse shuddered. A gasp of poisoned air escaped the dead man's parted, blackened lips, filling Max's mouth and nose with a cloud's kiss of decomposing flesh and fermenting shit. Max shook the dead thing by its chest hole. Bone cracked. Skin tore. Its head lolled back and forth, its hands fell away from Max's face, and it lay limp in his grip. Max threw the body to the side, knocking back the businesswoman with the knapsack.

Two more dead men, a police officer and a young man in a sweat suit, both shot through the forehead, bore down on Max, pinning his arms against his chest. He kicked and kneed them, breaking bones and joints, but not getting to the vital essence Rithisak had planted inside them. He lunged forward, bit the nose from the policeman. The sour taste of dead flesh curled around his tongue. He drew the creature closer until he could use his teeth and tongue on its eyes. The packed matter broke apart in his mouth, filling his throat with bitter herbs, tangy earth, oily chemicals. Max freed one of his arms as the dead man jerked back, then shoved his fingers into its eye sockets. Holding on to the skull, he forced the cop into the youth, knocking them both down and freeing his other arm. The pregnant woman stepped forward, along with a gray-haired woman and a broad, big-bellied man.

Max went down on one knee and let the corpses get to the Lincoln over him while he finished the policeman, then the youth, his fingers beginning to ache with the effort of dragging out the odd mixtures of substances and materials from body cavities. The corpses collapsed into their natural state under his ministrations. The Beast cried out in triumph. While not as satisfying as murdering the living, the work had its pleasures. The Beast understood ruined meat and gore-stained hands. The suffering was missing, but the result was the same: What moved stopped. Taking what it could from bodies, the Beast rose to the task of butchering the dead.

Max moved without thought, riding the swelling wave of the Beast's urgency, which eclipsed all other shadows and desires inside him. Deep in the heart of devastation, the circuit joining the Beast and Max closed. The Beast's appetite was his action, as it was in his best moments. The Beast's power and joy and cruelty were his, and Max savored the intoxicating rush of life he felt in death's embrace.

The big man's belly knocked Max back into the Lincoln's bumper. Max bounced off metal, swung out of the way of the dead man's relentless approach, pushed back and tripped several of the walking corpses approaching the car. The gray-haired woman, hanging on to Belly Man's shirt, stepped into Max's crotch with an oversize orthotic shoe as she attacked the trunk. Max trapped a leg with hands wrapped around its ankle, then shoved his shoulder into the shin. Gray Hair fell backward, arms reaching for the car, and landed with a crunch. As she tried to get up, a teenager in baggy clothes stepped onto its chest, the heel of a reflective-surface sneaker sinking into the hole through which the dead woman's heart had been taken. Gray Hair's head snapped back, cracked against the street. Rice sprayed up in miniature geysers from her eye sockets.

Max drove his shoulder into Belly Man's groin, nearly lifting him off the ground. Delicate structures snapped and burst within the bubble of the dead man's body, but his mass and Max's broken balance forced them both onto the back of the car. The weight of Belly Man's body, along with the corpses behind him, again pinned Max against the trunk. This time his arms were at his sides, and the press of bodies and Belly Man's arms held him in check. The pregnant woman flailed against the hood on one side of him; the business-suited woman smashed her knapsack against metal as if it were a sledgehammer.

Max stretched forward and closed his teeth over Belly Man's throat, ripping flesh and working the trachea loose as he worked his hands down into Belly Man's pants. Fingers curled into claws. Wound-ruptured skin oozing cold organic sludge parted under his pressure. He forced his way into the corpse's body, ripping through scrotum and belly, curling up into the enormous stomach where he pulled back from burning acid and worked through jelly-like fat and decomposing organs, under ribs and spine, until the stretched rents he had made in the skin tore and the reservoir of the dead man's insides gushed out with a wet gurgle, as if a drain had been opened in a backed-up toilet. Belly Man collapsed in Max's arms, reeking of a lifetime's bad habits. Max released its throat, reached into the heart's cavity, and pulled out the magical detritus Rithisak had planted to replace the life-giving muscle. The dead man slid against Max, lighter for the release of inner organs. Before the dead thing fell to the ground, Max poked out its bottle-cap eyes.

Baggy Teenager appeared before him, Gray Hair hanging on to his leg. Max lashed out with kicks, breaking hips and knees and spine. The teenager fell on top of Gray Hair in a twitching heap, and Max did not bother severing their ties with Rithisak, turning instead to the women by his sides.

He intercepted Suit Woman's knapsack as it followed a lazy arc to the car, redirected the bag's momentum, and sent it smashing into several of the dead behind her. The woman hung on to the knapsack as if it were her only connection to what she had once been. She spun with the change of arc and crashed into a wall of the walking dead.

Max whirled around and punched Baby Woman in the jaw, trying to draw her attention. He went for her eyes first, but her fingers closed over his face and mirrored his attack, digging at his own eyes. He broke her hold, kicked back a pair of closing corpses, stuck a hand in the slit across her throat that had killed her. He rammed his hand up into her skull and poked out the dog shit and tiny plastic drug vials replacing her eyes. He poked his other hand through the same, stinking mire in her chest hole and reached for Rithisak's magic in her viscera. Baby Woman drooped.

Another set of hands shot out from the torn fabric over her belly. Tiny fingers fastened on to his belt. Baby Woman threw herself into a final, frantic seizure as her infant fought its way out of her womb, as heartless and blind to the world as its mother. As Max fended off the woman's final spasmodic assault, the baby emerged from the widening rent that split her from between her legs to her chest. White, luminescent fluid spilled from the rent. An umbilical cord danced in the air. The baby closed in on Max, shooting for his genitals, striking and lashing at his manhood with pudgy arms and legs. Max took the infant by the skull, scooped the shit and vials from its eyes and chest, and threw the dead husk away.

The dead crumbled in his hands, faceless, nameless, no longer individualized in his mind by sex, body type, or clothing, as the Beast swept everything away in its path. Riding the Beast, their appetites synchronized, Max's killing moves fell into an easy rhythm of destruction, a tactical routine that hardly changed since his prey offered no variety in their behavior. Mindlessly, they went after their objective, tucked away in the Lincoln's trunk. Mindlessly, Max tore out the glimmer of animation Rithisak had planted in their bodies after killing them. He had reached the purity of state Mrs. Chan encouraged him to attain through focused meditation and practicing chi kung and t'ai chi. Mind and body, in harmony with the world and the Beast within, fused to commit a single, repetitive act. Time vanished and the killing went on forever.

But the narrow focus of forever scattered into a kaleidoscopic burst of now as the number of walking corpses dwindled and survivors proved more difficult to destroy. A soup of blood thinned by luminescent white fluid slicked the street. Smashed bodies, limbs, heads, and organs littered the ground, ready to betray footwork. Max struggled to keep his balance, which broke his killing rhythm and disrupted his communion with the Beast. The need for calculated thinking and caution collided with the clean fury of appetite's fulfillment. In the background, the wail of sirens intruded on the roar of raging spirits, drawing him further out of his perfect moment. And then, when only one enemy remained, the routine of closing with a corpse and reaching into its guts was shattered when the body danced out of his reach, screaming, and swung a machete back and forth as if it were more concerned with fending him off than reaching the prize in the Lincoln's trunk.

Reluctantly, the Beast yielded to the danger of change and left him to handle the threat of a shifting world. The wave of its power crashed. Max surfaced, stripped of the Beast, running with nothing but mortal spirit in his body and mind again. Training and human instincts took over, carrying his exhausted body into a probing stance as the figure in front of him whipped the machete around in a defensive pattern. Max slipped, fell. The figure shouted at him, holding up a hand. Max rose, the reality of night and cool air and stinking corpses crashing down on him. He staggered, wiped gore from his eyes. Sirens pierced his awareness. Time sprang up around Max, walls contracting, nearly crushing him with the need to get away from the street before authorities arrived and the last vestige of control over the situation crumbled. He sucked in air, aching for the feel of the Beast coursing through him even as it rattled its cage of flesh. The Beast's ride left him feeling empty, frustrated, and he could not remember the last time that had happened.

Max heard his name.

Lost it as the Beast, unsatisfied with its feast of dead flesh and thin blood, cried for the delight that usually followed the infliction of pain. It wanted something to rape. Max glanced at the bodies, whole and in pieces, scattered across the street. Too far gone, he decided. There was no more pleasure in the remains than there had been pain.

He heard his name again.

"What the hell's wrong with you? Max, it's me, Lee. We have to move out. Stop fucking with me, Max!"

Max squinted, focusing on the face in front of him. Features, lit by the last of the small flickering fires consuming garbage and dead men's clothes, coalesced into a familiar visage.

Lee. Guns and harness gone. Clothes ripped and stained beyond recognition. Skin torn by a dozen cuts, covered by a film of the dead's running fluids. But still Lee.

Max relaxed his guard. Lee lowered his weapon. The machete's edge dripped with the luminescent substance from Rithisak's agents. He had hacked the dead apart to reach Max, who had done his best to kill him.

Relief in finding Lee and overcoming the enemy mingled with a faint touch of shame over endangering his comrade with the Beast's blood rage. He had lost his professional composure and endangered the mission, something he had never done before. But stronger than shame was the sense of a missed opportunity. A part of him had wanted to kill Lee.

How much of the feeling found its root in the Beast's relentless appetite, his own ambivalence toward close companionship, or in Mani's subtle, covetous presence within him, Max was not certain. Only the unknown strength of the last source of emotion disturbed him. One Beast gave him strength. Two could kill him.

Lee stepped forward, eyes blazing, and took hold of Max's elbow. They ran for the Lincoln. The nearly silent wash of a stealth surveillance helicopter sounded from overhead, almost drowned out by the chorus of sirens rising from the neighborhood. Max made out a gray shape hovering above, faintly illuminated by the city's night lights.

"I called in as I came down," Lee said, breathing hard. He looked at his watch. "Police are on hold, but the situation's too fucking hot. Gang war, they're saying. People got their fingers on the trigger. We've got under a minute left to clear the fuck out." He shoved Max toward the passenger side of the car.

Max threw himself into the passenger seat. Lee startled him by already being inside, breathing hard on the driver's side. The engine rumbled, the car rolled toward the intersection. "I should drive," he said, slamming the door. Lee, his face red in the soft glow of the dashboard display lights, gunned the engine, spun the Lincoln around, and raced out onto the avenue with a squeal of tires. Max bounced against the door, then nearly popped out of the front seat as they sped over the sidewalk curb and the carpet of bodies.

"You almost bit my fucking balls off, you fucking maniac!" Lee screamed as they hit the intersection. "Are you in-fucking-sane? You want to get us killed? You lost it, Max. Lost it all, and I've seen you do some crazy shit. What the fuck did that bitch do to you?"

Max tuned the car radio to the police and emergency bands. Looking past Lee, he saw one of the surviving ambush cars turn a corner. As static crackled and nervous dispatchers cluttered the airwaves, Max pointed at the escaping vehicle. "We should finish the job," he said, the Beast speaking the unwise choice.

"With what?" Lee shouted, his voice cracking. "We're hot, we look like shit, we're out of firepower, and the shit we had was no fucking good anyway. This was not a clean fucking hit, in case you didn't notice. We almost got taken by a bunch of dead-ass motherfucking zombies. What the hell was that? I mean, have you ever seen shit like that? I been through weird shit, we both been through it, but fuck this, this was straight out—I don't even know what. I mean, it's one thing talking about ghosts and ESP shit, but it's a whole other game when I can't see nothing through my scope and I know I got targets walking around, and when I hit them they don't go down, and they ain't wearing no fucking armor. Hell, those were mostly fucking civilians back there. I don't know which was more fucking nuts, those dead motherfuckers walking around or you so far into your zone you were coming after me. You never come after me, no matter how kill crazy you get. What the fuck was that? You ain't been right since that bitch looked at you, you know that? You going soft on me, Max? Or are you losing it? 'Cause if you are, you better get the fuck out of ops before you take me down with you."

Lee's words shot through Max but did not touch him. They were truth, but the truth did not matter to him. He had the Beast. He had his hungers. He thought of Mani in the trunk.

Red lights strobed in the distance. White search beams from the sky swept across building facades. The cacophony of sirens was growing louder, merging into one voice. Fear's chill warned the Beast. Pain lancing through his temples alerted Max of the enemy he could not fight or consume.

A raspy voice rose out of the back of the car. Max reached for the glove compartment gun, remembered it was gone when his fingers closed on nothing. The radio squawked unit numbers, response codes, street names. Buried in the dispatch instructions, posted with recognition sequences, was their escape route. Lee stopped the car.

"You heard the radio," Max said. "We don't have time."

Lee remained frozen behind the wheel. "You fucking check that out."

Max turned on the ceiling light to investigate the voice in the back, but the real danger was outside the car, closing in. Razor-wire threads of pain laced Max's head. Time collapsed into a single, frantic, cutting here and now. The Beast's instincts drove it to fight, kill. Max's needs tempted him to surrender to the Beast one final time. The Beast's eruption was as certain as a death sentence if they were captured. Coupled in the heat of their blood lust, they would die, a rogue hunter-killer taken down by a pack of scavengers.

The Beast convulsed like a snake caught in the jaws of its enemy. It wanted to kill. It did not want to acknowledge the certainty of its own death on the teeth of authority, consequence, and punishment.

Max controlled his breathing. Following Mrs. Chan's meditation techniques, he cleared his mind. Mani's living shadow fell over his passion for killing. He welcomed her intrusive presence within him. Instincts and appetites calmed, leaving cold professionalism in charge of surviving.

He looked into the back of the car. He saw the outline of a plan in the play of what lay on the floor of the car, and in shadows, assumptions, fragments of knowledge.

"Shit, what a dumb-ass pair of stupid motherfuckers we are!" Lee glared at Max, sat up suddenly, and followed Max's gaze. He moaned. "No fucking way."

The voice gargled wetly.

Lee stared, then continued in a monotone, as if parts of him had been left behind in the dead-end street battle. "We didn't even check the car when we got in. Fuck me, but we're going to die from our own stupidity. Look at that shit back there. Should have smelled them, if I didn't have so much of that stink on me already. Fucking kids and their mom . . ."

As Lee babbled, Max considered bolting from the car and leaving Lee and the woman for the authorities. But he needed the car to get through the escape route. And there was the plan, an endgame gaining reality even though they had not yet survived the immediate danger.

"Drive. Let's get to Omari's. You heard where the opening is?" Max counted down the seconds until he had to kill Lee and take the car. The Beast trembled, ready to pounce, desperate to take control and kill someone not already dead.

Lee slid back into the seat, stared straight ahead, nodded, drove off.

"Give her up," a little boy said from the floor of the backseat. It had taken a few seconds for whatever had taken over the corpse to gain control of the body's breathing mechanism and vocal cords. If the boy had been alive, his raspy words might have warned of serious illness. Dead, Max knew the words were not the boy's.

Max studied the bodies huddled together like the remains of a modern ethnic cleansing crowded into a shallow grave. The older girl's jaw was broken, her mouth ruined by the blunt object used to kill her. The boy, still in his Catholic school uniform, his dark locks and high cheekbones casting him in the same feminine frame as his sister and mother, wore mottled bruises around his neck to show that his death had been slow, and perhaps enjoyed by his killer. The mother bore the familiar lipless mouth across the neck marking the majority of Rithisak's corpses. Pieces of their flesh hung on the shredded leather and padding ripped away from the rear of the car, and the armored trunk wall was scratched by their effort to get to Mani.

Three sets of eye sockets filled with tacks, crumpled aluminum foil, rat poison pellets, broken glass, torn name tags, and cigarette butts fixed on Max. Three chest holes blocked by tightly woven twig and dried-leaf walls torn from squirrel nests invited the Beast to smash through and rip out the magic mechanism of their afterlife. Their fingers, nails torn off and tips scraped raw from raking the trunk wall, were splayed across the seat cushions and doors, bracing the bodies for the ride. Rithisak's white animating fluid beaded on pale skin, reddish-brown meat and protruding white bone.

Max scanned the street for the surviving ambush car but found nothing suspicious. Line of sight was apparently not critical for Rithisak's work.

"She is not yours," the boy said. "You must give her back to me. Now."

Max recognized an inflection in the voice.

Lee grunted, took a sharp left turn. Gunfire erupted behind them. "I don't believe it," Lee said, life returning to him. "You hear that? We really *do* know this fuck, don't we, Max?"

A short, sharp burst of laughter escaped Max, surprising himself, the Beast, Lee. "He's come back to punish us for our sins," he said, barely containing a rising giddiness as he saw a Khmer face in a crowd of trainees countless years ago, anonymous except for a nasal twang some said was an American affectation and others claimed had its source in overindulgence of drugs, mystic chanting, or a blow to the nose by an unpaid whore. A sense of the situation's absurdity nearly overwhelmed him, as if it were a Beast of its own inside him.

Rithisak's resurrection in their lives was not a ghost coming back to haunt them, but another signal spike in the endless background static of sanctioned operations. Allies and enemies frequently exchanged places, and opposition forces on one mission often acted as facilitators on the next. There was no more meaning in his reappearance than in the civilian casualties scattered on the street they had left behind. It was not as if the victims of his pleasures were reaching out of their graves for him.

The tension laughter had dissipated sank cold, bony fingers into his shoulders and squeezed.

Lee spoke, turning again, weaving out of the circle of a helicopter's searchlight as they went down a street lined with burned-out lamps. "He didn't give us that goof name when we trained him, the little son of a bitch. Couldn't put together a decent patrol back then, can't pull off an ambush today. No wonder most of his people are fucking dead. Who the fuck would work for him?"

The boy held out a ragged hand to Max. "We are old comrades. She is nothing. Give her to me, and I will let you go."

"Let us go?" Lee said. "It ain't you that's kicking our asses right now, shithead."

"Fuck you, Rithisak," Max said, and reached for the dead little boy.

"Max?" Lee's tone made him turn. Ahead, a roadblock

of limousines and Jeep Trailblazers, all in black, cut off the street they were on. Lee slowed. Presidential seals decorated the vehicle license plates.

"Ah, shit," Lee said, "we're going to hear about this one."

A limousine backed out, leaving a hole for the Town Car to pass through. Secret Service agents chattering into their lapel mikes checked Lee and Max through the side windows and waved them through. No one inspected the backseat or trunk. Lee never let the car come to a complete halt, and slowly rolled through the roadblock. On the other side, police cruisers and uniformed officers mingled with men in paramilitary gear and helmets, bearing automatic and sniper weapons. Heads turned. Eyes bore into the Lincoln. Max switched the ceiling light off. Helicopters thrummed overhead, their vertical searchlights joining the horizontal beams from the police cruisers in a blinding dance.

As they slipped through the security checkpoint, Max ground his teeth. The resources his superiors had allocated to the emergency on such short notice impressed him. But he was nervous under the intense scrutiny, and felt himself on the razor's edge of danger in passing so close among men who would gladly kill him if they only knew his true nature. He wanted to kill them, but he had no chance, a lone hunter so deep in the pack of his enemies. The loss of control reminded him of Mani's intrusion, and panic nipped at his gut, driving his heart to beat faster. The Beast shared his discomfort, but as Lee eased through the thinning ranks of police, firemen, bomb squad, emergency units, and special tactical units, the Beast let loose a cry of triumph at its escape. The Beast's joy infected Max, confirming his freedom. The crushing pressure of now evaporated. The future opened up, and opportunity for fresh prey was not so distant.

"We don't have far to go," Lee said. "What do you want to do about that shit in the backseat?"

Max rubbed his temples as the Beast's sustained, piercing ululation replaced the pain of closing time for the moment. Lee accelerated after passing the last police cordon closing off traffic access and keeping neighborhood locals away from the scene of the action. The Beast exhausted itself. Max relaxed into the passenger seat. Cuts and scratches, and deeper wounds, from his fight with Rithisak's dead agents called for his attention. He pushed through the noise of needs from his own body, the Beast, Mani, Lee, and focused on getting through the next few hours. Mrs. Chan's admonitions to listen to his opponent, to give in without surrendering and draw out his opponents, rose from the memories of her lessons. For once, he heard the meaning of her lesson and almost understood.

He needed one of the dead, but not three.

He started turning, the Beast rising with its strength but not its accustomed enthusiasm for slaughter. The mother shot through the gap between the passenger and driver's seat, bone-tipped fingers curled into claws. Max clipped the woman's elbow with an instinctive blow, knocking her off balance and saving Lee's face. Before he could grab her, the daughter, snaking her way under her mother, took hold of his left forearm with both hands. The boy, crawling over the seat, slid over Max's shoulder and hung on to his right arm.

Lee cried out, fought off the mother, hit a breakaway lamppost, and sent it flying over the car. The Lincoln shuddered, wove back and forth across the street as the dead woman wrestled with Lee. Max smashed the children together, head first, tried to pull the woman off of Lee. They scraped a parked car, clipped a mailbox, and bounced off the side of a parked forty-foot tractor-trailer. Max reached over to help Lee fight off the mother, but the children exploited a wild turn of the car and pinned him against the door. Another shudder passed through the Lincoln from an impact with a loosely anchored chain-link fence pole, and they careened across a rubble-filled empty lot, crashing through a foot-high wall that crushed the front end of the car.

The children flew out of Max's arms as glass shattered under flying bricks and air bags ballooned. Max fought for breath as the children's heads pressed against his chest, driven by the safety bags. Metal crunched and clanged in the wheel wells as the car continued rolling. Lee's muffled scream broke into a string of curses. The car vaulted, landed front end first, and remained stuck, tail elevated. The sudden stop shot Max into the ceiling. Ears rang, vision narrowed. A shock wave of pain swept through his skull. His stomach lurched at the smell of burnt oil and gasoline mingled with the stench of guts and gases forced out of the dead by sudden pressure. The world blacked out.

Max woke, stunned, to the Beast's howl of outrage and the engine sputtering and grinding itself into annihilation. The dead children fidgeted against him, their fingers finding wounds to burrow into and widen. The children's teeth, loosened by the impact and Max's blows, gnawed at the meat of his limbs. Max clawed out of the fog in his head, instincts telling him he had been out for only moments, the Beast driving him to fight. The children reached for his eyes. Lee moaned, and sounds of a struggle dominated his side of the car.

The air bags ripped and deflated before Max's frenzied burst to rid himself of his attackers. He drove the boy to the floor, trapped his head against the floor of the car with one leaden foot, focused his attention on the girl. The Beast spat at Max's restraint.

Cursing faster than he could breathe, Lee fought his way out of the driver's-side crumpled window, dragging the mother out with him as she clung to his waist and tried to bite his crotch.

Max finished with the girl, freeing her body from Rithisak's enslavement, and heaving her empty form into the backseat. He ripped the air bag free by rubbing it against protruding, twisted shards of front-end metal, and bound the boy tightly with the plastic. He tried his door, surprised by the blood splattered against the glass and side panel. The Beast added its rage to his adrenaline rush, but their combined strength wasted itself against the car's mangled shell. He crawled to the driver's side, pulling the dead boy after him, and followed Lee into the night.

Max fell headfirst into a ditch. The boy slipped from his grasp. Lee grunted and cursed a few feet away as he imitated Max's tactics and tore Rithisak's controlling substances from the mother's body. Max tried to get to his feet and fell like a drunkard, face first, against the car. He tried again, failed, realized his legs were numb from the impact. He checked himself for broken bones and found none. Dizziness overwhelmed him, and he vomited.

"Max," Lee called, throwing off the mother's husk, "we only have a block to go. Get up, you lazy fucking bastard, you ain't hurt. I wasn't even going twenty at the end. . . ."

Max wiped his mouth, trading bitter bile for gore and his own blood splattered over his skin. A police cruiser sped past, sirens and lights carving the night, the officers ignoring the torn fence and smoking wreck in the empty lot. The Beast rose to answer Max's unspoken need, mobilizing every ounce of latent strength. His legs tingled. Pain, the beginning of life, crept through his body like rivulets of blood breaking a drought's parched earth.

Lee drew himself up. "Fine, you take a fucking vacation and I'll get your date." He leaned over Max, took out the car keys, went around to the back. "Ah, shit, I fucking hope she's still alive."

Max pushed himself to join Lee. Nothing happened. More, the Beast demanded. His body needed even more strength, more pain.

He tasted the blood on his fingers, the excrement and refuse, bits of other people's dead skin, the sticky residue of Rithisak's controlling substance trapped under his nails. Mani's shadow stirred inside him, deepening with remembrances, offering hope. Max crawled to the mother's corpse, lapped at the white matter running slow and thick like sap from her chest wound. Familiar flavors from the fight overlaid knowledge of tropical flora Mani had left in his mind, and a part of him began analyzing the ingredients Rithisak used. The Beast pounced on the substance, savoring the glutinous milk as if it were life's essence. Max devoured the residue as he would blood at the height of his lust, scooping out remnants from inside the carcass, scraping the body's inner walls, consuming like a madman starving for nourishment, dying of thirst.

Sap oozed between his fingers, crept on ten thousand

prickling legs down his throat, burrowed into his stomach. Wild seasonings lingered in his mouth. Within moments, time slowed, his heartbeat resounded like the footsteps of a god coming for him, and the surrounding reality's straight urban lines melted, folded, curled into a hellish maze.

For a moment, a window opened in a place beyond where the Beast resided. A vision blazed, filled his mind with a view looking out onto a land of death. Howls of agony and despair rose from a landscape of twisted bone partially hidden by flesh draped like the banners of ancient, fallen armies. Someone—something—called his name. Hatred hit him like waves of heat coming off the ground. Senses alerted him to a stalker.

Max closed his eyes, trying to filter the vision and isolate the enemy coming for him. He strained for a glimpse, a taste, the scent of his hunter, but even the frisson of a malevolent gaze brushing against him was absent. The Beast cast out its inhuman senses, but floundered in the territory between hallucinations and reality. Neither of them could define the enemy. What eluded their grasp was a shape of power, vast and slow, dotted with the hint of multiplicity, like the eye of a fly, and reinforced by the palpable despair underlying a concentration camp's cold hate.

The enemy was far away, but closing. Not Rithisak or Mani, who were near and familiar. Something new and terrible. The threat unbalanced him even more than all the assaults, from his official contacts, Mani, and Rithisak's army of the dead, he had suffered.

The Beast sucked the warped perceptions into itself, feeding on hallucination's excesses. The sense of being stalked faded, became irrelevant. Strength returned to Max's limbs. Pain blazed, then diminished into a manageable throbbing. Max stood, pulled the weakly writhing dead boy from the car, and dragged it to the back of the Lincoln sticking up out of the ditch, where Lee struggled with the lock.

"You into souvenirs again?" Lee asked, doing a double take at Max's approach.

Max let the body go, slapped Lee's hand away from the lock. "I need it."

Lee looked Max over. "I hate to ask what for. You got any more of the shit that's got you buzzed up again?"

Max reached into the boy's partially stoppered heart hole and took out a fingertip full of Rithisak's white life-giving fluid. He offered it to Lee, who winced and shook his head. Max stuck the finger into his mouth, then pushed a release point near the bumper while turning the key. The trunk hood popped open.

Max met Mani as she emerged, putting his hands around her waist and lifting her out. "Are you all right?" he said, surprising himself with the question, and the emotion behind the words. "The baby?" The Beast growled a warning.

"The child still lives inside me." She leaned into him after he set her down, hands traveling over his torn clothing and wounds. "Cambodians are used to suffering. Water flows where it can, where it must. I know how to protect what I carry. After all, you did not set off one of your smart bombs in the trunk, or beat and rape me for hours."

He examined her body by the dim glow of the trunk light, dabbing bleeding cuts with the cleaner shreds of her clothing, putting his palm against her belly to try and feel

99

the faint motions of life in her. His pulse quickened, and senses sharpened in the way they did when he closed on a kill. He felt the fetus inside her, cocooned in layers of unfamiliar tissue. He wondered what trick she knew to fool his senses, or what magic had grown a protective egg in her.

A slight tremor took hold of his hands. Unaccustomed excitement paced the flow of his newfound energy. A protective urge seized him, as if a bond had established itself with Mani as it had between him and the twins. He puzzled over this new, unwanted attachment, wondering how she might mean something to him. The Beast's shrill barking rose in protest. Max agreed with its jealous caution. There was nothing real between them, as there was between Max and the twins, and the Beast. She was only burrowing deeper into him, like a ravenous worm feasting on a corpse. The scope and strength of her influence surprised him, and the confidence he had held in his self-control waned like the moon slipping behind storm clouds. He thought of Rithisak.

He wanted to forget.

Lee tapped Max on the shoulder as he spoke into the secure cell phone, speaking hurriedly about cleaners and safe house ETA. Max pushed Mani away, leaned into the trunk, slid a small panel door open, and punched a code into a tiny electronic pad. A red light blinked.

Max picked up the boy and threw him over one shoulder, then ran across the empty lot, grabbing hold of Mani's forearm and dragging her along. Lee followed. Pain flashed through Max's knees and ankles with every step. Lee grunted as if he were finishing a thirty-mile hike with a full pack. Mani gasped and moaned for a moment, but then struggled to keep pace with Max in steely silence.

They were through the fence and on the other side of the street when the bomb went off. Max's skin prickled from the heat. Flames shot into the air through broken windows.

"There goes our DNA trace," Lee said. He pointed down a street. "Come on, you know the routine. Gotta run from all the trouble we caused."

They broke into limping trots, Lee on point, Max bringing up the rear with the boy wriggling on his shoulder, Mani between them, back hunched as if hauling RPGs for the resistance through her homeland's jungle. Helicopter rotors chopping through the air nearby, along with the sirens and shouting voices echoing through the streets, reinforced the sense of dislocation in time and space. People stood in doorways and windows, gathered on stoops and in front of bodegas, never straying far from cover but drawn to the street by the drama of police action. Eyes tracked their progress, alert to danger. Max shifted his burden to shield his face, and adjusted his gait and posture to disguise himself, as he often did during his work and his play. Fingers pointed at Max and the others, but no one came out to stop them or offer help. Old cars and a few trucks crowded the parking spots along the curb, but the street itself was empty of traffic. At their approach, the sparse neighborhood withdrew into its shell of homes, only to come out again in their wake.

Lee glanced over his shoulder and said to Max, "You know, you might make better time without the kid. It's freaking me out, still moving in your arms like that. Why don't you dump that thing?"

"I told you I needed it."

"Fine, bring your own lunch, then," Lee said, increasing the pace as they crossed an intersection. "I think you need to take some time off, Max, 'cause you're flashing back to bush time, only this ain't the bush." He glanced at Mani. "And you, why didn't you tell us he'd send dead people?"

"How was I to know?" Mani answered, more indignant than breathless. "I never took part in these kinds of operations. I was put to much subtler uses. And if I had known, and told you, would you have believed me?"

Lee looked away instead of answering, and pointed ahead. "Next block."

Max sifted through jungle memories, searching for just how much Mani knew of Rithisak's methods. His gut told him she was lying, and the Beast coiled inside him, urging him to leap at her back and break her neck. Max understood he was being tested, that Mani was assessing her newly chosen protector for the wider world she had entered. His rage danced with the parts of herself she had infected him with, and he could not see an immediate way out of the trap of her presence. He squeezed the dead boy's body with iron fingers. It spat gore in his face.

As they reached the corner, a police cruiser screeched to a halt in front of them. Overhead, a helicopter passed, light flicking back and forth across the street, then doubled back, pinning the three of them in its beam. Two officers tumbled out of the car, guns raised. Lights in a bodega went out, and a few people hanging out of windows vanished.

"What the fuck is this?" the closest shouted, while the other spoke into the radio mike.

"Shit," Lee said, looking from side to side as if an escape route might suddenly materialize. His fingers twitched, firing weapons he did not have. "Hold up, guys, let me make a phone call—"

"Shut up," the close officer screamed, fixing his aim at Lee.

Max could feel the man's urge to kill, though it was founded on motives alien to Max: fear and surprise and threat. The Beast rose excitedly to the promise of violence.

Mani straightened, walked toward the officer, whose face slackened as he stared at her face. He relaxed out of his firing stance.

Max looked up at the helicopter hovering above, hoisted the dead boy over his head, and leered for the camera he assumed was trained on them. Face twisted, teeth bared, he showed just enough of his true face to be recognized by those he needed at the moment. The Beast roared in triumph, and Max gave its voice his throat and lungs.

The helicopter searchlights switched off, and the craft veered away like a wounded bird driven from its nest by predators consuming its young.

"Let them go," the officer on the radio said, holstering his weapon. "They're on our side."

Mani stopped, lowered her head, and backed away. The nearest officer shook his head, resumed his firing stance. His partner, getting back in the cruiser, repeated the command.

Lowering the gun, the remaining officer stared as first Lee, then Mani, jogged past the car. Max walked, the bound dead boy over his shoulder, dripping natural and unnatural vitals from his eyes and mouth. Max gave him the same expression he had offered his employers hooked into the police video cameras. He heard the officer ask quietly, of no one in particular, "They're with us?" And then Max was past the cruiser and following Lee to the safe house. The police cruiser drove off, its siren silent.

The building was one of several in a row of five-story apartment buildings with windows sealed by cement blocks, and a steel slab for a front door. The block was mixed, commercial and residential, gap-toothed with empty lots and a burned out shell of a low warehouse. There were only a few cars parked on the street, and no people. Lee went up the front steps, pushed the door in half a dozen spots, stepped back. The door opened. Lee walked in. Max pushed Mani up the stairs and through the door.

Darkness smothered them as soon as the door closed. The Beast's instincts flared at the sudden change, but its rage found nothing to assault. Max's senses had already measured the hall and stairs. Rotted, water-damaged floors and walls sheltered scattering rats and bugs; dogs, cats, and squirrels had left scent markings; ragged snatches of carpet added to the mold and mildew smell and spores thick in the air. There was the scent of blood already spilled, human and animal, and cooking smells, as well as lingering sweat, cologne, and perfume, but nothing immediately dangerous.

Cursing under his breath, Lee searched a wall until a switch clicked. The glow from a string of small, dim red bulbs carved a winding entrail of light through the darkness, wandering through first-floor rooms, descending into the basement, ascending to the upper floors.

"Omari!" Lee called out. "Don't fuck with me now, man. It's hot out there."

"What the hell kind of fire you started?" a deeper voice answered from above, muffled by at least two floors.

They headed upstairs but had to stop at the first landing, unable to get past the next dozen smashed steps. Lee cursed again, louder, but inspired no further answer or guidance from above. He led the way through the maze of apartments and rooms connected by broken doorways and ragged holes in the wall, lit by red bulbs. Copper plumbing and wiring had been ripped out of the walls and ceilings, adding to the shelled look of the building's interior. A few pieces of furniture lurked in gloomy corners. After going through several dusty, graffiti-decorated rooms, they came upon an altar illuminated by a dozen colored glass-enclosed candles and Christmas tree lights.

Its unexpected appearance and overwhelming wealth of paraphernalia captured Max's attention, drew him in even as he pushed himself to keep moving. Pictures of Catholic saints, dominated by Peter, partially covered cracks and holes in the back wall. Bottles of wine, liquor, liqueur, and soda cluttered the altar's multiple shelves, almost obliterating the other offerings and ritual objects: a rusty machete, clay, plastic and glass jars, vials, bowls and cups, cutlery, sequined cloth panels and bottles, keys, doorknobs and handles, broken locks and chain links, a large G.I. Joe Tuskegee pilot, a cane, statues of mythological figures, a blue ceramic Kali figurine, handmade and altered commercial dolls, currency, cigarettes. The floor was covered by an intricately drawn cross accented by stars, curving lines, and a chalk stroke that reminded Max of the cane on the altar, or a sword. Max's hunting instincts searched for a hidden message in the altar's arrangement, but he found no warnings, prophecies, or advice. Max curbed the Beast's impulse to clear away the sacred site. There was no time for pointless destruction.

Small bones crunched underfoot as they went through the next room, and in another veils hung from the ceiling, which tickled his face as he passed through them. In a room where old bloodstains darkened the scuffed wooden floor and the air was redolent with the stench of spoiled meat, hand-painted signs splattered the walls. One sigil caught his attention by darkening as he passed, though he cast no shadow on it. As he turned and approached the wall, the graffiti sign's thick, crude lines describing a tiny circle surrounded by a concentric pattern of triangles encircled again by a flamelike design, bled down the wall. Drawn to the thick, running liquid, Max reached out, scraped the substance from the rough plaster. Electric tingling raced up his arm, buzzed in his ears, sparked in his eyes, pinched the nerves of his spine. The dead boy jerked and moaned. Max straightened, backed away. But the connection he had made with the sign's unknown meaning resonated throughout his body, provoking muscle spasms and ghost sensations of being caressed, bitten, held. Invisible arms and legs sprouted from his body and danced to a chaotic rhythm. For a moment, he saw inside his mind the Beast's vaguely human shape, as well as Mani's much smaller mental figure, limned by the glory and power of what he had touched. The Beast cowered at first, then widened and grew taller, feeding on the strange power's vast energy as Max had fed on Rithisak's dead-raising concoction. Mani's shell-self withered in the power's glaring heat, a lost entity trapped in a dead pool long after a surging tide came and left.

All he knew that was Max—memories, appetites, skills, emotions—merged with the exploding cosmic consciousness taking root in him. For a moment, he lost sight of the

Beast, Mani, Lee, his time and place in the world, in the sweep of the universe his narrow vision contained. Forces lurked at the edge of his awareness. Wars raged. Creation unfolded. And then the consciousness answered his touch with a touch, like a voice answering on a long-distance connection, and his vision burst to embrace new vistas. Rushing, racing, he tried to hang on to himself as he rode and was ridden by the discarded flotsam of a reality levels beyond anything he knew or understood, as he consumed and was swallowed by a slipstream of images and sounds and stimuli he had no organs to perceive but in the medium of higher consciousness recognized as sensations of a kind, as he was buffeted by storms and battles and lovemaking, deluged by the knowledge newborns at this level knew as instinct and weathered close to the dust of madness by the scale and scope and depth of his new surroundings. Only relentless speed saved him. His fragile dust mote bundle of concerns and appetites was cradled in a protective nest of attention, and the fleeting fragment of concern was enough to keep him from losing himself in any particular alien spectacle.

"For me," a woman's voice whispered in his mind. Not Mani, he knew instantly. Not one of Rithisak's dead agents. A thing in the guise of a woman because that was something he understood. The power behind the sign he had touched. She was accepting the sacrifice she thought he was surrendering. For a moment, Max thought he had inadvertently offered himself. The woman's laughter rippled through him, shaking him nearly to pieces. She saw the dead boy in his mind, he realized, and understood why he was carrying the corpse. She wanted nothing from him, was only teasing him. Their paths had inadvertently crossed, nothing more.

"Excuse the fuck out of me, Max," Lee said, slapping Max's shoulder, "but Omari's waiting for us upstairs."

The touch of power dissipated, mist blown apart by a gust of words. Max's world tumbled back into now, into place, and the truths and super-realities he had glimpsed slipped from the limited scope of his awareness. Back in the world defined by five human senses and solid boundaries, the Beast nuzzling the bloody corners of his mind, Max recovered, grateful the vistas that had filled him to bursting and nearly obliterated everything that was himself and his world were gone. He could not even recall the shadows or afterimages of what he had seen, and he was grateful. Oblivion was less distracting.

He knew enough not to reach for the melting sign again.

Lee brought his attention to the ladder next to the string of red bulbs rising through a hole in the ceiling to the next floor. They climbed, Max bringing up the rear as he maneuvered the dead boy up on his back. Remote-controlled antipersonnel mines threatened to turn the passage up into a killing zone, and Max wondered how many more they had walked through downstairs. They came up onto another sealed level, the immediate floor swept clean, the faint whine and hum of electronic equipment breaking the building's quiet. Several walls had apparently been knocked down to create a large chamber.

The man sitting at the keyboard in the middle of racks and shelves full of equipment and monitors connected and powered by a jungle of cables did not turn to greet them. He acknowledged their presence only after Lee brushed against the back of his chair on the way to the minifridge between a pair of dented file cabinets.

"You got any beer in here?" Lee asked, pushing through plastic canisters and bottles.

The man glanced at Lee, turned to Max and Mani standing by the ladder entrance. He flipped down the eye screen attached to his headset, took off the earphones first, and put them aside. Underneath the black kufthi he put on, large round eyes took in Max and the wriggling dead boy he dumped beside the entry hole, and the slight flare of his nostrils was all he gave up in judgment of the meaning of what he saw. Max gave him a nod of the head. Big, solid shoulders, potbelly, loose comfortable pants, and pullover gave the impression of softness. Hands too large for the keyboard contradicted the intricacy of the surrounding joined machinery. Max thought it might take more than the usual effort to kill him. The Beast let out a growl of curiosity, rising out of the languor that had settled over it after its brush with the power in the melting sign. Max did not need Mani's shadow to soothe the Beast. He was counting on its appetite for what was to come, and did not want either of them to waste energy on useless prey.

"Omari," the man said by way of introduction, voice pitched higher than Max expected for such a big man. "I've heard much about you. Your work in my properties has always been of value to me. Welcome."

"I never saw altars before," Max said.

"They come after a building has been . . . broken in. The Blood of Killers did this place for me. You boys been raising quite a bit of hell out there tonight." He pointed to a trunk next to the hole in the floor through which they had arrived. "Outside of showers, what you need is in there."

Lee joined Max at the trunk and pulled out medical supplies. "Ain't no beer in here," Lee said.

Mani knelt beside the boy and stared into its empty eyes. She reminded Max of a soldier separated from his platoon, lost in enemy territory, calling for help on a dead radio.

"You're late. There's business to be done," Omari said, closing down programs on the screens with deft taps on the keyboard and clicks of the rollerball. "And you don't need any damn beer."

"Is it here?" Lee asked, standing, peering into corners and staring at piles, searching for something apparently missing from the cornucopia of goods.

For a moment, Max thought he was still talking about the beer.

In the next room, on the edge of the glow of red bulbs, electronic equipment boxed in the original manufacturers' cartons was stacked in piles according to type, many marked for government use only. Weapon crates, some with Russian and Chinese markings, were stored farther away on the floor, nearly hidden behind rubble. Plastic bags with designer clothing name tags hung from rusty heating pipes. Cases of military M.R.E.s, Hooah! bars, and ERGO drink provided the foundation for a table set with bottles of wine, champagne, liquor and water, caviar tins and baskets filled with exotic cheeses, fresh fruit, pâté, crackers and bread sticks, and a variety of canned and jarred delicacies. Microwavable dishes lay atop the micro-wave along with the cappuccino maker on the shelf above the small refrigerator.

Omari leaned back in the swivel chair, watching the

surrounding screens power down. "Your people dropped it off before the fireworks began. They explained the preset timer to control effect-duration after you turn it on, the tracking mechanisms installed in the carrier box, as well as the instrumentation available to track what's inside. I was told what would happen to me and about a square mile of the city if I tried to break the security seals, and what would happen to the greater consensual reality if I actually let out what the seals are guarding. They also pointed out who my sons and daughters in Lebanon, Sierra Leone, and Wisconsin would be sold to and what would happen afterward if I didn't follow the established protocol precisely. Then they threatened my life if it wasn't here when they returned.

"And they took some of my inventory. Without paying for it."

Lee nodded, eyebrows raised in sympathy. "They were in a hurry; things are pretty crazy in the city right now. Sounds like they were short of equipment, too. You got off lucky. Most times, they give newbies like you demonstrations. Welcome to the club."

Omari stood, flicking power switches to shut off the computer web. "I thought you backed me with your employers. I thought you said, after years of loyal service hiding their shit, they'd trust me with their precious device."

"Don't take it personal. They check everybody out, Omari. They know people are going to exploit the thing, they just want to make sure it's done in ways that don't throw everything out of control. And they don't want you getting too big for yourself, either."

Omari cocked his head at Max. "They check him out?"

Max let the silence drag on until only Omari remained staring at him. "They only do background checks on what belongs to them," he said at last.

Omari snorted, turned away. Fists on hips, he surveyed his domain and shook his head. "The price for the privilege of belonging."

"Think of what you can charge those mumbo-jumbo priests you're renting chapel space to downstairs," Lee said. "Think of all the networks and outfits you're plugged into now, the cost savings on your payoffs and purchasing, the profit margins on your distribution."

Omari grunted. "Sometimes it's hard to see what kind of garden will grow from a field of fertilizer."

Max laid out gauze, bandages, scissors, tape, antibiotic salves, medical needles, and thread on a blanket, all drawn from the trunk. Mani joined him, took over setting up. Max glanced at the dead boy. He was still firmly secured, squirming weakly. Mani got several liter bottles of spring-water from the gourmet spread, then took the scissors and cut off the rest of Max's clothes, stripping him naked.

"Oh shit," Lee said, a wince turning into an expression of disgust as he looked away from Max. "Show me what they dropped off, and then take me to your bathroom, Omari? If I stay here any longer, I really don't think I'm going to be able to control myself."

"I suppose you'll all be needing a change of clothes," Omari said, heading for a section of interior wall partially obscured by shelving.

"And transportation for me," Lee said, following. "I've got things to do tonight."

"Additional services will cost you." He rummaged through cardboard boxes, tossed out packages of underwear and socks, then gave each of them a hard stare before returning to another set of boxes and pulling out jeans, sweatshirts, and sneakers, all with designer marks. Mani gathered their pile of clothes and put them aside, while Lee ignored the pile at his feet to watch Omari draw a thick aluminum case from under a floorboard.

Breaking into a broad smile, Lee said, "Hey, you're management level now. No more overtime. Open it up."

Omari shook his head, an expression of pain battling with regret on his face, and brought the case into the web of computers, clearing away a pile of keyboards and a cable switcher to lay down the case.

Mani began washing Max's wounds, drawing his attention away from the men. She hovered over him like a bee over a rosebush, settling occasionally to draw blood as if it were pollen, a precious substance from which she could sustain herself. And like a bee, her ministrations stung. The Beast grumbled. Mani's shadow settled over his mind, encouraging him to let her heal him with pain, for her. He saw the controlling path she was taking as she tested the depth and strength of her influence over him.

He wanted to refresh the memories she had sampled from him, show her how his victims had fought in their desperate final moments. He wanted to tell her not all the scars he wore were earned at his work. The twins' mildest show of affection toward him hurt more.

The Beast's grumbling grew louder, provoked by Mani's stitching of one of his deeper wounds. Excited by her scent, the feel of her warm breath and fingers on his skin, the appetite emanating from her like midday heat off white sand, he became hard. She was letting herself go with him, releasing all that was inside along the bond they shared. "The beisac spirits' hunger infected you," Max said.

"I know," she answered, tying him off. She moved across his back, treating a bite on his shoulder, coming so close he thought she wanted to match the wound tooth for tooth. The Beast moved through him, rising to her need, eager to pounce. Mani's shadow answered the challenge, matched the Beast in threat and atrocity, promised more. The two spirits within them twined in a destructive embrace, eager for battle. Blood. Gratification.

Max wondered who, or what, was really in control of either of them. "Can you be satisfied?"

"No."

He let out air slowly as she closed another bleeding cut. "I understand." He rode the rising tide of pain on the Beast's back, trusting its appetite would take him where they had to go, as it always did. But Mani's beisac hunger rode the Beast with him, and suddenly he was no longer certain where they were all going.

He was not supposed to kill her. He could not kill her. He had to control himself, deliver her to his employers. Keep her safe.

A cut pinched shut under an astringent. Her fingers stung like wasps along the ribs under his arms.

Consume her.

He focused on Mani's spirit hunger, dissecting the quality of its ancient rage, trying to analyze whether its driving force was vengeance, a demand for compensation, or simply the poison expelled from some primal wound. When he found himself drifting to what he would do to her in answer to her rough touch, Max tuned in to Omari and Lee huddled over the open aluminum case.

114

"—fucking zombies thick as flies, a million cops coming down on us, our mission locked up in the trunk, and this asshole comes after *me*. Man, I could've shit bricks. So, is this the button that—"

Omari smacked away Lee's hand hovering over the case. "I have no intention of being caught in the Nowhere House field and losing memory. There, are you happy now? Seen one of the great achievements of Western science?"

"You're just jealous."

"Hardly. Like the discoverers of this anomaly, you miss the obvious."

"Kiss my ass. I know this is some kind of quantum device they locked down because they couldn't control it, and it does something with collapsing probabilities that creates a short-range field that drops everything inside it outphase with that . . . that perceived reality, and it messes with your head, but—"

"Please, go back to your American comic books. Everything is so vaguely scientific in your world."

"Yeah, and in your world, what is this, a down-on-his-luck god?"

Omari leaned into Lee and spoke quietly, so that Max had to strain to hear his words. "What this is is a stone, no bigger than your fingernail, that is part of the compressed remains of a sentient universe that leaked into this one. Or was drawn into it. The old Arabic scholars disagree. As they do over the cause of the breach between our existence and this entity's: Allah's will, the work of djinn and demons, a transgression by Mankind so great it tore the fabric of space and time."

115

"Oh, that must have been the day you were born, huh, Omari?"

"Your wit is exceeded only by your originality. No, my comrade, this treasure has been in the world for many eons, possibly since shortly after Creation. For it is believed by some that Allah created many worlds, indeed, many universes, and in each planted the seeds of life that took shape in ways different from one another, according to Allah's will. In one such place, formed one nanosecond before our own existence, the universal laws allowed Creation's foam to spread evenly through the void, rather than cluster in galaxies and stars. The life that came to be was not confined to a single ball of rock, but glistened in the forever of that universe, encompassing all of its reality."

"So this *is* a god—"

"It is Allah's will, as are we all. But the breach occurred, and this wretched sentience was introduced to space and, most traumatically, time. It beheld our universe, perceived probabilities, the constant of Allah's ever-changing glory; it tried to hold on to a single instant, and was driven mad by the splitting of moments and possibilities, past and future, and the infinite multiplicity of nows. Whether through the intent of escaping the trap of endless transformation, or an accident that is merely the will of Allah made manifest, this universe slipped through the breach and entered our time and our space. The husk of its matter was shredded in the rough transition, its invisible mass distributed among endless probabilities. The brittle essence of this existence, the quantum consciousness of another reality's single collapsed probability wave—its soul, if you will—did not go to Paradise, but instead settled like a volcano's fine ash to infect our universe with anomalies caused by its latent laws of physics. And so, even on this brightest of jewels in all of Allah's firmament, there exists a few fragments of fallen, mad, alien intelligence locked within the crystallized, even traumatized, ether of another reality. This case holds one such fragment. Others are scattered in the world's sacred places, where aboriginal minds first communed with spirits through such a medium. A trove lies at the bottom of the ocean, in your Bermuda triangle, stolen by the Spanish from Aztec temples devoted to experimenting with time and space, but lost in a storm during transport back to Europe. Your scientists claimed to have discovered this substance, though it has been known and explored secretly throughout humanity's history. More powerful than shaministic hallucinogens, its effects on human perception and memory make its study problematic. All your scientists have managed to draw out from its nature is the ability to hide without detection. Very brave. Stunning ingenuity. I suppose, after the Siberian accidents, and all the men and equipment the Russians lost trying to gather its own hoard of material from the bottom of the ocean and from deposits on the Moon and Mars, your Western leaders decided to pursue a safer path through the mysteries of this matter's existence."

Lee's fingers tapped a labored, funeral rhythm on the aluminum case. "So. Do you actually believe even one word of this crap you're laying on me?"

"There are times when the will of Allah can only be approached through the gullibility of Mankind."

"You're so full of shit, you make me smell good. You know, I think there are parts of the world where you can get killed for talking that kind of shit."

"And you are the one who comes here talking of zombies, dragging a witch, an assassin, and a bound, twitching dead boy with no eyes or heart."

Max roused himself from the swelling and subsiding rhythm of pleasure and pain riding the currents caused by Mani's fingers: "You sound like two old men."

Omari shut the case and brought it to Max, along with a notepad and paper. "Then it is time to pay my respects to you, my elder, and move on. The protocol says you must write yourself instructions on what you have to do next before you turn it on."

"Of course," Max grumbled. He put the case between his feet. It was far heavier than its size conveyed. "But your recording devices aren't going to work, and you won't be getting any telemetry from the instruments you've scattered around."

Omari started turning his head to glance at one of the hidden cameras Max had spotted in a ceiling joint. "Perhaps I should stay, for the experience."

"You won't remember. And what notes you'd write if you stayed wouldn't make any sense once you were outside."

"Hey, you idiot," Lee said, pulling out a rack of recording decks hidden inside an unblemished section of wall. "What the hell were you thinking?"

Omari dismissed Lee's discovery with a wave of a hand. "They meet your people's specs. This is a safe house, after all. It's *your* people who want everything and everyone recorded."

"Well, if that's the case, I guess I don't have to be debriefed since I told you what happened. What a relief. That makes what I want to do a hell of a lot simpler. . . ."

Max wrote two words on the pad, tore the paper, put it

in the pocket of the larger pair of jeans in the neat pile Mani had made of their clothes. He wrote another note, folded it, addressed it to the Housekeepers who were scheduled to visit tomorrow morning after he left, and put it on Omari's seat at the heart of his computer network.

Omari took the pad and pen from Max and considered them, tapping one against the other. "I suppose if I stayed, I *would* have the experience of the Nowhere House. But in forgetting that same experience, what would I gain? My life is recorded; I lose nothing in terms of contacts and business done, except the joy of their accomplishment. Is it worth the loss of life's memory to say I experienced something I can never remember?" Omari sighed and tossed the pad and pen down. "Perhaps another time, when memory is a burden rather than a precious cargo."

Lee shook his head. "Do you always work hard to make life that complicated, or is it something that comes naturally to you? Listen, if you don't mind, I'm gonna call in before Max here turns that thing on, and then I'm going to let it flush me out. I got enough things in my head without tonight's shit giving me more nightmares." He picked up the pad, looked to Omari. You go ahead and bring the car around. I'll be out in five minutes." He snapped his finger and took the cell phone from its hip holster. "Check in. They'll have to brief me again."

"If I'm supposed to take you to your next appointment, you're going to take a shower and change into those clothes I gave you."

Lee waved at him and nodded his head as he spoke quietly into the phone. Omari disappeared for a moment, returned with a duffel bag full of cash he was still zipping closed. Mani dressed the last of his wounds as the Beast

119

strained at the leash of Max's bond to Mani's shadow self, and his duty to his employers.

Lee closed the phone, went to Omari, and whispered to him. Mani kissed Max's ear, ran her tongue over his spine.

Omari opened a file cabinet and handed a sheaf of papers to Lee, who brought them over to Max. "Sorry, you know how it is," Lee said, hastily filling in blanks on forms before handing them over to Max to sign. Max glanced at Lee's notations on expense reports, time sheets, receipts for Mani, the Lincoln they had destroyed, weapons, Omari's services. "It's for the status and expense reports," Lee said apologetically. "Otherwise, you won't get paid, much less reimbursed for the car and stuff you lost. You know how these clerks are if they don't get their *t*'s dotted and *i*'s crossed. . . ."

Max signed until there were no more papers. Lee put them in a portfolio Omari passed to him, scribbled instructions to himself, and jammed them into the portfolio, as well, then grabbed his clothes and went off in the direction Omari pointed for the bathroom.

Omari paused in front of Max. "May you live long enough to see your enemies buried."

"I already have."

Omari stared for a moment, smiled. "Then may you live long enough to see them all find peace."

He went to the opening in the floor, stepped over it, pushed a loose brick in a wall in the next room. A motor started. A shelving unit slid back, revealing a hole opening onto a space between walls. A metal pole stood out in the latticework of pipes, cables, wall frames. A motorized foot stand descended the pole, trailing a power cord. Omari smiled at Mani's gasp. "Things easily gained lose their value," he said by way of explanation. "Would you have found all of this so impressive if you'd taken the elevator up?" He grinned, squeezed into the space. The door slid shut and the tiny elevator went down. Moments later, a door slammed.

Max took it as the signal to activate the Nowhere House. He opened the case, pushed the only button on a panel filled with screens, dials, status lights.

He felt no different. The red bulbs did not dim; the walls, ceiling, and floor did not waver in their solidity. The Beast still danced inside him to the music Mani played on his body, appetite running as deep and endless as ever. Mani's scent, the heat of her body, the sound of her breathing, outlined in vivid detail the absolute truth of Mani's presence and purpose.

Mani's clothes rained down on him from above as she stripped.

Max took his pants off. Stood. Turned. The Beast raced through him, already leaping at Mani. She smiled, shook her head, put her hands on his shoulders, and gently pushed him back to the floor until he was sitting at her feet.

She moved, in the way and with the meaning that had clouded the air between them by the car on the dead-end street. Hips swiveled, shoulders rolled, arms and legs parted the air with the grace of wings. The slight swell of her belly invited attention, seducing the eye with the allure of its curvature, enticing the mind with its promise of new life. Balanced, flowing, powerful, her movements absorbed the bulge and weight of the early pregnancy, making the burden a part of the dance. Her gaze locked with his, forcing him to peripherally take in her quivering breasts, nipples promising the milk of his pleasure, and the slit of her sex opening and closing, urging him to meet her thrust for thrust. His erection throbbed, ached. But his nature followed another groove Mani cut into the space between them.

Their hungers crashed, fought, merged, fell apart in the empty places within them. Mani's shadow self deepened, solidified, until she filled a part of Max's emptiness, nuzzling up against the Beast. The roots she had established in him grew. Fresh shoots of her desire pushed deeper into him, wound themselves around the Beast, choked Max's thoughts and instincts. In a remote part of his personal void, a terrible wind howled, bringing with it the cold of mountain peaks and the stinging of icy clouds: the imprint of beisac spirits, exploring new territory. Lightning flashed in his eyes, momentarily blinding him as the dead kissed the inside of his skull.

The Beast roared, the sound and fire of its rage chasing away the wind, cold, lightning. It clawed eagerly at Mani's spreading roots, burning her. She stumbled. Her startled expression illuminated fragments of her first experience with the Beast, when she had momentarily exchanged bodies with Max. Tears pooled in her eyes.

Recovering quickly, Mani danced, weaving their hungers back together again with the motion of her body. A fan of black hair brushed against his shoulders, a smile that was like a crescent moon shined its meager light on him. Max caught himself yearning for the fullness of her radiance. He fought against the desire to bathe in the depths of her mind and body, rather than her blood. The last of her tears fell on his folded hands.

Take her, the Beast whined. Kill her. The Beast fought

against a stranger's intrusion in its territory, even as it approached its adversary, tasting, testing, unwilling to lose Max, but questioning the power of a potential new ally.

Max caught the hint of the Beast's curiosity in someone other than its host. For all of its murderous demeanor, the Beast's initial encounter with Mani had left behind a sliver of interest. Max felt the question turning in the Beast's core, unspoken, a dead fetus incapable of living in speech: What new appetites could be fulfilled in the body of another host? Max responded with his own question: What might he gain by giving up the Beast and leaving himself open for a relationship with a new entity, or even a person?

He remembered being torn from the Beast, existing with nothing but himself, ghosts, and Mani's shell. From what he had experienced of her, he decided Mani was not the one to answer his question. He distracted the Beast from its curiosity with memories of bloody rampages.

Mani drew closer to Max in his mind while keeping their bodies apart. Her torso undulated, muscles rippling under smooth-as-silk flesh, inviting him, challenging him. The sheen covering her belly caught the red light, brightening her skin. The thread of a new life worked its way into him, rising from the memory of being inside her, insinuating itself into the pattern Mani wove inside him.

She drifted inside his reach, teasing him, but eluded his sluggish grabs for her. Beads of sweat arced through the air when she snapped and whipped her body to the sudden explosion of tempo in the rhythm their heat beats. The droplets splashed against him, cool and stinging hot at the same time.

Max's appetite burned and boiled like lava, setting everything in its path on fire.

Gerard Houarner

Mani approached him once more, this time bearing a tray. Kneeling next to him, she fed him slivers of pâté and peppers on crackers, offered water from a labeled bottle. He tasted her gifts, and the fingers that held the food, but did not bite. He swallowed his fill of water. She poured the rest over him, and then, laughing, opened another bottle and emptied it over both of them. Leaping up to dance in an intricate pattern of steps, she took an armful of bottles and doused them both with springwater. Max opened himself wide to the fresh shower, challenging her to douse the fire burning in him. Water flowed over his face, blinding him as his own fire had, filling his nose and ears, backing out of his throat and mouth when he could not swallow any more. Their currents of fire and water mingled, and Max found himself floating, then flying through the vapor that was their appetites and emptiness transformed.

The Beast, his life, the world he lived in receded from his awareness. He sensed the alien life Mani offered him gliding through the mist like a shark. He felt the coldness of death, the bright spark of life, Rithisak's child. Both watched him, waiting for his submission. Fatherhood crept into his awareness when he realized his role with Rithisak's child. The idea of a child in his arms, whether or not it was his, shocked him. He backed out of her offering of herself, spitting out water, getting out of the way of her dousing. He found firm anchorage in his rage and the Beast's hunger.

Lee's voice worked its way into the elemental war. Max blinked the water from his eyes and looked to his comrade.

"Whoa—hey," Lee said, emerging from a doorway. "Hello, I must be going. Pardon me, no thank you, I'd love to join the orgy but I just showered and, really, duty calls." Lee shielded his face with the portfolio as he trotted through Omari's central room, pausing only to grab a handful of Hooah! bars. He scrambled halfway down the passageway to the lower floors before he stopped, looking up and away from Max and Mani. "You turned that thing on, right?"

"Yes," Max answered.

"Don't feel no different. Funny to think I won't remember anything about tonight. It was good seeing you again, Max."

Max said nothing, staring at the curve of Mani's inner thigh. He thought the skin over her belly writhed with the baby's turning.

Lee gave up a low laugh. "You know, that asshole Omari is just another guy from Bed-Stuy. He's not Muslim, or even African, the way he likes to play he is. But he goes through changes being a player in this business. Keeps looking for something to hang on to, I guess. Next time, I'm betting he'll be dressed up like some corporate geek and believing in the military-industrial rap. Or he'll be opposition, trying to put a bullet in us. Or me, at least. But it's good to know some things stay what they are, you know what I mean?" He glanced at Max, hunched his shoulders against the dead boy's weak twitching, and wiggled down the hole. "Don't change," he called out.

"Some things never do," Max said.

"Some do, whether you want them to or not," Mani added.

Max looked to her, surprised by the wistfulness in her voice, then turned to Lee. But he was already gone. And in the moment he realized he was Mani's only protection against her enemy, he missed Lee, his last tie to the world he considered normal.

"Do you trust yourself with me?" Mani asked, giving voice to one of the questions on Max's mind.

Max kept the obvious answer to himself. The downstairs door shut with a resounding slam. They were alone in an invisible house, except for the children, one dead, one not yet born, both Rithisak's making.

"You shouldn't," Mani said, throwing away the water bottle in her hand. She stood over Max's lap, settled over his cock, engulfed his head in her bosom.

Mani's baby, Rithisak's seed, floated in its amniotic fluid inches away from him.

The dead boy jerked and bucked as if he were being whipped.

Max opened his mouth. What about the kid? he nearly asked. The Beast howled its indifference. Instead, Max filled his mouth with one of Mani's breasts. There was no more need for control.

He dug his fingers into her back and drew her closer. She arched her back, put her feet on his hips, pushed away. Max held on, surprised by her strength, and bit her nipple. She gasped, pulled his head closer, worked her fingers into his neck. Pain shot like a geyser into his head, and he released her. His own nipples tingled. The Beast snapped at the sudden shock of pain. Leaning back, she pressed her thighs against his ribs, still gently riding and squeezing him.

Max winced, though the pressure on his ribs was slight. He grabbed her thighs, fingers curled into claws and sinking into her flesh. She moaned, swayed, reached for him with outstretched arms and fingers.

Max felt the vibration of her voice in his throat; the pressure of his own viselike grip on his thighs; the warm, hard flesh-and-blood rod of his cock pushing between her hips, driving into her belly. The Beast's howl confirmed Mani's revival of their bond. Baptized by Mani's shower of water, their connection required more than an outburst of rage to be severed. Max's confidence in his ability to control the shadow cast by Mani in him began to waver.

Max released Mani. Slow, rhythmic grinding of bodies constructed a bridge of tension between them, allowing the syncopated traffic of pressure and release to flow back and forth in a free, open, and endless cycle. The pain vanished, allowing the sensual slick warmth between her legs to take his body over. Tickling, throbbing, pulsing sensations doubled, echoed, countered one another as they spread from the tip of his cock to its root. Contradictory impressions of penetrating and being penetrated filled his body to bursting. His mind stretched, encompassed the new, embraced the old. Heat suffused his belly and hips, as well as real and phantom organs. Electric tingling crept down his legs, up through his chest and arms, bursting at the base of his neck in small, flarelike explosions illuminating a range of sensory experiences he had never known.

The Beast chased the invading sensations, pounced on them, wallowed and submerged itself in their exotic variations. For both Max and the Beast, it was like discovering a new way to kill, a fresh means of experiencing blood and life leaking from a broken mortal shell. Max followed the Beast, but fought against abandoning himself to the orgy of perspectives and flavorings on familiar acts. The strangeness threw him off balance. His lack of control over the situation inhibited him. The image of self-penetration inspired a fear of self-insemination, and he wondered if, lost in the mystery of Mani's joining, there actually was a way to give himself a child, or pass her child to him.

A moment's rational thinking exposed the fear as ridiculous. But the murky depths of their lovemaking blurred the boundaries between the imagined and the real, the possible and fantastic. The logical conclusion slipped away and fear returned, as Max realized the superimposition of Mani's sexuality, as dim as it might be, was itself impossible and should not be happening.

"You see?" she whispered in his ear, her moist tongue teasing the cartilage, playing with the fleshy lobe. "You can be more than your animal spirit. You can escape the bonds of your human spirit. Be something more... yes..."

Hands stroked his body, fondled and probed ears, mouth, balls, anus. Her mouth found clusters of nerves at the base of his neck and set them on fire; her tongue traced the routes of his nerves, laying down the boundary of her territory, encompassing him, overwhelming him with the riches she offered. The power of her dance across his body drew him into her reality, seduced him, and promised him all that he could ever wish. But when he wished for a victim's anguished scream, he received pleasure's moan and gasp. Mani's pleasure. And when he fought against her appetite, when he stoked the rage and mindless appetite that lived within him, the Beast rose, foundered, collapsed, suddenly without direction or purpose, gorged on the banquet of her sensation, as rich as any feast it had ever consumed with Max.

Max lifted her up, freeing himself from the enticement of her motion, breaking the spell she wove over his body and instincts. He tried to throw her back, but her legs snaked over and around his shoulders, ankles locking. The shadowed petals of her pleasure's source parted before him as if he were the life-giving embodiment of the sun, or a bug to be used to propagate her species. Hips rolled, inviting him to sample the musky depths of what lay between them. Max traveled the length of her legs, inhaling the subtle perfumes mingling in her sweat, savoring her skin's texture, tasting skin seasoned by fear and death, rubbing his cheek against the strength of her dancer's legs. She balanced herself in his hands, gazed at him from the floating perch of his hands. Mysteries swam in the depths of her eyes. The salty tequila taste of her sex intoxicated him, driving him to consume the hallucinatory worm of her clit. She cried out, mystery turning to raw truth for the moment. The Beast screeched in glee.

The moment leapt across their bond, locking them both in a lightning flash of brilliant ecstasy. The beat of her heart, the pulse of her life and pleasure, flowed through him along the well-worn channels of his own fulfillment. His crotch warmed in the flood tide of her excitement. The Beast chased ghost organs. His face flushed, and shivers shot up his spine in an empathic mimicry of her orgasms.

He saw and felt himself through her, and was both drawn to and repulsed by the brutish mass he perceived himself to be through her eyes. Senses merged and consciousness melded, drawing them together in an inescapable embrace. Pieces of their lives reflected one another, or stood out in stark contrast to each other: death to death, life to death, hunger to appetite. Commonalties as broad as death joined them, and even oppositions as stark as their sex brought them closer together. Whether in the city or the jungle, alone or in the midst of village life, the essence of their lives was not so different. They had both been touched in their youth by terrible powers, and both carried the weight of appetites not entirely their own. In another life, she might have been his sister.

The lightning vanished. Cast out of rapture's clarity, Max tumbled back to the world of flesh and blood. He rode the wild current of their wedded passion gushing from the meeting place of their hungers.

Awakened to a new level of self-awareness by their communion, the life she carried in her stirred, parting darkness, separating itself from her, from them. To Max's horror, it rose like fish to bait, seeking out the primal sustenance of their mutual gratification. A toothless mouth opened onto an appetite as great as the Beast's or Max's. The residue of their joining vanished into the maw.

Rithisak's child moved in Mani, in Max, eager to throw itself into their dance. Mani's beisac spirit ran thick through the child, already poisoned with Rithisak's blood. The taint of its corruption sent waves of nausea through Max, like a piece of spoiled meat curdling in his belly. He wanted to expel the warped shell stunting the spirit it housed, but the child was not in him to push out. He wanted to tear the baby from Mani, tell her the creature she carried demanded too high a price for granting her freedom from Rithisak. The *beisac* spirit rose, protesting Max's urge. Its voice drowned out Mani's child. The Beast heard the terrible call and answered, raising its own voice, demanding its fill of pain and suffering. Mani's appetite responded, along with Max's base desires, until a cacophony of cries deafened him. Heightened by nausea, the noise in his head stunned and dizzied Max. Confronted by a pool full of snapping jaws shoving each other out of the way in their desperation to catch what crumbs of agony and pleasure he found to throw to them, a sense of helplessness crushed Max. Appetites, all taking, demanding, grabbing, trapped him in a feedback loop of inescapable frustration. No matter how many he killed or tortured, no matter how much pleasure he took, there would never be enough to satisfy them all. Too many hungers crowded their two adult mortal shells.

Max threw her away, sending her crashing into a stack of cardboard boxes. Cans of paté spilled out with a clatter. The bond between them weakened with the distance, but like the ocean at low tide, did not vanish. Max still felt the cold, relentless *beisac* spirit reaching out for the living, as well as Mani's own hunger. Even her appreciation of his harsh treatment reached him, though he was not surprised with her familiarity with the infliction of cruelty. Rithisak did not impress him as a gentle lover. Her child lay stunned within her, however, still alive but caught unprepared by the world's harshness.

Max got up, stalked Mani as she crawled among the boxes, slapped the back of her head until she turned, then fell on her. The Beast settled into its own predatory hunger, reinforcing Max's appetite, though Max heard the plaintive edge to its brutal cry. It reached for Mani's shadow self, pawed over the bond linking their two bodies, desperate to reopen the floodgates of sensation. It wanted more than prey. The Beast enjoyed the new perspective of living inside its prey's pain and terror, demanded more.

Max fought against the inexorable flow, as thick and hot as lava, opening between Mani and him. He threw himself into assaulting her body, raking and striking her, savagely thrusting into her, feeding off her cries. But she fought, as well, surprising him with her strength, her skill in avoiding the worst of his blows, as well as her own brutal strikes to the wounds she had just tended. They wrestled in their lovemaking, Max racing ahead of the charging wave of their overpowering bond, and though he dominated, Mani held her own. She showed him she could survive, even thrive, under his attention, with or without the distraction of their linked minds and spirits.

Even the child rode out his assault, Max noted, suspicious of the fetus's durability. Mani's subtle body shifting provided some protection from the worst of his abuse, but when Max used their bond to test and taste the child's life, he discovered the separate current of life coursing in Rithisak's blood child. Through the lens of Mani's shamanistic powers of perception, he saw the threads of power connecting mother and child that, when called upon by Mani, had allowed Rithisak to track her. Pushing deeper into the womb, he saw power flaring to shield the baby from his weight, thrusts, and blows. A latent tangle of spells and incantations woven by Rithisak, founded on the power in the blood and spirit that was his share of the child, formed thick walls as tough as leather to cushion copulation's random violence.

Max withdrew from the tangle of alien worldviews and understandings. Seeing himself through his own eyes, Max dismissed the fantasies of magic and supernatural interventions. He had no doubt he could physically force his way past Rithisak's ephemeral safeguards and kill the unborn child. He did not believe in magic, despite Mani's apparent abilities. He had never seen a spell to stop a bullet or a knife. Something lodged inside him protected the child.

Focusing on the unfamiliar in his usual arsenal of emotion, Max found, to his astonishment, that he did not want to hurt Mani's baby. A nascent need to protect it from his own brutality had taken root in him. The Beast, captured by the wealth of Mani's sensations, had not focused on the child as prey, allowing the protective instinct to grow. Mani's acquiescence to his appetite curbed his naturally destructive impulses toward the child. But what shocked Max was the discovery of a maternal bond he now shared, along with so much else, with Mani. In the polluted corners of his mind, Max felt as much a mother to Rithisak's offspring as Mani.

His realization opened the floodgates for more of Mani's self to gush into his mind. Max roared along with the Beast as Mani's interior world enveloped them once more. Max continued to lead their dance, biting, clawing, lapping up the blood she spilled, even as Mani channeled his emotions, and the beisac spirit cast its cold regard across his life, and the child stirred, hungry again. Instead of trying to hold off the chaos, Max concentrated his strength in keeping a tiny part of himself detached, riding the onrushing tide of their intimacy, watching the play of spirits and minds to catch weaknesses and vulnerabilities.

And as the savage play of their bodies wore on, with neither he nor Mani giving in or dying, Max realized that making love did not necessarily have to end in death. Both he and the Beast could be satisfied with something else, though the alternative was like nothing he had ever seen in the mortal world. He wondered what came after the lovemaking ended, and how long that period lasted, and what happened if he got tired of making love to Mani over and over again and really did want her to die. Would she just walk away? Could he? And if they parted, which was the only certainty to Max, even in the heat of their lust, who else might survive his appetite?

A violent spasm rocked Mani's body and threw Max off. Blood smeared across her face, Mani looked over her body, stared at Max, and smiled. Her laughter reverberated inside Max, invited him to pounce on her again.

The Beast leapt, but Max remained still. The room's balance was off. Something was missing. He surveyed Omari's lair, taking in the minor damage caused by their passion. Stopped.

The dead boy was missing.

Eyes adjusting to the real world again, Max got up, checked the malfunctioning surveillance equipment, and inspected the top floor. Mani called out after him twice, but by the time he returned she was curled up in a nest of their clothes gathered in a tight space between shelving racks. Bruises darkened her face and body. Blood seeped from cuts. Her body trembled, as if anticipating more gestures of his affection. Their connection shriveled as Mani retreated into herself, leaving Max's mind with a final impression of beisac spirits closing in on both of them. Terror descended like a fog to seal her off.

With her living presence gone from his mind, both Max and the Beast ached from her abandonment. Caught between lust for blood and the crash from an intoxicating rush of emotion and sensation, the Beast sought comfort in Mani's shadow self. Max sank for a moment into the past, recalling a little boy lost on a city street full of noises he did not understand, packed with people and things far larger than he.

The dead boy. What happened to the dead boy?

An explosion rocked the building, shooting a deafening blast through the stairwell and ducts. Max bounced as the floor jumped, then sprang to his feet. Plaster rained down on them, along with loose insulation, wooden planks, dust. One of the shelving units against the wall tipped over, spilling cartons and papers over a bank of computer towers. Broken glass tinkled. Altars on the lower floors crashed.

Max remembered his plan. Rithisak had arrived, guided to the Nowhere House by the dead boy. It was time to end their duel.

Max stopped by one of Omari's weapons caches and picked up a shotgun, leaving a .45 he wanted for backup because he had no place to put it. Pausing only to load shells, Max descended to the second floor.

He dropped down ready to fire, but the floor was clear. He waited, listening, heard only his own breathing, his heart beating. A cleared swath cut through the dust and refuse covering the floor. Advancing through the altar rooms, Max followed the dead boy's trail, checking corners and under tables for signs of the corpse or intruders. He picked up the stench of the decomposing body, as well as Rithisak's animating compound, but the boy had gone ahead.

Someone else was watching him. He felt the gaze hot on the back of his neck.

Finger on the trigger, he waited for the ambush. He lowered the shotgun, pretending to relax, leaving himself open for an instantaneous reaction to the attack that refused to come.

Max moved on, drifting away from the dead boy's trail, knowing it could only lead to the stairs. He was more interested in catching his observer. He wondered if Rithisak wanted to negotiate a truce and settle for a farewell meeting with Mani. Max could not decide if he'd let them meet before he killed Rithisak, or simply eliminate the shaman as they went back upstairs. The Beast, coiled to attack, wanted to spring at first sight of their enemy.

Smoke drew him to the altar piled with statues, toys, and candles they had passed on the way up. Spilled candles ignited cigarette packs, money, and plastic, starting a dozen small fires. Max took a step toward the altar, stopped, suddenly chilled, feeling his nakedness for the first time.

The altar's Kali statue moved. Blue skin shimmering in the flickering light, skull necklace swinging, skirt of severed arms exposing her thighs, the statue sidestepped through the clutter of baby and animal dolls dressed in homemade patchwork clothing. With each step, the statue grew, until it stood as tall as Max atop the altar. Looking down on Max, Kali smiled, flicked her tongue out at him. In her eyes, Max saw the sign on the wall he had touched.

The cracked wall behind the altar burst apart. A tall, naked, muscular black man pushed through the wreckage, a body under each arm. The ruined eyes and chest hole of the corpse the stranger carried under one arm declared its undead loyalty to Rithisak. The twitching, bleeding Asian man under the stranger's other arm wailed and pleaded in the Khmer tongue Max had heard earlier in the evening.

He did not need a translator to understand the dying man's plea.

Max brought the shotgun up. The Beast screamed. Max fired twice, peppering the walls and altar with shot. The Kali figure twirled, hissed, eyes blazing. The tall man, his body untouched by the pellet spray, threw the corpses down at Kali's feet, distracting her.

"You are at a crossroads," the man said, embracing Kali from behind as she scooped out Rithisak's compound from the corpse's eyes and chest hole and consumed it. "Choose carefully." Kali picked up the freshly dead man, tore the head off, raised the body overhead, and let the blood pour over her.

The figures coupled under the blood shower as Max backed away. The Beast urged him to join the pair. They both looked at Max as if hearing the Beast, sensing Max's temptation. The man nodded, laughing. Kali opened her mouth wide, ready to consume him. Max raised the shotgun to fire again. His erection pointed like a dowsing stick at the pair, distracting him. He tripped, fell backward through a doorway. The gun went off again, blowing a hole through the ceiling and sending down a blizzard of dust and debris. Sitting up, Max checked the altar room. The two figures were gone, though the small fires scattered through the shaken collection of relics and offerings had spread. Wood crackled, plastic popped. A burnt chemical smell made him cough. His own gun smoke stung his nostrils.

Something moved under his legs. The dead boy, still bound, squirmed underneath him. It twisted, bit his calf. Pain enraged the Beast and shocked Max into action. He blasted the dead thing's head apart, then shoved the barrel into its chest and excavated its torso with another shot. The Beast roared with joy. Wiping blood from his leg and splatter from his skin with the dead boy's shredded clothing, he traced the corpse's crawl path back to the stairs. From the broad trail on the steps, Max saw it had already gone downstairs. Blast marks scarred the floorboards and walls. Wisps of smoke blew up the stairs on the breeze blowing in through the open door and the Nowhere House warping veil.

The boy and, if the altar scene had not been a hallucination, two more dead agents lost to Rithisak. How many more of the corpse puppets had survived the alley, he wondered, and how many living agents?

It did not matter.

Max stood at the top of the stairs, shotgun at the ready, daring Rithisak to show himself. The Beast reveled in his nakedness, eager to bathe in the blood and guts of its enemies. Max drew upon the shadows and ghosts in his head to distract and contain the Beast, and managed to keep the Beast from driving him down to the first floor and tearing it apart in a sweep for Rithisak. He listened to the creak of wood as he shifted his balance, the rasp of his breathing, his own heartbeat. And when they were a part of him, invisible, he listened for anything else. The altar fire, spreading slowly, sputtering, choking on objects of spiritual importance before finding mundane fuel, rustled in the background. Rats scurried behind the walls. The madness of an alien entity screamed between the layers of reality shifting through the building. Max listened for the slide of metal on metal, the whisper of a bullet being readied to fire.

He waited, feeling Rithisak seethe in the darkness beyond the string of red lights. His cock grew hard once again at the thought.

The bulbs went out, casting the safe house in darkness. Max knew only of the light switch by the door. He was certain there was another upstairs, in Omari's den. But going for the lights meant giving ground, letting Rithisak closer to Mani. Max kept to his post, weathering the Beast's frenzy to attack.

No living men shot at him, no dead men lunged for his throat. Rithisak's agents were gone. Max understood guns were not the sorcerer's weapons, and waited for more tricks to manifest themselves.

He fired a warning blast into the darkness and waited. The blast rang with satisfying harshness in his ears.

Hungry spirits howled in his mind. Mani's shadow self stirred.

"Mani," a voice called from the darkness.

"No," Mani shouted from above. "Stop."

Max turned to tell her to shut up, stopped as a mental wave of thoughts and emotions slammed into him. Their bond opened as Mani reached for the strength to resist her old lover. His chest constricted as her grip on him tightened. He felt the weight of all her fears like an anchor pinning him to the spot. Desire and dread flooded him. Something cold brushed the inside of his skin.

A gentle rapping dragged Max back into the real world, and he fired another shot. The flash showed no one on the stairs. Max sat on his haunches and went back to waiting, the Beast and Mani both heavy on his mind. Mani's memory of beisac spirits filled the back of his head like a glacier, its weight bearing down on his thoughts and nearly crushing them.

Four loud raps from the bottom of the stairs startled Max, and he fired again.

No, he thought he heard Mani say. He's using us. He's with us, in our minds, through my old bond with him.

"What?" Max asked. The house remained silent.

But in his head he heard Mani say, He's using your own power against you. Watch—

Or was it Mrs. Chan trying to teach him her way of defeating an enemy with his own strength. But Mrs. Chan was not here. Mani was not using her voice to speak to him. There was no one else close by in the darkness. Ghosts and magic did not really exist.

The Beast's roar was edged with panic. Death muffled its voice, suffocated its explosive energy, reflecting the horror the Beast delivered to others. In death, the Beast feared it might never be satiated again.

Light drew Max's attention from the psychotic war of voices, memories, and feelings being waged in him. Gratefully, he stared down the stairs at the fuzzy column of light growing, expanding, solidifying out of darkness into a woman. She glowed, illuminating herself but not the blackness around her, like a star in the depths of space. Dressed in an open robe that slowly lifted and snapped in a breeze Max could not feel, she struck a familiar pose. Plump thighs and wide, heavy hips led to a rounded potbelly and full waist. The wide aureoles of her breasts focused attention like flowers to her erect nipples, which she pinched and stroked with small, thick-fingered hands. A faint smile creased her smooth, round face as her half-closed eyelids fluttered with the dream of an imaginary lover. The cascade of her auburn hair fell over cheeks and ears to land in a riotous pool across her shoulders.

The Beast remembered her. Max had raped and killed her weeks ago. She was one of his victims, an unconscious and unwitting offering seen through an apartment window and taken by himself and the Beast to satisfy their appetites.

Her eyes opened. She looked up. Max felt her gaze pass through him, fix on a sight that teased a wider smile from her lips. She nodded.

Max went down the stairs.

Machinery started up in the distance. Elevator, Max told himself. Danger. He knew there was danger, but did not understand how he should react. The Beast focused on the woman before them, anticipating the taste of resurrected prey. Go back up the stairs, he told himself. Go back to Mani. A plan unfolded in his head on a chessboard design of the Nowhere House: a threat to the flank, forcing him to react and retreat back up the stairs to protect Mani from Rithisak on the elevator. But it was a feint. Rithisak was here, on the ground floor. Max smelled him on the shining woman. He felt the man's jealous breath on his neck.

The woman cocked her head to the side, floated away from the stairs. Max followed.

He hunted, the Beast casting its sensory net wide for Rithisak. It reared, withdrew, confused by the emptiness. Max pushed on, chasing the woman by sight through the ground-floor warren of rooms and apartments. She disappeared around corners, appearing farther off as soon as he made the same turn, lengthening her lead. Her flight challenged him, and he taunted the Beast, which no longer begged him to give chase but instead circled restlessly, lost, hungry, sullen. He broke into a run, reveling in the lead he was taking over the Beast in the hunt, showing his inner döppelganger that he was still strong, he could provide for them even if the Beast failed. He did not need its rage; he had enough of his own.

The woman vanished. Max stumbled over a beam, crashed into a wall. The shotgun went off, its sudden discharge shocking him. He fell, disoriented, stabbing pain shooting through his ears into his head. Old wounds opened, new ones stung as he rolled naked over bricks, concrete, wood, glass, nails.

Voices called to him. Women's voices, strained by terror and pain and anguish. Gagging, coughing, choking, spitting out fluids and teeth, they spoke his name. Max started to get up, but their voices drove him back to the ground where he covered his head to shield himself from the invisible flurry of his own name beating him down. And when they were done calling, they laughed. Cackled.

Like a shower of broken glass, their voices cut him.

Beside him on the floor, a figure grew out of darkness, bone and sinew and muscle blackened to a radiant absolute deeper than night, brighter than the shine of polished ebony. The thing had no face, and the holes for its eyes, nose, and mouth were warped out of true shape and locale. It whimpered, on the edge of death but undying. Beyond it, a tiny, undernourished boy sat at the center of a crossroads, filthy, weeping, alone. Himself again, with some version of the Beast either from the past or the future in the foreground.

A scream sounded, the faint recapitulation of theme in the symphonic chorus of laughter. Max listened closely, realized it was his own.

Another scream erupted, faint, dissonant, a minor variation of pain he dismissed at first as something of his. But the voice persisted, growling louder, taking its place in the cackling. The edge of its pain was sharper than anything Max had ever experienced or inspired. The voice had suffered its torment for a long time, but it seemed to him that it had only just found a shape for the scream of its release. Or perhaps the voice always knew the shape of pain and had been held in check by limitations of flesh and mind. Perhaps, by encountering Max, the voice had finally crossed a threshold beyond which it was free to express its inner self. Max was certain only that the scream inside his head was not his.

The scream grew louder, a pure and intense note, rushing through a private pipeline from its source to him, until its intoxicating pitch became a line, a road, a boundary, and a gate. The Beast awakened from its stupor, sensing a return to appetite and its fulfillment. Max focused beyond the moment and its cutting-glass laughter, inspired by the promise of a route out of his paralysis. The scream stretched out, its path through him weaving laughter and pain into one, bringing order out of the chaos, introducing the clarity of vision beyond his suffering.

And in that moment of clarity, Max remembered Mani. Upstairs. The sound of the elevator working. Rithisak.

The spell broke. In its shattered pieces, Max recognized Rithisak's hand corrupting the link he shared with Mani and seeding his mind with the poisons of doubt, guilt, fear.

He stood and ran.

Mani's scream was real, shattering the safe house's silence. It guided him back up the stairs, floor, ladder, to Omari's technological aerie.

The red bulbs were on, illuminating a cleared space

among the racks of equipment and supplies where Mani moved.

Danced.

Mouth open, eyes wide, the scream a ceaseless river of sound gushing from her throat like blood, like the Beast's roar, like the pain and pleasure of living, Mani danced to the accompaniment of her own droning voice. Muscles twitched beneath red-tinged skin as her arms and hands snaked through the air, fashioning invisible signs, warning and inviting at the same time. Hips and shoulders rolling, thighs glistening with sweat, she stepped lightly across the small space of her stage, delicate and graceful, untouchable and powerless: like mist in moonlight.

And at the mouth of a corridor between two rows of packed shelves, a thin, bald, Asian man stood in a baggy set of casual clothes that made him appear much younger than the lines on his forehead and the corners of his eyes declared him to be.

"Rithisak!" Max shouted, closing the distance between them.

Words pummeled Max from the inside out, forcing him to stop, bend over, and absorb the blows: Do not stand in the way of our love, unless you wish to be consumed by it.

"Fuck you," Max muttered.

The Beast rose to Rithisak's challenge, overcome by the flesh-and-bone promise of true prey. Max stood, lurched toward Rithisak. His hands reached forward, fingers curled into claws.

You challenge an àp thmòp, naked and unarmed? The question came riding the crest of voiceless laughter, though not the cutting kind Max had just escaped. The wave crashed, blinding Max in a maddening jumble of perspectives, voices, thoughts, feelings. He saw himself through Rithisak's eyes: nude, scarred, wild-eyed and dangerous, flailing now as if fighting off a storm of wasps. He saw himself through Mani's eyes: wounded, vulnerable, enticing. And he saw himself through the death-cursed creature Mani carried, though the meaning of the infant entity's psychic perceptions eluded him while leaving a residue of nausea.

The little man jumped forward, producing a small wax figure from his pocket. Ducking under Max's grasp, Rithisak rubbed the figure against his body, catching blood and sweat and bits of skin. He backed away, drew out a pin, stuck it into the figure while whispering to it. Pain shot through Max's ribs, burst in his stomach, in correspondence to the area on the doll pricked by the sorcerer.

Too late, Rithisak told him in a gloating thought before returning his attention to Mani.

Too late, Mani said. Our time together has passed.

Max was not certain if she spoke to him or to Rithisak. Pain lanced him again, this time from the side of his neck to his hip. He kept moving, pain fueling rage, his own and the Beast's; rage fueling motion, in the physical world, and in the mad universe trapped in the meat of his brain. Mani slid out of his way as her scream wore on, passing so close to him he heard her cycling her breath to sustain the note.

Do you love her as I do? Rithisak asked.

"Never," Max answered, using the word to strike Rithisak in place of his hands.

The scream stopped. Max staggered, as if its absence had knocked out a vital underpinning to his balance.

Someone grunted.

A tiny wail answered.

"No. . . ." A man's wavering voice. Rithisak's true voice, escaping the weathered husk of his body.

Max's head and vision cleared as the flood coursing through the bond he shared with Mani subsided. Rithisak stood a few feet away, and Max rushed forward, striking the doll from the man's hands. The wax figure fell headfirst to the floor. A blow to Max's head stunned him, dropped him to his knees. The Beast urged him back to his feet.

Rithisak moved away, leaving the doll behind. The sorcerer's mouth hung open. Tears streaked his face. A high-pitched whine escaped from his quirked lips. He ignored his danger, the fallen doll, transfixed instead by something out of Max's peripheral vision. Max turned.

Mani held the blood-drenched placental tissue and minuscule, twisted corpse of her expelled fetus in her hands, which she held out in offering to Rithisak as she fell to the floor.

Max moved to her. The Beast rebelled, pushed him to Rithisak. Max went for the sorcerer, intercepted him as he dove for the child. Max caught Rithisak by the shoulders, whirled him around. Where are your tricks now? he wanted to say. Instead, he scooped one of Rithisak's eyes out, then the other, in mocking mimicry of the ritual defilement the sorcerer had performed to animate his corpse agents. The Beast roared with pleasure at the irony, and made Max pop both morsels into his mouth. Max rejoiced in the spiced flavorings in Rithisak's blood, the sweet milk of his eyeball fluids, the stringy meat of torn flesh and ligament. The song of Rithisak's agony made his heart race, made the Beast convulse with pleasure.

Something wrenched free inside Max. The trickle of foreign thoughts and emotions stopped. Max nearly let go of the sagging Rithisak. Where once he and the Beast had been more than enough to fill him, it seemed to Max that they were alone in vast and silent cavern. The Beast, oblivious in the heat of its passion, pressed for more blood.

Farewell, an echo of Mani whispered to one of them, any of them, none of them. A final breeze of her thoughts passed through Max, like a dying exhalation. He caught the hunger of beisac spirits, and loneliness, and terror of abandonment. Their passage resonated within him, made his flesh crawl. And he caught a last word, prãy, and an image, a ghostly woman and child, taken too soon from life, filled with hatred for the living. He recoiled from the image even as the thought passed.

On the floor, Mani's shoulders sagged. The fetus fell from her hands, landed wetly on the floor. Her eyes closed. A rattling escaped her lungs.

Cold darkness blanked Max's vision for a moment. The sparse shadow self nestled in him disintegrated into a brief twinge of anxiety, and the burden of their bond dissipated, leaving a hollow still warm from her presence.

Rithisak screeched, Mani's death propelling the sorcerer into new realms of torment. Anguish carved a carnival of terrible expressions on Rithisak's face. Max watched, the Beast consumed. When the physical pain of his absent eyes regained ascendancy in the hierarchy of suffering, Max threw Rithisak to the floor. He grabbed an antique bayonet from a stack of edged weapons on a shelf, carved Rithisak's chest open with savage thrusts and manic rips backed by his body weight, and pushed his hand into the gash he made in the sorcerer's torso.

The Beast devoured atrocity, drinking deeply from its

147

excess, as Max straddled Rithisak and rode his desperate convulsions. Max found Rithisak's heart, tore it out, ate it.

When Max was finished with the meat, and had moved past gnawing at bones, chewing on gristle and tendons, lapping at blood, and thrusting his cock into empty eye sockets of his enemy, Rithisak was a withered bag of skin between Max and the floor, emptier than the corpses he had brought back to serve him. The Beast lay sated in the kennel of Max's mind.

Max rolled off the body. Stared at Mani.

The Nowhere House embraced them. Max thought he might never leave the moment, never escape the walls of the tomb he had created for his enemy, and for the woman he had been made responsible to protect. He wondered what would happen if he smashed the Nowhere House case. Would he be trapped forever in a space between worlds, a time between moments? With the Beast quiet, his body exhausted, his mind raw, Max did not think his entombment was a bad fate.

A shadow moved. A strand of Mani's hair fell away from her face. The tiny head on the nearly translucent fetus jerked.

Above Mani, the air wavered like a desert horizon in midday heat. Max crawled away from Mani's body. The shimmering air brightened, leaching color from the red bulbs, hurting Max's eyes. A gust of cold air blew over Max, and through the emptiness left inside him in Mani's wake.

A woman appeared, transparent, hovering over Mani, an infant at her feet. Her hair was long, as were her nails, and her mouth opened into a feral grin. The face was vaguely Asian, obscured as if a filtered lens or warped window separated the woman from the rest of existence. The baby dripped blood from its eyes and ears. Both glared at Max. The Beast stirred, stimulated by the apparition.

The gust returned, strengthened, until wind whipped through the floor with sudden hurricane intensity, sending shelving and racks crashing to the floor, launching papers, plastic, nails, and knives into the air. Laughter reminiscent of what Max had heard downstairs, chasing Rithisak's decoy, joined the wind's howl.

Max curled himself into a ball, covered his head. "Mani," he shouted, and again, with all the force he could raise, stretching the word so that it was as long and plaintive as the wind, he shouted, "Mani!"

The wind died away. A brief shower of objects clattered back to earth. The woman and child looked away from Max, then faded. Vanished.

Leaving Max alone, again.

Spent and ravaged, he slipped into a sleep without dreams.

When he woke, he thought at first that everything he remembered happening was a dream. The remains on and around him brought reality into focus. Max sat up, tried to shake out the detritus of a waking nightmare. As he sorted through memories, separating his own from Mani's and whatever else had taken root in his mind, he paused at the horror that had coalesced over Mani's body. Like a scavenger digging up a grave, the memory dragged another piece of the past out of him: the woman haunting the foot of the stairs. More tumbled into the light of consciousness: the faces of women he had killed in the service of his appetite. They surrounded him, smiles turning into rictus grins, soft eyes hardening into stones of petrified terror.

He had already slaughtered the undead. He wondered what it would be like to kill again what he had killed and consumed.

The Beast released a contemptuous snarl. Memories fled.

Max showered, dressed in the clothes Omari left for him. Soap, water, and fresh clothes could not touch the raw wounds left by Mani's passage through him. The Beast seemed small in the space carved out of him by all that had happened. Max's own appetites revolted him, as if the shape of Mani's former presence corrupted his self-perception. The taste of blood and flesh soured in his mouth. His balls throbbed, his cock felt like a shriveled root exposed too long to the sun. Worms of doubt and guilt squirmed in the turned earth of memory, exposing bits and pieces of the undigested past. His body ached. Sadness suffocated his mind, crushed his chest, decayed in his gut.

He quelled his flaring temper over the strange feelings, telling himself and the Beast they would soon be gone.

As he started climbing down the ladder to the lower floors, he surveyed the wreckage left behind. The stench of bodies perfumed the air. Roaches and rats darted from the walls, eager to sample the new feast laid out for them. Flies buzzed. He smiled at the bloody mystery his superiors would discover when the Nowhere House machinery turned itself off. Whom could they debrief? It was the kind of joke Lee would appreciate, and Max regretted not being able to tell him about it.

Or even remember that the trick had been played.

At the door to the Nowhere House, Max decided he needed a vacation. A restless new hunger rumbled beneath his sadness, though he could not put a name to it. He needed a change, though he did not want to change himself. Perhaps if he took the twins away, if they explored new places and appetites together, the world might be cast in fresh colors, and new tastes might be found to satisfy him, and the Beast within.

He opened the door. The city lay restless under night's cover, muttering and squirming in a nightmare's grip. Streetlamps glowed like distant, fuzzy candles through the Nowhere House shielding. Confident the taste for new adventure would stay with him, though he could never recall its genesis, Max stepped through the doorway.

The world spun around Max's head, his stomach lurched, and for a moment he forgot who he was, and where, and why. He landed on concrete, scraping his cheek and palms. When he got up, he did not know where he was, or why he was unarmed. The Beast, startled by the sudden loss of balance, cried out in protest. Max judged by its sluggishness that he had recently feasted, though he could not recall stalking prey. His body's condition told him he had just finished a serious piece of work for his employers, though his target and the assignment's difficulties were out of his reach. Light-headed, almost giddy, Max had a feeling it was better that he not remember. The Beast curled itself around forgetfulness like a pup at a teat.

He dug into his pockets looking for car keys, wondering at the false identity he had picked requiring the cut and make of clothes he wore. He found a piece of paper on which he had apparently written two words: GO HOME.

Max crumpled up the piece of paper and tossed it away. He took off along the street, checking doorways and rooftops and cars for signs of ambush, but finally trusting himself not to leave himself in obvious danger without more detailed instructions. He did avoid the patrol cars cruising through the neighborhood, in case he had something to do with the heightened police presence.

The elevated highway and street names oriented him. Knowing he was in the Bronx, he worked his way past police checkpoints and patrols, taking alleys, rooftops, sewers, and utility conduits. While searching for an unguarded subway station, he found a phone and called the twins to check on them, and see if he had left himself a message with them as to what had happened and what he was supposed to do. Alioune answered the phone.

"Where have you been?" she demanded, then passed the phone to her sister before he had a chance to answer.

"I don't know," he said to dead air.

"Are you all right, Tonton?" Kueur asked as she picked up the line, her tone gentler but, like Alioune's, stressed by worry.

Max vomited. His stomach's rebellion surprised him, as did the mix of undigested morsels of flesh and food he regurgitated. He hated wasting prey, even if it proved too corrupt to nourish him. Especially, among other things, an enemy's heart, as he judged by the meat on the sidewalk and his reaction to it.

Alioune continued when he came back on the phone. "We heard what happened in the Bronx. It's on the news."

"What happened in the Bronx?"

"Well, it sounded like you. Did you take care of our package?"

"What package?"

Kueur sighed dramatically into the phone. "Tonton Bébête, why don't you come by. . . . We have a fresh pot of palava and mint tea."

"I never called you tonight?"

"*Non*, Tonton, you did not."

"I think I'll go home. I'm very tired for some reason."

"Will we see you soon?"

The music of her voice raised his mood. The Beast rose, happy to bask in her attention. A police siren blared nearby.

"Yes, Kueur. I'll see you soon."

"Good. Maybe we can get away. It's been so long since we went on a vacation, even if it's only for a weekend."

Max hung up. The idea did not sound bad.

He wondered what they would hunt together.

Part Two

The Beast That Was Max

Chapter One

"No," Alioune replied. She met Max's gaze without flinching, letting her sweetly seductive African-French accent take the edge from her denial. "We do not want her. Not now. Not like this. Not from you."

"But you said you were interested in her," Max protested. "I brought her just for you. I haven't touched her. Not a bit."

The four of them sat in silence for a few moments. Nicole, sandwiched between the twins Alioune and Kueur on the couch, stared out the ten-foot window behind Max. The crimson sunset warming his back and suffusing the vast loft with the red of a fresh wound also colored her pale face and tinted her blond hair. But her eyes were as dull as the waters of the Hudson River twenty stories below. As empty as the expressions on the twins.

Max held his hands out in a pleading gesture. "Is it

because she's sedated? The drug will wear off in a few hours. Put her in the Box," he said, with a nod to the open door leading to the soundproofed room next to the twins' bedchamber. "When she comes to, she won't remember where she is or how she got here. She'll have no idea what's going on. We can play any game we want with her. I have other drugs, mixtures. From the rain forests. The sea. To heighten the experience for everyone. In the meantime, we can sit, have dinner, relax. We haven't talked about Paris in a long time. We can reminisce. You can tell me about Dakar again, and Morocco, and what you did to the crew of the freighter that brought you to—"

"Tonton Bébête," Kueur said, putting her elbows on her knees as she leaned forward.

Max's heart jumped at the old name; at the play of muscles under Kueur's smooth, golden brown skin; at the flash of affection in her voice. He remembered long ago feeling their weight as he bounced them one on each thigh during his visits to Lycée. Remembered the heat of their bodies as they snuggled up against him, and the heat of their lips when they kissed him. Sweetly, innocently. Not a hint of forbidden passion. Not a stirring of hunger for illicit pleasure. That had always been for others. Never for their Uncle Beast.

More than ever, Max, and the Beast that was his hunger, wanted them. Needed them. And the special thing they did between them that he saw only in the eyes of their lovers, before they disappeared.

There was nothing in the world left for him to taste, except for his beloved twins. He tottered on the edge of a precipice, emotions and appetites giving way under him, drawing him closer to falling over the edge into unknown territory.

"Tonton Bébête," Kueur called again, waving her long finger to catch his attention. "It is very thoughtful of you to bring her. We are grateful for your kindness. But, Tonton, what you are doing is wrong. We're sorry, but we cannot accept your gift."

"You're afraid your friends will wonder about her disappearance. Think of our flirtation at the Carlisle party. Investigate. Discover my hand, my tracks, and trace her back here." Max shook his head. He paced back and forth in front of the sofa on which the three women sat. "I may be old, but I haven't lost my skills. Do you remember how I took you by surprise that first time, in the Bois? No one, not even the gypsies, ever caught you like that. I was the one who showed you the lure-and-trap trick. Who do you still call for your disposal needs, if not your old Tonton? Do you think I can no longer run with my little adopted nieces? Trust me, please."

"Why do you do this?" Alioune asked. She sat back, long legs crossed, hands in her lap. Her almond-shaped eyes bored into Max from someplace far away. Farther away than where the twins' Senegalese father and Vietnamese mother had been born.

Words caught in Max's throat. He became aware of standing with his mouth open and turned to look out the window, and close his mouth with dignity.

"If we wanted Nicole, we would seduce her ourselves," Alioune continued. "She is your payment, no? For what, our bodies? Is that all that drives you? Lust? Appetite?"

Max turned back to face them. "No. No, my babies. I do this out of love for you. To please you. To deepen the

159

bond that's kept us together all these years."

Kueur stood. She came to Max, gripped his shoulder. Her musk scent, spiced with curry from the lamb she'd had for dinner, made his heart beat faster, his stomach churn. Warmth flushed through his groin. "Tonton, you will destroy what we already have if you insist on pushing this woman on us."

"Do you want me to send her away. Is that it?" Max brushed past Kueur, eager to escape her smell. He grabbed Nicole's arm and pulled her up. Alioune's scent, rich and exotic and exciting like her sister's, enveloped him and he hesitated, stared at the woman still sitting on the sofa. Like a wild animal caught between two hunters, he glanced back and forth between the twins. Wanting them. Aching to turn, snarling and raging, and take them. Use them. Throw them away.

But he was their Tonton Bébête.

He could not bring himself to tear away the seductively cut silk robes draping their lean, wiry models' bodies. He dared not taste the salty dampness of their private darkness, or feel the strength of their bodies struggling against his. The warm, electric texture of their skin, the shock of their touch, were snapshot memories he shivered at the dream of exploring any further.

They were his only family. They did not share blood, or flesh, or appetites. But the spirit of the predator lived in them. Spoke to him. Ever since that first time in the Bois de Boulogne, when he'd seen what they did, what they were, he'd felt the bond of kinship. And in their way, the twins felt the bond, as well. They'd followed him after his visits to the Lycée, where he'd put them to learn what he could not teach. They'd seen him satisfy the Beast that was his hunger for sensation, for stimulation of mind and body and soul. They knew exactly why they called him their Uncle Beast.

They loved him. As much as they had, and could, ever love anyone. And he loved them, as well. Alioune and Kueur. His solitary treasures. The shadows of his spirit. His reflections caught and shaped by some kind of magic mirror, better than him, closer to perfection. He could not, would not take them. He would sooner kill himself.

The depth of his passion surprised him. The Beast complained, unaccustomed to Max's drifting attention. The terrain of his inner life had suffered transformation since he recently found himself in the Bronx, surviving what his employers told him was a custodial assignment that had ended in a massacre. Frustrated by the new territory of himself, rage shot through him.

He slapped Nicole's face. The woman's body jerked. He let her go, and she took a few stumbling steps back.

"Go home," he commanded. "Sleep. Forget everything. You have been ill, feverish. This has been a nightmare. You will return to your life, and tell no one of your foolish dreams."

Nicole straightened, turned, walked unsteadily to the vestibule leading to building's elevator. When the automatic doors had shut and the locks clicked back into place, Max turned to the Alioune.

"There. Happy? I offer to give you something precious, and what do you do with it? Throw it away. Unless . . ." Rage dissipated, leaving a terrifying emptiness not even the Beast or a murderous riot of violence could fulfill. Stunned, he looked to Kueur, who had drifted to the window and was staring at the sun sinking into New Jersey.

161

A premonition chilled him, rattled the Beast. "Unless things have changed? And you didn't want to tell me? Something has happened, a disease, an accident, and you can no longer—"

"We have not changed," Kueur said. "But you have."

"Well, and what's wrong with that? What's wrong with giving instead of taking? It's all I've ever done. I could've easily taken that woman for myself. Consumed her. Feasted on the pleasures she had to give, on her blood, on her flesh. But no. I made her a gift to you. To show my love."

"We know you love us," said Alioune. "In your way. You don't need to drag home your kill like a cat to show your feeling for us. Unless something in you has changed. Unless you want something more than what we have always given each other."

Max stared down at Alioune. Into her eyes, razor-lined pits ending in black velvet cushions. His gaze slipped to her lips, moist, parted. He tried to see the pink of her tongue, but the darkness was too deep. Then he looked away. Cornered by her question, he searched for a way to escape over the bare marble island countertops in the darkened kitchen at the back of the loft; in the silent clock hanging in separate, colorful pieces of abstract swirling design on the long wall to his right; through the grain of the oak floorboards. He found nowhere to run. Instead, he plunged into the chasm at the heart of his new self. He floundered, falling without landing through space excavated by a lifetime of living with appetite and its satiation, the Beast, and mysteries that had carved their way through him, changing him, leaving no memories, only tracings of discontent.

Talk, he screamed at himself, inside. Tell them what you feel. You want them. You always have. Since they were girls. Now more than ever. Admit that things have changed. You've run through everything there is in the world. There's nothing left except for them. But you're afraid, you've always been afraid. Of them. Of their power. You want the thing you've seen in the eyes of their lovers, before they vanished forever. But you're afraid.

Of vanishing.

Of loving them.

The Beast that was Max howled. Cried for release.

Love.

lovelovelovelovelove

The Beast did not want to be caged. It did not want to be killed, or tamed, or exiled to some lonely place, or hunted until it dropped and died choking on emotion. The Beast wanted the ecstasy of sensation. The pleasure of pain, the pain of pleasure.

He was hard. His heart beat wildly.

The Beast screamed for release.

Max timed a leap. Checked the sofa for weapons, the twins for jewelry and accessories they might use to fight him. More than ever, he wanted to take from them what he wanted. Give them the only thing he really knew how to give.

But he had not survived the years by letting the Beast have its way with every impulse. Nor had he devoted his life to the twins, protecting them and nurturing their relationship with him, only to snuff them out without getting what he really wanted. Not their bodies, but the thing they did together.

He was not a madman. The Beast was not all of Max.

He wanted, needed, more than what the Beast desired.

Alioune's scent filled his lungs. Kueur's gaze bored into the back of his head. Max closed his eyes and remembered Emile, who had taken a liking to them and broken into their hotel room in Lisbon to take them one night when he knew Max was out of the city. Max missed Emile, and still felt the scar on his abdomen where Emile had cut him during a friendly barroom sparring session in Singapore. He missed him, though he would have killed Emile himself for attacking his charges if the twins had not managed the task by themselves. Unlike his old comrade Lee, age had dulled Emile's awareness of his limitations.

He took a deep breath and thought of the condition of Emile's body when he'd come to collect the corpse. The twins had never cared for the details of cleaning up, and he really did not mind. Not for his twins. The task allowed him the vicarious pleasure of seeing the results of their handiwork and recalling that night in the Bois de Boulogne. He remembered the twins were also a beast, and fantasized what that beast might do to him under the right conditions, and what would happen if he was not careful.

The Beast growled, and spat, and hissed. Circled. Settled, curling in on itself, tail twitching. Claws retracting. Eyes glowing. Watching. Waiting. Knowing that the Beast's way was not the way to get what was wanted. Needed.

His heart slowed. He softened, though the warmth did not leave his groin.

Max opened his eyes and found Alioune still watching him. There was no hint of fear, impatience or boredom in her expression. Her face remained a blank mask. He looked back at Kueur, and found a reflection of Alioune framed by dusk.

Their blankness tore truth from him. Words spilled out like blood from a wound, surprising him.

"I want to be with you. To be a part of what you do. I want you to give me what you've given those you've used and thrown away. You won't hurt me. I have the strength, the stamina, to take whatever you have to give. I just want to be . . . closer. No barriers between us. Do you understand?" His question hung in the air, fell without an answer. His voice had sounded strange, distant, as if someone else were speaking. He'd never heard himself beg.

Kueur's gaze shifted to Alioune. Max turned back to the sofa, his eyes brimming with tears. He wondered how long it had been since he'd cried. He wondered if he wanted to cry because of the desperation tearing at his gut, or because he felt as if he'd surrendered a part of himself.

"We've never given anyone anything," Kueur said gently, her voice drifting out of the fading light. "We do not give, nor do we take."

"Let me watch, then. I'll get Nicole back, and let me see what you do."

"As you did that night in the Bois?" Alioune asked.

"Yes."

Alioune stood, hips tilted and arms at her side, like a model. "And what did you see?"

"Two little girls. The two of you. That prostitute, a Brazilian boy. His dress ripped off, his breasts slashed. Alioune cutting him, Kueur kissing his wounds. The blood on your faces. And him. That kid. Crying for you not to stop. Begging for you to keep going. Demanding that . . . that you rape him."

165

"What did you understand?" Kueur asked. The nearness of her voice startled him. She was standing five feet behind him.

"That I—" The Beast howled, drowning out what he might have said: loved you? No, he would not have said that. Could not.

"Why now?" Alioune asked.

Max looked back and forth between the twins. "Because I'm getting old, and closer to death," he whispered. "Because I've tasted everything. Tried to feel . . . something, besides what this Beast inside me feels. Anything. There's nothing left to try, except for you."

He waited a few moments for them to fill the silence. Then he walked to the door, defeated. Weak. Stripped of illusion and dream, carrying only bleak reality.

The elevator came, and he went in. The twins stood next to each other, looking at him. The elevator doors began to close. Night flooded the loft through the wide window behind them. The doors closed, and Max went down.

Alioune picked up the phone on the fourth ring. It was their bedroom line. Unlisted. No message machine.

"Hello?"

"I'm going to kill her," he said. "I'm watching her right now. She's in the McDonald's on Seventh and Thirty-third. You'd think she'd have better taste. When she comes out, she's going to stop at the Barnes and Noble, then walk over to Thirty-second to her office. I'll be waiting in the stairwell. She'll be found on the roof. There'll be headlines, I'm sure. Midtown Consultant Found Dead. Murder Comes to Midtown. Maybe the detectives will come to question you. I know they'll never target me. But she doesn't have to go that way. You don't even have to use her. Just give me—"

Alioune hung up the phone. Max followed Nicole but did not wait for her in the stairwell next to her office. He went instead into the subway, traveled to the Lower East Side, lurked until evening among the old tenement buildings, and left a body behind but took with him the Beast of his unsatisfied appetite.

Max kept the answering machine line busy speaking into the digital storage unit, filling it with threats and pleas and promises, until Alioune finally picked up the phone.

"Tonton Bébête," she said, her voice soft, full of sorrow.

Max growled. "You know I'll come up there. You know what I'm capable of. I'll make you do to me what you did for the others. I can do it. I'm a hunter, a killer, and I am hungry. Only you can give me—"

Kueur's voice sliced through his words, cutting him short on an extension. "You cannot hunt us. You cannot hurt us. You have helped us, and we appreciate your aid and support. But at the age when you were killing your pet collie Pat, torturing your adoptive mother by cutting yourself in the comfort of your American suburban home, and beating up lower graders in school for money, we were learning to survive in the streets of Dakar. When you were setting fires under parked trucks, we were making our way across Africa. Alone. And at the age when you learned to control your urges, refine them so that no one knew what was going on inside your head, we were in Milan, Lisbon, Marseilles, finally Paris, learning to control our own urges. In public. And we survived, Tonton. Without television, without parents to buy us food and clothes and shelter,

167

without the police and jailers and counselors to teach us our lessons. We survived the women who shaped your appetites, the men who taught you how to satisfy your hungers. How can we not survive you?"

"I'm your uncle," Max said, his throat dry. "How can you deny me the secret of your pleasure? Why won't you give me my last chance to feel something?"

"Not this way, Tonton Bébête," Kueur said.

"What way, then? What do you want me to do?"

He hung up after he could not stand to hear the quiet, steady sound of their breathing over the phone.

With the doorman huddled in a corner, staring at him with wide eyes, Max rang the intercom to the twins' loft until Kueur answered.

"I'll kill myself if you don't give me what I need," he said. He surprised himself, sounding like a desperate junkie. "Right here, right now. People will have to step over my body to get into this building. I'll write a suicide note in the guest book, addressed to you. Telling everybody how cruel you were, denying your uncle what he needed."

"You always give," Alioune replied. The intercom hissed, and her words carried a mechanical overtone. "You give so much. And you take. But do you ever share, Tonton? Have you ever shared? No more than you have ever felt, I think. No more than that."

Max held his finger against the speaker button but said nothing. Tears burned his eyes. He started to weep. Sobbing, he escaped to the street and ran.

The Beast howled as it gnawed at its own guts.

* * *

He'd kept Nicole for an entire day and night at one of his secret places on the West Side, downtown, where the smell of raw meat hung in the air like mist. The place was small, the paint on the walls peeling; the floor was filthy, but there was an alcove with a working toilet. A cold, rat-poison-scented breeze blowing in through a six-inch-wide grated vent opposite the steel door that opened onto a forgotten service duct leading up from the basement. A single low-wattage bulb illuminated the space. Refrigerated rooms surrounded the secret room on all sides, and above and below, insulating them against the world.

Nicole was hung spread-eagled in a harness suspended from the ceiling. He stared at her unconscious form as he lay, naked, flat on his back on the floor, trying to feel something. Anything.

He'd tried ordinary pleasure. He'd ridden her silky warmth, thrust himself into the portals of her body. But after his initial excitement, the sweet prize he'd sought receded and his erection had failed.

He'd tried his imagination. He'd allowed Nicole to regain full consciousness while restrained, suspended himself beside her and tried to ride her terror and panic as she became aware of her situation. He screamed when she did, and cried, and begged, and struggled. Letting himself down with a push of his release button, he'd taken and given hallucinogenics smuggled out of a desert government laboratory; tried a device that allowed Nicole to shock him with jolts of electricity with a trigger in her ball mouth gag; listened to her curses and pleas for release. But the pleasures he'd felt were no more than passing shudders, as if from a chill breeze running through a warm house. His imagination, too, had failed him.

Nothing moved him. The curves of Nicole's body, the dark wetness of her sex, the brown honey spots on her breasts, left him cold. Neither the fear and pain in her eyes when he tortured her, nor the ecstasy in her face when he drugged her, excited him. He'd offered everything in him he had to offer. There was nothing left to give.

He'd finally given up, feeling as if he were only going through the motions of pursuing sexual pleasure. As he had for a long time, whenever he took on the role of a lover.

He'd returned Nicole to her drugged stupor and wearily settled to the floor to consider his options. He'd wondered what would happen if he stayed in the secret room. Never came out again. Let the both of them die slowly of starvation. Of if he set a fire in the room. Or locked the both of them in one of the meat freezers. Or let her go, without scrambling her memory, and let the authorities and panicked employers try to track him down.

For the first time in his life, Max did not know where to look next to satisfy his hunger for sensation. The Beast paced restlessly in the cage of his body, until, exhausted, it settled in a corner and stared at the blank walls of his imagination. And whimpered.

A hand caressed his forehead.

Startled, Max jumped up, swung one arm up in a defensive arc while searching the floor for a weapon with his free hand. Alioune blocked and redirected his arm as she knelt by the open steel door. Kueur put a hand over his as she settled beside him. Wearing dark designer jeans and pastel silk T-shirts, the twins looked like a pair of exotic models posing on an industrial set.

"You see, Tonton, we are not without skills," Kueur said with a smile.

"Alioune? Kueur? What are you doing here?" Goose pimples crawled over his flesh as a chill breeze blew in through the open doorway. The stench of spoiled meat flooded the room. Oil dripped from the door hinges.

He smiled, despite his shock, at the craft of his two adopted nieces.

"We think it is time," Alioune said, letting her caress travel gently up his arm, to his shoulder and neck. "You are ready for us."

"Ready? For what?" He tensed. His cock shriveled, his genitals pulled up into the shelter of the hollow of bone between his legs.

"Do not worry, Tonton," Alioune continued. "Our building is discrete. The door man and the tenants who saw you will not betray us. As for Nicole, her friends believe she is on a vacation. Searching for herself. They believe, from the way she's been acting lately, thanks to you, that she is in crisis and needs time for herself. There is no one who will interfere with us."

"What are you talking about?" Max asked, his voice small. The Beast listened, trembling.

Kueur's fingers traveled along the length of his arm, glided across his shoulder, circled his left nipple. "You have learned some things, no? We denied you, and you did not let loose the Beast on us, or on another. And, after all these years, you finally tore down the wall between us and surrendered a part of yourself to us. We could not have come if you had not done that."

"Surrendered?"

"Share is the word closer to the truth," Alioune said.

She slid up to Max, legs stretching out on either side of him. "For you, giving is only half the equation. There is also the taking. You give to receive something that will feed the Beast in you. But when one shares, there is no expectation of a return. It is an act of selflessness. It is an act beyond the appetite of the Beast."

"I don't understand. What did I share?"

Kueur pressed her palm against his breast. His heart beat faster.

"Your self," she said. "Your pain and desperation. Your most intimate desire."

"And what would that be?"

"Death," Kueur said with sadness. She kissed his left nipple. Her hair brushed against his skin. The warmth of her body burned him.

"Is that all you wanted?" he asked, his voice tremulous.

Alioune pulled her T-shirt off, then drew his head back between her small breasts. "Not what we wanted," she said. "What was necessary, for what you ask."

"You want us, Tonton Bébête. And we would give ourselves to you. But what we do has requirements." Kueur leaned back, took off her T-shirt and unzipped her jeans. She was not wearing panties.

Behind him, Max felt Alioune maneuvering out of her jeans. "It is like an electrical circuit. We need the proper conductor. A creature beyond the care of pain or pleasure. A man, or woman, who has stopped caring about themselves, their hungers, their needs. Through desperation, or joy, or despair. Or, quite simply, because they have forgotten what they need in their drive to please others."

Kueur, naked, pressed the heel of his hand against her sex. Her pubic hair scratched his skin.

172

"Like the prostitute you saw us with, in the Bois," she said. She brought his hand up to her mouth. Put his thumb in her mouth, ran her tongue along the edge of his nail. Sucked.

Bit.

Max flinched and tried to pull his hand away. But she was strong, and his thumb stayed in her smiling mouth.

Alioune circled his neck with her lean arms and whispered, "Do you remember his eyes, Tonton?" Her hot breath sent a shiver down his spine. She thrust the tip of her tongue into his ear, then gently kissed her way down the back of his neck. "Do you remember the look of his pleasure? He had given up ever feeling anything again. From trick to trick he went, selling himself for nothing, for the money to feed himself. So he could survive. So he could live for another night of searching for what he'd given up finding. Until he met us." She thrust her tongue against the hollow at the base of his neck, pulled back enough to speak. "We felt our pleasure through him, and he felt ours. But he was not as strong as you, Tonton. He did not last. None of them ever do. But you will. You will, Tonton."

Max moaned, sagged against Alioune. She supported him as she worked her tongue up and down from the hollow to his ear and back. He looked up at Nicole suspended above them. Her eyelids twitched.

"You had to leave the narrow path of your life before you could find what you needed," Kueur said, twisting his hand into a wrist lock.

He cried out and jerked his free hand over to try for a release. She let him go before he could strike her.

Alioune pulled his hand back, pressed it against her

173

breast. "Because the pleasure you seek is ours, channeled through you," she said.

"Our conductor of flesh and emotion," Kueur whispered, driving her nails into the flesh under his arms. "Of sensation, and pleasure."

"Our soul. Our Tonton."

"And here, I think," said Kueur, looking up at Nicole's vacant-eyed form, "we have two such special conductors."

"Thank you, Tonton." Alioune settled Max's head on the floor. "We have never tried with four." She stood, lowered Nicole, unbound her.

Kueur reached for Nicole's hand. Nicole whimpered, stared at Alioune, then at Kueur's hand. Finally, she took it, allowed Kueur to pull her down to the floor beside Max. Kueur slapped Nicole's face with one hand, scratched Max from armpit to hip with the other. Max gasped, Nicole grunted.

Kueur smiled and said, "We should have known that when your time came to be with us, Tonton Bébête, you would make it special."

Alioune settled between his legs like a butterfly in the cup of a waiting flower. She kissed his balls, ran her tongue over them, licked his thighs and hardening cock. Her hands caressed his legs as he squeezed her body between his knees.

Kueur turned to Max and kissed him, pushed her tongue into his mouth, probing. She tasted like lemon ginger. He breathed her in and swallowed her taste.

Nicole, responding to Kueur's encouraging hand, rolled over his body. She lay on top of him, arms at her sides, legs on the outside of his. Her hair fell across Max's eyes, found its way with Kueur's tongue into his mouth.

174

Alioune moved his cock into Nicole, maneuvered the woman's hips from side to side. A faint moan escaped Nicole.

Kueur pulled away from Max, leaving him gasping for more of her kisses. She drew Nicole's head up by the hair, scratched Nicole's cheeks and drew blood. Suddenly, she slammed Nicole's head into his chest. Max grunted from the impact of her forehead on his collarbone.

The shock and pain of bone hitting bone traveled through Max, and he kicked his legs instinctively.

"Yes," Alioune whispered, her voice hoarse. She shuddered between his legs, then pushed Nicole's hips back and forth to a faster rhythm. The warm moistness of her mouth covered him where Nicole's did not.

Pain evaporated. Max gasped at a sudden shot of pleasure running through him, exploding from between his legs. He forced himself up, saw Alioune had jammed her fingers into Nicole from the rear.

Kueur cried out, laughed.

Max looked to her. She grabbed his hair and banged his head hard to the floor. He heard a crack, and his vision blurred. Pleasure shattered like a crystal vase thrown to the floor. The knock on the back of his head sent a cold wave down to his toes.

Alioune moaned.

"Do not be shy, Tonton," Kueur teased, nuzzling his neck.

Max shook his head, grabbed hold of Nicole's shoulders and threw her off, then climbed on top of her, ignoring Alioune's twisting body between his legs. He thrust himself into Nicole, bounced against her hips, grasping for the pleasure that seemed to be rolling back and forth through his body like a tide, just out of his grasp.

Alioune jammed her hand into him. He arched his back, reaching for sensation. Kueur sighed, caught her breath, then scratched his back, drawing blood. Max cried out, but the pain drained out of him as Alioune began to pant.

"Work harder, Tonton," Alioune commanded, massaging his butt and back with one hand while the fingers of her other hand still worked like snakes inside of him.

Max complied, his body tingling as the pleasure and pain passing through him was beginning to carry him along on its surging waves.

Kueur drove her finger into a nerve cluster at the base of his jaw, sending a sharp dagger of pain into his brain. Almost immediately, the pain was consumed, absorbed, sucked away by a powerful undertow. He did not have time to cry out; it was Alioune who screamed. He felt the pain blossom in her. It was like watching a nuclear detonation from a distance. Moments later, the aftershock rushed through him, propelled by Alioune's massaging fingers and eager tongue. He was carried by the wave front of sensation headlong into Kueur's next torture: biting his earlobe. Back he went, driven by pain, to Alioune. Faster, he jerked between them, between extremes of sensation, the back-and-forth tide rising, trapping him in its tempest waves.

And beneath him, barely conscious, her humanity stripped until she was responding to him on only the most primitive levels, Nicole grunted and moaned, her pain and pleasure a shifting bed over which the storm cycle of sex and sensation raged.

Alioune screamed for Kueur, drinking the pain from him and Nicole.

Kueur cried out for Alioune, downing their pleasure, as well.

Together they shouted his name. Tonton, they called. Bébête.

Max.

And the Beast howled as sensation filled the pit of its appetite. Blood pounding in his ears, the smell and taste of sweat and sex and blood on his tongue, body heat burning his skin, Max surrendered to the Beast, to the storm, to Alioune and Kueur and the dark sorcery of their sex. The thunder of their ecstasy boomed through him. His own pleasure screamed like a hurricane wind, amplified beyond limitations in the twins' all-encompassing bond. He thrust and grabbed and tore, choked on what he put in his mouth, shut his eyes against the lightning-bright flashes of over-whelmed nerves. He shook and trembled, and finally con-vulsed, as the twins rose to their climax like two goddesses on pillars of volcanic fire.

He came as if he were in a dream. Hot, pulsing, endless. A throbbing beam of joy cut his body in half and scram-bled his mind until he could do no more than moan and mewl and twist his body, stretching for one more pulse of pleasure. And when the beam faded enough for him to think, the first thing that came to his mind was the certainty that what he had experienced was as pale as a distant star compared to the glory of the sun that had burned in the bodies of Alioune and Kueur.

"Sweet Tonton," Kueur whispered between gasps for breath. She crept away, bloody, hair matted, and braced herself against a wall, legs folded under her.

Alioune said nothing, but crawled on all fours to the bathroom, coughing, her sex swaying casually. She cast razor glances over her shoulder. Her body moved with primal, carnal strength. Like a jaguar with its mouth still painted with the blood of its kill.

Max stood up on trembling legs. Muscles twitched randomly in his back. He ran a hand over the back of his head, felt the bumps and cuts, checked his wounds. None were serious. Nicole's, he noted, were fatal.

She looked like any of the twins' lovers he'd cleaned up after one of their wild nights.

"Your place is just as good as our Box," said Kueur. Her breathing had slowed to normal. "So private. But of course it would be. You are our Tonton Bébête."

Max picked up a piece of the blouse he'd ripped off Nicole when he first brought her in, and wiped his face.

"I hope this doesn't mean I'm falling in love," he said with a glance at Kueur. "People might talk if they knew I'd turned to incest." He cocked his head back and laughed, feeling giddy. It was as if he had been transformed, as if he had been crawling like a worm through daily existence, and suddenly discovered one day that he had become a butterfly, beautiful and glorious. A butterfly capable of tasting the sensual depths of any flower he wished to taste.

"Do not worry," Alioune replied from the bathroom. She turned on the tap and splashed water on her face. "Love is no more a part of your future than guilt was a part of your past. You are beyond the shallowness of emotions, Tonton. More so now than you ever were." She shook her head, flinging water and blood on the walls. "You are a part of us. Your Beast is tamed, your hunger fulfilled."

"For now," Max said.

"Forever," Alioune replied. She turned and faced him as she slicked back her hair.

Max stood still, let the blood-soaked blouse fall to the floor. The Beast was quiet. Invisible. Consumed.

Max suddenly felt light, almost insubstantial. Like a butterfly fluttering in the air. His future without the Beast flashed in his mind: drifting from flower to flower, aimless.

"But," he said, his voice thick, "I need my hunger. It gives me strength, it drives me, makes me fight for life."

"We are your strength, now," Alioune said. She braced herself with one arm on each wall of the small bathroom. The curving lines of her slim, dark body stood in sharp contrast to the filthy, flat surfaces and straight lines surrounding her. "We are your hunger. We are your reason to fight."

"You killed the Beast yourself, by sharing," Kueur said. "We only consumed its corpse."

Max crouched, stared down, considered the bits of rubble and refuse littering the floor. He felt as if he had been gutted and nothing remained of him except for a dry husk drifting on a breeze.

"Our bond is much deeper than love or hate, Tonton." Alioune walked to him, put her hand on his shoulder. "We belong to one another. There is only us. You felt what we are like, what we do. How can anything else be important? How can anything else matter?"

Her pubic hair brushed against his cheek. The smell of her filled his lungs. Her hand warmed his shoulder. He searched for some reaction in himself, a glimmer of feeling, but found none. He knew then that only when they were joined together in their singular act of love would he taste sensation again. Their sensation. As the conductor of their passion, he had no feeling left for himself. The twins could ignite his capacity to feel, but they would also consume it, allowing him to feel only after they had used his body and nerves and mind to fulfill themselves.

They were his Beast and his prey. And he, like the more fragile lovers they had taken on over the years, was the hunting ground on which they played.

"Sex, love, death, they are all the same, Tonton," Kueur said. "Pain, pleasure, what is the difference? Words. Little labels people put on the things they find to distract themselves from what is important." She sat up against the wall and spread her legs, opening her sex to him. "We are what is important, Tonton. The rest, they are the feast we consume."

Kueur's honey laughter rolled over Max as he looked away from her and met Alioune's razor-pit gaze. He broke off quickly and, sinking to his knees, hugged Alioune around her hips. Kueur came to them and embraced them both, and the pulse of their life beat in his ears.

In that moment, he was surprised to discover he had surrendered so much, surprised he had possessed so much to give. And he wondered at the hunger he would never feel again, the hunger for the love of Kueur and Alioune that had driven the Beast that was Max to its destruction.

Chapter Two

"Time's catching up to me," Max said, slipping into a white terry-cloth robe on his way out of the Box. "I should stop trying to keep up with youngsters like you." A spasm seized his back muscles and his legs felt weak. He stopped and leaned against the marble counter separating the kitchen from the rest of the loft. Time, and the blur of lives he and the Beast had claimed, left him breathless.

Kueur Ba swept past him, a golden brown blur of lean muscle leaving a wake of laughter. She threw herself down on the black leather sofa facing the picture window looking out on the Hudson River and Jersey. "Tonton Bébête, you know you can't help yourself. We're all bound by desire to our fates." She looked over the top of the couch at him, smile wide and almond eyes bright. A patina of sweat glistened on her skin. With a wink, she drew a large towel around her shoulders and lay back down on the couch. "You are not as old as you believe, nor we as young as you think," Kueur's twin sister Alioune added as she shut the door to the soundproof Box.

Max looked back. Alioune stood framed, tall, naked, curving lines from an armory of scimitars accented by shadow, in the closing doorway to the pleasure chamber the sisters had constructed in their loft. Suspension harnesses still swung back and forth, and the rubber sheets on the bed below were twisted into a bas-relief map of their strange passions. Devices and equipment lay scattered across the floor. Trophies, offerings, sacrifices, and mementos decorated the walls and hung from the ceiling: skulls and bones from beasts and humans, some broken, others whole, bleached or stained or dipped in gold or studded with jewels; spears and knives constructed of wood and stone and decorated with feathers, hair, bone fragments; shrunken heads, hands, feet, ears, and other parts clustered together and strung up like dried peppers. The scent of sweat and incense blew out on a gust of fan-blown air. But there was no blood. Nothing to clean up.

A sense of relief passed through him as he turned away. Since he had inserted himself into the dark equation in which his adopted nieces found sexual gratification, there had been no need to help them dispose of bodies. Nor had it been necessary to satisfy himself with street prey. Their new relationship, still a shock to him after so many years of serving as their secret guardian, fulfilled them all—and even more astonishing, left them alive. Balanced between pain and pleasure, life and death. Unlike all the fragile innocents he and the twins had sacrificed in the temples of their appetite.

No death. No killing. Max was grateful, because the

terrible thing inside that had allowed him to kill so easily was gone. Consumed by the new bond between Max and the twins. He could not go back to the old ways. Without the Beast inside of him, he could barely perform his craft. The simple blood work of carving a body for transport, sterilizing a kill site, burying or cremating the remains, turned his stomach. In the six months since he and the twins had started seeing each other regularly, he had taken only two assignments. Both times, screaming migraines had paralyzed him for days after the jobs. On the last job, he had allowed an old homeless woman to witness the work and had been forced to eliminate her. He had been paralyzed in a pitch-black room for two days afterward. Even their bizarre and relentless lovemaking tested his limits more than he had thought possible.

Max reached into the robe pocket for something to wipe the sweat building on his forehead. His fingers closed on cool, smooth silk, wrapped around a folded sheaf of stiff paper. The note he had found that morning on his pillow, in his apartment, where no one should have been to leave him anything.

A short, breathless walk brought him to the sofa opposite Kueur. The Box's locks and seals sighed into place. Max closed his eyes. Alioune's bare feet slapped against oak floor as she walked to the kitchen. He pulled out the silk-wrapped note and held it loosely in his hand. "The world has become a harsh place," he whispered.

"But it's always been that way," Kueur said.

"What would I do without you?" he asked, overwhelmed for a moment by an image of being naked, crippled, and lost in a maze of narrow, razor-lined walls. "Where would I be, what would I do?"

"What you have always done," Alioune answered from the kitchen. Pots clanged, glasses clinked, cutlery tinkled as she straightened out the kitchen with ferocious energy.

"But perhaps with less care," Kueur added.

The purr of her voice made him open his eyes, meet her gaze.

"What is this thing that flavors you with melancholy today?" she asked.

He took out the note and tossed it across the space between them. The towel draping her body fell away as she snatched the red silk out of the air like a hawk catching a helpless bird.

She read: " 'No one will ever love you the way I will.' "

Kueur looked to Max, who slipped his gaze down to the red silk in her hand. Alioune came over, took the note. Her eyes flicked back and forth over the paper. She turned it over, examined the blank side, then took the piece of silk, rubbed it between her fingertips, smelled it. She handed both back to her twin.

"Certainly not a designer scarf's quality of silk, and that color would never be fashionable," she said. "Some cheap Chinese import."

"It's the color of blood," Max said.

"Fresh blood," Kueur corrected. "The paper's mark—"

"Painfreak," Max said. "I know."

"An invitation," said Alioune. She strutted back to the kitchen, taut legs and long arms swinging with aggressive energy. "A challenge."

Max found himself aroused and looked to Kueur. Her full lips were slightly parted. She brushed back her short-cropped hair, ran the nail of a fingertip from her forehead, down her high cheekbones to the corner of her mouth. "Who is she?"

"I don't know." He told them where he had found it a week ago. "It could have been a bomb, or poison, or there might have been someone in the room waiting to kill me."

"But it wasn't, Tonton. Perhaps it's from some old admirer? Someone you worked with? Someone who . . . survived your attentions?"

"I doubt it, but I can't be sure."

Alioune spooned tea from a tin into a kettle. "The Painfreak connection? Is the club in town? Have you visited it lately?"

Max scowled. "Painfreak moved into an abandoned warehouse in Brooklyn a week ago. And no, I haven't gone. I don't want to go. That place was a den of dilettantes and amateurs in Saigon thirty years ago." He glanced at the back of his left hand, where the invisible mark of entry and participation was supposed to remain for the rest of his life. "It was a disappointment. I'm amazed it's still in business."

"Twenty-five years ago, in Cairo," Kueur said, holding up her left hand as if the mark would suddenly appear with the memory.

"It was a new world for us," said Alioune, filling the kettle with water and setting it on the stove. "But it quickly became boring."

Max shook his head. "You weren't even born—"

"Tonton, why do you never listen to us when we talk of our past?" Kueur interrupted.

"But you were such little girls when I saw you in the Bois, what, fifteen, twenty years ago?"

Kueur wrapped the note back in the red silk scarf. "We

did not have to age, in Africa, in the jungles and cities and desert. And we were afraid to grow old, to take on the risks and responsibilities. We had enough power to protect ourselves. Even in Europe, life was simpler as children. When you found us, revealed your self and appetite and the life that could be ours, we understood that change was not as fearful a thing as we believed. We grew up with the other girls in the school you left us in, learned the ways of modern society and culture. Paid what price we had to pay for change. Adapted. Of course, since we left the school, we simply have not gotten older. We have not had to. We are as we wish to be. Surely, you noticed."

"Well, until recently, I've only come when you needed me, and I didn't think—You're right, I didn't want to know. Not really. I wanted to believe you might have had some innocence to you at some time."

"Alioune and I were never innocent. And neither were you. Being born was a corruption of our souls." Kueur wrapped the towel more tightly around herself. "It is only one of the things that bind you to us, Tonton."

"Why are you afraid to go to her?" Alioune asked.

"I don't even know if it is a her. . . ."

"There was a time when nothing would have stopped you from finding out what this message means," said Alioune, turning back to the kettle.

"I'm not as hungry as I used to be. Your fault," he said, almost smiling.

Alioune bowed her head. "Neither are we, and we are grateful. But someone," she continued, waving the red-wrapped message, "wants you, and it is dangerous to ignore such a summons. These things build power over time. We know."

"But why me?"

"Are you afraid?"

A chill passed through Max. "I don't know. I don't think so." He laughed, shrugged his shoulders, stroked his wide palm with cold fingers. "I've never been afraid before. I think what I feel is something else. Like something is waiting for me, and I don't know what it is, what it wants, how I will deal with it. My world, inside and out, has changed. I feel . . . uncertain?"

"Dread," Alioune said, pouring boiling water into cups. She stared intently at the stream of steaming liquid.

Kueur came to Max, put the letter back in his robe pocket, settled herself in his lap. Her arms snaked over his shoulders, around his neck. A leg twined around his. She was hot, even through the towel and robe. Her breath smelled of sex. When her tongue probed his mouth, he tasted his own cum.

"You must face this haunting," she whispered in his ear.

"Stalking, surely."

"In times of change, the past sometimes comes to haunt," Alioune said, appearing suddenly beside them offering a tray of cups.

"*Merci*, Alioune," Kueur said, taking one. To Max, she said, "You must, or the cost will be terrible. And we do not want to lose you, Tonton Bébête. Especially now that we have truly discovered what we can be to each other."

Max took a cup, sipped the tea. Alioune's mixture went down like a caress and sent soothing fingers of warmth through his body, into his muscles, along his nerves. A feeling of calm settled over him. He exhaled a long breath that released all the tension his body had been hoarding. Alioune pressed against him as she sat, cup in hand. She sipped, then rested her head against his shoulder. "You must pay the price for change," she said gently.

"I thought I already had," Max answered, thinking of his Beast.

"That was only the beginning," said Kueur.

They finished the tea and sat huddled together as the afternoon passed in silence, like a hunter circling its prey.

On his way back to his apartment, walking on Leonard Street with the river, sunset, and brisk fall breeze at his back, Max struggled to remember how time had passed before and after meeting the twins in Paris's Bois de Boulogne. The moment he saw them with the young Brazilian boy masquerading as a woman remained vivid in his mind, like an explosion of light and emotion. Like Creation's Big Bang. Seeing them carve into the prostitute while at the same time pleasuring him, one feeding on pain, the other on ecstasy, had awakened feelings he never knew existed. In the twins, he caught a glimpse of a part of himself in the moment, and in the future. The reflection tantalized him with its differences, seduced him with possibilities. Raised hope, which remained even after the consummation of their relationship, so that he wondered what he was hoping for in staying with them. Fired a need to protect, as if the twins had emerged fully grown from his own loins. Cast a cold shadow over him at the thought of losing them.

In that moment, Max remembered making the first clear, conscious decision of his life. He would not interrupt their play, or kill them, or run away from something he did not understand. He would not become their victim, or allow them to control his life. Max vowed to help them instead.

He would watch what they became. Be their friend, their guardian. But at a distance, so neither his appetite nor theirs would interfere with their relationship. And so the Beast that had been Max would not corrupt their development, and their blossoming would not distract him from his work.

That moment was so different from the random paths of death he had followed before and after that it hardly seemed to belong to him. And since that moment in the Bois, his life had been shaped by his visits with the twins. The years spent killing, for himself and others, was a fog of vague memories. The days shared with Kueur and Alioune were light-filled islands of life. He was old in time without the twins, and young in time with them.

Max laughed to himself, wondering if there was a way to borrow from the young to make the old feel better.

"Why laugh alone?" a woman's voice asked.

Max froze, focused on his surroundings.

He was alone on the tiny island of Finn Square, waiting for the light to change. The streetlamps had just turned on, and the crisp autumn air was tainted by exhaust from cars accelerating to beat the red signal. The open space gave him a view down West Broadway, up Varick, and up and down Leonard. A few pedestrians walked in the distance. Neon restaurant names glowed between closed storefronts. Darkened office building windows reflected the closing darkness while spilling the emptiness they had contained through the day onto the streets.

The breeze gusted. Something cool and smooth settled over his ear and cheek. Max jerked a hand up, startled, and brushed away the sensation. A red scarf fluttered away.

Max checked the windows again, peered through a hole

between boards protecting subway construction work abandoned for the weekend, then patted himself for a planted transmission receiver. He found nothing. But the voice was real. Someone had spoken to him, from nearly right next to him.

He waited. Shadows stretched, twisted, scurried before cars and trucks, blossomed under streetlamps. At the next corner on Varick, one shadow hesitated before vanishing up the street. Max followed.

Buildings loomed over him, doorways yawned. Homeless men and women looked out from cardboard shacks and dens fashioned out of accidental juxtapositions between steel and concrete. Max examined them as he passed, searching for the elusive maker of the shadow he pursued. Startled cries and moans of fear greeted him. He moved on, stalking sudden movements on the periphery of his vision. The streets shortened as he broke into a run. The echo of his footsteps chased him as he hunted his unknown prey, turning corners, threading his way through traffic.

At last he stopped, lost and confused. He searched for street signs but found he could not read them. Traffic streamed past every street corner except the one he stood on. A woman's laughter rained down to him as if from a great height, and the scent of a sweet perfume pooled around him until he thought he would choke.

"Who are you?" he screamed. "What do you want?"

"You all right, mister?"

Max spun, faced an old woman. Dark eyes looked up at him from a grim-crusted, wrinkled face. Strands of white hair escaped from her tightly drawn coat hood like smoke trails from lost rockets. Her thin lips were twisted into a smirk. The stench of her filthy clothes and body dispersed the scent of perfume and made him gag. She seemed familiar, but Max dismissed the feeling. The streets were littered with her kind.

"What?" He looked past her, at the street sign he could understand, the cars passing, pedestrians glancing quickly in his direction as they crossed the street.

"She told me to give you this," the old woman said, pressing a red package into his hand.

He grabbed hold of her coat, shook her once, dragged her close. "Who?"

She hissed, and her breath filled his lungs with corruption, his head with the smell of corpses fished out of swamps, cut open on autopsy tables, chopped up and drained of blood and fluid and maggots. He pushed her away, coughing. He wiped his face and spat, but the flavor of decayed flesh and exposed, rotten viscera remained with him. When he looked up the old woman was gone. A red scarf danced away on the sidewalk.

The package in his hand, another red silk scarf with its ends loosely folded over, fell apart as he held it up. Inside, a swatch of pale leather he recognized as human skin was tied tightly into a bundle by dried sinew, like a fetish pouch filled with sacred matter containing magical spirit and power. He worked the knot loose with a fingernail, opened the bundle. Bone fragments, ends jagged, tooth marks scarring the stained surface, clattered as he shook them in his palm. He picked up a fragment with a jewel embedded in the center of a rune etched into the bone. His fingers became cold, and the cold spread like spilling blood over his hand, arm, shoulder, chest. He shook the other bones in his palm again, found a bloody rear molar. On the inside of the leather, under the bones, a message had been scrawled. Moving under a lamp, he read: *No one will ever love you the way I will*. Next to the words was the sign of Painfreak.

Bones. Pieces of old enemies, prey, sacrifices. His, Alioiune's, and Kueur's, taken from the Box in the twins' loft. A tooth, no doubt knocked loose from one of the twins. His hands trembled. The cold creeping through his body seized his heart, nestled in his gut and groin, and ran its icy edges along his spine. He wanted to run to the loft, but did not want to see the locks broken, the Box ransacked, the sanctum of his most precious intimacy raped. Most of all, he did not want to know he had lost Kueur and Alioune.

Frozen to the spot, Max understood he had been discovered by fear, and that it had filled every empty space inside of him that had ever held rage and hate and cruelty, and all the other sharp fangs and talons of his old inner companion, his Beast. Knowing the name of the thing he felt did not help him dispel or even control it. But knowledge released his body to act and follow the impulses of habit and training even as his thoughts ran tight little circles around the hope that Alioune and Kueur were still alive.

He ran to a nearby phone, called the number to the loft reserved for him by the twins. Someone picked up before the line had a chance to ring.

"Tell me, are they all right?" he asked. "Because if you've hurt them . . ." He ran out of words, fear consuming the spark of his rage. The Beast that would have known what to say, and how, to make his enemy come forward. . . .

A woman laughed. Another joined. And another. And still more. Until the phone blared with the piercing laughter of countless women, even when Max held the receiver away from him, even when he hung up the phone. The laughter continued, running on and on, gaining voices, taunting him with sudden swells.

The breeze gusted once again. Another red scarf flew out of the faint remnants of sunset. The breeze pinned it against the phone for a moment. The night looked as if a fresh wound had been cut into its side. Then the scarf flew away and the laughter died, and the world returned to a steel-and-concrete focus where sidewalks were hard and streetlights held back darkness, where cars and passersby moved restlessly in a city so full of harsh reality it had no room for dreams or nightmares.

Max held the package the old woman had given him against his chest, as if the bones of prey might protect him from fear. Invisible, icy fingers dug through his flesh and closed around his heart. He threw the scarf and leather swatch away. Bones rattled against concrete. There was only one thing that could keep him safe and save the twins, if they still lived. But the Beast was dead. And someone, or something, else wanted to love him.

He headed for the subway, driven by fear and the need to control it by exerting his will. Pursued by the red-veiled visage of a love like no one else's.

The two men at the entrance stared at Max. The taller, wider doorman, bald and scarred, kept his hands by his sides. His loose black suit and T-shirt gave him plenty of room to move. The other man, Asian, slightly built, dressed in a long, gray tunic with slits on the side, trousers, and a tightly fitted cap, kept his hands folded in front of him. Except for a few more scars on the larger man, they looked no different from when he had first visited the club thirty years ago.

"You look familiar," the Asian doorman said. "Have you been here before?"

Max remembered the mark and held up his left hand. The tougher-looking doorman stepped forward, guided Max's hand forward, stopped. The Painfreak sign, the same he remembered from years ago, the same that had accompanied the messages he had been receiving, appeared on the back of his hand. His skin tingled.

"Welcome back," the smaller man said. "It's been a long time."

"I've been invited," Max replied.

"Of course," he replied, closing his eyes. "A message was left for you. What you need is in the House of Spirits. Follow the sign." He opened his eyes, met Max's gaze.

Max bowed, then passed through the doorway as the two men stepped back into waiting shadows.

The club was buried at the end of a maze of tunnels and stairwells. Thick, slow-burning candles barely in each other's line of sight marked the path. Footsteps had cleared dust and debris from the floor. Rats squeaked and scattered at his approach. A thread of pulsing, liquid beats wound through darkness, calling to him, drawing him to the heart of his search.

A giggling couple, apparently lost, stumbled against him near a candle, sobered when they saw his expression in the flickering light, and followed quietly as he made his way to the club's double steel doors. They hurried past him as he entered, faces flushed with excitement. He doubted they would survive the night. Their high-pitched voices and sex-sweat scents were quickly lost in the storm of sounds and aromas that slammed against Max as the doors swung shut behind him.

The faint throbbing pulse that had echoed through the empty warehouse exploded into a cacophony of rumbling bass, screeching guitars, driving percussive rhythms that pierced flesh and bone and grabbed hold of an intangible part of his being. And squeezed. The stench reminded him of Bombay's poorest quarters. Every human biological activity was represented: shitting, pissing, digesting, fucking. The pungent aromas formed an offensive cloud that repulsed him at first. Moments later, the sensory assault whetted his appetites. His stomach grumbled for meat, bloodred and warm. He had a taste for salt. His parched throat ached for the cleansing burn of liquor.

Skin tingled, anticipating touch. Muscles twitched, reacting to ghost pain and pleasure. Nerves screamed, craving sensation. Excitement. Every part of him wanted Kueur and Alioune. Needed them.

Max stepped away from the entrance, prowled the bar area. Naked, vacant-eyed barkeeps and waitresses offered herbal concoctions, painkillers, stimulants, hallucinogens, and other substances he could not identify. Multicolored lights flashed stroboscopically through clouds of smoke that were acrid in one breath, sweetly scented in another. People stretched out singly and in groups on circular couches resembling inverted mushrooms. In a shadowy corner, a constant stream of people squeezed through a small doorway no fire marshal would have approved.

The club's layout was the same as it had been thirty years ago in Saigon. The music was louder, the space bigger, the gossamer glamour more polished. But the atmosphere of death and decay was as heavy on his spirit as it had been in the middle of that war. A willowy man with rings in his nipples, nose, and along the bottom of his erect penis tried to kiss him, but Max hoved him away. Even with the Beast alive in him, he would have found no prey in the club. Everyone in Painfreak was already dead.

Finding no red scarves to taunt him, no guide or House of Spirits, Max pushed his way through Painfreak's helpers eager to put him into another state of mind. He passed through the narrow entrance to the heart of Painfreak.

On the other side, the floor of the vast, hangarlike space was studded with circular stages set at various heights. On each stage, performers enticed a gathering of devoted attendants.

Men, women, hermaphrodites and eunuchs, costumed and naked, danced against the pulse of the music, seemingly possessed by their own rhythms. Some stood bound and twitching. Performers reached down from high stages and touched, or slapped, or whipped members of their following. Others, set on lower stages or in pits, allowed the audience to touch them.

One woman was being crucified by a couple in nun's habits driving spikes through her hands and feet. Three men in suits licked the blood from her wounds. A small, hairless man swam desperately in a plastic sphere of water rotating in randomly shifting directions. He chased the air bubble trapped at the top of the sphere while fettered by one foot to a point on the globe's inner surface. A figure half hidden by cables and electronic equipment moved for a collection of men and women connected by wired pelvic and hand gloves, helmets, boots, and skin pads to a massive block of interconnected components and digital read-outs.

Max studied the performers, searching for Alioune and Kueur among the victims, for a guide with a red scarf among the tormentors. Restless spotlights, incense smoke, and the layout of stages made it hard to see much detail from a distance. He made his way through the performances, pausing at each, taking in faces and body motions.

He let fear lead him away from a man slashing himself with a razor while video monitors played back scenes of genuine torture and murder all around him. Away from the woman hanging bound upside down in a black rubber suit connected by a mask to an air tank controlled by her audience. Away from the electric arcs sliding across flesh and the stainless-steel mechanical lover servicing a dozen admirers, and the tiny operating theater with a leering, mis-shapen surgeon holding up shiny, bloodstained instruments while begging for more volunteers to join him.

A flash of red fabric drew him to a part of the floor where the lights did not shift so restlessly, where the music changed from a relentless, bass-driven roll down an endless mountain to a hypnotic string of airy notes floating on the edge of awareness. Men and women danced slowly in this part of Painfreak, their bodies gliding with the music like hawks staying with a breeze. Veils and loose, flowing robes replaced the other participants' more complicated costumes. Only one or two admirers, kneeling or prone before each stage, offered attention to dancers who remained aloof, involved in the sensuality of their own movements.

Another flash of red drew him to a grouping of veiled dancers. The music climbed an octave, gained several beats per second, shadowing his racing heart. Lighting dimmed. The dancers swung their hips and waved their arms for no one. Beyond them, the stages were empty. Max stopped, stared at the platforms, grew agitated. His fear sharpened until its edges sliced every coherent thought free from his mind.

A red scarf snapped out from behind a rounded corner. A brown hand held the scarf, drew it slowly back. Beckoning.

Legs shaking, palms damp and mouth dry, Max followed.

On a knee-high stage, a woman danced slowly, sinuously, covered by red scarves. Her eyes, one brown, the other green, locked onto him as soon as he rounded the corner. His gaze traveled the length of her body, followed her hips, her hands—one brown, the other alabaster white—the roundness of her thighs pushing through scarves to flash black skin once, then reddish brown the second time. Her feet were visible as the corner tips of scarves brushed against the tops of her toes. A yellow-tinged, delicate foot rotated on its ball while the other foot, larger, reddish pink, and scarred, ground its heel in counterpoint to the first. He tried to look away, but found he could not. Drawn into the hidden corner, he felt the curtain of her attention fall around him and cut him off from the rest of the club, the world. Himself.

Bumping the edge of the platform, Max stopped. The dancing woman filled his eyes, his mind. The swaying curves of her breasts pushed scarves one way, then another, but always the red silk veiled the flesh underneath, leaving only the impression of softness. Ripeness. Erect nipples. Her head was swathed in scarves, leaving only her eyes visible. Eyes that were like hooks, planted firmly into the tender, vulnerable parts Max never knew existed in him; eyes that held him, frozen.

Max found the urge to fight. His body chafed at bondage, wanted to move. For a moment, he managed to hang on to his thoughts, and he wondered how the scarves could hang on the woman with no visible support; and he wondered why the flesh and shapes of her hands and feet were so different; and he questioned the reasonableness of the fear that gripped him, when he had found himself in far more dangerous situations in his life and never felt afraid.

The woman came to the edge of the platform. A sickly-sweet scent blew into Max's nose and mouth and turned his lungs cold. Her brown hand rubbed a scarf against his lips, eyes, ears. She went down on one knee, still moving back and forth, rolling her shoulders, her elbows and wrists rotating through small circles in the air, and she pushed the scarf into his mouth. Once again, his feeble grip on thoughts and instincts gave way.

He tried to keep his mouth closed, tried to clamp his jaws shut. When her cold fingers pushed against his tongue, and cool silk rubbed against the insides of his cheeks, he tried to bite down. But his mouth would not obey him. His hands would not leap up to bat away her arm. His eyes would not shut against the relentless glare, fury bright, of her eyes.

She finished stuffing the scarf in his mouth and caressed the side of his face. Jumped down from the stage, pushed her body against his.

He tasted chemical dye and worm shit. He tasted his own gorge rising, until she traced a line from his chin down to throat to solar plexus, ripping open his turtleneck with her nail. His bile receded, burned in his stomach. Guts twisted, boiled, shivered with the urge to explode, as if filled with an acid enema. Skin, where she touched it, stung as if opened by a razor's edge.

The woman embraced him. Max tried to draw his head back, but his neck would not the obey instinct. Her arms, suddenly impossibly long, circled around him and linked somewhere between his shoulder blades. Her breasts pressed against his broad chest. Dancing on the stage of his body, her legs entwined his, rubbed him up and down. Her pelvis slowly thrust against his crotch and hips. But instead of lust, her frigid presence made his penis to shrink and genitals draw up.

Her eyes bore into his, filled his mind. Red scarves brushed against lips. Kissed him.

"No one will ever love you the way I will," she said. Her voice was many voices, as her body belonged to many corpses. She laughed, as she had on the phone.

Reason dropped away like a stone thrown over an endless cliff. Max tried to hang on to the image of Kueur and Alioune; to the sound of their voices; the feel of their hands on his skin; the hot, slick, welcoming darkness of their sex. But memory slipped out of his reach, spun away into a numb and empty void. Vanished. Max tried closing his eyes, shutting the holes of his prick and anus. He willed his ears to be sealed. Stopped breathing. Anything, everything, to stop his self from being ejected like sperm into a dead and infinite womb.

But with her eyes and her touch, the woman drained him.

Nameless, empty, alone, he screamed. But the scarf in his mouth allowed no sound to escape. His voice echoed in the hollow world left to him until even sound was lost to him. The walls of his hollow world collapsed, and darkness followed. But the terror never died.

Max woke with a cry, walking and naked.

The veiled woman led him on a leash of scarves the length of his body through a short, dark hallway ending in a spiral, metal staircase. The scarves were not sewn or tied together, but instead merged into one another through interlaced folds. It ended in a tight noose around his neck. A taut string of scarves linked his neck to his bound genitals, looped between his legs and between his cheeks to his fettered wrists and elbows. Rising out of the stooped walk in which he had awakened brought a sharp pain that forced him to resume a stiff and only mildly painful gait.

The hallway was cold. Stepping onto the staircase sent frozen spikes up his legs and spine.

The woman glanced at him over her shoulder. Dim light from a bulb hanging at the base of the stairs illuminated the pallor of the skin around her eyes. The rest of her was a shifting cloud of dark red.

"We are not done, my love," she said, one voice rising out of many. "We have not even started."

They climbed the stairs. Max began shivering. His shoulders and elbows burned with pain from his arms being twisted and tied behind his back. He opened his mouth to ask the woman what was happening, found it stuffed with fabric. Silk.

He remembered fear and terror. He remembered losing his name, memories, sanity. Discovering bits and pieces of them again gave him no comfort. Max. He was Max, searching for Alioune and Kueur, in Painfreak. He was

201

alive, and the creature leading him, he was certain, was dead. The world and his life beyond those facts were hidden in the mental fog and sharp threads of pain binding his mind.

They reached another floor, walked along a winding hallway with uneven walls and ceiling. Soft, violet lights over mostly closed doorways lit their way. A shriek erupted from one open doorway, where murmuring dhol chants praising Ahtu rolled out of the absolute darkness within. The stench of gasoline and burning flesh flowed from another doorway opened to reveal a room in which a naked couple sat, legs wrapped around one another, holding hands. A pillar of crackling flame consumed them, blackening and rolling back their skin, exposing red tissue and flashes of white bone for a moment before these too were charred. Their heads rolled back, lips baring teeth in a fiery grin, liquefied eyes staring at the roiling cloud of many colors above their heads drinking in the angry smoke of their sacrifice. Shaken, Max looked down at the worn, stained floorboards. He managed not to look into several more open rooms until he heard his name whispered. He looked to the veiled woman, who walked ahead and gave no sign of calling him. Again, someone called his name. He turned to the left. A four-armed woman stood in a boat floating in a pool of blood that lapped at the edge of the open doorway. Her skin was black, her smile terrible, her eyes filled with Max's reflection. A necklace of heads hung from her neck, and one set of hands held an iron hook and an upturned skull brimming with blood, which she sipped. In the other set of hands, she held a lotus and a sword, which she presented to him. Her blood-smeared face broke into laughter as Max, drawn to her offer, stared at the pool's edge and wondered how to reach the boat. The leash pulled him forward. He stumbled after his captor.

The doorway was left behind, but the woman's image burned in his mind. Blood pounded in his ears, flushed through his body, and drove off the cold. For a moment, he almost recognized the four-armed woman and his fright withered. Hope flickered. He searched for meaning in the image: a path to escape, a force to rescue him from his entrapment. He found nothing except fog, confusion, and pain. Hope died, and darkness filled the hallway.

A series of tugs on the leash forced him to trot forward until the walls and ceiling were lost in absolute darkness. Max could not tell if he had entered a room or was still in the hallway. Suddenly, the tension in the leash eased. The sound of flapping wings surrounded him, then vanished. His arms dropped to his sides. He stood straight, his bonds gone. Except for the tightness around his genitals. He reached with numbed fingers for the scarf tied securely around his balls, his hard cock. Found a slack leash trailing to the ground.

Max shook out his arms, stretched, rubbed himself to generate heat. When life had returned to his fingers, he dug into the scarf tied around his cock for a knot to untie. Finding only unyielding silk wound tightly around him, Max began to back out, trying to retrace his footsteps.

"Welcome," the woman said, all around him. "To the House of Spirits."

Max stopped. "Alioune," he said. "Kueur."

"Come, my love. Find me." She laughed, teasing him like a fickle lover.

He took a step forward. Anger roused him, and for a lucid moment he knew what he wanted, and what he would do to get it. "I want the twins," he growled.

"Forget them."

"I can't. I won't."

"Yes, you can. They're safe, at home."

Anger crumbled as doubt made his voice quaver. "I called—"

"But never reached them. I answered instead."

"But the tooth, the bones—"

"A lover's lie, easily forgiven." Bone fragments rained down on him. He covered his head against the downpour. A few bone pieces fell in his hand. He felt the arcane symbols etched into bone, the inlaid jewels and precious metal coatings. "You wouldn't answer the invitation. You had to be drawn here. With a lie. But I knew you'd understand. You've told so many, after all. Forgive me, as I've forgiven you. For the lies."

"Who are you?" Max shouted. "What do you want?" He walked, arms outstretched, eyes opened wide to catch any glint of light. His foot caught against something solid. He lost his balance, slipped in a puddle, fell. A charnel stench engulfed him. Coughing, he struggled to rise. His hand closed around cold, stiff fingers, then jerked away.

A flash of red light illuminated body parts scattered around him. For a heart's beat, he saw limbs and a pair of torsos. The flash burned in his eyes. Spots, like circles of blood, floated in his vision. The light flashed in his mind again, and he remembered seeing the faces of two severed heads among the body parts. The old woman who had given him the bone bundle and a younger woman whose eyes over a veil of red silk had captured him.

And suddenly, the faces were familiar. He had seen them before. Arms, hands, legs, the different shades and textures of skin, the odd coloration, scratched at his awareness, as well. But memories eluded him. He got to his feet, walked gingerly through the body parts, careful not to slip on fluids and decomposing flesh.

A faint, angry howl ripped through him. His hands twitched, closed around imaginary throats. His body ached for the pleasures of sensation.

The Beast was dead. It did not sing in him anymore. Yet he heard it, like an echo from another time. He broke into a sweat, though he was colder than he had been when he had awakened.

"Come to me," the woman said.

Was the Beast's cry hiding in the susurration of the woman's speaking voices? Max wondered. Or was it lost. Trapped.

"You want to, you always have."

"No," said Max, turning, searching for an exit in the pitch blackness.

A flash of red light froze an image of wood floor, cavernous ceiling, and distant walls of exposed pipes and conduits and support beams in his mind. The spill of broken bodies was to his left. Something had moved at the center of the flash.

Max ran toward a wall, stopped when another flash of light burst in front of him. A shadow at the center of the light writhed. Flapped.

"You see?" the woman's voice whispered, near and far. "I'm not angry over your lies. I understand you're afraid only because you don't recognize me. But I know you need to find me. Follow the light, my precious. It's a game we both must play. Hunter, and hunted. Follow the trail I leave for you, as you did when we first knew each other."

"I don't want you."

"But you do. Surrender to that part of yourself. Don't fight against your nature. Don't throw away what is already yours."

Max ran in the direction opposite from the last flash.

"Earn my love. Track me down. I know you can do it. Because of all that we've been to each other, I know you can find me."

Max skittered to a stop. He should have reached a wall by now, but there was nothing. "I love the twins," he shouted. "I'm going back to them.

"No. You belong to me. The one you took. All of the ones you took. Then abandoned. You've come to us."

"No. I've never been with anything like you."

"Another lover's lie." The sound of fabric snapping in a wind rose out of silence, turned to laughter. "You made us. Left us. But we found what you lost. Or perhaps it drifted to us, after you drove it away from yourself. The thing you loved us with. It's with us. It teases us. Hurts us. But without the flesh, the heart, the soul, the mind of its master, it can't satisfy us. So we tracked you through this monster. It is a fine monster, eager to please, sensitive, gifted. Hungry. Are you proud of your prey turned hunter? But only so we can return this part of yourself. Make you whole. And then you can love us as you did. Give us pleasure. Pain. We will love you as no one ever will, if only you would love us as you once did."

The Beast's cry drove Max to his knees. He covered his ears, but still the Beast's roar filled him.

"Who are you?"

"All that's left."

Another flash. Red pierced his eyes, staggered him.

Scarves danced at the center of the light. Moved fast and slow, spun, whipped, waved, all in the shape of a woman. A woman with enormous wings spreading out from her back. A woman with long, flowing hair. No face. Limbs, but no hands or feet. A thing made of scarves.

In the darkness after the flash, the Beast roared. The woman's voice, all their voices, screamed.

A fragment of memory he thought lost in the terror that still rang through him rose out of the roar, and the scream. He remembered a woman in Calcutta, many years ago, sacrificed to the Beast's appetite. She had been sold to him by a father lost in addiction's haze. Had there been a red scarf? Some cheap, frivolous accessory tied around her neck, or head, or arm, to make her more attractive to him? He shook his head, but the memory would not expand into a coherent tale. But the image remained, connected to the scarves haunting him, and to the voice. And the old woman: not a morsel tossed to the Beast, but someone who had witnessed his work a week ago; caught and disposed of with barely a thought. Startled by the sudden remembrance, Max discovered other reminders of the past. The voices under the dancing woman's voice: he had heard them before. The scarf woman's eyes, her limbs, body, all the enticements that had lured him deeper into Painfreak: They were pieces of some of the women consumed by him over the years since the Calcutta woman, preserved in rage, and pain, and desire.

They were shards of lives he had shattered, spoiled drops of souls left over from his passion. Ghosts who found each other in the wake of his passage. Ghosts bound to him by their passion for the pain and death he had granted them. Ghosts clothed in the symbol of the eldest spirit's degradation: a red scarf. They were perfect prey to the Beast's perfect hunter. And they had used the part of his spirit he thought he had slain, the Beast, to hunt and capture him.

The leash around his cock jerked. He looked down. Found himself holding the leash. Pulling it. Forcing himself to stand up. His hand drew the leash around, stopped, pulled him forward.

The red light blossomed in the darkness before him, lingered, allowed him to study the apparition at its heart: an angel made of scarves crowded together, their folds and parts as curved and delicate as the lips of sex. Her arms stretched out to him. She filled the light, had nearly become the red glow. When she vanished again, his heart twisted with pain.

"Yes, my lover," the angel said out of the darkness. "You know you must come to me."

He wanted to say no, but his mouth would not open. His hand betrayed him, as did his feet. He moved to where the light had been. He followed his pain, and to his horror, he knew his hand and feet had not betrayed him. He wanted to go to the woman, to all the women he had slain. He needed to join the Beast. Take the women. Relive, again and again, the moments of their deaths. Bask in their suffering, savor their agony, drink in their deaths. As he had done when they were alive and the Beast had been his guide.

The light grew all around him, shading his skin in the red of the scarves encircling him.

"Here we are," the angel said. The leash left his hand, snaked into the mass of scarves before him until his sex was connected to hers. A hand, true in form until it came near and separated itself into dozens of individual dancing scarves, caressed his face and body. Her mouth—four scarves rolled into sumptuous curves—pressed against his face. Cool, smooth silk rubbed against his skin, cupped and massaged his balls, circled the head of his dick in tight little circles. His body shivered, muscles relaxed, hard flesh became even harder.

"No one can ever love us the way you can," the voices said, crowding one another, slightly out of synch. "No one will ever love you the way we will."

A storm of scarves erupted around him. The Beast roared. Its ravenous appetite filled Max, and he eagerly accepted the familiar blood and sex rage. Something inside of him was better than nothing.

The spirit of the Beast moved through him, awakening dormant senses, pumping blood into seemingly forgotten internal organs. Each ghost in the roiling cloud came into focus for Max, and he was able to see all the twisted shapes of pain he and the Beast had made. His body yearned for the taste of blood pumping into his mouth, for the wail of despair born from torture. His heart pumped from the excitement of stalking prey through countryside, towns, cities. He burned where another rib, a second heart, a third eye, a womb enclosing a monstrous prodigy, a cunt, might have been. The stench of a freshly carved carcass engulfed him. The slick, warm envelope of a second skin moved over every inch of his body.

Max roared with the Beast. The ghosts screamed and yielded their pain. Images flickered in Max's mind, like pieces of dreams caught in daylight. Brief, mad moments of struggling bodies in his grasp mixed with sudden explosions of violence with knife, ax, pick, scalpel. The wild orgies of feasting on bodies living and dying washed through him, stoking his appetite for more. He moved to the rhythm of ghost hips struggling under his, arms and hands lashing and slapping at him, legs flailing. He shuddered, and electric arcs of pleasure racked his spine and guts and heart and brain, as he came again and again.

Max rose into the storm of scarves and spirits, back arched, arms and legs spread wide, like a helpless baby lifted out of the crib. And like an infant, he cried for more. Hunger drove him into a desperate frenzy as it burrowed into his stomach. The need for violent sensation drove spasms through his body. He wept, he pleaded for more even as memories of the pain he had caused played themselves over in his mind in an endless loop. With every death, his appetite increased. Every soul consumed drove him deeper into starvation.

The Beast roared again, but its voice was smaller, its presence a dim reflection of what it had been in life, and even of what it had been only moments before. And as its presence shrank, the emptiness inside Max grew, as if he were feeding on himself.

He tried to rein in the Beast, but just as when it had been a living part of himself, he could not curb its appetite. He could only hang on and ride, keeping his sanity by letting it take him wherever it wanted to go and joining in its desperate consumption.

His bones felt like ice. His sense of smell clogged, his skin's sensitivity died. He tasted ash. The leash of scarves around his cock pulled, relaxed, pulled again, drawing him deeper into the silken petals of ghostly sex. He thrust harder, forced himself deeper, but his mechanical passion only heightened his feeling of emptiness. He wanted to stop, but could not. He wanted warmth, life, Kueur and Alioune, but his actions denied them. Horror insinuated itself into the hollow world expanding inside of him like a balloon growing to encompass a vaster emptiness with every spastic pump of his hips. Horror became his world as the ghost of his Beast, frustrated, blinded by hunger, turned on him, raped him, penetrated and violated him through every orifice, soiled every organ, thought, emotion, memory. He was the horror as, riding the Beast, he raped and violated himself.

Max tried to scream, but the scarves worked themselves down his throat and nose, into his ears, up his ass and into his penis, as if jealous for the fruit of his attention.

No one will ever love you the way I will, they all whispered in his mind.

Max wanted to black out. Die. But the darkness never came, or the peace of death. He could only suffer. That was the death his angel granted him.

He searched for something to hold on to, a weapon with which to fight back. A statement, a curse, a feeling. Nothing came to him that might touch the ghosts. Even remorse eluded him.

He tried to remember intimate details about his victims, so he could separate them in his mind and distance himself from their need for pain. But the dancer's kiss had drained him of his past, and all he had of them was their own memories of death and the Beast's primitive hunger. Even the events since he had awakened as the dancing woman's captive were fading. Max fought to hang on to what he had just seen on his way to the House of Spirits: the pile of body parts, the pillar of flame consuming contemplative lovers, the woman with the necklace of severed heads.

They were all that defined him. No matter how seductive their appeal, he was not the fear and suffering of his victims, not the rage and appetite of the Beast. Max was something else.

But what? Fire and body parts suggested nothing but the idea of suicide. The woman on the blood pond, she had offered him a sword and a lotus. A weapon, a flower. Death, and life. He was death, like the angel. And a part of him was dead, as well: the Beast, returned to him by the ghosts, rooted in him as if it were a living part of him. But he was life, as well. Still flesh and blood, still alive. The spirits of his victims were dead, and only dead. There was an advantage in the lack of balance.

They had no bodies. There was no way they could hurt him. But they were hurting him.

The scarves. The spirits had taken possession of the scarves. The red silk had become the symbol of their unity and purpose. There was still the body of the old homeless woman, and enough body parts to form an enticing dancer, and perhaps a few fragments more scattered throughout Painfreak. But the scarves were the key.

Max found the Beast inside him, tiny, its roar reduced to pitiful mewing, but still savage and relentless, sparking lust for blood and pain, firing up spirit memories of death and dying. As small as it had become, there was still no holding back the Beast. It was rooted firmly in Max's own desires. But the Beast could be directed, with effort and will. He knew it could be done, knew he had done it, though he could not recall when or how. Using the Beast, he was certain, was at the heart of Max.

He urged the Beast on, focusing on the spirits. The Beast roared, though it sounded like a squeal, and initiated a new cycle of pain and suffering among the spirits of its victims.

Max felt the threads of his sanity fray from the pain searing every orifice, twisting his gut, squeezing his heart.

Wrong. Not the spirits. Stupid. The scarves.

His arms jerked forward, plunged into the mass of red silk. Fingers closed around fabric. He pulled, ripping silk with all of his strength.

His hands tore at the scarves crowded into his mouth, teeming at the other ports to his body. He bit and he sliced with his nails and he tore with bleeding hands. The screams changed pitch. The Beast cried out in triumph, joyous in creating a new kind of pain. All the colors of fear rose out of Max like smoke, scorched out of existence by the Beast's blinding presence.

The storm of scarves flew apart, scattered, drifted to distant corners of the House of Spirits. The angel dissipated, releasing Max. He fell suddenly to the ground, rolled, got up. Scarves pulled out of his body, flicked away from his skin. The pressure around his cock and balls vanished as the scarves released him. The Beast growled, caught the scent of silk from all corners of the world, coarse and weathered and cheap. The red glow dimmed, sputtered. Spirit fire shimmered wherever whole scarves settled.

Heat rose through Max. Hot fire erupted in his belly, heart, mind. Riding the Beast, he hunted each scarf down, tearing every one he caught to shreds. With time, the Beast's strength waned and its appetite died. It was not as strong as when it had been a living part of Max. But as a dead spirit housed in his body, Max found it easier to live with. He continued the hunt, pushed himself, until there were no more whole pieces of silk. Until the spirit fires had gone out, and the voices of his victims no longer screamed.

With the ghosts banished, Max gathered the torn silk scattered around the cavernous storeroom he found himself in, by the light of a few half-dark banks of fluorescent lights. He went down the hall, found the room in which he had seen the pillar of fire. The lovers were gone, as was the cloud of many colors near the ceiling. The silk burst into flames and then vanished in black, foul puffs of smoke when he tossed the pieces into the fire. He made a dozen trips back and forth, until every piece was gone, as well as the limbs, torsos, and heads.

When he was finished, all he wanted to do was curl up in a corner and sleep. But he was naked, and hurting, and far from safety. With the Beast sleeping quietly next to his soul, Max started back to Painfreak's main rooms. He paused at the room he thought belonged to the woman with the sword and the lotus. The door was closed. He opened it, and blood spilled out over his feet. The boat and its passenger were gone. He left the House of Spirits and tracked bloody footprints back down into Painfreak.

The Asian doorman smiled politely as Max emerged from the warehouse wearing what he had picked up from the club floor in clothes discarded by patrons in the heat of sexual frenzy.

"I trust your stay with us was more satisfying this time," the doorman said. "Please, do not wait so long to visit us again."

Max paused, looked down at the man. "I'll never come back."

The larger of the two doormen stepped out of the shadows, exchanged a glance with the small doorman, and laughed.

The Asian doorman maintained his smile and gave Max a slight bow. Max moved on. "That was what you said the last time," the smaller doorman said.

Max looked back. The Beast he had just regained grumbled. But both doormen were gone. His shoulders sagged, and he staggered off into the Brooklyn night in search of a taxi.

Kueur's eyes widened when she opened the door. Alioune froze for a moment as her gaze met Max's. After their initial shock, they both rushed across the threshold to embrace him. Max shrugged out of their arms and entered their loft, eager to shed the ill-fitting clothes he had gathered. He walked gingerly to the couch facing away from the picture window and lay down, naked. The twins came to him, Kueur sitting on the edge of the sofa, Alioune standing by his head.

"Do you still feel old?" Kueur asked. Her eyes darted as she catalogued the cuts, burns, and bruises on his body.

Max started to say yes, that he was tired, that a thousand raging ghosts were chasing him and wanted to give him their terrible love. The colors of fear shimmered in his mind. He almost said he wanted to die, and the plea for them to finish him and consign his spirit to some safe and secret place began forming in his mind.

The Beast, familiar, comforting, but alien in him after so long an absence, sounded a thin, faint howl. And Max realized that with the thing he had cast off back inside him, the ghosts would have no way to track and find him. To draw him to them. They might find new scarves or another symbol of their death to inhabit. Fleshy parts of his victims might dig their way out of graves, quickened by their dying emotion, hungry for his touch. But Max was out of their reach, at least until they found another way to renew their bond with him.

He was safe from that hell. And the Beast was with him. Fear dissipated like graveyard fog in the morning sun. Whatever was left of the Beast was enough to keep fear at bay for a while. The blur of time and victims no longer made him breathless. He sat up on his elbows, looked over his body. Probed past the pain and exhaustion and soreness, past the physical and spiritual wreckage of his rape. And he found excitement, satisfaction, energy. The Beast was where it belonged.

"No," he answered, surprising himself. "I found something I thought I'd lost forever, in Painfreak. In the House of Spirits. I don't feel so old, anymore." He met Kueur's open gaze, glanced at Alioune. Smiled. "I think I'm as old as I truly am, however old that's supposed to be, and not as old as I thought I was."

Alioune put her palm across his forehead, pushed him back down. Her cool skin was soothing. She smelled of lemon, and saffron.

"The thing you took back is dead," she said.

Max started to protest, stopped. "I know," he said.

"It cannot fit itself back into the rhythms of your life. It cannot grow with your spirit, cannot learn, or take nourishment from your experiences. It will forever be apart from you."

"But I need it," Max said, nearly pleading.

Kueur took his hand. "Maybe you needed it dead, and

not alive. I think the price you paid for the change was fair, *non?*"

Alioune ran her fingers over Max's face. Kueur took his other hand, kissed the spot of Painfreak's invisible mark, and said, "Welcome back."

A phone rang: Max's private line, which only he could access. None of them moved to answer it. In the age between each ring, Max thought of the scarves and worried that he had forgotten some key factor in severing the ties with his past. Dread struggled against the Beast, churned again in Max's stomach. The answering machine picked up the call.

A harsh, cutting voice spoke over the speaker, which crackled and whined and hissed in protest. "Tread gently on the paths of the dead, my son," said the voice. "They are not as generous as the living, nor as forgiving."

When they went to replay the message, they found the phone and answering machine burned to slag.

" 'My son?' " Kueur asked.

"I'm an orphan. I never knew my mother or father." He remembered the woman in the boat, the blood, the sword, and the lotus. A chill rose like mist from a lake up his spine.

"Then it's too bad she did not leave you her number," said Alioune. When Kueur and Max looked to her, she took Max's hand and led him toward the Box. Kueur's laughter followed them.

"Be gentle," Max croaked as the Beast roused itself.

"As gentle as we can be," Kueur reassured him, with a sharp slap across his cheeks. She slipped his old white terry-cloth robe over his shoulders.

Max stopped at the entrance to the Box. He reached into

the pocket, drew out the first scarf he had found in his apartment, its message still wrapped in red. His heart skipped. The Beast roared. Max smiled.

"Let's play a game," he said, ushering Kueur in after Alioune. "A game with fire, and silk."

Chapter Three

Acrid smoke rose from the muzzle of Max's .22-caliber
Ruger. The dead man lay sprawled in the snow pile on the
edge of the curb, illuminated by an overhead streetlight.
The first shot, to the temple, had been in the service of the
triad contracting for the man's death, and had left a blackened hole in the skull. Max dumped the gun under the
nearest car and walked away, staying close to the cover of
buildings and away from lights. He stripped off latex false
hands and dumped them in a bag with his wig, facial latex,
and the rest of the disguise he had used to stake out the
killing ground. His mind was a clear pool reflecting sights
and sounds. Gazing into the pool of perceptions, Max was
pleased. The job had gone without complications so far,
and there was nothing near to cast a shadow on the water.

The second shot, in the neck, had been for the Beast in
Max. The Beast screamed in his mind and ran hot in his

veins as the man's blood flowed from the neck wound into the snowmelt running along the gutter. Pressure built in Max's chest to cut off Johnny's head, hands, feet, sex. His genitals ached with the need to satiate the Beast through atrocity. He glanced over his shoulder to give the Beast a last look at the work, grateful that he had once killed the Beast in him, and recently found and taken back its ghost. He had missed the Beast's strength in the work he did, but its madness had made his love for the twins, Kueur and Alioune, a deadly passion. With the Beast a dead thing inside him, unable to touch all that was living in Max, it could not rule him as it had in the past. He was free from the compulsion to satisfy the appetites he shared with the Beast at every opportunity. The twins were safe in his love. And Max had Beast's power and vision to take him through the darkness of the tasks he chose to perform.

The Beast's scream subsided. A chill seized the base of Max's spine and shot up his back, setting off icy star bursts in his head. Ripples of fright broke over the waters of his senses.

A white mist was rising from the man he had just killed. Max froze. Not from the man, but from the flow of blood and water in the gutter. Max continued automatically to strip away his disguise, reversing and shortening his coat, taking off false soles, while he leaned against a building stoop and watched the mist rise, thicken, form into a human shape.

Instinct urged him to run. The Beast wanted to kill. Max fought against both. Though there was danger in lingering near a job, he needed to understand the mist's nature. Assess its threat and capacity to hurt him. He had learned about ignoring the past. The Beast, and the ghosts of victims who had tracked him through the part of himself he had discarded, had taught him.

At first he thought the mist was the manifestation of his target's ghost. But as he continued to watch, the mist took on female characteristics. Perhaps the spirit represented a defensive curse about which he had not been briefed. He snarled to himself, thinking of what he would do to the contractors if they had led him into a trap. But the spirit's form refined itself into the image of an elderly woman, Asian, dressed in loose pantaloons and a long blouse. She caught his eye, waved, mouthed words he could not hear. He felt no danger in her presence. Something else? Max scanned the surrounding buildings for observers, but the windows in the mixed residential and commercial Queens neighborhood were dark, as they should have been at this time of the night. Something buried in the snow pile, he reasoned, hidden for the past week and only now, during a January thaw, coming out: a homeless woman, dead; or a mugging victim; or a ghost locked in a broken piece of discarded furniture. Max was tempted to go back and kick the pile loose, to make certain. The Beast, confronted by a reminder of its captivity and how easily other spirits and its own appetite had deceived it, grew quiet, watchful.

Voices cried out. A car turned the far corner, screeched to a halt, sliding first on a patch of melting ice. Two men came out of the car, handguns drawn. More men emerged from the alley entrance facing the dead man's resting final place. A rapid-fire argument erupted. Guns were pointed. Someone knelt over the body, glanced at the ghost, screamed. The men cocked their guns, but no one fired. A man grabbed hold of a stick, passed it through the form, and threw the stick away. A cluster of men surrounded the ghost and the body, gesticulating wildly as they raised their voices. Others made the sign of the cross and drifted into the street, looking up at the roofline and windows, behind and under parked cars and trucks, into doorways. Max cursed, finished his transformation, eased around the stoop and crab-walked along the walls, careful to avoid trash cans, bottles and cans, snow mounds and ice sheets ready to crackle under his weight.

Shots rang out from across the street. Bullets slammed into the brick face above Max, spraying concrete dust down on him. He ran, reached the corner, glanced back as he turned it.

Men with coats flying open and weapons drawn pursued him. The car's tires screamed as they fought for traction, finally found it and took off down the street after him. The ghost floated past the pursuers and bore down on Max, crying out in a high-pitched voice that carried over the angry curses of the men below her.

"Wait," she called, "I must speak to you. There is terrible danger—"

The fastest of the pursuers broke stride and flinched as the ghost passed over him, shot at it once as its foot grazed his shoulder and finally slipped and fell. Max put his head down and sprinted around the corner.

Wheels taking a turn too sharply warned Max that the car was closing in. Even as the car momentarily lost control and slammed against a parked van, a hail of Uzi fire raked the sidewalk and walls around him. Max pulled a string from the bag in which he had stowed his disguise, twisted a cap on a bottle sticking out of a side pocket. Metal ground against metal, snapped, and then the engine gunned as the car finally freed itself. Max turned and threw the bag. Its arc took it through the ghost and into the car's windshield. The incendiary and fragmentation devices exploded on contact, consuming the evidence of his alternate identity and destroying the front portion of the car. The flash turned night into day, the fireball made the winter summer, both for a moment. Neither scathed the ghost. It was almost on top of him, reaching a hand out for him, its wrinkled face twisted into a hideous mask. The spirit still called to him. Max heard the burden of fear its tremulous voice carried and wondered what might frighten something insubstantial.

Max continued to run as the car, burning, crashed into the back of a parked truck. More pursuers rounded the corner and skipped, slid, stumbled, when confronted by the spectacle of flame and twisted metal. More shots rang out. Bullets whined past Max.

The ghost hovered by his shoulder like a marker made from luminous mist. "Wait, I must warn you, or they will be lost—"

"Fuck off!" Max shouted.

"Their father wants them—"

"Leave me!"

"Their father has found them—"

The rear window of an old Jeep shattered as Max passed the vehicle. "You'll get me killed!" He wanted to curse, to lash out at the creature, drive it away with his rage. The Beast, he was surprised to feel, was quiet within him, like a cat confronted by unpleasant mystery, haunches down, tail flat to the ground, its instinct to run paralyzed by curiosity. It had not done well by ghosts and spirits, and neither, Max realized, had he.

"Their father has taken them," the ghost continued, "and

they will die for his desire. I do not want to lose my children."

Max spared the spirit a look. She had descended and was floating alongside him, effortlessly keeping pace with his frantic sprint. Her substance shimmered, thickened and thinned like a roiling cloud, and was veined with faint traces of red. Strands of ghost hair fell from her balding head to her shoulders, unaffected by her moving through the physical world so quickly. Her thin lips trembled and her mouth was open, revealing more mist and gaps in her two rows of teeth. Tears brimmed her eyes, crawled down her elevated cheekbones.

Max reached the next corner, found the stolen car he had left for his getaway, threw himself against it. He was inside without remembering unlocking and opening the door. The engine turned as soon as he started it, and he peeled out of the parking space and down the street. The dull thunk of a farewell bullet clipping the bumper accompanied his turn around another corner.

Sirens wailed over the sound of the car, and Max slowed, continued to drive with his lights off through a few blocks of industrial buildings, stopping to check for oncoming police at every corner. He focused on the wheel in his hands and the empty streets while he drove and caught his breath. He did not look at the woman's glowing form sitting next to him, did not listen to her incessant whispering about daughters and fathers and killing.

Max did not relax until he was on the parkway, heading for Manhattan. He took a deep breath, arched his back, and slammed his fist into the seat next to him. His hand passed through the old woman and cracked the seat back a notch.

"What?" he shouted. "What are you? What do you want with me?"

The old woman turned to him. Her form shifted over the cushion like a restless television image trapped in a screen as the car took gentle curves, slowed and sped up with traffic. "I am their mother."

"Whose mother?" Max met her gaze. "Someone I killed?"

"No, the ones you love."

Max tightened his grip on the steering wheel. "Alioune and Kueur?" He peered into the night unrolling in front of him.

"The ones I brought into the world."

"How did you die? At birth, or did their father kill you?"

The ghost laughed. "I am not dead. Though I have come close over the years."

Max shook his head. "The twins said they were orphans. Their mother was supposed to be mortal, and Vietnamese."

"That is your name for my land. I am Chiao, the dragon. My true form sleeps in a maze of forgotten tunnels and bunkers dug by fighters during the last war."

"You don't look like a sleeping dragon to me."

"Dreaming, I take on an aspect, just as, killing, you take on an aspect of yourself." The Beast howled and squirmed under her attention. "The people of my land know this part of me as an old woman who comes to judge the wicked and save the innocent. I raise the water, to kill and protect."

Max poked her belly with his finger. "Your womb doesn't seem up to the job."

"My daughters were not born from this substance. During the last war for unity and identity, your people shook my earth with weapons, rained fire from the sky, spewed nightmares into the spirit world. So many conquests, so many wars—I had to fly from the blood and metal and nightmares. I found a young woman raped and left for dead. Her soul crippled. I joined her, and we traveled together. Found a way to leave the country, and had our adventures in the world."

"And one of those adventures was in Africa?"

"Many, in Africa. So many spirits, so much life. I thought, once, foolishly, I might make it my home." The spirit looked out her side window. They passed a minivan, and children looked out from behind the driver and made faces and gestures at them. "But I was tricked. Used, by their father. Driven away by so much pain that my adventure had become worse than what had disturbed my sleep. I fled back to my homeland. I left the woman in Saigon, and she spent her last days in an opium den. I returned to Chiao's sleep and let the other parts have their chance at adventure." She turned away from the scenery of homes and cars and night, focused on Max. "Do you believe me?"

"Is it important that I do?"

"It is, if you love my daughters."

They passed La Guardia Airport, St. Michael's Cemetery, descended into a wall-bounded collection of lanes, and emerged onto the Triboro's ribbon of steel and concrete suspended in the night over water. Manhattan's towers glittered to the left. The jagged horizon before them seemed to reach out for the car. Water slipped under the bridge like oil. Wind keened at the windows. The Beast was quiet in Max, watching the spirit.

Chiao ignored the city, staring instead at Max. "I do not have much time," she said. "You are their only hope."

226

"I know," he answered. "I've always known that." They rolled into a plaza leading to tollbooths. The Beast growled in Max. It ached to hurt the spirit, sensing Chiao as kin to the ghosts who had recently tortured it. Max took a deep breath and reasoned with himself that, whatever the spirit claimed to be, it was not what had caused Max and the Beast so much recent pain. Besides, he could see no way to kill it. Max chose the machine booth lane. "What do you want from me?" he asked.

"Do you listen? Did you hear what I said when I breached the wall between our worlds?"

Max smiled as he dug out a token from the coin box under the seat. "That's what they say to me sometimes. 'Don't you listen, Tonton, when we speak of our past?'"

"And do you?"

Max waved his hand. "Sometimes I get distracted. The Beast, the thing inside me, you know, it makes me hungry. I find it hard to concentrate."

"You are afraid of what they are."

"I know Kueur and Alioune, what they are," Max spat, angry. "I am a part of them. We belong to one another." He threw the token into the toll basket. The Beast screamed in outrage. As they went down a ramp and onto the highway by the river, Max fought the urge to crash the car into the guardrails.

"Your fear and love are their doom," Chiao said, gazing at the water and the lights from the other shore reflected in the flowing darkness. "My own fears and loves have already cursed me. I should have dared to go to their father and fight him, though he has the power to kill this part of Chiao, as you do not. My own fear of death and my hope for your strength drove me to find you, as surely as my love for them. I was stupid." Chiao veiled her old face behind gnarled hands.

Max glanced at her. He could see through her more clearly. "You're fading."

"It is not easy coming into this world. In my own land, with my own people, there is belief to sustain me. But in this land, where there is hardly any faith, I must await my opportunities. Death. The passing of a spirit. Running water, for I am a spirit of water. We make do with what we can, even if all there is is blood and water. Or blood and flesh housing an enraged, dead spirit."

The work for the night ahead flashed in Max's mind. He took an exit, drove on the service road and side streets until he found an abandoned corner by the towers of a housing project. He stopped the car, knowing he had to abandon it, keep moving, distance himself from the slaughter. But he could not walk Manhattan's streets haunted by a ghost. "If I were to believe you," he said, eager to end the dance between them, "if the twins really are missing, what can I do?

"Find them first." Her arm shot out, and her hand passed through Max's blocking arm and into his head before he realized what had happened.

The Beast leaped, and Max smashed his fist into the passenger-side door. Cursing, Max pulled back, squirmed against his side of the car. Chiao's hand withdrew. The world spun for Max for a moment. Images of roads, lights, buildings superimposed themselves on each other. Nausea seized his stomach.

"Can you see?" Chiao asked, fading more quickly, ghost hair and clothes a wisp of mist, the red tracery of her form only a suggestion, like the afterimage of a firefly's flight.

Her voice sounded as if it came from one of the nearby building's windows. Blood-tainted water pooled on the car floor.

"What? I don't understand. What am I supposed to do—" A leering face exploded like lightning across his consciousness, vanished, leaving him shaken.

"I have nothing of my own, except for them," the old woman whispered, now only a dissipating column of mist thinner than a smoker's hurried puff.

"Was that him? Their father?"

"I should have stayed with my children," wailed the spirit in a voice nearly drowned out by the wind-driving rush of cars from the nearby highway. "I should be stronger than the pain . . ."

"Who is he? Why is he taking them? What does he want?" Max shouted, jumping into the damp passenger seat, straining to hear the voice, to feel the spirit's touch in his mind again.

". . . not follow your fear, or your love . . ."

The voice was gone, like the spirit. Max kicked the steering column in frustration, shattering the housing and rocking the car. He threw the door open and burst out, slammed the door shut again, headed for the nearest telephone booth. A cluster of youths, camouflaged in dark clothing and hoods, eased out of the shadows around the telephone. The Beast rolled out of Max as his stride lengthened and his fists balled. A frail, young voice cursed. The youths scattered. Max called the twins' loft, his own private line to them as well as their general number. The answering machines picked up. He did not trust himself to leave a coherent message. Instead, Max strode downtown, searching for either a cab or a car he could steal, riding the Beast's and his own rage. He had never liked threats against the twins. People had died for the hint of mistreating them when they had only been his charges. Now that they had moved beyond that relationship, now that he was tied to them in ways he had never thought possible, danger to the twins meant more to him than his life. He could not, would not lose them. He would not lose that part of himself he had found in them. Death was nothing compared to that loss.

The dim voice of reason warned him. He had acted rashly before when it came to the twins. And suffered because of it. The last time—But the last time, he had been influenced by ghosts. Allowed his senses to be deceived. This time, he was going to make sure the twins were in danger.

A gypsy cab stopped for him, took him downtown on the West Side. The doorman to the twins' building was missing from his station. The door to their loft was ajar. Inside, dishes and glassware lay shattered on the wooden floor. Something burned on the stove. The celebratory meal they had been arranging for his triumphant return was ruined, and they did not answer his call.

Reviewing the recordings from the cameras he had installed for their security, he saw a man, dark-skinned, tall, with a drawn face and slightly bulging eyes, enter the lobby. He lashed out with a lightning-fast blow at the doorman's head. The doorman fell. The stranger dragged him to a side room. The stranger took the elevator up, smashed through the loft door, entered. The twins had turned to face him. The stranger looked up at the camera, smiled. And then the monitors went dead.

Max paced the loft for a few moments, trying to filter

another truth out of what he had seen. But he could see no trap, no trick. The twins were gone.

He sat on the couch facing away from the picture window, head in his hands, remembering. Sifting through the images Chiao had given him. Tunnel. Water. Highways. Buildings. Max stood, went to the window, looked out across the Hudson to the Jersey shore. Kueur and Alioune were on the other side.

Max went downstairs, roused the doorman. He went to the nearby parking lot to retrieve one of the cars he kept for work: an old, black Buick Le Sabre. The Beast's roar, as loud and constant as the sound of a mighty river going over a fall, followed him as he drove to find the twins and bring them back.

The part of Max the spirit had filled with knowledge of the twins' location drove through the Holland Tunnel. Traffic was light, and the stuffy air tasted of exhaust. Driving with the window open, Max let the wind rush through the car, blow through his short-cropped hair, whip against his cheek, and cry in his ear. That part of Max which held his instincts, skills, and talents was filled with joy as it moved his body with cold purpose. He was preparing to kill again. He knew his target by the visage he had glimpsed in the flash of Chiao's memory, and he knew his enemy's location. The certainty of purpose was all the confidence he needed.

Another part of Max listened to the wind, watched the tunnel unwind before him, felt the pressure of water bearing down on the walls, and could dwell only on the part of death that meant loss to him. He wondered if the wind carried their death cry, if the road they traveled was as closed and endless as the tunnel appeared to be, if the weight of all the lives yet to be rushed to fill the hollow space of their existence.

Max slapped the outside of the door until his palm stung, trying to drive away the dull, agonizing threat of loss. He did not want to think of the twins as gone. Nor did he want to feel the tug of sympathy and hurt for those who had suffered from the loss of men and women he had made his victims. Madness stirred in dark corners, in the shadows of awareness, as he almost felt the connection between his pain and theirs.

The tunnel mouth appeared at last around a bend, opening to night trimmed with streetlamps and service station signs and distant lighted windows. He wondered if the Chiao spirit had felt the same elation and surge of freedom when she had separated from the rest of the dragon buried under bombed, defoliated, and napalmed earth. Max spat out the window, hating that he had bothered to wonder.

The car climbed up a ramp, proceeded along a skyway. His heart jumped at an exit sign for Bayonne. Images fell into place one after another in his mind.

Like a commuter gliding through radio stations looking for a comforting song, Max searched for memories of himself with the twins and found the first, as he always did, almost immediately: two young, brown-skinned girls torturing a transvestite prostitute in the Bois de Boulogne. The prostitute cried out in pain. And pleasure.

Max's erection grew with the fear and desire from that distant moment. Max shuddered as he went down the exit ramp, paid the toll, and pulled over to the side. The fresh memory of their first time together overwhelmed him: Kueur, giving him pain while Alioune teased pleasure from him; pain spiking through him to Alioune, while pleasure drained into Kueur; the flow reversing, coming back through him to them. He barely remembered the other woman with them that first time, though her body had served to amplify the experience before their passion had consumed her life. The nova brilliance of sensation did remain, however, etched into his mind and body.

The memory of that sensation was enough to blind him for a moment. He bowed his head, caught his breath, shifted in the seat as his erection shrank into a warm pool in his lap.

The part of him that was the ghost of his old Beast, still strong enough in death, Max understood, to drive almost any other mortal insane, let loose a roar that rose from his genitals through his guts and reverberated in his heart.

Max took off again, winding through Bayonne streets, momentarily drained. Sad. Beyond the love he claimed for Kueur and Alioune. On the edge of his true desire: death. He wished for the heat of the twins' bodies, for the bright sound of their voices, the intimacy of their hungers playing over his senses in the Box, to drag him back to life.

The images in his mind clicked into place on Bayonne's west side beyond Kennedy Boulevard. The roar of jets sounded from across Newark Bay; their lights danced in the black sky. Run-down warehouses and factories loomed all around him. Max hit the brakes. The car slid on the icy street, coming to a halt by colliding lightly with the only vehicle parked on the block: a small, windowless van. He stepped out, a hard, cold wind coming off the water to cut through his coat and chill his bones. Snow mountains loomed, spread over sidewalk and street.

The building he wanted faced the water. He broke in

through a boarded window, crept along the wall surrounding raw, unlit space, following the echoes of a fight and the cries of Alioune and Kueur up a flight of stairs.

Five fires burning in punctured drums arranged in a wide circle illuminated the second floor, its barren expanse broken by the occasional piece of ruined machinery and ancient office furniture. Sparks sputtered on the concrete floor, smoke swirled under the fifteen-foot ceiling before being whisked out by the breeze through breaks in the boarded windows. Max stepped into the circle of flickering light behind the twins.

"Who's this?" asked the black man standing at the center of the circle atop a fallen file cabinet, hands on hips, shirt and pants ripped, face scratched, eyes torn from his face. Max recognized him from the security tapes: the face was the same, though his black leather jacket was a shredded heap by one of the light drums, and his blue jeans and gray sweatshirt were dirty and torn.

"Tonton!" Kueur cried out, maintaining her stance and guard facing the man.

"Be careful," Alioune warned, "it's not human."

"Tonton? An uncle?" The man cocked his head in Max's direction. "I didn't know I had a brother." He turned to Kueur. "Or is he your mother's brother? I'm having trouble tracing the lineage." He sniffed the air, turned again toward Max. "Looks like a white man to me, but smells, well, mixed. Or is the confusion just in his mind?" The man laughed, jumped down from the cabinet, feinted toward Alioune, dipped, drew out a drawer, and hurled it at Kueur with unnatural strength and speed.

Kueur ducked and rolled as the drawer spun past her and crashed into a lathe. The clatter of metal echoed through the building. Alioune jumped forward, lunging high with her fist, then with a roundhouse kick, forcing the man to hunch low. She pivoted when her kicking foot landed, thrust her other leg straight out, landed a smashing blow to the man's head.

He was hurled backward by the kick. Kueur screamed in rage as she charged, bringing a steel tool half her size over her head with every step until she swung it over just as she reached the fallen man. The metal bit into his skull and drove his face into the concrete. Kueur kept running, jumping over what Max took to be random flailing of his arms and legs. The twins circled to the other side of the informal ring. Max watched them, noting the scratches on their skin, the puffiness of their faces, bruised knuckles, scraped elbows and knees peeking through the loose, gauzy one-piece outfits they frequently wore when relaxing at home during the evening. Their feet were bleeding from cuts suffered walking barefoot on a floor littered with pieces of metal, wood, and glass. Max was surprised the man had gotten the twins this far, and had punished them as even he had never been able to manage during their sparring sessions.

The sound of the steel tool crunching into concrete brought Max's attention back to the stranger, who had tossed aside Kueur's weapon and was getting to his feet. His deformed skull righted itself, as did the position of the skull on the neck.

The man turned to Max, grinned. "We've been at this for hours, Tonton. My daughters are very inventive in their foreplay." He pointed to his eyes. "For instance, I never knew I could not grow back a human's eyes until they forced me to try. Now I make my way in the world with

235

only a god's senses. Though fine for the spirit world, they lend the material realm a certain air of mystery. But what better way to bring excitement and pleasure to what must be done?"

"It says it's our father," Kueur shouted from across the way. "It wants to rape us—"

"I want my sister!" the stranger screamed. His expression transformed suddenly as the pits of his eyes grew deeper, wider; his skull elongated; his nose and mouth elongated into a poor mimicry of a snout while his cheeks and chin receded. The air crackled around him, and the flames in the drums leapt and hissed.

"What is it?" Max asked, circling until he felt a fire's heat warming his back. He focused on the man, searching for weakness while reining in the Beast's urge to attack. The Beast's roaring was a dull, insistent headache behind his eyes.

Alioune wiped blood from her forehead as she spoke up. "Some kind of mad monster. It surprised us, broke into the loft, threw powder over Kueur as I was preparing dinner. I tried to fight it, but the powder it blew into my face put me to sleep. We woke up here, with this thing ranting about seed and wombs, a damned twin—"

"Don't speak of her," the stranger said, glancing at Kueur and Alioune. He returned his attention to Max. "Children. They have no respect."

"If you're their father, I can see where they got it from."

The man's visage returned to normal. The play of firelight did not penetrate into the darkness of his eyeholes. "Why are you here?"

"I'm taking them back. They are my charges."

"They're your lovers."

Max hesitated, nodded his head in acknowledgment. "They have become that, yes."

"A fine choice, for all concerned. Any children?"

Startled, Max answered too loudly, "No."

"Too bad. A little girl from their blood might have been enough."

"For what?"

The man took a step toward Max, then one to the side, another toward Max. He walked slowly, with no trace of martial preparation or stealth. He sniffed the air again. "I smell Chiao on you. But you're no relation to her. Has she has spoken to you?"

"Warned me. Told me where you'd taken them." To the twins, who had exchanged puzzled looks, Max said, "Your mother."

They exchanged looks, lips parted in surprise.

The stranger ignored them, stared at Max. "Indeed. But she didn't come, herself. Didn't even offer you any help. Do you hear, daughters?" he asked, turning suddenly back to them and taking a few steps in their direction. "Your mother has abandoned you again. Left you to me. So you see, you have no choices in the matter. It's what we both want. Your mother always knew how important it was for me to get what I want." By the time the man had stopped talking, he had come around back to Max, two steps closer than when he had started.

"You haven't answered my questions," said Max. "Who are you, and what do you want with the twins?"

"Oh, I haven't answered you?" The man tore off his sweatshirt and tossed it at Max, who knocked it down. "A god hasn't answered a mortal's questions?" Boots came off, flung quickly at Max's head. He hopped as he took off his jeans, circling around, forcing Max to turn, until the man stood between the fire and Max. "Perhaps the god being questioned is fortunate to be speaking at all, considering his maker stole his shape and voice, his name and nature, turned him from Ogo to Pale Fox, for the sins of eagerness and appetite. For wanting to live beyond the bounds of a universe full of rules and petty order." The jeans snapped through the air as the stranger threw them at Max.

Max caught the jeans, held them in one hand. His heart raced, and the Beast paused in its roaring.

"But as you see," the twins' father shouted, slipping out of a pair of boxer shorts, holding up his arms, spinning in place twice, rolling his shoulders and hips provocatively so that his genitals bounced, "I've a shape I can speak through again for a short while. And for as long as I don't forget my new self. Do you like it?" He stared at himself, played with his penis, looked up at Max. "Terrible thing, this circumcision. Did you know my own brother bit off my foreskin as part of my punishment?"

Max whipped the jeans out toward the man once, as a warning. His gut churned, alerting him to the danger of distraction, the need to strike back in order to ward off the stranger and buy a few more moments to find a way to truly hurt him.

Max gazed into the man's empty eye sockets, forced himself to stare past the torn skin and blood, the viscous fluid and muscle sticking to the rims, through the ruined gates that, in humans, led to a soul. He dove through the darkness he found, straight and hard and fast, ignoring random waves of pain and pleasure, the wail of a trapped mortal spirit, and a ravenous burst of hunger that nearly overwhelmed him with its intensity. The Beast cried out, trying to answer the hunger with its own, but the Beast was dead and the burst of appetite came from something ancient but living. A god, Max understood, not stopping at the realization. Afraid to be pulled into the same seductive trap of belief that had caught the man's soul and allowed the god to sink roots into his soul and take his body. Max pushed on, until he thought he could see a seed bursting in a vast emptiness, an egg growing out of the energies contained in that seed. Max burrowed deeper, seeing growing figures in the egg: two couples on either side. The Beast howled, sensing the vulnerability of something young and true. Max did not flinch, did not back out of the nightmare dreamscape of an alien mind, though he wanted to vomit, and cry, and forget what he was experiencing as if he had lived that moment of creation. One of the figures moved. Struggled. Tore at the egg's fragile membrane before the imprint of the universe had been written on its walls.

The stranger shook his head, and Max lost contact. He tumbled back into Bayonne, landing in the warehouse's reality. Smoke scratched at his lungs. The twins hung on to balance and defensive postures. And the naked black man who had already changed shape once, taken more punishment than an old-fashioned cartoon character and who was more than he appeared, much more than seemed reasonable, or acceptable to a modern Western mind, remained at the center of Max's small, focused world.

Max stood firm and exhaled slowly. A part of him felt kinship with the creature before him. The rest of him wanted to destroy whatever threatened the twins.

A smile teased the man's lips, faded. He sniffed at Max,

then said, "As arrogant as their mother. As full of himself, and as ignorant of the world, as that dragon dream floating in a demented woman's head."

Smoke from one of the other drums drifted between them, making Max's eyes tear. The stranger waved his hand in front of his face, coughed. "There's more than Chiao's smell to you. But don't think that because you carry a god's touch, you're a match for me. You're not, no more than they are. Children is all you are. I am a god. Ogo once, then yurugu. Pale Fox. Do you see me inside this pathetic form? Even the gods are afraid of this. Even the gods."

The Beast was filled with shadows of Max's fear and rage. It cried to be set loose. Max was not ready to release that part of himself.

"So you're a god," Max said. "You want your sister. What does that have to do with them?"

"What do you care? I could kill you, if I had time. But this flesh wastes quickly as I ride it, and when the flesh is gone I must go back to my world. Legba will not favor me again with entry into this land through his followers, and there are none of my own worshipers here to use. So I'll let you live. Be grateful. Isn't that enough? Isn't that what you mortals care about? Living? Keeping these putrid, fragile, stinking bags of blood and bones and shit alive for another day?" Pale Fox spread his arms wide, spun around, took a few more steps to the side and one in toward Max. His penis swung heavily, partially engorged. He spat on the sweatshirt and briefs, slapped his naked chest for emphasis.

With the fire once again at his back, Max retreated a

step, sank slightly at the knees, kept his arms loose and to the front in a low guard.

"I could keep you busy," Max said. "Make you use up your precious time."

"You could try." Pale Fox feinted with a clumsy jab, laughed at Max's overreaction. "I should have saved some of that zombie powder I used on my daughters. It wouldn't have worked on you any more than it did on them, but at least it would have kept you quiet long enough to get rid of you."

The twins glide-stepped forward, closing in on Pale Fox's back. Max snapped a front kick, retreated quickly, whipped the jeans back and forth to create space between himself and Pale Fox. His heel kicked the fire drum. His back prickled from the heat.

"Why don't you ask them for what you want," Max said, letting a trace of desperation creep into his voice.

Pale Fox paused in his circling advance. He straightened, and his expression relaxed into a human mask of surprise. "Ask?"

"Explain what you want. Tell me, and we can come to an arrangement."

Pale Fox regarded him suspiciously, shook his head, but said in a cautious tone: "The human way? Humans lie. Particularly you white men. If I had eyes, I would see your soul as you glimpsed mine, and know the truth of your bargain."

Max moved to the side of the fire drum, unable to tolerate the closeness of the heat.

"Talk to the twins, then. They're your daughters. Your blood. Use the bond between your spirits, instead of just taking whatever it is you want. Wouldn't it be simpler?"

Gerard Houarner

Pale Fox turned. Kueur and Alioune kept their guard but stopped closing in. They exchanged looks with Max, waited.

"Daughters?" Pale Fox began, turned partially toward them. "Daughters! Do you know how much I envy you? I understand the connection you share. I remember the purity, the feeling of completion, invulnerability. Because I had a twin once. Yasigui. We shared the same womb, the same sustenance. Her heart beat in rhythm to my own; her soul nestled in our womb next to mine. We slept together for an age, growing, gathering strength for the task of creation. But in the long age of waiting, I became restless. I was eager for life, to shape the energies I felt all around me. I burst out of my mother's womb, desperate to be born. The others said I raped her, but the gods will say anything against me. I thought my sister was with me as I made my way across the universe. And when I realized she was not, I called to her, searched the depths of this earth for her, pleaded for her to join me. When I couldn't find Yasigui, I stole the Creator's seed, thinking to make another sister to join me. But I was caught. Punished. Stripped of my place among the gods, my place in creation. My foreskin torn from me. Agony of mind, body, spirit. But the pain that tortures me is my sister's absence. Yasigui, my other half." Pale Fox hesitated, and for a moment the mortal host's face started to change back to the spirit's animal essence. Pale Fox gasped, snarled. "Can you understand my pain, my emptiness?" he asked the twins, then turned back to Max. "Half of me is missing. I must get it back."

The god's pain resonated in the place where the Beast had once lived in Max, bringing back memories of the emptiness he still felt on occasions when the Beast's ghost was not enough to fill the void. Max fought off the seductive persuasion of Pale Fox's voice and words. "How can we help you get Yasigui back?" he asked. He held the cuff of a pants leg in each hand. Wrapped them slowly around his wrists. Forearms.

"I need only to plant a spirit seed, through this body's physical seed, in my daughters. My seed is a fragment of the original fonio, the seed of the world, which I took with me at the beginning of all things. The fonio will take root in their wombs, twins will grow, and from both sets of children I'll choose my Yasigui and kill the rest. As the child grows, I'll shape her into what I am not, make her my sister, and she will make me whole. I'll be healed, and the curse of jealous gods, this yurugu, will not hold me any longer. I will be Ogo once again."

"And what's to happen with us?" Alioune asked, voice hard, eyes narrowed. "The same death that took our mother?"

"What do you know about your mother?" Pale Fox asked with contempt.

"No more than what we know about you, Father," said Kueur. "Our Jola mother never saw her when she found us in the bush. She only judged a mother had left us, by the weave of our baskets and blankets, and the gold hidden next to our bodies for our care. She judged the father had driven the mother to do this, and that our mother must surely be dead, for the basket's weave showed the kind of love that could only be broken by death."

"Your Jola mother was as quick to judge as your real mother," Pale Fox said with a dismissive gesture.

"Not quick enough, if she was with you long enough to have us," Alioune spat back.

Pale Fox swept his clawed hand around, as if to lash at their faces. When he opened his mouth to speak, his teeth flashed, longer and sharper than they had been moments before. "Chiao came to me while I was in the body of a man. I had the habit in my own domain to take the body of a follower for a few days, so I could taste the old shape and the old ways of perceiving. She had sought me out, sensing my presence from afar, drawn to my power, knowing I was more than what I seemed. The moment I saw her, I knew she was also more than what she seemed. We talked of innocent things, then of her land, and then of mine. I told her Ogo stories into the night, and when she asked, we loved each other's bodies. That was when we discovered the godhood at the heart of our souls. That was when I, in a moment of passion and hope, planted a fragment of the fonio seed in her, to see if her godhood might bring forth another Yasigui.

"Your mother spoke of love, of leaving her land and the places and things to which she belonged. She felt the emptiness in my heart, and thought she could fill it. She thought she could become my twin, and share what I had shared with Yasigui in the womb of creation at the beginning of our universe.

"I waited, saying nothing—"

"You did not encourage her?" Alioune asked, incredulous.

"You didn't fill her with dreams and fantasies?" Kueur added. "You made no promises? You didn't seduce her with your pathetic Ogo stories?"

"Words!" Pale Fox shouted. "Talk! All empty, meaningless. We were gods enjoying a time of peace from the dreary reality of mortals. To talk of a future, to build palaces of pleasure and wisdom out of smoke was to say nothing."

Alioiune nodded her head. "You lied to her."

"You've no understanding of the ways of gods."

"We know enough," Kueur said with a contemptuous edge.

"Your mother knew. I can't help what she chose to believe, but she knew what I wanted. The seed grew quickly in her womb. Nine days we stayed together. Then you came. Twins, instead of the one daughter-sister I needed. I wondered what I should do—find some way to combine the two of you? Kill one, raise the other to be my twin? But which? It was all new to me.

"Your mother went mad with my dilemma. She cursed me, told me I could never re-create what I had thrown away when I escaped from the womb. She wouldn't listen to my reasoning. She didn't want to understand. I told her to leave me. One night she did, with you two. She left me a message, whispered into a mango that split open and let her words escape when I woke. Her children would not die or be used by my hand, she said. But she could no longer walk the world of mortals and raise her children because of the pain I had shown her. So she would see that the children would be cared for, and left me with a final curse: I would never know the spirit of the sister I left behind.

"I hunted Chiao, but she was clever. She led me to a river, which with her power she caused to swell suddenly, sweeping away and drowning my host. By the time I could secure another, her trail was gone.

"For years, I've searched for my daughters. I've paid for the meager help of the old land's dying gods with the souls of my own followers. Bargained and begged for the aid of gods born in this new land from the blood of the old land's people. I have served demons and ghosts, caused plagues and wars, for the knowledge of a few miles of trail taken by my daughters. And during the time of my hunt for you, I considered what happened with Chiao, and what I would have to do when I found my twins."

Pale Fox stared at Kueur and Alioune for a few moments. "You are not your mother," he said at last. "She was only a dragon dream, after all. You know pain, thrive on it, as far as I can see. What are children to you? Burdens. What can you lose by letting my fonio seed blossom inside you? Nine days is all I ask. You will have my gratitude. Come to my land, and I will protect you. Perhaps I can even arrange for Legba to favor you with one or two of his blessings. Whatever I can give, I will. Can't you sacrifice just a piece of yourselves for your father's happiness? Can't you find your own joy in the knowledge that you helped your lost father find his?"

Only the crackling of fire disturbed the quiet that followed. The Beast in Max had fallen under Pale Fox's spell, lulled by words and stories, and the god's power behind them, to a grumbling ghost of rage. Max silently approached the nearest fire drum, jean legs wrapped as another layer of insulation around his hands and arms.

Kueur spoke. "You know we'll have twins, because that's the seed's power. But you only want one child. What if we want to keep the one set's remaining child, and the other pair?"

"You don't."

"But if we do?"

"You can't. When I sacrifice the others, I'll merge their spirits with the one I've chosen. Purge the mortal influences of your flesh, along with the taint of the bodies Chiao and I possessed when we made you. Even Chiao's magic of dream and water and justice will be cut away. All that will be left is my essence, purified of all foreign poisons, shaped in a woman's form. In a short time, and under my guidance, she will become Yasigui."

"You should've kept looking for your birth twin," Kueur said, a touch of sadness in her voice. "You never found her, so she may still exist. Only she can fulfill you."

"If she was ever born, then the others hid her from me. No price I paid, no bargain I made, ever revealed what happened to her. The bond between us is broken, and she is dead to me. I must make my own twin. Your answer, daughters?"

"We'd rather die," said Alioune.

Pale Fox's head transformed once again into an animal's, this time with white hair growing over the canine skull shape. Pale Fox bared his teeth, crouched, moved to face Max.

The shift in shape had broken Pale Fox's hypnotic spell and roused the Beast, but Max had already picked up the fire-filled drum and started charging toward the god. With the Beast's roar rising through him like a searing lava flow, Max lifted the drum over his head and brought it down over Pale Fox.

The crash of metal, fuel, and fire staggered the god. Flames burst out of the drum's holes and open end as the fire bit into the god's flesh and singed Max's clothes and face. Alioune rolled forward, thrust a leg out, and swept

Pale Fox off his feet. The god rolled, still in the drum, as soon as he landed. Kueur brought up the steel tool she had used before as a weapon and began to hammer at Pale Fox's legs. Max freed himself of the jeans, found a length of steel tubing, and, using it as a spear, drove it through a gash in the side of the drum and jabbed the tube's end repeatedly into the god's body. Alioune joined them with two short lengths of steel pipe, which she used in rapid succession like a drummer on Pale Fox's legs in between Kueur's swings.

The sounds of metal clanging on metal, thumping against concrete and bone, mixed with heavy breathing, curses, and inarticulate cries from the twins. Max was surprised to hear himself joining them, with a voice that was not all Beast. He wondered if his expression was as contorted as theirs. Pale Fox remained silent as he rolled, tried to climb out of the drum, threw out burning wood. The smell of burning flesh wafted across the old factory floor.

Suddenly, Pale Fox withdrew his legs. The fire burned brighter in the drum. Max, sensing a trap, drew Alioune away from the opening, which she had been preparing to probe with pipes, and signed to Kueur to step back. At that instant, the drum rumbled, shook. Max dove, taking Alioune down with him. Kueur followed their example. The drum burst, sending fire and jagged steel in all directions, stunning Max for a moment with the sound and flash and shock wave of the explosion. The force of the explosion traveled up his legs and torso and blasted into the back of his head. Metal shards rained down after bouncing off the ceiling.

Max roused himself when he felt the fire burning through his clothes. He stood, swayed unsteadily, patted out flames coming from his coat and pants, glanced at the twins doing the same. The sting of wounds distracted him, and he felt along his body for any serious cuts from the shrapnel. A scraping sound alerted him. His hands rose instinctively, and he hunched his shoulders to receive a blow.

Pale Fox, his borrowed body hot, smoking, still on fire in places, dove into him. The god drove his head into Max's stomach while wrapping his arms around Max's waist. They wrestled, stumbled, and then Max felt his feet give and his balance shift backward as Pale Fox pushed him toward the one of the boarded windows. He cracked Pale Fox's shoulder with a knee-kick and elbow smash even as they fell backward, but the blow did nothing to curb the god's power or charge.

They passed out of the circle of lights, smashed once into a heavy piece of equipment. Metal corners dug into Max's back, and his head whipped back. Pale Fox pulled him away from the machine, and Max reached down, trying to break the hold. But his grip slid from around Pale Fox's neck, and the god quickly tightened his hold around Max's hips. Max tried to sink his center of gravity, sinking his body until he was almost kneeling. But Pale Fox charged again, legs churning and driving with inhuman power, and Max fell back, unable to find his balance or stand up to the god's strength. Kueur and Alioune chased them, but they were too far behind to help. Max felt himself lifted into the air; his feet left the ground. His fists and elbows sank into Pale Fox's burnt back, into flame and charred flesh. Bones and discs broke and cracked, but just as quickly mended. He tried to bite, scratch, kick. Pale Fox came on like a wild tempest. The Beast screeched with frustration.

The cold air struck him first. Then the sensation of flying. Wood splintered and broke all around him, and the dull pain from breaking through glass and wooden boards spread like a slow stain from back to spine to the base of his skull until the world blacked out. He woke falling, Pale Fox still holding on to him. Air was forced out of him when he stopped, when wet snow just starting to refreeze crunched under his back and Pale Fox landed headfirst on top of him, in the gut.

Max lay stunned in a mound of snow, his body twitching, frigid snow kissing the back of his neck and his hands. Pale Fox rolled off, threw snow and ice on himself, then got to his feet. Skin had been burned away, along with hair, leaving raw muscle and even bone exposed. The wounds had no apparent effect. Pale Fox pulled slices of metal from his body. Blood dribbled, stopped. Cuts and tears knitted closed, though skin, like eyes, would not grow back where it had been eaten away in large patches.

"Tonton!" Kueur shouted from the window through which they had fallen.

"Don't worry," Pale Fox said, leaping to the side of the building, clambering up the brick face like a spider, "I haven't killed him. You can have him back, if you live after I'm done with you." The twins drew away from the window as Pale Fox entered. The sounds of fighting drifted down to the street. Max groaned, concentrated on shutting down the Beast's rage so he could think. Slowly, he rose, pain shooting from ribs and back. His body had taken worse punishment and survived, even thrived, in the pursuit of work, and of pleasures. And when even his unnatural resilience and stamina had failed and he suffered injuries, the Beast had carried him on. But he was older, and the Beast a ghost. Max forced himself toward the door, staggering slightly, pushing himself for the twins. Driven by his love for them, and by the fear of losing them.

Love, and fear. Chiao's warning returned to him. Love and fear were driving him to his destruction, and condemning the twins.

He stopped at the door, leaned against the jamb. A slight tremor seized his legs. He had little enough left to fight the god, not enough to save the twins. Unlike his enemy, he could not heal his own bruised and broken ribs, much less shattered bones. The Beast urged him on, eager for blood and pain, but reason made him think. He was not afraid to die. A part of him welcomed the promise of darkness. But he could not follow his love and fear to a useless sacrifice, leaving one or both of the twins for Pale Fox. Max hammered the steel door frame once with his fist. He could find no advantage to help him against the god. Looking down, searching for an answer, he saw Pale Fox's footprint in the snow. The god's elevated body heat had melted a layer of snow, and a few specks of blood floated in the water. Blood and water.

Max nodded to himself. He might not know how to stop the twins' father, but he knew someone who might have an answer. He just needed a flow of blood and water. And a mother who cared enough to come across worlds to offer help.

Max went to his car and drove off, hunting for a source of blood. The Beast danced in the haze of pain behind Max's eyes.

* * *

Corners flashed by, mostly abandoned, locked in cold darkness illuminated by lonely streetlamps. Prostitutes ventured through snow and ice when he slowed to cruise by them, cursed when he sped off. A parked tractor-trailer with a driver slouched against the truck cab window tempted him. A police cruiser turning back toward the highway tugged at his restless rage and reckless instincts. He had counted all of their professions among the victims demanded by his work and his appetite, at one time or another, but hesitated now to pursue any of them for his need. The Beast jumped at the sight of each, just as his reason urged him to get on with what he had to do. They were all meat for the slaughter. They all held the blood he needed to summon a spirit. But something held him back from making the necessary sacrifice, and it was neither pain nor weariness.

Max shook his head, irritated by his paralysis, angered by the apparent birth of a drive to kill for a reason beyond his personal necessity. Even saving the twins was not enough. And though the Beast, in its ghost state, was strong enough to aid him in his work, it lacked the power to drive him into the state of frenzy he needed to be in to kill indiscriminately. It was as if the glimpse of Pale Fox's torment over the loss of his twin, and the god's abandonment of any reality except the one in which he could find her again, had driven a wedge between Max and his appetites.

Max's grip on the steering wheel tightened as a realization struck him. He did not want to kill an innocent. He did not want to follow Pale Fox's path and drag in a helpless bystander, like the man whose body Pale Fox had possessed, to get what he wanted. He needed to find some-one that needed killing.

Without thinking, he drove toward a block well-lit by a yellow corner bodega sign, a bar, and closed pawnshop and used furniture and clothing warehouse. He parked on a corner around the block, within sight of the bar. Waited. A tall, husky blond man singing and waving a short pea coat over his head emerged, accompanied by two shorter, stocky men laughing, kicking at street debris, throwing snowballs at the singer. A bus pulled in to the corner, obscuring them for a few moments. When it pulled away, they had quieted. A woman, bundled up in a long coat and hat, carrying a pharmacy bag, quickly crossed the street in front of Max and headed up a quiet block of six-story apartment buildings. The blond man put on his coat. They spoke among themselves, then split up, the blonde leading while the other two trailed on either side of the street as they went after the woman.

Max turned off the headlights and followed them through the cold, abandoned streets.

They caught her as she fumbled with keys at the door to an apartment building. While two kept watch on the street, the blonde jumped up the steps to the entrance and hooked his arm around her neck. Her cry was choked off and she was dragged off her feet, swept down the stairs, surrounded by the others, and carried struggling down the street. The pharmacy bag and its contents lay strewn across the stairs. She had no chance to cry out. Max was reminded of wasps stinging a worm into paralysis and dragging it off to plant eggs in the body.

They took her into an alley between two buildings, one shuttered and abandoned, the other closed tightly with curtains and blinds against the night. By the time Max reached the alley mouth they had beaten her into stillness and removed her coat. The woman was sprawled across garbage bags, half in the light from the streetlamp facing the alley. Her jeans were pulled down below her hips, sweatshirt rolled up to her shoulders, breasts flattened against her body, brown face bloodied, eyelids fluttering. The men jostled around her, glancing up occasionally at the windows shut and gate-locked against winter, thieves, and the stench of garbage. Max ducked back, anticipating one of the men looking back at the alley entrance. Moments later, Max looked back in. Night sucked the harsh sound of the three men's breathing out of the air.

Max raced his shadow to come up behind the closest man to the mouth of the alley. He snaked his hand under the chin, pushed his knee into the back of the man's knee, pulled with one hand clenching the back of the coat, and pushed with the chin hand. As the man flailed and gasped with sudden vertigo over the shift of balance, Max drove the head into the brick wall. The man groaned as he slid, stunned, to the ground. Turning, Max caught the second man charging with a kick to the knee. As the second man staggered forward, grimacing, a quick side step and arm trap gave Max the advantage. He led the assailant into the same brick wall into which he had thrown the first man.

Max sank at the knees slightly and raised his hands as he caught sight of the third man as a blur of motion coming quickly up on him. The attacker's fist deflected off Max's raised shoulder. Max redirected the blow past his face with one hand, reached low with the other as the man's solid body crashed into him. Max sank deeper, letting the man roll up on his shoulder. His high hand grabbed hold of the attacker's lead arm; his low hand hooked around the crotch. Max pulled, pushed, stood up. The third attacker, carried by his momentum, went up easily in Max's arms. He cursed, and the smell of alcohol blew out with his condensing breath. Max flipped him over, sent him to the ground headfirst, hard. Bone cracked. Fluid and blood dribbled from torn skin and a broken skull, staining the man's blond hair and making it clump.

The Beast howled with its victory, though Max had hardly needed to call on its rage and power. Without a god to lend them power and overcome their drunkenness and lack of skill, they were no match for Max. An invigorating rush of energy washed through Max, a consequence of the Beast's elation. Max took a deep breath and savored the partial and temporary relief from pain and exhaustion.

The fight had been quick and quiet, and no one had been alerted. Max wondered if anyone would have noticed if there had been noise. He went to the woman. She opened her eyes, stared at Max. He tried to give her a reassuring smile, but the Beast lurked behind his eyes, twisted his lips into a sneer, rumbled in his throat. Her fingers dug through the taut plastic of the bags under her. Her mouth opened, eyes widened. Her feet sank between the garbage bags as she tried to push herself away from him. The scream was coming, rushing out just behind the terror contorting her brown face and blinding her vision. Max raised his fist. The blow was sudden and unexpected, he was certain. She would never be able to separate his face from the other three and describe it accurately.

The Beast rose up, ravenous. Max's erection pushed un-expectedly against his pants. The woman's legs were spread apart, and her panties dug into the flesh below her belly. The scratches on her breasts inflamed the Beast; the puffiness around her eyes and the bloody cuts on her face incited wild appetites, promised savage pleasures. The Beast's call was answered by his own lusts, and Max took a step toward the woman while his hands fumbled with his pants.

He remembered the twins and his love; Chiao and her warning about letting love and fear lead him; Pale Fox and the god's terrible need; his pledge not to sacrifice innocents. Max hesitated. The Beast rode over his resolve, but Max hung on. He turned, stepped to the alley wall, punched bricks once, twice. Hanging on to the pain, Max wrestled the Beast down into darkness. His own desires he swallowed, until his gorge rose and he had to vomit thin and bitter acid. Stomach fluttering, Max went back to the woman and pulled her clothes together with trembling hands. He replaced her coat, found the little purse she had carried in a pocket, as well as keys, and put them in her hands.

One of the attackers moaned, and Max went to the two shorter men and knocked their heads into the wall again, until only soft breathing escaped their slack mouths. The big blond man was dead. Max dragged him farther back into the alley, where a snowdrift accumulated against the back wall. He set a fire in a small trash pile he built in the drift. Snow melted, water flowed. Max dragged the dead man to the drift, cut a gash in his throat, and let blood join the water's flow.

"Chiao," Max whispered. He listened for sirens, for the sound of a car on the street.

The old woman came after a few minutes, pale, transparent, veined with rivulets of blood. She looked like the dream she had claimed to be, her form shifting and wavering two feet off the ground.

"The god is stronger than I am," Max told her.

"My daughters . . . not safe . . ."

"I know. I tried to save them, but I don't have the power. Can you help me? Enter me, give me some of your strength?"

". . . restless sleep . . . can't . . ."

Max kicked a garbage bag. "Call on another part of yourself, Chiao. A warrior, or a magician, or something useful."

". . . too far . . ."

"Too frightened." Max glanced at the man he had sacrificed to call the god, wondering if he should have gone through all the trouble. "Give me something, damn it! You warned me, but gave me nothing to fight him with. What can I do to stop Pale Fox?"

". . . trick . . ."

"Trick? What kind of trick?"

". . . trick the trickster . . ."

"How? With what?"

". . . his pride . . . his need . . ."

"What does he need?"

". . . everything . . . my . . . daughters . . . his . . . sister . . . a host . . ."

"The man he's using, Legba's follower, his body's being used up. The eyes are gone, and some skin. But I can't wear Pale Fox down. He'll kill me before I finish the job."

". . . make an offering . . . draw him out . . ."

"Another body?"

". . . a form . . . a soul . . . to be . . . possessed . . ."

"But I don't want him stronger, damn it!"

". . . catch him . . . in form . . . he cannot use . . ."

"A dead body?"

". . . won't come to death . . . only life . . ."

"So what are you saying? Tell me—"

"—offer . . . what he needs . . . but in . . . stranger . . . when he comes . . . take it away . . . he will be caught . . . in between . . . trapped . . . in soul . . . follow it . . . as he followed me . . . to his death . . ." Chiao drifted toward him, reached out with curled fingers, faded before she could touch him. A mist of water and blood settled to the ground.

Max glanced at the bodies in the alley, still searching for a plan. The only one that occurred to him was to some-how trick the god into believing the woman was one of the twins, lure him into trying to plant his seed in her, and somehow kill the host body while the god was distracted. The woman's chances of survival seemed poor. He shook his head, dismissing the thought.

Max left the alley to retrieve the Buick. He opened the trunk, laid out the thick plastic he kept for blood work, hog-tied the smaller of the unconscious men, and put him in the trunk with a half-formed hope of using his soul to bargain with Pale Fox. As an afterthought, almost as a part of his habit of cleaning up after his pleasures, he put the dead man in, as well. The third he bound, gagged, and secured to a drainpipe bolted into the wall. After closing the trunk and starting the car, he went back and roused the woman by pressing snow against her face. He left before she fully regained consciousness, and before the Beast could further inflame him with its appetites. On the drive back to Pale Fox's hiding place, Max could think only of Kueur and Alioune.

* * *

The building was silent when Max returned, dragging the two men in with him. He brought them to the foot of the stairs, checked once again on the one still alive, tugging at the binding knots, went upstairs.

The twins were sitting naked, cross-legged and opposite one another in front of a single fire drum. The others had been overturned and their fires had spilled out and extinguished on the concrete floor. The twins' heads were bowed, their hands upturned in their laps. They might have been meditating, except for cuts, bruises, swollen joints, and the blood splattered over their bodies and faces. Pieces of foreign flesh clung to their bodies, and their mouths were framed by gore. Even from a distance, Max could see them trembling.

Pale Fox was not sitting with the twins. Max peered into the shadows, careful to stay in them, until he found the god silently pacing at the far end of the floor, appearing and disappearing behind a massive machine that reached nearly to the ceiling. Pale Fox made no sound until one of the twins moaned.

"Shut up!" Pale Fox screamed. Long, limping strides took him out of the darkness, into the flickering light. His body was ravaged: burned patches of skin across his back and chest flapped in the air; several fingers and the tip of his nose were gone; bone lay exposed at his cheek, the top of his head, and at an ankle. Dried blood and viscous, white fluid surrounded his wounds.

"Bitch," he continued, standing over Kueur, sniffing the air through his ruined nose. "What can I do now?" To Alioune he said, "Kill you? Is that what you want?"

Kueur managed to spit at Pale Fox. It was then, watching her thin spray of saliva strike the god, that Max noticed Pale Fox's genitals had been ripped away. A wide gash lay open between his legs, dark and moist with blood.

"You think you've won," Pale Fox continued. "But you should pray I find a way to plant my seed in you before this body dies. Because if I can't," he said, kneeing Kueur's head, "I'll leave you crippled and helpless, waiting for my return. And I will come back. If I have to drive my own followers across the ocean, I will come back. Now that I've found you, my sweet daughters, I'll never let you go."

It came to Max that he was not the only one who could be led to his doom by what he loved and what he feared. He looked at the two men at the foot of the stairs. A trick came to Max; a disguise, and a chance to put Pale Fox on death's road. The Beast snuffled, paced like a predatory wolf trapped in the confines of his head, eager to break out and kill something. The disguise was desperate, and the trick to get rid of Pale Fox lacked the certainty of a bullet or a knife's edge. But then, he did not know how to kill a god. No one had ever taught him. A chance was all he could hope for. Max went down the stairs, throwing his doubts about the sanity of what he was about to do to the Beast.

The cutting and peeling went quickly, his hands working with the skill and quickness of careful training and practice. Pale Fox stomped overhead, kicking loose rubble and screaming in frustration. The smell of blood and organs and guts hung in the air. When Max was done, he stripped, piled his clothes neatly in a corner against his survival, and slipped into the skin of the man he had killed. He was grateful for the man's size, which made the skin's fit loose and allowed freedom of movement. Next, he made certain the second, smaller man was still unconscious, then stripped him and tied clothes together into a harness. Using the harness, he secured the second man to his back, spine to spine. Hooking his feet around the man's ankles, Max brought each up so he could tie their legs together. Tying the man's ankles to Max's calves provided enough freedom of movement while maintaining the crude illusion of being joined. To link their arms, Max used a pair of loops made from the man's socks to keep their hands back to back. When he was done, Max was carrying the sacrifice he hoped to offer on his back.

"What is this thing that comes?" Pale Fox cried out from above as Max took the first step up the stairs. "Meat, touched by gods, like the one before?"

Max focused on climbing the stairs, grateful for the second man's smaller size and weight. He lifted each leg carefully, and pulled himself along by finding handholds in the crumbling stairwell walls. The unconscious man's arms tied to his limited his reach, but Max did not let go. He wanted Pale Fox to sense only one body, clumsy, with little threat.

"I smell Chiao's hand in this!" said Pale Fox. "An abomination. Twins, but brothers in place of sisters! Joined? Do you mock me, Chiao? Are you hiding in this monstrosity? No, no . . . I don't think so. You're just another agent, aren't you? Something failed, I think. A final, desperate gesture from a frightened mother."

Max reached the second floor and trudged toward the twins, afraid to stop. Stopping might invite collapse. Max shivered from the cold, from the pain of metal and glass and loose concrete pricking the soles of his feet. The dead man's skin slid back and forth over Max's body with each step, its restless movement aided by lubricants of blood and fat and sweat. The dead man's face and scalp sagged over Max's face. Eyeholes slipped out of alignment, partially obscuring Max's vision. Despite the pain and the cold, he headed for the dance of flames flickering through skin with his confidence rising. Pale Fox caught only the scents of strangers and Chiao, as Max desired. He still had a chance to save the twins.

Kueur and Alioune turned, stared at Max. Their expressions transformed from shock to revulsion to wonder. They gave no hint that they recognized him.

Pale Fox moved to intercept him, arms stretched out, fingers grasping. Max stepped sideways, circling around the god.

"Can't speak?" said Pale Fox. "Two mouths, two souls, but nothing to say? Or are there too many words, too many ingredients in this stew?" Pale Fox froze, sniffed, cocked his head, listened to Max's shuffling steps. "Are you here to challenge me? Save my daughters from me?" The god shadowed Max's movements, keeping himself between Max and the twins. "Don't be afraid. Chiao's last agent couldn't manage, but you're bigger. Stranger. Far more interesting. Filled with possibilities. Come, don't be afraid, let me feel your strength." Pale Fox held his hands up, inviting Max to charge.

The Beast made Max lean forward, shuffle his feet. Max strained to hold the extra weight on his back, and to hold back the Beast. Not yet. Give the god what he wants.

Pale Fox barked and sprang forward a step, challenging Max. "Come, now. Surely I can't be that intimidating. After what my daughters did to me? They finished the job my brother started when he nipped me down below," Pale Fox said, passing a hand over the emptiness between his legs. "But you don't know about my brother, or my daughters, or anything else, do you? You're just meat. Stupid. Dull." He sniffed again, strained to listen, shook his head and stamped his feet. "These pitiful flesh senses. Hardly anything left even of them. But there's two of you, sure enough. Both touched and warped by spirit powers. But one is stronger than the other, no? One seethes with energies and power. Rage. Part of you wants to kill me. But another part wants . . . my daughters!" Pale Fox cackled, hunched forward as if he were carrying as heavy a weight as Max. "The other sleeps. Chiao was not as generous with that one, I think. That one is weak." Pale Fox's laughter was high-pitched and short. "Twins, mated to my twins. What a nest that would make for my Yasigui."

Pale Fox withdrew. He reached back, felt for the twins. He caught Kueur by the ear, turned her toward Max. Kueur grimaced but offered no resistance. She kept her gaze lowered, as if the god's hold reached inside to dominate her spirit.

"She's beautiful," Pale Fox said, in a hushed, inviting voice. "Under the blood and filth. You want her. Yes, part of you does. Don't lie, I can feel your desire, hotter than the flames. Forget what Chiao told you to do. However she made you, whatever she gave or promised, you owe her nothing. She's betrayed you by sending you here. You know you can't kill me, or hurt me any more than they already have. So forget Chiao. She's abandoned you just as she did my daughters. There are more important things for you to do, like satisfy your hunger. Take this one," he said, shaking Kueur's head. "Take them both," he added, pointing to Alioune with his other hand. He threw Kueur down, whirled around the fire, stood behind the drum.

Max approached the twins. Kueur looked up while Alioune crept forward and put a protective arm around her sister. Neither of them recognized him. They stared, wonder long faded from their faces, waiting for whatever was going to happen next. Max recognized the price the twins had paid to hurt Pale Fox, and it was as terrible as the god's emasculation. Their hopelessness frightened him even as their passivity incited the Beast.

"Kill us," Alioune said, in a low, flat whisper.

"He'll use you if you let him," said Kueur, the musical lilt of her voice flattened. "Then he'll kill you, too."

Max carefully adjusted the mask of flesh over his face, allowing the twins to catch a glimpse of him underneath the dead man's skin. Their faces lit up. Shoulders rolled back, spines straightened. Alioune glanced at Pale Fox and licked her lips. Max's love for them stirred as they took strength from his return and mended their broken spirits.

"No, you don't want to die," Pale Fox said. "I can feel your interest, your passion. You want each other. Don't deny yourselves. Give in to your desire. Give yourselves the pleasure you want. I'll just take what I need, you won't even notice me."

Kueur and Alioune came to Max. Following his lead, they helped him to the ground where he lay on his side. Kueur embraced him, kissed him through the layer of death so hard he felt her lips through the dead man's flesh. Her teeth tore at the second skin, her tongue probed the holes for his eyes, nose, mouth. He almost released the unconscious man's arm to hold her to him, but remembered in time that the moment had not yet come. He satisfied himself with tasting her tongue in his mouth, feeling her teeth rub against his lips and her thigh against his crotch.

Alioune joined her sister, moaning into Max's ear as her fingers kneaded his neck. She straddled his hip, rolled and pumped her own hips gently as her mouth closed around his ear.

The dead skin rippled over Max's body. The ancient hunger he had touched when looking into the empty eye sockets of the god's host caressed him, murmured soothing sounds in his mind, darkened his thoughts. Fragile spirit tendrils barbed with sharp hooks of hunger sank through him, searching for a soul to catch. Seeking a life in which to sink roots. Max resisted Pale Fox's entry into his mind. The Beast roared, leapt, savaged the delicate tendrils of spirit insinuating themselves into Max's mind.

Finding no follower of gods, Pale Fox drew away, reached for the unconscious man's mind. During the few moments of transition, Max caught a glimpse over the shared link between their minds at the other man's darkened consciousness. At the floor of the empty cavern of the man's awareness, a shallow pool of memories reflected the faces of women, some drunk and laughing, others screaming. The images of sex, short and violent, rippled across the water. Along the edge of the pool, a few stones appeared carved in the images of a man and a woman. The faces were smooth and their expressions severe. The rest of the stones were shaped like the man's ideal of his own sexual organ.

Pale Fox hesitated, searching for the familiar structures of belief and ritual he was accustomed to finding in the people he possessed. In that moment of distraction, Max saw the seed Pale Fox carried: a dense fragment of idea and emotion; an endlessly coiled snake devouring its own tail, its mottled skin a codex for creation. The Beast strained to consume the seed while Max drew away from the vision, awed and humbled by its immensity.

At last, Pale Fox moved into the unconscious man's mind. Before the link broke, Max had an impression of the god's anger over the unfamiliar terrain of the man's mind, and his horror over a soul that not only did not believe in ancient African gods but held no faith in any spiritual life. Pale Fox floundered in the alien mind. Max held his breath, trying to suppress his fear that Pale Fox would run back to his follower's body rather than follow his appetite. But the god's hunger came, as deep and unstoppable as the Beast's had been when it was a living part of Max. The link broke. The unconscious man coughed, barked, kicked, and struggled against his bondage to Max.

Max signed for the twins to go to the man. As they settled over Pale Fox's new body, Max released the loops and slipknots holding them together. Kueur and Alioune entwined themselves around Pale Fox, sparing Max a brief glance to confirm what Max wanted them to do. He nodded.

Max's erection, already stiff from the twins' brief foreplay, ached at the sight of Kueur biting Pale Fox's new neck and drawing blood. The god cried out, then gasped as Alioune stole his cry as well as his sensation of pain with a kiss. Pale Fox turned to Alioune, distracted from the fact that bonds to Max no longer limited his movement. The god's erection grew as Alioune rubbed herself against him, her body undulating like an eel's. She rubbed her breasts in his face, then crept down to bite his nipples while her hand massaged his genitals. Once he was hard, she slipped him into her sex. Slowly gyrating her hips, she moved to his awakening urge, licking blood from his neck, kissing his eyes and lips.

Pale Fox thrust his hips forward, pushing himself deeper into Alioune even as he arched his back and reached for Kueur, drawing her closer. The gore and blood Pale Fox had shed on the twins during his struggle with them mingled with their sweat and, as the three pressed their bodies against each other, painted the pristine, white skin of his new host. The smells of burnt wood and paper, rusted machinery, and concrete dust gave way to the tang of blood, sweat, and the lubricating fluids of sex. Pale Fox grunted with each thrust, and his eyes changed subtly to his animal form's feral shape.

He maneuvered Alioune's hips with eager hands and gasped for breath through clenched teeth, driving toward his climax. But Kueur, her head thrown back and eyelids fluttering, stole his pleasure through the long, slender brown fingers with which she caressed his body and herded his senses to greater ecstasy. Pale Fox cried out in desperation, and Kueur answered him with clawed fingers raking and tearing skin from hips to underarms. His eyes opened wider in shock. Blood pulsed from his wounds. Bone peeked out through loose flesh. He opened his mouth to scream. Alioune pounced, covering his mouth with hers. She closed her eyes and shuddered as Pale Fox's erupting scream died into a moan.

Max reluctantly left them to their building rhythm of pain and pleasure, dragging his and the Beast's hunger away. He moved to the fire drum, where a voice whimpered over the crackle and snap of flames.

Pale Fox's original host lay on the ground, curled into a fetal ball. His arms swept down protectively into the devastated region between his legs. He smelled of urine and feces. Weeping, the man looked up at Max. Blinked. Cringed. "Please . . ." he whispered before his chattering teeth made speech impossible.

Then the unconscious man Pale Fox inhabited woke up. His scream mingled with Pale Fox's startled yip. The twins drew their heads back, leaving their limbs still coiled around him while they studied, with narrowed eyes and pursed lips, the conflict escalating in the god's mortal house. Pale Fox's host twisted and bucked, his arms and legs strained against the floor and the twins' grip. Bones cracked. A snout stretched out of the man's face, and his ears grew into points. Another scream wrenched his throat, followed by a spray of blood that splattered across Alioune's face. The blood startled her into action, and she resumed the rhythm of thrust and counterthrust, drawing an eager response from the man's body even as souls battled for its possession. Kueur bit, slapped, and prodded flesh, fueling and guiding the frenzy of the body's appetite for sensation. The tidal play of pain and pleasure resumed, washing the body's spirit combatants back and forth.

Max kneeled beside the god's former host and smoothly broke his neck. The Beast blew through Max like a sandstorm: blinding, stinging, hot. Max tore off the man's arms and legs, using a jagged length of metal to saw tendons and sinew. He broke bones, separated joints, drew out the man's blood-slick heart and felt its spasms die out in his palm. The Beast, ravenous, made him eat it. When he was finished, he sank his fingers into the man's bowels, drew out his entrails, threw them into the fire drum. He yanked organs out until the torso was an empty cavity, then severed the head and threw all the remains into the fire. The fire brightened, sending up thick smoke redolent with the stench of charring meat. And in that smoke, Max imagined the soul of the man sold by the god Legba into Pale Fox's mad service rising to freedom, testing the direction of the cross-breezes, and finally escaping on a cold wind into the black night. Free to fly to the spirit world the soul had been shaped to expect after death.

Without a god rooted in its soul-form, fleeing death as it had done when Chiao drowned its host in rising river water.

As the Beast vented its rage and triumph, Max watched the twins still using the god's host, killing the mortal flesh with their love. Neither god nor man had yet assumed control. And without the god's will, the mortal flesh would not survive the twins' attention for much longer. Max understood what it took to survive the twins. He knew how the brain and muscle and organs were reacting in the riptide of sensation. Sanity and physical stamina were being drawn farther out beyond the boundaries imposed by the physical world. Each affirmation of life, every sliver of pain and pleasure, was sending the man's body closer to death.

Max waited for the moment when Pale Fox realized he had lost the soul of the one who believed in him. Without that soul, Max was certain Pale Fox would not find his way back to the spirit world of his creation, and so lose the path to his own followers. Without followers, Pale Fox's hunger for the twins would have no means of satisfying itself. Kueur and Alioune would be safe. The plan had fallen into place instinctively, in an instant, as soon as he had seen what the twins had done to Pale Fox's first host. Chiao's words echoed in his mind. Her form danced at the edges of his vision.

Only the slightest touch of doubt chilled Max as he basked in the Beast's exultation.

A seizure suddenly racked the man's body. His limbs flailed, and his hands and head smashed repeatedly against the floor. Then his muscles locked, stood out under his skin, fully flexed. Veins popped up. His hair stood up on end. The animal form receded. A choked cry escaped his wide-open mouth.

Alioune released him, pulled away. Kueur quickly untangled herself from his rock-hard limbs and embraced her sister. As they collapsed to the ground in each other's arms, Pale Fox's host surrendered to an orgasm. A pale geyser exploded from his raw, red organ. Human seed splashed on concrete and metal and bloody, torn skin. Max imagined the fragments of fonio seed unraveling, the snakeskin codex scrambling into hissing, static clouds. The waste saddened him, and made him feel small and insignificant.

The twins convulsed, looked to Max with surprise in their faces, then closed their eyes and balled their fists. Their skin rippled.

Of course, a part of their souls believed in Pale Fox. In them, he might find safe haven.

Max started toward them, but Kueur held out her hand without opening her eyes. The twins breathed steadily, deeply. The skin rippling subsided.

Chiao, Max thought. Prayed. The part of them that was not Pale Fox would give them strength to fight off the god.

The tattered remains of second skin hanging from Max's

270

body twitched with life. A darkness entered his mind. Spiked tentacles of hunger searched for his soul.

"You've seen, you believe," said Pale Fox. The Beast leapt at the alien entity intruding on its territory. Through the tenuous bonds the god was trying to forge with his mind, Max saw the soul of the second host disappearing into a nimbus of light. Still rooted to that soul, Pale Fox's spirit stretched between the light and Max. "Let me in," Pale Fox pleaded. "He's taking me with him. I fought too hard for his body. I'm caught in his soul. I need help to free myself. Just let me root in you until this mortal's soul leaves. Then I'll release you. I promise. Swear. Please, this soul believes in nothing. He drags me to oblivion. Spare me. Spare the father of your lovers. Can you live with them, knowing you killed their creator?"

Max closed his mind against Pale Fox's influence. The Beast stormed along the borders of Max's self, cutting loose every hold Pale Fox tried to take. Savaging the spirit with cruel ghost spikes and sharp ghost teeth.

"I'll find another way to bring Yasigui back," Pale Fox said, his voice diminishing as the link between them died. "I won't ever attack them again . . . please . . . help me . . ." His words turned to frantic barking.

Pale Fox's form stretched to an infinite length between one world and the next. Max caught a last glimpse of Pale Fox's stolen fonio seed. Smaller now, and shrinking as it went with the god into the unknown, it still had the power to move Max. The knotted snake vanished into the light, and the last grip Pale Fox had on Max came loose. The god dwindled like a train barreling into mist-veiled mountains.

As the light began to fade and Max's hold on reality

returned, a sound rose up in Max's mind like an echo traveling from a valley on the other side of existence. The Beast's cry of victory nearly overwhelmed the echo, which Max thought first was a grumbling bark, and then a word in some foreign tongue. At last, with the breeze picking at the torn suit of skin and chilling his blood-soaked flesh, Max understood he had heard the god call out, in a voice filled with hope and surprise: "Yasigui?"

"You look like hell," said Kueur, washing herself with warm water melted from ice held over the fire drum's glowing embers.

Max scraped his skin with a sharp-edged piece of metal he had cleansed with water and fire, flicking away the last of the gore still clinging to him. "I'm getting too old for this," he said. The Beast rumbled in protest but returned to its sated, drowsy state, curled in a dark corner of his mind and dreaming ghost dreams of torn bodies and the taste of blood.

Alioune sifted through a pile of clothes salvaged from those discarded by everyone over the course of the night's battles. "You always say that," she said. She found Pale Fox's original jeans, burned and torn, and put them on.

"At least lately," he added, turning to his own pile of clothes he had brought up from downstairs.

"Maybe now you'll listen when we talk about our past," said Kueur with a rueful smile that faded quickly. She donned the jeans Max had used as part of the harness he used to bring up his living sacrifice to the god. "Do you think he's dead?" she asked, holding up two ragged sweatshirts and looking from one to the other.

"The gray one doesn't have blood on it," Max said.

When Kueur looked to him, he nodded his head. "He's gone. I don't think he'll be back." After another pause, he asked, "Will you miss him?"

Kueur laughed. Alioune answered in a serious voice, "We didn't know him long enough to miss him. If we had, we still would not miss him."

Suppressing her amusement, Kueur added, "But it is good to meet one's father."

They finished dressing and hurried to the car, all three crowding into the front. With the heater running high, they drove through an ice-locked world with the wind whistling at the windows, and left Bayonne for the lights and life across the river.

"You met our mother," Alioune said as they went through the tunnel. She was sitting in Kueur's lap, staring at the tile wall streaming past. Limbs entangled, bodies pressed against one another, the twins looked like a pair of lion cubs exhausted from their play of chasing future prey.

"Tell us about her?" asked Kueur.

Max did, recalling every detail and impression as he took them to a safe house in Chinatown, where they changed into clean clothes and drove out in a Lincoln. On the final ride back to their loft, Max stopped at a red light, frowned, turned to them. He spoke the question that had been haunting him, prepared to flinch at the answer.

"Did you really want to keep the children?"

Alioune met his gaze. Kueur, now sitting in her sister's lap, closed her eyes. Neither of them answered for several moments. The light turned green and Max accelerated, thinking he had escaped their response.

"Perhaps," said Kueur, her eyes still closed, as if envisioning another life. "After going through all the pain of conceiving and delivering them, it might've been interesting to keep them, raise them. Who knows what pleasures there are in giving our children what we never had?"

Max swallowed his answer and kept his silence. By the time they reached the loft, the edge to his fear had been dulled by the claw-edged purr of the twin's presence. He no longer felt compelled by restless anxiety to go back out to the dead drop and pick up the rest of his money for the night's earlier work. A peaceful exhaustion had settled over him, blanketing even the Beast in a layer of sleep's deadening sand. The money could wait until tomorrow. He headed for the bedroom, his love for the twins casting the idea of children in an alien but not entirely discomforting light.

Kueur grabbed his hand and pulled him toward the Box. Alioune held the door open. Waves passed through crimson veils lining the walls.

"I'm getting too—" Max began, then stopped himself. He allowed himself to be pulled into the Box. "It's time to change the decor in here," he said sheepishly, thinking of a serpent motif, with a very specific pattern for the skin of his tail-eating snakes.

"Some things never change," Kueur said, wriggling out of her pants.

"And some things do," said Alioune, closing the door.

Part Three

Truth and Consequences in the Heart of Destruction

Max roused himself from a chant-induced and dream-laced slumber. The Australian oknirabata, a white cloud of beard masking his weathered face, paused in his ministrations. He looked up from Max's bloated stomach, his lips still pursed from his attempt at sucking out the malevolent Djanba spirit he claimed had come to reside in Max's belly. The other shamans, healers, and wise folk scattered throughout the loft glanced at Max lying naked on the prayer rug draped over the sofa.

Max tried to sit up, but a wave of nausea and dizziness forced him back. Nothing had changed. The mysterious ailment plaguing him for the past two days had not yet been exorcised. He was as helpless as when he had first been struck down at the airport while assassinating a diplomatic courier attempting to take stolen computer chips out of the country.

The Beast whimpered, its spirit writhing in the storm of sorceries washing through Max like a cleansing flood. He soothed the ghost of his murderous impulse, reassuring the Beast that it was not the object of the magical assault. The Beast, having already been slain once by Max, snarled with distrust and squeezed itself into a dark pit of rage in Max's soul like a poisonous snail withdrawing into its shell.

The men and women scattered throughout the loft turned back to their own work. The oknirabata lowered his head and smacked his lips, preparing to use his power once again, but Max shifted and waved him away. With lowered gaze the holy man stuck two fingers up Max's anus and pulled out the magic mabanba stone he had implanted earlier. Then he walked away, bare feet slapping against the wood and tapping the mabanba stone against his bare chest, shoulders hunched in his worn, dark, two-piece suit.

Kueur hurried from the kitchen carrying a cup of tea fragrant with ginger, deliberately bumping into Dex, the New Age crystal guru in European-cut sport casuals drawing out his finest stones from their leather pouches and laying them on the floor. Max scowled at the fool who had taken great pains to introduce himself when he arrived. He knew most of the healers in the room, but their names were indistinct shadows in his mind. He needed their skills and powers, not their familiarity or fawning attention.

Kueur's twin, Alioune, watched her sister's flirtation from behind the dining counter with her arms crossed over her chest, shoulders hunched, the exotic beauty of her Asian-African features distorted by a frown.

"Tonton," Kueur said, the music of her voice soured by quavering, "how was your rest?" She cradled Max's head

278

in her lap and helped him take a few sips before putting the cup down on the long, low, glass coffee table.

"More of the same," he answered curtly. He opened his mouth to say more, shamed by his harsh tone. They deserved better than his helplessness and short-tempered moodiness.

His mouth stayed open, but nothing came out. He wanted to tell Kueur about dreams limned by healing fires, shadowed by blood desires. He needed to talk to the twins about images haunting his dreams: fanged monsters lurking in caves; cherubic infants steadily devouring his limbs, sex, torso, and finally his face; the sensation of worms tunneling through his body, devouring organs and tissue, caressing his bones with their soft, plump rings. They had to hear of the endless pursuit through sewers by wailing creatures that moved like a horde of slick-haired rats but, when they finally trapped him against a drainage grating overlooking the sea, looked up at him with innocent eyes set into round and smooth-skinned faces.

Max closed his mouth, then his eyes. Dreams spun a cocoon of paralyzing fear around his mind. Reality dipped and tilted as if uprooted, and the strength Max had always counted on to face the dangerous and the strange drained from his body. Words broke apart, spilling memory, thought, and emotion. He could say nothing.

He opened his eyes, met Kueur's gaze, felt the strength of her arms and and legs holding him, the power of her womb beating in his ear. A fit of rage rose from where the Beast had burrowed into hiding. Kueur's solicitousness stung his raw nerves. Alioune's pensive pose insulted his sensibilities. Worse than his illness, their physical and emotional imperfections were driving him mad. Be strong, he wanted to scream. Don't worry about me. Go on with your lives. Did I raise you to be weak?

"Lee called on the secure line from Albania," Alioune said. "He said you should wait to die until he comes back, because he was rolled over to another assignment and cannot come to your funeral. He also said you owe him money."

"Fuck Lee," Max said.

Kueur spoke up quickly. "Dr. Plummer left some referrals after you refused hospitalization." A sweep of her hand encompassed a stack of papers on top of a low glass coffee table. "He said to come in when you're ready to give up witchcraft."

"Medical science won't help, I know that much," Max grumbled. "Something darker than my body attacks me." He turned away, reached for a bowl of fruit. He spilled them on the floor and held the bowl to his face in time to catch the vomit erupting from his mouth.

After he was finished, Max set the bowl down and collapsed against Kueur. As she wiped his face and body with the moist towel Alioune had brought over, she said, "Tonton, the government man wants to see you. Do you want me to send him away?"

Max stared at the security squad camouflaged in dark suits in the alcove leading to the loft door. Flinched. Their hard, black presence blighted the currents of gentler energies flowing through the air. "Let him come," Max said, eager to get them out.

Kueur held her index finger up to the group. A broad-chested official wearing faint, tailored pinstripe spoke briefly to a bespectacled Chinese man, then wove a path past Dex and his crystals, four weathered Navajos—one

ancient, two old, and one no younger than Max—in faded
jeans and dusty boots softly chanting around their sand
painting, the Australian listening with closed eyes for the
evil spirit he sought, and a short, dark-haired mambo in
long skirts and peasant blouse, hunched over and leaning
on a cane. The loa spirit riding her form leered at the
government official as he passed, and the Navajo shamans
looked up with hooded glances in his wake.

Kueur and Alioune's faces lit at his approach. Alioune
put a fist against her hip and spread the fingers of her other
hand across her bare, brown stomach. Kueur ran a palm
over her short, red-tinged hair and smiled. The government
man flashed a grin and winked at the twins, exuding eye-
twinkling charm that ballooned like a chemical cloud
around him.

Anger shook Max as the twins' focus of attention shifted
away from him. He knew the hunger they were feeling,
the appetite that was driving them to draw prey into the
bed of their desire. But he was sick. Unable to satisfy them
by joining in games of love and pain they saved for each
other in the Box at the back of the loft. He needed their
attention. He might be in danger. They were being selfish,
abandoning him for their lust, ignoring his pain, his need.
Ungrateful, after all the years of attention he had given
them—

"Leave him," he snapped, unable to contain his irritation. "He's not for you."

Alioune jerked her head to the side, hurt a twitch catching the corner of her wide lips. Kueur looked down at him.
"Tonton?" she said.

The government man's gaze captured their moment of
stunned silence. Kueur slipped out from under Max and

gently propped his head with a cushion. As she picked up the bowl of vomit, her face a mask, Max felt shame redden his face. Alioune wrapped the prayer rug around him, making sure his crotch and belly were covered, and he nodded, wondering if that was enough of an apology. The twins stood, ignoring each other and him, turned to go. The government man came to a stop at Max's feet.

"I—I'm sorry," Max said, stunned, lost in a dense fog of irrational fears and inconsistent emotions.

The twins stopped, looked at each other.

"I just don't know what's happening to me," he said. "I can't control—"

"I understand," Kueur said softly, flashing a smile at Max. "It's not easy acting human."

Alioune nodded once, took the bowl from Kueur, and went to the bathroom. Kueur headed back to the kitchen, ignoring the stir the sway of her long, elegant arms created. Dex and the men at the alcove followed her walk until the kitchen counter shielded her from their view. The mambo's loa cackled and shook its hips in a crude pantomime of provocativeness.

Max turned to his latest visitor, who moved a nearby stool to sit at the foot of Max's improvised bed.

"Hello, Mr. Johnson," said Max. It was not his real name, but since the government man had never shared any personal information, Max had named him George Johnson, based on no one he had ever known. Having only a shell of worldly power granted by those who worked for him, and for whom he worked, the names of Mr. Johnson and the other major representative in the alcove, Mr. Tung, came easily to Max. "I didn't realize you knew my new address. I thought the drop was as close as you cared to come to my affairs."

"If you liked fingers up your ass, Max, all you had to do was ask," Mr. Johnson said, wiggling two fingers in Max's face. He laughed and patted Max's distended belly. "I thought I'd drop by when I heard you were under the weather. Of course, I knew about you moving in with the girls. I keep track of all of my good friends. Never know when I might want to give a surprise party." Max's gut twisted. The Beast rose for a moment, hauling with it rage and power, and a knife stroke that would have opened the government man from neck to groin. No one spoke to him that way, ever. No one threatened his home, his family. Who was this? Dizziness swept away Max's outrage, leaving him feeling small and vulnerable before the representative of vast but unseen powers. He realized in that moment that Mr. Johnson was as much a shaman as anyone else in the loft, though his soul and magic were both rooted in material planes.

"Since when are you and Mr. Tung associates?" Max asked, looking to the alcove at the Chinese man who did not care if anyone knew his name. Max hoped he was hiding the extent of his illness from Mr. Johnson's quick and greedy eyes.

"We've been elected to represent your contractors, Max. All the sides. Everyone knows what happened at the airport. There are rumors. Concerns."

"So soon?"

"It's the age of technology, Max. Modems and computers."

"I completed the assignment."

"You crawled into a baggage mover and called the girls

to fetch you. Didn't even clean up after yourself. You were lucky, working outside the main terminals. Thank God for cell phones, eh, Max?"

"It's the age of technology, yes. Your concern is touching."

"I'm sure." Mr. Johnson kept a steady gaze locked on Max.

"But you're too early for my funeral."

"We want to be sure what happens, happens. Whatever that may be."

"In a roomful of magicians, you want certainties?

"When it comes to life or death, Max, trust me, Mr. Tung and I can tell the difference. We brought experts. Equipment."

"I never took you for a healer."

"I'm not." Mr. Johnson's lips set into a thin line, and his eyes hardened.

Max scowled. "Your secrets are safe."

"Normally, yes. We've all trusted you to take what you know with you in case a job went bad. But now you're vulnerable. So's your information. If things don't go well for you, what you know might be ... excavated ... by whoever has gained power over you. Odd things happen in your world, Max."

The Beast paced among Max's thoughts, restless with the verbal fencing, eager for action. Death. It nuzzled images of Max jumping up, ripping Mr. Johnson's throat out with teeth and nails, cracking the man's skull open and sifting through whatever government secrets he kept hidden in the flesh off his brain. But Max's body remained leaden, paralyzed by a lack of strength. The Beast howled in frustration, and Max seethed with sympathetic rage.

Kueur appeared, as if sensing his crisis. She placed burning incense the Indian sadhu from Flushing had brought to clear the air of bad spirits on the coffee table. Alioune glided to a halt behind Mr. Johnson and stared over his shoulder at the floor between him and Max. The men in the alcove stirred, but Mr. Johnson shook his head once. Alioune came around and stood behind the couch, by Max's head.

"Do you think you can finish whatever was started against me?" Max asked. Words of challenge did nothing to mollify the impatient Beast.

Mr. Johnson's shoulders relaxed. He gestured with his hands, as if clearing a game board of pieces. "Max, you're taking this far too personally. We know the dead can be made to speak. If you die, we want only to make sure you don't talk. If you live, we have work for you."

"And if I live but can't work? If this is the best I can do for the rest of my life?"

Mr. Johnson leaned forward. "Max, it's been my experience that when things start to go up or down, they reach some kind of climax, one way or the other. I don't think you'll let yourself crawl toward death. You'll either get up and walk, or roll into a hole in the ground."

Max's silence echoed his resolve.

Mr. Johnson patted Max on the thigh, stood up, started to turn. He faced Alioune, who did not make way for him. Mr. Johnson glanced over his shoulder and pointed a thick, rigid finger at Max's crotch. "Well, at least I know the appeal you hold for the young ladies," he said with a leer. He spun smoothly around Alioune and headed back to the alcove, telling the suited men to go ahead with the operation in a loud, commanding voice that sent ripples of unease through the loft.

"Why can't we take him into the Box?" Kueur asked.

"He wants to go," Alioune said in a low, grumbling voice. "He is one of those who thinks he can survive our affection. Let us. Join us. Perhaps it will help to—"

"Leave him. His death would cause more problems than it would solve."

"Maybe he's the cause," Kueur whispered, bending close to Max's ear. "Wouldn't he, or Tung, or the others do anything they could to take what you know and gain the advantage over the others?"

Another wave of nausea came crashing down on Max, and he slid to the couch and lay on his side, drawing his knees up and facing the kitchen. He breathed deeply and concentrated on talking to distract himself from feeling sick. "They don't have that kind of power over me. They only have electronic toys and ordinary men. And even if one of them, or some faction, stumbled onto something to use against me, how long would they have to pick me clean of codes and drops and contacts? Victims, past and future? Operations they don't even realize happened? There's too much information. They'd hardly know what to look for. They barely know each other, really. Corporations, faiths, secret societies as old as civilization, shadow governments, all scrambling in the darkness looking for an advantage. I'm their light. A light that illuminates a little corner of the universe they want to know every time I kill."

A sharp pain cut into the small of Max's back, bled a dull ache up and down his spine, around his hips and belly, into his groin. He curled more tightly into a fetal position while holding on tight to the prayer rug. A spasm seized his stomach, and he dry-heaved, shaking and sweating, until the nausea exhausted itself and his body relaxed. The Beast, its lust for death unsated, pulled back from his body's betrayals and sulked in a pit of hate.

Alioune's eyes opened wider, as if to contain the tears pooling in their corners. She gesticulated frantically as she said, "He's just another distraction. They are all distractions. I am sorry, Tonton. We were just so frightened, we have never seen you this way. We called everyone we knew in the city, hoping—"

"I understand," Max croaked. In a moment of clarity between attacks of illness and moodiness, he saw fear breaching the cool, sensual surface of the twins' demeanors. A chill seized him, touching him more deeply than the wild fluctuations of his own body heat. He knew for that moment what they felt for him, what the twins meant to him. He saw the abyss that would swallow them all if the bonds between them were broken. Tears burned his eyes. A moment later, understanding dissipated like mist under the sun's scrutiny, leaving behind the raw edge of appetite, the driving fury of need.

"Perhaps we should send them all away," Alioune continued, her eyes darting, searching for something to fix on.

"No," Max said, surprised by the exhaustion in his voice. "Let the healers work. Let the vultures circle."

"Do you feel the evil spirit troubling you yet?" Kueur asked hopefully, taking Max's hand and squeezing it.

"Aside from the Beast, no. But something sucks the life from me. If only they can find the hole my enemy has made in me." Nausea crept like a slow, cold mud slide over the borders of his awareness. Max rubbed his slightly distended stomach and asked, "Who's next to try their skill?"

Kueur and Alioune surveyed the loft. They were each about to speak when a disturbance drew attention to the alcove, where Mr. Johnson and Mr. Tung, along with their associates, surrounded a small, thin figure with a cane.

Max thought at first a child had come bundled in a ski jacket and scarf, but then saw the straight, silver hair slipping out from under the newcomer's baseball cap and falling to the figure's slightly hunched shoulders.

"Mrs. Chan," Max called out. Her name burned in his mind almost as brightly as the twins', though she was not a lover. One of the healers brought in to help him, she was also the latest in a long line of teachers whose wisdom and talents substituted for the mother he had never known.

The woman glanced in his direction and nodded curtly, then turned on Mr. Johnson, who was holding a handheld metal detector and trying to sweep it over her body. Mrs. Chan whipped the cane around in a circle, striking Mr. Johnson's wrist sharply. The detector flew out of his hands, and he gave out a yelp, seizing his wrist and taking a step back. One of the dark-suited men stepped forward, reaching for the cane. She slid her grip down to the end and swung the cane, curved handle first, down on the man's face. He staggered sideways, both hands covering his bleeding nose. A third man danced forward, arms, head, and torso moving snakelike from side to side. Mrs. Chan feinted a thrust to the solar plexus. The man froze, ready to embrace and trap the strike. Mrs. Chan's front foot glided toward her opponent. She dipped, impossibly quick and agile, and hooked the cane handle around the man's foot. With a snap of her body, she pulled the cane and sent the man flipping backward. He landed on his shoulders with a surprised grunt, recovered quickly with a kick-up, but assumed a low, and unmoving, guarded stance.

Two other men pulled guns. More agents crowded the outer door, coming from the hallway. Racks of electronic equipment in the alcove shook from the sudden action. Mr. Tung called out in a sharp voice. Everyone froze except for Mrs. Chan, who resumed a normal grip on the cane and brushed her silk pants and windbreaker as if a dust devil had just passed over her. Mr. Tung bowed and spoke softly. Mrs. Chan replied curtly, sparing him a brief, glowering look. Mr. Tung bowed once again and waved her into the loft.

Mrs. Chan walked briskly past the others. The Navajos, without breaking the rhythm of their chanting, watched her go by with bemused expressions. Dex gathered his crystals and moved hastily out of her way, while the mambo hooted and called out, "Make way, bad spirit, here comes your master." The mambo waved her cane in mocking imitation of Mrs. Chan's fighting style, thrusting to a finger's breadth away from the elderly woman's arm as she walked by.

Mrs. Chan ignored the antics of the mambo's loa and stopped beside Max. Shaking his hand, she smiled and said, "Good afternoon, my friend. Not feeling well, I hear." She released Max, slowly ran the palm of her hand a few inches over the length of his body. "Have you been practicing your chi kung exercises?" she asked, the smile fading from her face. Her eyes narrowed, her hand trembled, and shadows seemed to gather in the folds of her flesh.

"Every day, master," Max replied. "Until this."

Mrs. Chan reached under the prayer rug and pressed her

palm against his belly. "So. Something blocks the chi. Thought? Spirit? Body?"

Warmth blossomed below Max's belly button. His stomach settled, and a sense of well-being surged through him. Feeling suddenly stronger, he started to get up.

"Body," Mrs. Chan said, pushing him back into the sofa. "My friend, you have a most interesting problem. One I cannot help you with. But do not worry, it is not serious. It will pass on its own, and quite soon. My congratulations."

Alioune and Kueur closed in around Max. The Navajos stopped chanting, and the other shamans and healers scattered throughout the loft broke through the veneer of their aloofness and stared at Mrs. Chan.

"What is it?" Max asked.

"You are pregnant."

The silence was a stone no one seemed strong enough to break. Max opened his mouth, closed it. A smile flickered through his surprise as it occurred to him that Mrs. Chan was joking. But her appraising stare sobered him, letting him feel truth spread through him and numb any conscious reaction. He waited for what was coming next.

"Good luck, my friend," Mrs. Chan said, squeezing his hand as she prepared to leave. "When this is over, you must be certain to return to your chi kung practice."

Max bolted to his feet. Mrs. Chan withdrew, flowing backward like an exhausted wave from the beach. The prayer rug slid down his body and fell to the floor. The twins grabbed hold of his arms, pressed themselves against him.

"Tonton!" Alioune shouted, trying to hold him back.

"Be careful!" Kueur screamed, pushing him in a circle

so he would find himself back at the couch.

He shrugged, and they fell away. Thoughts sparkled like a thousand stars scattered across the darkness of his mind, remote, unattainable. Emotions rumbled through him, raw and intoxicating. The twins, his work as an assassin, his past of rape and torture and killing, the unfolding mystery of his future, spread before him like an endless savannah. He felt the power of creation coursing through his veins, felt a bond to everything that lived. He was a hunter surveying his territory, a god looking over what his hand had made. The world belonged to him for a bright, burning moment, and nothing seemed impossible.

Joy made Max cry out. As if through a fog, he saw Mrs. Chan waving her hands in his face, the oknirabata and the sadhu and the mambo and all the rest staring at him, mouths shaping chants and spells and curses. In the distance, Mr. Johnson and Mr. Tung stared up from their handheld electronics, faces sundered by expressions of astonishment. A moment later, the golden brown visages of Kueur and Alioune, skin smooth as polished wood, eyes deep as pools in the depths of undiscovered caverns, fell across his sight like a curtain.

Tears flowed, forging cold tracks across his cheeks. Terror shattered the foundations of his power. He collapsed into their arms, and the twins eased him back onto the couch. It was all too vast, he realized. Too much to hold, to own, to bear. Even the spark he carried that was his own life was too heavy a responsibility. So much more dire, then, was the bud of life Mrs. Chan had identified in him. How could he bring another life into the world where everything was his to destroy?

Max cried out again. The Beast, cowed by the intensity

of his visions and the glow of life within him, keened in mourning.

Thoughts extinguished. Emotion ran dry. Max surrendered with relief to the blackness closing around him.

"He's only fainted," the mambo said, and only stopped slapping Max's face when he opened his eyes. She picked up the end of the prayer rug and began chewing at loose threads.

"Someone should feed the loa," said the youngest of the Navajo shamans standing behind the crowd huddled around the couch.

Max grunted, feeling as if he had just woken from one nightmare only to stumble into another. Faces bobbed around him like multicolored buoys warning of secret tides and underwater reefs. His stomach lurched, and the room seemed to spin around his head. He clutched at the edge of the couch while Mrs. Chan pulled the prayer rug back over his naked body.

"I'll get something for the god," Kueur said. She patted Max's hand but avoided eye contact. She stood and left the immediate circle around him, with Alioune following wordlessly in her wake. Distracted healers filled in their places.

Mrs. Chan took up Max's hand. His fingers tingled. A river of warmth traveled up his arm and through his torso, settling his stomach and pooling in his belly. He rubbed the mound of flesh, looked up at Mrs. Chan.

"Is it true?" he asked, horrified.

"Do not worry, my friend," she said. "The young ladies felt further involvement by Western medical professionals might lead to personal complications for you. I have assured them that, with the assistance of some of these good people, we can deliver your child. Everything is quite natural, I assure you. Except, of course, for you."

"It's true," said Max, shaking his head.

"I have had some experience in the delivery of little ones, although," she said, with a wink and a pass of the hand over his crotch, "the mechanics were not the same." She laughed at his expression. "My friend, you will survive to make children in the more usual fashion, perhaps with your two lovely companions?"

"How could this happen?" Max asked. "Why?"

"We might be able to answer those questions," Mr. Johnson said, waving at Max from the background. At his side, Mr. Tung nodded his head. "Private hospital, a medical research team with the latest technology—"

"Thank you," Max said, "but I'm not ready to sell myself to you."

"A most interesting condition," the sadhu said, thrusting his head to the forefront of the group. "Have you engaged in any unusual activities lately?"

"Your dreams, have they spoken to you?" the oknirabata asked.

"Been fucking spirits?" added the oldest Navajo shaman, an emaciated sliver of flesh and bone.

"I will see you in a few days, a week at the most," Mrs. Chan said. "You will know when the baby is ready to come out."

"So soon?"

"Better nine days than nine months," the twins' own healer, a Moroccan shuwwafat in robes and a veil, muttered as she got up. "Allah is always merciful to men. It must be that he knows men are not as strong as women."

"And, my friend, I would meditate a great deal if I were you," Mrs. Chan added, "to prepare for the pain."

Mrs. Chan bowed to Max, presenting a fist in hand, then picked up her cane and, after a word with the mambo and a few others, left. Her departure signaled an end to the search for spirits for many in the loft. The Navajo shamans destroyed their sand painting; Dex gathered his crystals; others picked up bones, feathers, grimmoires, and other paraphernalia, picked through the mound of coats, jackets, and hats piled by the alcove, and drifted past the suited men on their way out.

Kueur stepped out of the pantry at the back of the kitchen, opposite the walk-in freezer, and studied the departing shamans. Alioune, holding a woven basket, straightened at the dining counter and held her head high, as if she were sniffing a scent in the air. The twins watched the group like a hunting pair of lions paring down a herd to the most vulnerable prey. Separating companions and friends from casual acquaintances, men and women carrying true power from those who only wore it.

The Beast's ghost growled. Max tasted blood in his mouth and realized he had bitten his lip in a moment of excitement.

"Dex?" Alioune called out.

Kueur dumped the armload of fruits, cheese, bread, and pastries she was carrying into Alioune's basket and rushed to the New Age healer's side. "We were wondering if you could show us your crystals," Kueur said with a touch of breathlessness.

Alioune placed the basket among the branches of the ficus tree in a planter at the center of the loft, between the couch and the scenic window overlooking the Hudson. She guided the mambo toward the tree, and as soon as the woman began eating, Alioune glided back to take Dex's other arm. Together, they brought Dex to the kitchen counter, where they leaned against him, casually brushing legs and shoulders and breasts against him as he took out his jewels, held them up to the light, and droned on about their properties and use with the vigor of a faithless priest performing the ritual of transforming a wafer into the host of his savior. His interest, like his gaze, was drawn to the twins themselves.

Max found himself drawn into their game of seduction. He shuddered at the scratching of long nails at the back of Dex's neck, swayed in rhythm to the dance of slender fingers across Dex's chest, twitched in response to the tweaking and pinching of nipples. Dex fumbled a crystal, let it fall. It bounced on the floor, until Alioune stomped on it with the heel of her short, black boot. The sound of crystal breaking and crunching underfoot carried through the loft, momentarily distracting the mambo from her gorging and the suited men in the alcove from the growing latticework of instrumentation. The tail end of the departing train of shamans glanced at the twins. Unlike Max, they did not linger to watch the show.

Alioune smiled at Dex's shock. He started to hunch down to pick up the pieces, but Kueur grabbed his ponytail and pulled him back up while Alioune pressed against him and wrapped a leg around his thigh. Stones clattered onto the floor. Dex forgot to close his mouth, and Alioune kissed him, long and hard, the muscles of her neck and jaw working as she probed him with her tongue. Max's mouth watered with the taste of her, his nose filled with the sweet and musky scents of her body, his body warmed in the spots she leaned against on Dex with sympathetic heat from the undulating curves of her body.

Alioune broke the kiss, pulled back while keeping her leg around his thigh. Dex chased her, eyes half closed, sweat giving his face a sheen. Kueur palmed his chin and drew him back, took his ear into her mouth, ran her other hand down the front of his shirt. His eyes widened. Suddenly, he cried out. Blood streamed down his neck. Kueur giggled as she drew away, lips and teeth bloody. Alioune gave him a sharp knee blow to the groin, and Dex doubled over, hand over his ear.

Kueur unzipped the front of Dex's pants, reached in, and pulled out his balls. Dex moaned, started to go down on one knee, but rose back up as Kueur's grip did not follow him down. He tried to bat away her arm, but his blows fell without effect and became weaker, like a fly slowly succumbing to a spider's venom. Alioune rubbed her body against his as she went onto her knees in front of him. Licking skin left uncovered by Kueur's hand, she picked up Dex's fallen stones with one hand, shattered pieces with the other. Like a snake on a tree she crawled back up his body, shook the broken fragments of gem from her palm into Kueur's hand. Kueur kissed him on the eyes, nose, cheek. Then she slapped him, and ground her hand against his face. Dex's head rocked to the side. He swayed away from her, but she held him close by his penis. Alioune grabbed his hair and drove his face into Kueur's shard-covered hand. He sobbed as his blood mingled with Kueur's.

She took her hand away after she had rubbed Dex's head with gem fragments. Licking her hand, she swallowed blood and crystal rock. When she was done, her hand was clean and whole. Taking a deep breath, she reared her head back. Then she spat, spraying Dex's face with more blood and broken precious stone. He gasped, then sagged against Kueur.

His sex in hand, she led him toward the Box's sound-proof door between the kitchen and the bedroom. Alioune supported him as he took small, stumbling steps. She rubbed his back at first, then ripped his shirt with her nails. Dex shuddered where she raked his flesh. They led him like a crippled beast into the Box, cooing and crooning tenderly about the healing powers of their love into his good ear. Kueur paused at the doorway, started to turn her head, but stopped suddenly before Max could catch a glimpse of her face. Alioune hurried forward, pushing Dex before her. The door to the Box closed only partway, as if they had forgotten all their training in discretion and safety for the modern Western world.

The winter's weak afternoon sun was streaming into the loft. Max picked up the remote control and drew the horizontal blinds across the scenic window. The mambo lay curled around the tree's planter, eyes closed, sucking on an orange. Mr. Johnson and Mr. Tung had both withdrawn, leaving only two of their associates monitoring equipment. Max wondered if their remote-sensing devices could hear the Beast within him, feel his lust stiff and hot between his legs, see whether the life growing inside him was a boy, a girl, or a monster.

"How?" he asked no one in particular. "Why?"

No one answered. Not the twins, not the legion of men and women walking on paths of supernatural wisdom, not the far-off databases linked to the faintly humming portable computers in the alcove.

Alone.

Looking down the length of the prayer rug at the bulge, he had to laugh. No, not quite alone. He put his hand under the rug, on his belly. His skin was hot. He pressed down gently with his fingers. Inside him, something moved. Kicked.

Max drew his hand away, sucked in breath, waited. Nothing else happened. The past few days of nausea and paralysis came into focus, and he pictured himself carrying an alien other, giving it sustenance, nurturing its existence with his life. He felt as if a wandering ghost had come to live in the worn shell of his body, making painful demands, promising nothing in return. Worse than a demon, whose bold needs and overt methods offered the challenge of battle, the thing within him had insinuated itself into his life without his ever being aware of the intrusion. It enjoyed a subtle intimacy with his body without his knowledge. It used him, robbed him, with every breath he took, as it built a fresh new form for itself out of the antique remnants and battered ruins of his body.

It was as close to him as the Beast had ever been, but at the same time remote. He did not know its feelings or desires. It sapped his strength instead of providing him with power. It did not answer his questions, explain its meaning. By the speed of the entity's growth and silence, it wanted as little to do with him as possible. Max had never felt so old or useless. There was nothing to fight, nothing to do but wait for the baby to leave him.

The child moved again. This time the Beast rattled the bones of Max's body, hissing at the realization that it had to share its host with another. Fed by the Beast, Max's sense of abandonment grew into fear, then revulsion.

Fingers curled, nails scratched at skin. The Beast's rage stoked the fires of Max's resentment, built on fear, until he wanted to tear away his belly and rip out the parasitic creature that had dared nest in his body. He raised his hand. The rug fell away. He stared at his rounded belly, then looked up at his thick, blunt fingers poised to attack.

A knife. He needed a knife. He sat up, thoughts speeding beyond his control, the Beast barking and yipping, driving him every time nausea or dizziness or instinct urged him to pause, consider, stop. Pushing himself off of the couch, Max prepared to hurl himself into the kitchen.

He took a step. Another. Then his legs gave way as if bones and muscle had been sucked out and replaced with fat. He collapsed, broke the fall with his forearms, rolled, came to a halt on his back, breathing hard. The Beast gnawed at his will and snapped at his emotions, but Max lay still, momentarily exhausted, empty.

"Need help?" one of the alcove attendants asked, stepping into the loft with his assistant.

"Fuck off," Max said, letting the Beast into his voice. The two men stopped. Reached up as if to adjust missing sunglasses, straightened ties instead, withdrew.

"It hasn't got a soul, you know," the mambo said in a low, lazy voice, squeezing words past all the food she had eaten. "That's why you can't hear it inside you. That's why you can't feel the bond that links it to you. It's a dead thing, though it has a heartbeat."

"What?" Max asked, raising himself on his elbows. He crawled around the couch on his back until he could see the mambo at the foot of the tree. "Who talks?"

"An old friend."

"I have none. Only dead enemies."

"Not so old, then."

"Who?"

"Legba." The mambo opened her eyes, smiled, waved fingers at him. Drool and chewed bits of food fell from her mouth. "I caused you some inconvenience not long ago."

"Ogo," Max said, remembering the African god, the twins' father, who had recently tracked Kueur and Alioune to America and attempted to use them in fulfilling his quest for his lost twin. Legba had opened doorways for Ogo, as was his power to do.

The Beast urged him to continue to the kitchen, but Max forced himself to focus on the mambo. Instinct told him to sift through the veils of sensation, delusion, and illusion; to listen, reason, understand what was happening.

"That was business. Favor owed."

"I didn't think it was personal. I've never involved myself with you. Why do you care about what's happening to me?"

The mambo shook her head from side to side. "Not necessary to care. Not necessary for involvement. Things happen. Places come and go, like the Nowhere House." The mambo's face suddenly tightened, and her eyes blazed with penetrating focus. "Doors open and close. Like the doors in the House of Spirits, in Painfreak," she said, her voice a guttural growl warped by an odd accent.

The first reference eluded him, but the second clicked. The recent trip Max had taken to the floating, undying sex club in which he had thought the twins imprisoned flashed past him. He remembered finding his way to one of its many wings, the House of Spirits, and walking down a hall with doors, some open, revealing rooms, one with a pool of blood and a four-armed, black-skinned woman wearing a necklace of heads. She had offered him a lotus, a sword, and his reflection in her eyes. The image of her offer had opened the way to his escape from the House of Spirits, but not to his redemption. A chill raced up Max's spine. He shivered, covered his genitals with a hand.

The mambo's face relaxed into its normal visage of possession by the loa. "Sometimes a hand reaches out across doorways. Favors asked for are favors to be returned." The mambo shrugged her shoulders. Her head lolled to the side. "Followers come and go, rise, mostly fall. I'm an old man. I like my steady meal. I help the balance here for someone else, and somewhere else the balance is helped for me."

Max grunted as he made his way back to the couch. As he climbed back on, the mambo stretched, went on all fours, shook crumbs from her blouse and skirt like a dog shaking water from its hair. She stood, leaned on the cane, and looked to Max.

"So who asks you to help me?" Max asked.

"She does not want her name revealed," the mambo said, glancing at the men in the alcove. "But she feels you are not so ignorant as to forget a phone call she once made to you."

Max nodded. Returning from his misadventure in Painfreak's House of Spirits, the same voice that had ridden over the loa had left a message that melted his phone and answering machine. The words were etched in his memory by the smell and smoke from burning plastic: "Tread gently on the paths of the dead, my son. They are not as generous as the living, nor as forgiving."

"Won't I ever be rid of the dead?" Max whispered, then

laughed at his own dullness. Not as long as I kill, he answered himself silently.

"Not as long as you kill," whispered the mambo, half mocking, half growling in the other's voice.

Max stared at the mambo, her words reverberating inside him. He decided he could trust her loa more than he could most mortals and spirits he had dealt with, except the twins. He gathered the prayer rug and covered his lap, asking, "So what is the favor you need to do for me?"

"Keep watch," she answered, slowly coming around the couch. "See what comes through the doors, what leaves."

"Anything lately?"

"Oh, yes, much traffic." Her eyes darted back and forth dramatically, and then she giggled.

"What did this to me?"

"You did," she said, pointing her cane at him.

"If you're here to help me, do it. Stop playing games."

"You're the one who's played games. For so many years, you played with innocents. Rape, torture, murder, games like that."

"I stopped. I'm no longer ruled by my Beast. The innocents don't have to be afraid of me anymore."

"But should you still be afraid of the innocents you killed?"

Fear tripped Max's quick answer. He thought he had left his past behind in the House of Spirits. Had he been found again? "The scarves," he said, glancing around the loft. Fighting down panic, he expected to see the scarlet silk that had housed the ghosts of his victims and lured him into Painfreak, into their embrace. The Beast whimpered within.

At that moment, Dex screamed. His cry pierced the loft,

startling the men in the alcove. Even Max jumped, half turning and raising his arms to defend against a blow. Pain in the small of his back came as a second surprise, and he eased into a prone position on the couch. The mambo came around, eyes closed, mouth puckered as if savoring the long, drawn-out release of mortal suffering. She felt her way to the table with her cane, then knelt as if in prayer until Dex was silent.

The scream continued for Max, until he realized he was remembering the sound of his own pain when the scarves had seized him in the House of Spirits, when the ghosts of the women he had sacrificed to appease his own and the Beast's hunger had taken him. Entered him. Raped him with his own dark needs and their pain.

No one will ever love you the way I will, the scarves had said.

"The scarves . . ." said Max, giving up his search for red silk. He stared at his belly. Raped. With no seed or womb, what did the spirits of women have to plant in the flesh of living men?

The memory of women and their wombs. The sorrow of giving birth to children, loving them, leaving them behind in the midst of joy or anger, regretting things said and unsaid. And most potent of all, the terrible yearning for the children that might have been brought into the world.

The spirits of the dead had planted the shade of their life-giving power in their life-taker's flesh. The pain of missing not only their own lives, but the lives they had or might have created mingled with his twisted appetites. In the heat of his suffering, on the forge of his agony, the two needs had twined together and linked like strands of

DNA. And like DNA, the product of that joining had haunted and shaped the living matter of his body, constructing something new following the secret design of merged desires.

Max wiped the sweat suddenly beading on his brow. Fever burned like glowing coals, as if thoughts leapt and raced so quickly they were setting fire to his flesh. With sickening clarity, he saw how the past had reached out to plant the promise of the future in the living present. What grew inside him now was an idea, an emotion, a potential lost; the union between material and ghostly worlds. What would the future bring?

Was he harboring the avenger of the innocents he had killed? Was the thing waiting to be born so it could kill him, or was the creature in him working its vengeance on his body as it grew, tormenting him, slowly destroying him? The Beast roused itself from its terror and barked an alarm, pushing Max to take action.

"Took a while for the child to take root, didn't it?" the mambo asked, startling Max out of his reverie. "What else can you expect from ghost seeding human, and neither one with the right tools or plumbing? The poor thing's lucky to have taken at all." The mambo hesitated, glancing at Max's belly. "Or unlucky. The bridal bed must have been a place of power."

Dex screamed again, thin and high-pitched at first, his wail tumbling into a guttural, gasping series of cries, as if something vital were being plucked out of his body. Kueur's laughter bubbled out of the Box. *"C'est bon?"* she asked. Alioune's voice wove through theirs, binding sounds of pain and pleasure with the grumbling of raw, inarticulate hunger.

Max shook his head. "I have to kill it," he said, the urgency rising once again in him. "Get rid of this thing. Now." He started to rise, throwing off the prayer rug.

The mambo pressed her hand against his naked belly, pushing him down. The palm of her hand was like a blazing iron on his skin, and he shifted away from her on the couch.

"That's not what you have to worry about yet," she said.

"Get out of my way, loa."

"Your child is an empty vessel. It's all the spirits of the dead could make."

"You're riding the mambo too long, too hard, Legba. You're killing her. Leave her, leave me."

"Your child is no danger until it gets a soul."

"I'll kill the mambo quick if you don't get out of my way. And then I'll kill this thing inside me."

"Don't you hear me, boy? It's your baby's soul you have to worry about."

Max picked up one of the couch cushions and kept it between him and the mambo. He stood, pushed the cushion into the mambo's hand. The smell of burning leather was carried up by wisps of smoke.

"Not if the vessel is dead, loa."

The mambo struggled, pushing back against Max. The cushion crackled as her hand passed through the leather cover and into the filling. Seconds passed. He began to feel the heat from the mambo's hand as she cut through the cushion, and he braced himself for a killing stroke to her throat. The Beast urged him: Now, go, kill. Then she collapsed, groaning, taking the cushion down with her to the floor. Sweat soaked her clothes as the loa rode its mortal mount to ground. "The vessel won't kill you," she whis-

pered, hoarse, eyes fluttering, reaching for him as he
walked around her.

"No?" he said, trudging to the kitchen, words and the
loft and the cold winter world outside spinning around
him. "What will, then? The ghosts of my victims? They
had their chance in Painfreak."

"No . . ."

"You?"

The mambo gagged, tried to get up, wilted under the
effort. "The spirit . . ." she said, and was silent. Her eyes
fluttered, and for a moment the mambo's earthly person-
ality looked out through reddened eyes and a pale face
twisted by fever's pain. Then she faded like a meteor burning itself out in the night sky, and Legba abandoned his
human ride.

Max threw himself against the counter, knocking down
a stool, and rested his head against the cool marble top.
The knife. On the other side of the counter, in the kitchen
itself, the block filled with knives, and the garbage disposal
at the sink, and dish rags and running water, for the blood,
and the gash . . .

"Tonton?" Kueur stood at the doorway to the Box, naked, droplets of blood spattered across her thighs. "*Non,*
Tonton. Don't kill the little one."

Max turned, crouched, fingers curling into claws. The
sounds of pain and pleasure had stopped from the Box.
There was only Dex, whimpering, crying, saying,
"Please . . ." and "More . . ." Max bared his teeth, the Beast
a shadow eclipsing the light of his self. "Why not? It's
mine."

Kueur stared down at him. "The child also belongs to
Alioune and me. As do you."

The Beast strained against Max's tension-locked body, lost in a blood dream of tearing Kueur apart. Alioune pushed the door to the Box wide open and joined her sister, naked, hands and fingers dappled with blood. The Beast leapt at them, but Max stood his ground. The Beast whirled around in his mind like a starving wolf caught in a cage, teased by prey just beyond the bars. Max straightened, relaxed his fingers. The Beast, forgetting that its bond to Max had been severed by death, howled in rage over the betrayal of the flesh it had so often mastered. Max remembered the first time he had seen Kueur and Alioune, in Paris. The Bois. The young Brazilian. What they had done to him, what had been left. The Beast skittered to a halt, seduced as it had been that first time by the discovery of kindred spirits. Max remembered the more recent metamorphosis of his relationship with the twins, from his role of protective "Tonton" to lover, and the sacrifice of the Beast's uncontrollable appetites on the altar of his passion for Kueur and Alioune. The Beast quieted.

"Would you kill me too?" Kueur asked.

"And me?" Alioune added.

Each twin snaked an arm around the other's waist. They leaned into each other, hips pressed together, breasts like dark plums ripened to bursting with sweet juice and meat; twin sexes like crevices at the roots of mountains, veiled by brush, promising secret passage to the mysteries of life and death.

Lulled by the scents of blood and musk, the Beast settled into its place of submission in Max's mind. For punishment, Max recalled his sojourn into Painfreak and the Beast's retrieval from the House of Spirits.

At last, Max awoke as if from a dream, and the love he

had for the twins blazed again, chasing away the Beast's ghost to its place in the darkness of rage and pain. Max sagged against the counter.

"I hate this," he mumbled, rubbing his neck and head with both hands. "I'm out of control. This thing," he said with a dismissive gesture at his belly, "it's killing me."

The twins picked up paper napkins from a stand on the counter and wiped themselves, then turned back to him.

"I understand," said Kueur, coming to one side and supporting Max.

"Not necessarily," Alioune said, going to Max's other side to help him stand. "You are suffering no more than any woman does."

"How would you know?" he said, then bit his lip at the harshness of his voice and words.

"I know pain," Alioune said softly.

"Your discomfort will pass with the child," Kueur added. Together, the twins led Max back to the couch.

"How do I get rid of this thing?" asked Max.

"Why, you deliver it, of course," said Kueur. She tsked at the ruined cushion and left Max to Alioune. After moving the coffee table aside, she jogged past the alcove to a storage closet hidden in the wall. The men in the alcove stopped pretending to only occasionally glance up from their equipment and, with fingers poised over keyboards, followed her progress with lips parted, eyes narrowed. She rummaged through the linens and pillows at the front, leaving alone Max's stockpile of professional equipment stored in neatly piled containers at the back. Finally, she pulled out larger throw cushions.

"Abortion?" asked Max.

Alioune shook her head fervently. "Ill-advised," she admonished. "You are too far along."

"Are you sure?"

Alioune turned her head, and her eye was a finger's length away from his, filling his vision. Looking into its depths, Max felt a chill, which he savored. "Our shuwwa-fat taught us to know enough while we were with her in Africa. They say you are pregnant, they say you will deliver in days. The child is obviously not of mortal origin. It will have enmeshed itself in your system, merged with it like a parasitic demon."

"Careful, sister," Kueur said, looking back at them as she filled the space left by the burnt sofa cushion with smaller throw pillows. "Let's not make it any worse for him."

Alioune cleared her throat, helped Max to the sofa. "You cannot simply rip it out of you. The shock of separation would be fatal for both of you."

Max fell on to the repaired couch and lay down. As Kueur secured the prayer rug over him, he said, "Maybe that would be best for me, and for you, as well."

"No," Alioune said firmly. "The child must leave you when it is ready."

"We go where our paths lead us," Kueur said gently. She picked up the ruined cushion and strolled to the alcove. "Stray off the path, and you invite a deeper doom."

"I can't live like this," Max said, rubbing his belly, fighting back another wave of nausea rising out of his gut. "It was the scarves, the spirits of the women I killed, that did this. This is the price of appetite—mine, and the Beast's. But what will happen when I deliver this thing? And what's this business about souls and spirits? Was the loa saying the Beast might possess this thing to kill me?" A sliver of pain worked its way from temple to forehead, and he rubbed bone through skin. A thread of fear followed the pain. "Has the Beast betrayed me? Turned into an agent of the women I killed? Have they found me again through the child they planted in me? Is it the instrument of their vengeance, or just an accident? When will my past stop reaching out to me?"

"I do not know," said Alioune, sitting and letting Max's head rest in her lap.

Kueur handed the ruined cushion to one of the men in the alcove. "*S'il vous plaît?* The trash is by the elevator." The man lowered his head and withdrew. His companion kept watching Kueur as she went to the mambo, kneeled beside her, ran her fingers through the woman's black hair. "Think about it too much, Tonton, and you'll turn into one of these mad Americans, with their grassy knoll and their Roswell, seeing something sinister in the flicker of every shadow."

"But there is," Max said, turning his face into Alioune's stomach, seeking solace from his headache and confusion in her hot, silky skin, in the strength of her body, her taste of salt and spices and blood and semen.

He closed his eyes, letting Alioune's gentle massaging of his temple, upper neck, and shoulder seep into him, dispelling pain and sickness. Hearing movement, he turned to catch sight of Kueur lifting the mambo, her clothes a pile on the floor, in her arms and carrying her toward the bedrooms opposite the entrance alcove. Sunset painted their bodies crimson and lavender. Dust motes danced in their wake. He blinked.

When he opened his eyes again, Kueur was sitting on

the floor beside him, her head on his belly, eyes half closed like a cat's. Dusk had thrown its veil across the window, casting reality's firm lines into illusion's doubt. But even in the darkness, Max could see the bulge of his belly and wondered if it had grown while he was asleep; if the weight he felt pressing down on his intestines was entirely Kueur's head. The faint whine of power running through electronics announced the nearby presence of his employers' observers. They were still watching him.

Nothing had changed. He was still burdened by the life he carried.

Max stirred. Alioune rubbed her warm, dry palm across his chest while Kueur gently massaged his genitals.

"Do not worry, Tonton," said Alioune. "We will take care of you."

"Tonton, we're sorry for the way we've been acting," Kueur added, lifting her head and taking his hand in both of hers.

"You saved my life a little while ago," he said.

"Before. When Mrs. Chan said . . . when we found out you were pregnant."

Max looked from one to the other, waiting for laughter. They showed him curiosity, tinted by shame and other, less obvious emotions. "I've been difficult, myself, I suppose."

"We understand, Tonton," said Kueur, squeezing his hand. "What your body must be going through, for the baby . . ."

"The plumbing's wrong, as Legba would say."

Kueur gave him a blank look.

"You're upset," Max said gently. "The both of you. I'm your lover. A man. I was the one who was supposed to give you babies. Remember, after your father tried to rape

311

you, you were thinking about what it would be like to have children? Give them what you never had?"

"Yes," Kueur said. Alioune remained silent.

Max hesitated, uncertain about the territory he was exploring, how deeply he should probe this area of their mutual needs. For all their physical intimacy, for all the appetites they had shared and satisfied, there were worlds they had yet to map in the universe of their relationship. Max reminded himself that men and women who did not have their powers or pedigree had as much, if not more, difficulty in navigating through the fog of deceit, delusion, fear, insecurity, and all the other frailties that haunt the living.

But the living he knew were not sired by ancient spirits of power. The living had not been visited by a forgotten god seeking to reunite with a lost sister through the womb of his own children. The living he knew had very different lives.

Max took a deep breath. "You're angry because you both wanted a child, and I'm the one carrying it. You're angry because you knew the instant you heard I was pregnant that you had nothing to do with its conception. You feel betrayed. By me. By whatever passed the gift of life to me." Max felt drained, as if he had just handed over a part of his heart to strangers. "You're afraid the child will take me away from you," he heard himself say, wanting to stop, unable to silence the thoughts.

Tears welled in the twins' eyes. They looked as startled by the upwelling of emotion as by his words.

"I know," he said, hoarse, shaking his head. "I understand your fear. Because that's how I'd feel if you had children. Mine, or another's. Afraid."

"Tonton, making a life, it's such a large thing," Kueur said.

"Larger than any gods and demons and spirits we have ever met," Alioune added.

"We've been thinking of children, of what it is to be a woman, a bearer of life. That part of a woman's role in this world. Alioune and I have wondered if having children is what we must do to be women, truly women, as much as any mortal female you've been with."

"You mean, you want to be like the women I've killed, the women who've cursed me with this," he said, glancing at his belly.

"It is the act of creation we desire," Alioune said.

"But you don't need to have children to be women," Max said.

"We've heard the act is necessary," said Kueur.

"On TV," Alioune added, "though there has been debate. And terrible danger. We have studied how women and children are treated. On TV, the streets, families. Studied statistics."

"We weren't encouraged," said Kueur. "The cost is high."

"They are prey," Alioune said.

Max remembered. The Beast growled its agreement.

"If it's any consolation, I don't want it," said Max.

"No, it isn't," Kueur answered. "But we want to be a part of the act, Tonton. Part of this new life you're bringing into the world. We want to know the joy a new life brings, and the terror."

"Even if it wants to kill me?"

Kueur patted Max's chest. "We didn't let you kill the child. Do you think we'd let it kill you?"

313

"We will protect you, as you have always protected us."

A warm sensation passed over Max, touching the doubts and uncertainties he had felt about talking to the twins. Part of the tension inside him relaxed. But emotion still roiled in his heart as he discovered words had only skimmed the surface of the meaning he wished to convey, and he could think of nothing to say that would bring him closer to the twins. Nor could he summon the questions that would penetrate the mystery of their natures, pinpoint the exact hurt that needed attention, and raise answers to heal the wound they carried.

The temptation to point to the weave of threads that tied them together and label it with a word like *love*, or *passion*, or *desire*, was nearly irresistible. He craved the power of a spell, a curse, an anthem, anything that might summarize and contain the part of his feelings he wanted to communicate. But the clumsy phrases of mortal lovers not only failed to describe the content of his relationship with Alioune and Kueur, they could not even point to the path he walked in their company or to the boundaries of the world in which they traveled. Stumbling through the rituals of everyday love would cast a pall over what he valued more than his life. Belief in the stunted vocabulary of mortal love would sunder what had been created when he sacrificed the Beast for feelings he thought were love and passion but were in truth more primal and vast. Frustration provoked him, rousing the ghost of the Beast. He wanted to lash out with violence, sweep away the source of his irritation with an act of brutality. Kueur, Alioune. The baby. Himself.

Killing was easier. The equation of appetite and its satiation was much simpler to understand, and complete.

Max closed his eyes, concentrated on the twins. The warmth of their bodies. The fragrance of their sex. The musical lilt of their accents echoing in his mind.

The Beast, a cold spot that could not be warmed by the embrace of any bond, including the one to its host, subsided with a cantankerous growl.

Frustration dissipated. Rage dissolved. Relief gave Max a moment of respite from the chaos of his emotions. The brief taste of a strange new intimacy rooted beyond physical realms had left him and the twins unscathed, as far as he could tell. And thirsty to drink deeper, to reveal more of himself and try once again to sink into the depths of the mystery of others.

"Can you really protect me from the baby?" he asked, letting fear into his voice. "Nothing coming from being raped by the women I killed can be contained. It hungers. It feeds on me. The thing is wild, uncaring, demonic."

"You make the child sound like us," said Alioune. "Before we met you and started changing."

"Maybe that's what I fear most. The change. Even if we—I—survive, our lives will be different. The baby, whatever it is, what would it mean for us? What would we do with it?"

"Raise the child," Kueur answered.

"We'll have to take care of it, manage it somehow. . . ."

"Tonton, we are as lost as you are. The road you once walked has ended. Another beckons. You did not know the choices you made in the past would bring you here. You can't go back. The road forces you forward. And you are afraid. Alioune and I, we understand. We are with you on that same road. Helpless to ease the pain, relying on the help of others. It is as hard for us as it is for you."

"You're not pregnant."

"But we are with you. Losing, with every step we take, the delusion of freedom from the consequences of the past. Discovering we are not as independent as we thought we were."

"You're free to come and go. Both of you. I'm the one that's a prisoner of this thing inside me."

"*Non*, Tonton. You're wrong. In the past, we always took care of ourselves, even with the Jola mother who found and adopted us. Through Senegal, West Africa, the Sahara, to Europe, we survived and fulfilled our needs. It was when you discovered us in Paris, became our guide and showed us we could be more than wandering cubs, that we chose another path. As you did. We all tricked ourselves by coming and going as we pleased, thinking we controlled our destiny by satisfying our appetites, trading recklessly in lives and desires. But when our lives joined, we left our old paths and went off on a new road together.

"Alioune and I didn't think of what we were leaving behind when we left the Bois de Boulogne with you. We found ourselves in a world full of possibilities we had never imagined existed. The excitement, the hunger for newness swept us up. And for you, Tonton, discovering us filled the emptiness in you that the Beast, even when it lived, could not fill. None of us considered what lay ahead, what would change, what we were giving up. You continued your work of killing, and satisfying your appetites. And we moved through the world, adopting the mask of humanity, thinking ourselves invulnerable, as if more than you and our powers protected us.

"But we'd made our choice and did not see the world close in around us, the path we walked become more defined. We did not see that the price of straying from that path grew higher the longer we walked together.

"When you came to us months ago, wanting us, our lives came into focus. You had chosen us, and we you, that day you found us in the Bois. Since then, through the time we spent in Paris and then here, you had walked beside us, letting us mature, until we were ready to truly belong to you, and you to us. If we had refused you when you wanted us, we would have had to leave you forever.

"The cost of that choice was too high. We stayed, demanding our price so we could survive in your company. And you paid that price, sacrificing the Beast for us. Another road opened, and we took it together. This time, at least Alioune and I did not hide behind illusions.

"When you came back from Painfreak, and again when you saved us from our father, we realized how much in our lives was beyond our control. How much we had to lose because of what Alioune and I, and you, had chosen. Though our nature called for us to be wild and act as we wanted, we became afraid. We saw the perils of the road we had chosen.

"We've talked, Alioune and I. We've seen mortals on TV wrestle with the consequences of their decisions, and with threats and disruptions in their lives. We hoped we might be stronger, better, than what we saw. But we feel as helpless as any weeping mother, any broken child, any rageful man from the programs we watched. We feel as helpless as you, Tonton.

"With every decision, there is something lost for something gained. The road we take changes, and we can't always see what's ahead or what was left behind. This is what frightens us. And you, too. The baby is a threat, and a promise. It is the past come to haunt us, and the way through which we must go to find the future. The child hurt us all, but maybe it will heal us a little, as well. Too late now to jump from the path, Tonton. We walk the same road together."

This time, it was Max's eyes which burned with tears. "I feel old with all this talk of roads taken and given up. But maybe not so afraid."

"So do I." Kueur said.

"And I," said Alioune.

Max gasped for breath, as if he had dived into dark waters, plumbed warm depths with a grazing touch of soft sand, and surfaced stunned by daylight and desperate for air. He blinked, surprised the tears gathered in his eyes had not fallen. For a moment, he was confused. Emotions surged through him. Some he recognized as his own. Others, he was surprised, belonged to the twins. The Beast's insatiable rage rushed past, as well as the terror and despair of its victims. For that moment, he did not need bonds or words or spells to feel close to Kueur and Alioune. He was them, and others, and they were he.

The moment passed, leaving behind only the doubt that it had ever come. Max sat up, forcing the twins to shift around him.

"Are you all right?" Alioune asked.

He almost laughed. He pressed fingers to forehead, reassuring himself of his solidity. "I'm fine. I should just be more careful what I wish for."

Kueur smiled, pinched his arm with a seductive look. "Not too careful, we hope."

Max sat back, let the twins cover him once again with the prayer blanket. He looked up, drawn to the restless, red-tinged candlelight leaking from the Box into the loft's darkness. Dex stood, naked, with his back to the open door, legs spread wide, arms extended to the side and elevated over his head. In each hand he held a thick red candle. The melting wax dribbled along the candle sides, on to his fingers, down his arms, leaving red tracings on his flesh. Another candle burned on top of his head, and others on each shoulder and on his feet. Hot wax flowed over swollen joints, raw bruised skin, into open wounds. A fine tremor shook Dex's body, as if he were only a conduit for the pain and not its final reservoir. The columns of thin smoke rising from the flames curled and swayed to the frequency of Dex's trembling. Under the monotone hum of electronics in the alcove, Max could hear the New Age crystal healer whine.

The Beast showed no interest as it lay in Max, cowed and shocked by the moment's communion with the twins. Dex's superficial resemblance, in his finery of pain and red glowing candles, to the image presented by ghosts of Max's victims in the House of Spirits, could not be comforting for the Beast, either. An angel of death, Max recalled, made of red scarves. He turned away from the memory with a shudder.

"If Legba was right," Max said, "I should wish for another soul."

The twins gave him a blank look. Alioune asked, "Why?"

"The child needs one, according to the loa riding the mambo. If I had another soul, I could give it to the child, and then it wouldn't want to kill me."

Kueur put her hand on his belly. "The spirits of your

319

victims, you say they're the ones who gave you this. Perhaps they wish to possess the baby?"

"If that was their intention, then I ruined the plan when I escaped from the House of Spirits. I don't think they've found me, or they would have entered their creation by now."

"We could find the child a soul," Kueur said, looking to Alioune, and turned to Dex.

Max shook his head. "No more innocents. I have enough to pay for."

"Dex is not an innocent," Alioune said, standing, putting a hand on her hip. "He has lied. Let people die when he could not help then with his crystals, when he could have taken them to other healers. And he has used what small powers he has to spread illness, and kill, for others as well as to satiate his own petty hungers. He told us. Freely."

"Even worse. His corruption in this baby? I might as well seek out the ghosts of my past."

"We could cleanse him." said Kueur. "Prepare him for you. Bind him to all of us so the child and its soul would never harm us, could never become an agent for the dead."

Max scoffed. "He'd never survive."

Alioune shook her head. "His strength comes from the depths of his depravity. Desire is strong in his heart. He wants so much, so badly."

"Look at him, Tonton," said Kueur, standing, strutting toward the doorway, presenting Dex like a game show hostess sweeping her hand across a stage full of prizes. "Look at what we've done to him, how long he's waited, suffering. And still, he stands. For us. Is that not right, *mon petit* Dex?"

The healer whispered, "Yes."

"Louder!" Kueur commanded.

"Yes!" Dex screamed, sending ripples of agony through flame and smoke.

Kueur raised an eyebrow and placed a fingertip at the corner of her mouth. She glanced at the alcove, winked, cocked her head toward the Box, smiled at the reaction she received from the suited men.

Max did not bother to look over at the men. He studied Dex, trying to understand the hunger the twins had uncovered in him, wondering if he wanted the soul of such a man in his child.

His child. He smiled at the slip, at the thought of passing something of himself on beyond his death. His amusement quickly vanished under reality's harsh glare.

"You see?" Alioune said, joining her sister.

"Let us do this for you, Tonton."

"I don't think I want to rely on his soul to protect me."

"It will not be his soul when we are done with the harrowing," Alioune said. "It will be a small spirit, with sins and corruption burned away. The hunger will be left, yes, but do we not all have appetites? The child could hardly be a part of our family without appetites. The spirit will be strong, and that is what is important. Strong, and imprinted on the three of us. We will work hard, make certain the soul is worthy of you, and your child."

Max considered, reluctant to hope. "What if the child is a girl, or some kind of monster?"

"The soul, Tonton, will be pure, and take without protest whatever shell it receives."

Nausea twisted Max's stomach. "How long? Is there enough time?"

Alioune went to the Box, leaned against the door and

looked in. "We have enough time, if we work straight through to the time of your delivery." She looked to her sister. "If we work true, cut with precision, and release the soul at the proper moment."

Kueur went to her side. "No sleep for us, my sweet sister. We'll feed on his delicious pain and pleasure, rest in the darkness of his veiled desires. And we'll see who dies first, us, or him." She laughed, then sobered. "We'll have to watch for interference. The dead."

Max curled up on the sofa, huddled under the prayer blanket. Hope was too demanding, with its possibilities of elation and despair. He stared at the twins, remembered the time he had spent with them in the Box. "Is he as good as me?"

"Who could be, Tonton?" Kueur replied. "But he is good enough, for now, until you can join us again."

"Still, he has desire," Max acknowledged, feeling the twins' distance from him.

"Stunted and twisted, but yes, Tonton, he has that. He hungers. And we will satisfy him. For us. For you. For the little one." Kueur turned to Alioune and said, "Shall we?"

The twins went into the Box, leaving the door wide open, sharing the intimacy of hunger's satisfaction that had turned into the joy of their work for his child. He watched the twins bracket Dex, undo his ponytail, run their hands over pain-mottled skin. The physical aches and discomforts of Max's body faded as he lost himself in Kueur and Alioune's attention to drawing Dex's secret heart out and purifying his soul. In the background, the men in the alcove remained quiet and still while tiny motors whined, extensions unfolded, mounts turned, lenses refocused.

Kueur laughed sweetly, removing the candles, dripping

hot wax pooled under flame onto Dex and setting them on top of a rolling metal cart. Alioune reached down to a lower cart shelf and removed a harness with a double dildo secured at the groin, the smaller, crystal-encrusted phallus pointing outward.

"Remain as you are, my sweet, and tell us what you want," Kueur said when she was done. Alioune reverently inserted the large, knobbed and twisted dildo into Kueur's vagina. The hint of a smile passed between them; its subtle light might have cast the shadow of amusement on the figure in the Louvre's most famous painting. They both shuddered slightly as Alioune completed the insertion, the leather and metal harness rasping on satin skin. While her sister carefully adjusted straps and closed locks, Kueur continued speaking, her words a soft, seductive song. "Beg us for what you want. Don't make us angry, or we'll set you free. Do you want to be free, do you want to leave? Or do you want what we have to give you? Do you want to surrender what you have for us? Tell us," she said, raking her nails along the wax burn marks across Dex's shoulder.

"Tell us," echoed Alioune. She shifted on her knees from Kueur to Dex, teased his red, erect penis with her tongue.

Dex moaned, shuffled closer to her, began to lower his arms.

Alioune reared, bared her teeth. "Stop!" she commanded.

"Don't move!" Kueur growled. "You were told to stay still. How dare you disobey!"

Dex stiffened while his erection drooped. The twins stepped away and behind him. Stood silent, legs apart, Alioune with her arms crossed over her breasts, Kueur with her hands behind her back. Dex cried out, called to them, pleaded for them to return, to let him please them, all while remaining in his original position, arms out and feet spread wide. "That is all I want to do," he said, hoarse from his ceaseless, desperate cry for their return. "To please you. Tell me, what do you want me to do, what do you want me to say, so I can feel your touch—no, just be in your presence—wait, so I can just serve you, to know I'm a part of your world, no matter how small, because I can't go back, do you understand? After what you've done to me, shown me, I can't go back to what I was. I can't . . . please, don't leave me here . . . alone . . ." His words lost themselves in wet, inarticulate blubbering.

"Do you want to leave or do you want what we have to give?" Alioune asked.

"Take what we have to give," said Kueur, "let go of what we want. Or we will throw you in the gutter, and you will live the rest of your life in the depths of your worthlessness, this golden moment of life gnawing at every scrap of meaning you try to hold on to until they are all lost in the emptiness that will be your life without us."

"Let me stay . . ."

"Tell us what you want . . ."

". . . beg for what you need . . ."

". . . please . . ."

"Is it this?" asked Alioune, draping herself over Dex's shoulders, hooking a leg around his thigh, grinding her body against his.

Kueur stepped up behind Dex, positioned the dildo, rammed it into him. "Or this?" she said into his ruined ear, slowly pumping and rotating her hips. She snaked her arms under his, interlocked her fingers behind his neck. His arms were forced out of their outstretched positions, hitched up, hands held high. Bone cracked.

He tried to keep his feet positioned wide, but slipped as Alioune slid her leg down, drove the heel of her foot into the back of Dex's knee, put her foot down, reached around him and held on to Kueur's hips. Dex lost his balance, scrambled, legs flailing.

"Yes?" asked Alioune. "This?" The power and rhythm of the twins' gyrations managed to lift Dex off of his feet.

Kueur, her back arched, her head in profile, eyes half closed and lips parted in a feral smile, said, "And this?"

The twins moved, danced a slow, rocking dance, sinking in tandem into a crouch and then rising smoothly, the muscles of their thighs and calves and backs flexing under glistening skin. Their feet stomped the floor as they circled, carrying Dex between them skewered on a phallus of flesh and blood and plastic. Blood dripped from his anus, blood smeared across the twins' bodies. Kueur hummed a hypnotically repetitive tune while Alioune chanted, low and guttural.

They drove Dex back and forth between them, his flesh slapping against theirs, their sex joined on an axis of pain and pleasure. The magic circuit of hunger and satiation sparked as the twins' power, born from African and Asian spirit gods, flowed through Dex's conductive flesh, through his desire. Their eyes glowed, their faces were flushed.

Max gripped the couch, jealous. The ghost of the Beast was silent, hiding in some dark corner, cowed by unwanted intimacy.

Dex's cries rose above the twins' song. His writhing

struggle fueled the dance, sending Kueur into a biting frenzy, provoking Alioune into a sinewy counterpoint to her sister's brutal pumping.

"Tell us, please, why won't you," said Kueur, spitting Dex's blood as she looked up from the raw wound on his neck. "What do you want?"

"There," Alioune said, then fixed her gaze on Dex's, made him stare into her eyes while bringing up a hand to hold his head in position by the jaw. She moaned when he did, opened her eyes to reflect his startled expression as a new corner of pain opened for him, a different source of pleasure erupted within him. Her mouth shaped the same O as his lips, and the play of fine muscles beneath her face captured the twitches and scowls and grimaces running across his face.

Kueur joined in the mocking, gasping, "Yes, yes," to her stroke, and then to Alioune's. Sensations rebounded through him, to them, back and forth. At last they gasped and, instead of falling into a deadly embrace, trapped him in the cascade of pleasure and pain that only Max and the Beast could survive, they stepped back. Released Dex. Drew him out, and drew out of him.

He fell to the floor, lay on his back, still crying out, body convulsing spasmodically. The twins circled him like proud, long-legged cheetahs inspecting their kill.

"Not yet . . ."

"Too soon . . ."

"You haven't told us . . ."

"You must tell us . . ."

And words spewed out of Dex like a hot jet of lava, fiery and desperate and bearing the chewed-up and molten pieces of himself carried from the depths of memory and desire and conditioning and genetic design. A primal howl, like a poet's consumed by rage, filled the loft, and in that howl parts of a life boiled away, vanishing in air.

It took several minutes for Max to catch the rhythm of Dex's rapid speech and parse the sense in his ragged voice.

"—I let her die I did I could have told her she needed a real doctor damn bitch but she was so fucking rich she just sat there and ate it up her and her stupid daughter the pair of them not a brain between them so fucking stupid afraid of doctors hell I told them I did that doctors were only here to help even if they did more damage than good with their knives and tubes and medications and there I was talking in a roomful of crystals and the sun was shining in through the glass walls and the colors were everywhere and the air was warm and scented from these little burners I have spread all over the place and I was talking and letting her feel the cool glass and stone against her dried-up old skin and telling her daughter on the side that she could get some if she wanted to 'cause my dick was blessed with healing powers and could make her feel alive and like a woman instead of the slut bitch she felt like after years of living in that crazy old woman's house waiting for her inheritance while her uncles banged her and I told the old bitch she didn't have to trust the doctors all she had to do was trust me and have faith because the crystals would absorb and refract and boost her belief and heal her and she signed the papers because she believed and when she died I put crystals in her caskets to heal her on the other side and spent the rest of the money on a nice ranch in Arizona and her dumbshit daughter is still wondering how she wound up living with her youngest uncle entertaining his brothers when they come for a visit—"

"You do not believe anything you preach," said Alioune, probing his genitals with her toes.

"—believe yes I do I do the power its in stones I feel it—"

"Then you do not believe in yourself."

Dex paused, mouth moving but not speaking.

"Do you?" She pressed her heel into his groin.

"No no no no no no—"

"That's a good beginning," said Kueur, crouching over his chest. She traced the path of tears and cuts on his body with the tip of the crystal-encrusted phallus, then brought it to his mouth, pushed it into him. He opened himself, tongue flicking over edges and points. She pushed herself in, thrust slowly but steadily into his throat until he gagged, spat up blood, and swallowed crystal shards and dust. Back and forth Kueur went, then withdrew when Dex's heaving body and reddened face showed he was on the verge of passing out from lack of air. She undid the harness, Alioune helping, and removed the apparatus, placing it on the cart. Once again she crouched over him, her damp pubic hair brushing against his skin. Dex filled his lungs to bursting, pushing his chest closer to her, straining for breath and touch.

Max felt a warm, slick spot of memory open on his own chest.

"But only a beginning. We have much to peel away, so much to uncover." She sat on him, leaned forward, breasts brushing against his face. She licked the lacerations on his face, kissed his torn nose, his ragged lips.

"—please take me let me give take it take it all—"

"Because you want to?"

"—yes yes yes yes—"

"Because you believe?"

"—yesyesyesyesyesyes—"

"Yes." She closed her mouth over one of his eyes, and when her kiss was done and she drew back to smile at Max, Dex's eye was gone. She reached over to the cart, took Dex's bag of crystals from the bottom shelf, drew out a smooth ruby-colored stone and placed it in the dark red socket. She kissed the other eye and replaced it with another stone, purple and faceted. And then she sat up on his chest, slid up to his chin, covered his mouth with her sex, and let him whisper the sins and horrors and petty wrongs of his life into her, from his lips to hers. She closed her thighs around his head, embracing him, welcoming the seed of his corruption into her womb. She closed her eyes, as well, and let her head fall back, mouth open, ready to receive wisdom from the heavens.

Or perhaps, Max thought, to allow the eyes she had consumed one final sight of heaven before they sank into eternal darkness.

Alioune straddled Dex's stomach, her back to Kueur. She spread his legs wide with a rough push, lowered her head, took his erect penis into her mouth, bobbed up and down, taking more of him into her, dipping closer to the crux of his legs, until she was taking all of him, from his balls to the head of his dick, into her again and again, faster, faster, until suddenly she stopped and reached back for the bag of crystals Kueur held out for her. Alioune reached in, took out two clear stones, dropped them into the raw pit from which Dex's sex had grown, and then again she reached into the bag, and this time took out a hexagonal rod and thrust it between the stones.

And Dex arched his back and pushed his hips high into

the air, his butt cheeks quivering from the strain of reaching for something forever beyond his grasp.

Max wondered if what was left of Dex after the twins had taken what they needed for the baby would fall forever in darkness, or if Dex's New Age powers and spirits would greet his tattered remnants on the other side and raise a shadow of their follower. If there were crystal deities waiting to present Dex with salvation, they would find little of use in Dex's spiritual remains. The twins had picked their victim well, culling the most fragile of the healers from the herd that had come to help Max. With the core innocence of his soul stripped away, the crystal powers would find only the flaw of uncontrolled appetite surrounded by the self-absorption and delusion grown over a lifetime pursuing power and satiation. Max wished he could see through crystal eyes and watch over the soul the twins were paring down to make sure they did not offer too much to Dex's spirit powers, or too little. He wished for something, anything, to do that would fight the feeling of helplessness and contribute to the work of making certain what remained on the mortal plane would serve him and the child.

The baby moved inside him. Max rubbed his hands over his belly, certain he could hear the alien heartbeat. His belly had grown, like a pustule stretching skin to contain fluid. He closed his eyes. Sounds coming from the Box faded. Exhaustion sapped his will to act, watch, even imagine. Darkness closed over his mind. He sank quietly into sleep.

In the dreams, a clawed hand ripped his abdomen from the inside out. In his dreams, worms crawled through his veins and intestines. In his dreams, small, sharp teeth gnawed incessantly at his nipples.

The fall of a body woke Max.

The solid thump of a fleshy mass on wood floor penetrated his sleep and dreams, galvanizing nerves and muscles. He opened his eyes slowly, let them adjust to the faint light in the loft and his field of vision. He listened for footsteps, breathing, the rustle of fabric.

The twins, with no audience but the men and equipment in the alcove, had closed the door to the Box, sealing in the sounds of Dex's torture. Cutting them off from Max. The mambo behind the closed door to the bedrooms was useless.

Max waited. Missed the sound of surveillance electronics from the alcove. Mapped the possible avenues of assault, focusing on an attacker coming at him from over the couch.

Slowly, he slid down from the couch, turning his head to sweep the loft. Blind spots behind the couch and counter captured his attention. He took a cup from the coffee table as a weapon.

His attacker still did not come. Max crept along the floor on his side, feeling awkward and unbalanced by the shape and weight of his belly. The child moved again, and he imagined tiny hands scraping the inner wall of skin holding in his guts, playing with the coils of his intestines, pinching organs, bones, muscle.

The floor behind the couch looked clear as he came around, approaching the alcove. He stopped when he saw the two suited men slumped against their equipment racks. Dead or immobilized, they were useless. With the surveillance equipment partly or completely disabled, Max assumed a remote monitoring station would sound the alarm and estimated help would arrive in minutes. The assassin needed to act soon. Now.

A soft scrape of cloth on tile by the dining counter focused Max's attention on the kitchen. A small, dark lump twitched by the edge of the counter. Stupid, Max thought. Shadows exploded. Max turned. A slab of night bolted out of the darkness gathered on the other side of the alcove, from a trick of angle and shadow and the glow of city light coming in through the window. Stupid, Max thought, seeing what had happened in a vision as he tried to roll but was stopped by his stomach. Something he might have done: a tiny electronic motor controlled by remote in a beanbag, tossed on the other side of the room, its landing masked by the body falling. At the right moment, with the push of a button, the sound of miniature mechanical legs or wheels churning through filler to crawl on the floor was enough to be distracting.

Now.

The slab of night loomed over him. Max had time to brace himself, check for the glint of metal from a knife or gun, and then a weight crushed him.

Fingers closed around his left wrist, pushed that arm back to the floor. A point of darkness bore down on him. He rolled, protecting his face with his hand, swinging his elbow around. A black blade edge cut his left shoulder as he deflected the angle of attack from his throat with his elbow. Close work. Silent work. Coming back with his right hand, he caught the knife wrist. Their legs scrambled, hooking and kicking. The assassin slid along the side of Max's distended belly, and Max managed to bring his hips

332

up, snake his legs around his attacker's hips, and hang on.

Strength on strength, desperation against cold rage, they struggled. Max held on to the knife hand, pulling himself up while exchanging grips and taking hold of his opponent's right hand. The assassin staggered back, twisting and bucking between Max's scissoring legs. Unbalanced by the shifting weight, the assassin fell back on to the couch. Max held on, tried to squeeze, but managed only to pull himself up as his attacker broke out of his grip. They struggled, wordless, panting. Cushions flew off into the dark. They sank into the sofa's guts, locked in a killing embrace. Forehead to forehead, heads slipping on each other's sweat-slick skin, faces too close to view, they tried to steal each other's breath, tried to give each other a kiss of death.

Max expected the Beast to rise. Moments passed, and it remained slumbering. He called for it to fill him with a rage deeper than the one that drove the assassin. But the Beast did not answer. He felt as he had after he had killed the Beast for the love of the twins: empty. He felt as he had at the airport: confused, weak, the Beast a silent ghost.

The Beast wanted the child dead. Needed it dead. To keep Max for itself.

The assassin surged on top, legs spread wide, pinning Max under him.

The Beast wanted the assassin to kill the child. It was willing to risk Max, risk its own tenuous hold on existence, just so it would not have to share Max's attention.

The attacker reared. His face loomed over Max, features blurred by night and sweat in Max's eyes. But the features, the angle of cheeks and jawline, were familiar.

333

The Beast, jealous, had betrayed him. Withheld its power.

The assassin's knife bore down on Max. Muscles strained, thoughts flailed wildly, searching for reason, finding only betrayal.

The twins were gone, involved in their pleasures. The Beast sulked. There was only the assassin's face above him, eyes like black pools of water sucking him in. Someone he knew. Lips parted. Smiled. In the moment of Max's recognition, his strength faltered and the knife point came to within a finger's width of his left eye. But the killer's identity made no sense to Max. Why would Mr. Johnson kill his own men to come after him? Why would Mr. Johnson try to do the job himself? What had happened to Mr. Johnson's eyes?

"Mérde!" Alioune shouted.

"Tonton!" Kueur cried out.

At the sound of their voices, the Beast revived. Not jealous, not betraying its host, the Beast had merely been lying in the depths of Max's soul, stunned by unwanted intimacy with others. Roused by echoes of pleasure and pain and passion raised by the sound of the twins, it roared in defiance. Strength flowed through Max. The knife point was forced back.

Kueur landed on Mr. Johnson's back. One hand pulled Mr. Johnson's head back by the hair, the other reached under his chin. Alioune struck a blow to Mr. Johnson's ribs. Kueur pulled, twisted. Alioune gripped Mr. Johnson's head, added her strength. Bone cracked. Mr. Johnson sagged. Alioune reached over and intercepted the knife as it fell from his hand.

Ideas and fantasies and emotions flew like a startled

flock of birds through Max's mind. Nausea erupted, hot and bitter and withering, through his body. The Beast howled, wanting blood, searching for blood, feeling somehow cheated.

Max opened his mouth to vomit, thank the twins, give voice to the flock of questions and emotions and thoughts fluttering in his head. Before he knew which was first to pass his lips, his vision tunneled to a bright pinprick of light surrounded by darkness. He saw wings spread wide, white instead of the red he had seen in Painfreak, at the end of tunnel. And then he saw nothing more for a while.

Rumbling voices drew him out of the darkness. He opened his eyes, tried to focus, managed only to catch his surroundings in fragmented glimpses. He was on a bed. A large bed. The double-king in the loft's bedroom. On the quilt, naked, belly larger than he remembered. A double arm's-length away lay the mambo. Facing away from him. Covered by a blanket. Beyond, people bustled. Voices rose and fell. Kueur and Alioune shouted and cursed. Hissed, spat. Lights burned like tiny suns. Floated toward him. Aluminum, extending booms stretched over the bed, bearing the lights. Instrument pods. Lenses and probes.

A brown arm flashed over him. Metal jangled against metal. Plastic tubing rattled. A lens shattered. Max cringed, closed his eyes, waited for the shower of glass. When he opened his eyes, the metal arms arcing over him were gone, the bright lights out. Kueur and Alioune were screaming their outrage, and men's voices rose in angry reply. Max grabbed at the quilt. Tried to sit up. Failed. Looked to the edge of the bed, where Alioune swept away a lunging hand, struck back with a knife hand. Someone gagged, coughed, choked. Max looked back the other way.

Into the mambo's open, bloodshot eyes.

Her pale face.

"Do not fear this one," the loa whispered. Sweat beaded on her forehead, and her hand trembled. "I will guard her. But watch the weak ones, the hollow ones the spirit can possess."

"What . . . spirit?" Max asked.

The mambo passed out.

"Legba . . ." Max called, and joined her in oblivion.

Max heard himself shouting, "Rip it out, help me, take it out, I'm going, mad, please, I can't think, why, the feelings, too much inside, the Beast, where, please, stop this . . ."

The litany of pleading droned on. As if from a distance, he wondered if he had passed out while the twins were making love with and to him, and had merely continued crying out automatically, prodded by their tender attention.

But his words jumbled, his voice faded. And then he heard nothing more.

Until Mrs. Chan spoke to him out of the darkness: "I said meditation, not exercise."

"Is he hurt badly?" Alioune asked.

"He will be fine."

Kueur asked, "And the baby?"

"As far as I and the others can tell, the child was not injured. But there might be complications in the delivery."

"Kueur," Max croaked. "Alioune."

No one heard.

*   *   *

Voices argued from a world away. Two women, a man.

"I thought we settled this."

"Destroying equipment and hurting my men settled nothing."

"You are to leave. Right now."

"Threatening me won't help, either. Mr. Johnson and I represent a much larger body of interested parties."

"Mr. Johnson no longer represents anyone."

"But I do. There are questions to be answered. The monitoring equipment . . . failed at the critical—"

"Your Mr. Johnson sabotaged the equipment. We know what happened."

"So you say. But there are matters of proof. Documentation. Accountability."

"We were protecting our Tonton."

"You've been doing rather a poor job of it. This pregnancy, and then his near death. There are associates of mine who wonder about your role in these affairs."

"There's no time for this. We're busy working on something that will help him."

"We are not interested in your experiments in bizarre sex games. We require answers. And until we get them, he must be secured."

"He will be secure when he is left alone, under our care."

"That is not acceptable."

"Do you wish to fight over him now, in his condition?"

"If that's what you twins want."

"We will kill you."

"Death is the risk we take, the price we pay for what we want. Are you willing to take that risk, now, with him so vulnerable?"

337

In the silence that followed, Max believed with dream-like logic that he had lapsed into unconsciousness. He was startled when one of the twins spoke up.

"You will stay."

"My men—"

"You. Only you. Your men will set up surveillance equipment above the door and provide the Box with monitoring equipment so we can keep our own watch. The door to the loft will be locked. No one else will be allowed to remain inside. Your men can listen and watch and study their instruments from whatever remote location they wish. You will sit there, by the door. You may use the bathroom, kitchen, whatever you want from the rest of the loft. Take one step toward our Tonton, and you will die."

"I am glad you trust me."

"We do not. We trust our power over you."

"You have no . . ." A moment after he stopped, the man let out a startled cry.

"Do you like our touch?"

"The sharpness of pain?"

"The sweetness of pleasure?"

"Yes?"

"Yes?"

"Say yes."

Voices moaned, whispered, sang, shrieked. Max swam through the sounds buoyed by the possibility that he might be making them, driven to discover what would happen when his mind connected once again with his body. The sounds drifted away, returned, faded. No longer bound by time, he followed the current made by two women and one man, until he ran aground on a word.

"Yes."

A word spoken by a man.

"Step beyond the chair at the door, and you will die. Yes?"

The man grunted.

"Tell us, you will die if you try to harm him."

The man groaned. Wheezed. Whimpered.

"Tell us, Mr. Tung."

"Yes."

"What?"

Words barely made themselves understood between the man's weeping and his weak voice.

"I will die if I step beyond the door."

"If you try to harm, or cause harm to be done."

"If I try to harm or cause harm to be done . . ."

"Very good. You see, our trust was well-founded."

"Thank you, Mr. Tung."

Max followed the wail of despair as it wound into a nothingness.

When he woke, Max's first sight was of Mr. Tung sitting in a chair by the door to the loft bedroom. Face scratched, hair disheveled, Mr. Tung remained still while a trickle of blood ran from his hairline to cheek to jaw and dripped onto his ripped and rumpled tailored blue silk suit. Blood spatter, indentations, and streaks peppered the wall and door behind him. A cluster of lenses, microphones, and instruments hung above the doorway like a hunting technophobe's trophy head. An ozone tang sharpened the thicker odors of sweat and blood and semen.

Mr. Tung held up his hands, palm facing Max. "Do not be alarmed, sir. I am unarmed. Your lovers were quite thorough in searching me."

Max looked to the mambo curled up on the other side of the bed, her back to him. "I'm sure they found nothing useful." He scanned the windowless, fortified bedroom that was the loft's most secure area, checking the ventilation screens for tampering. Shadows wavered across eggshell-colored walls, cast by light from thick candles laced with medicinal herbs and potions placed on the two night tables, the Chinese lacquered chest at the foot of the bed, the low dresser and some folding tables distributed across the oak floor.

Mr. Tung's lips twitched. "There are more important matters to discuss."

"Mr. Johnson?"

"He is no longer with us. My associates have disposed of his body. They have not, however, been so successful eliminating the questions surrounding his death."

Max tried to sit up, but the weight of the child kept him pinned to the bed. It sat on his guts, pressed against his spine, pushed his stomach up into his chest. When the child kicked, Max gasped as if a heavyweight champion had surprised him with a dig to the belly. A vague feeling of unease still haunted him, spiking in sudden moments of dizziness and nausea. But the physical torments that had been ravaging him seemed muted, banished to the periphery of his awareness. In its place, a sense of well-being radiated from his center. From his belly. The feeling permeated his body, relaxed his muscles and nerves, suffused his bones and organs with warmth. He felt stronger than he had since the disaster at the airport. Only the shadow of the thing inside him, and the inescapable consequence of its intrusion, sent occasional shudders through his body.

He carefully slid his body up against the massive, curving headboard, propping a few pillows against his back. "We had to kill him."

"Why?"

"Because he was trying to kill me, Mr. Tung. Didn't you record what happened to the guards?"

"As a matter of fact, no, there is no documentation of what occurred."

"You had everything but a spy satellite in here, and you didn't catch sight of anything?"

"There were some . . . odd readings prior to the blackout. Shadows appeared on the Bohm material frames. Anomalous paradoxes coalesced in the Schrödinger Box. Paradigm shifts were implied in changes of properties of orientation in the Penrose scales. Odd nuances flashed in Poincaré field, but did not hold long enough for a strong image to develop."

"A demon? A ghost?"

"The technology is new. Our database is still being developed. None of the readings correlate to anything observed during séances, exorcisms, invocations."

"How about ordinary video and audio? Mr. Johnson is a material mass, not some insubstantial entity."

"Nothing before the blackout. Besides, the instruments were focused on the loft. It is possible you or one of your lovers managed to slip out, attack the guards from behind. Mr. Johnson might have discovered your ruse, tried to stop you."

"What ruse? Why would we want to kill him or the guards? Besides, I'm incapacitated, and the twins are obviously preoccupied. How were any of us supposed to escape your scrutiny?"

"Tricks and illusions. They are a part of your craft. You are well known for them."

Max shook his head, exasperated. "What would be the point?"

"Perhaps you do not wish us to understand what has happened to you. Or your . . . condition may might be part of a plan to deceive us. Distract us from your true intention."

"Which would be?"

Mr. Tung leaned forward. Worry lines creased his face. Eyes narrowed, lips pressed together, he seemed to strain against invisible bonds. "Are you joining sides?"

"What?"

Mr. Tung glanced up at the cluster of instruments above his head. With a sharp edge in his voice, he continued. "Mr. Johnson's death has had serious repercussions. Alliances are forming where none existed. Territories are being violated where peaceful coexistence was the rule. Some believe you have been bought, or blackmailed, by members of the group I represent. You must see that your recent involvement with the twins might lead some to think you have become vulnerable, or perhaps wish to change your status. Others suspect you are escalating traditional rivalries for your own gain, or for some other party trying to establish their own niche in the ecology of power."

Max's head spun from the play of intrigue and conspiracy implied by Mr. Tung's speculations. All he could think of was the child, its life entwined with his, growing, becoming a larger part of him. Becoming something that might be his death. Or, if he dared believe the burgeoning sense of belonging to something vaster than himself, his new life.

Mr. Tung watched him, eyes flicking up and down the length of Max's body. His expression softened, and he wrung his hands as if his life depended on Max's next words. "Did you kill Mr. Johnson, Max? Are you working for one of the factions I represent? Are you going to declare yourself as our agent? You need to tell me now. Forces are being set in motion. Vows are being made. Your position must be clear." When Max did not answer, Mr. Tung pressed on, his face darkening. "Or is there something else going on? Are you coming after me next? Don't think you can survive alone, or depend on whatever new allies have pledged their protection. Even you can be killed."

"I have no friends, Mr. Tung," Max said, suddenly weary. "I have no interest in your politics. I'm merely one of the many tools your kind use, like your Poincaré field and computers, your banks and corporations and other temples of the faith. I'm content with my role, Mr. Tung. I have no ambitions. All I ask is for honest work killing your kind, and to be left alone to handle my affairs." He waved a hand over his belly. "Like this."

"I wish I could believe you."

"What if Mr. Johnson sabotaged your equipment, killed the guards. What if he was the traitor, and my death was part of the plan to unravel the order of things. For whoever. For whatever master plan."

Mr. Tung sat back, crossed his arms over his chest. "I need evidence."

Anger roused Max for a moment. "Where's your evidence against me?"

"You're the one left alive. If Mr. Johnson had lived, he would have been the one to answer the questions."

Max slipped back into warm, rolling sea growing inside him, overwhelmed by the endless permutations of meaning, the folding and crumpling of reality to fit whatever need and agenda ruled the moment and its dark, nameless masters. It was easier to listen to the pulse of blood beating in his ears, feel the rush of blood coursing through him, bringing sustenance to the life within him. It was better to float in the briny ocean, beneath a sky filled with light and stars, waves carrying him gently to a distant shore, currents drawing, guiding him to an unknown but inevitable destination. He did not care.

Somewhere, a storm raged, thunder roared like a wild animal, and lightning lashed the world. Winds howled with outrage. Water heaved like a beast trying to break out of a smothering net, trying to lift the weight of lies and guilt from its hungering ghost of a soul. But the storm was far away, its voice a distant echo. The sea was all around him, lulling him in its rocking embrace, seducing him with its wet caresses. Water whispered promises of life as it lapped at the boundaries of his self. He wondered how the strange and fickle sea would keep its promises to both him and the thing growing in him.

Max struggled to keep his eyes open. "If you won't accept my answers, I've nothing else to offer you."

"Then I will stay at my post and keep watch over you until I find the truth."

"I didn't invite you to stay here," Max said, finally succumbing to drowsiness and shutting his eyes.

"Mr. Johnson explained our concerns."

"Yes. And I told him they're not mine." Max's words slurred together.

"You are not in a position to refuse our help."

"A lot of good your help's done me, so far," said Max. He didn't hear himself speak, and heard nothing more.

Max floated, bobbing up and down, buoyed by the sea itself. Stars shined above, hard and piercing in their brilliance. The sky and water were both dark. Occasionally, an enormous swell boosted him high into the air. For a few brief moments, he saw mats of phosphorescent vegetation floating in the distance. Something probed the blanket of light and matter, pushed it up like a child trying to escape from under its parents' comforter. Or like a shark nosing a net blocking its escape from a closed channel into open sea.

Down Max went with the passing of the swell, coasting into a trough, hurrying into deeper night, haunted by the creature trapped beneath the sea.

Moaning drifted like clouds over the dark sea of his mind. He thought the sound was his. A restless moment in the waking world found him staring at the mambo as she writhed and flailed and moaned on the bed next to him.

Again, he rose out of the sea for a moment, into her eyes as she stared at him, her face shining with sweat.

"The loa . . . still holds my reins . . ."

Max tried to answer, found himself slipping away.

". . . you must be important . . ."

He closed his eyes, heard her weeping.

"I'm dying . . ."

He wanted to call her name, but did not know it. No, he wanted to say, don't sacrifice yourself. No more innocents on my soul. Please.

But the sea took him down to itself again, and thoughts

fell away, and he forgot the touch of guilt and pain over the mambo's dying.

". . . outrageous conduct, totally irresponsible . . . endangering lives . . . report . . ."

". . . our responsibility, our Tonton . . ."

". . . paid to take care of him, and paid well . . ."

". . . and I have my ethics . . ."

Max thought he heard a gull cry. Or perhaps it was a scream.

". . . have your life, for now, Dr. Plummer. Just tell us . . ."

". . . hormonal imbalance, losing muscle mass but his breasts are enlarged, and he's burning up . . . impossible to say . . . survive . . . cancer . . . parasite . . . bizarre accelerated pregnancy you claim . . ."

". . . tell us what we can do . . ."

". . . intravenous feeding, and antibiotics, and I'll need some monitoring equipment—"

"—can be of assistance in that area, Dr. Plummer . . . associates can . . . wired directly to our equipment—"

"No," Max grumbled. "Mind your business."

"Just help our Tonton survive his ordeal, Dr. Plummer. Bring him to term. And don't concern yourself with diagnosis or prognosis."

"Who is in charge of his treatment, then?"

"We are. You are outside the bounds of your training and expertise."

"Aren't we all."

"Now about the mambo . . ."

*　　*　　*

The insistent tapping on his hip broke into the rhythm of Max's floating journey to his distant shore. A line of darkness, deeper than the rest of the surrounding night, lay ahead on what he thought was the horizon. Something tapped again, and he reached down, suddenly afraid of what might be nudging him under water. Remembering the thunder, the struggle of something under a blanket, he felt only the ocean's warmth.

Then he felt an arm, and a voice brought him out of the dream of belonging.

"You want to die?" the mambo asked, voice warped by exhaustion and the loa riding her. Max brushed her hand away from his hip. Their plastic IV tubes slapped against each other. Antiseptics scented the air. Bedpans bumped together at the foot of the bed as Max stretched and moved his legs. Medical status monitors displayed pulse and other physical readings, emitting dim beeping sounds that were shadows of heartbeats. Mr. Tung sat by the door, his jacket hanging on the back of the chair, shirtsleeves rolled up, head and shoulders slumped forward. But his eyes were half open, and he watched the bed with the languorous attention of a snake mesmerized by its charmer.

"What?" Max said, fighting the pull back to sleep and dreams, trying to orient himself to a world of words and dry, unmoving land.

"It all right," Legba said, rolling the mambo on her side to face Max. "Many mothers have sacrificed themselves for their child."

"What are you talking about?" Max flailed his arm and legs, feeling as if his body had been stolen, replaced by a bloated, bulbous bag of fluid.

347

"The big empty needs filling," the mambo said, pointing to Max's belly. "The child's a pit, drawing what it needs to itself. Your soul."

"No."

"Or your secret companion."

"No."

"Ah, then you'd best rise above the tide that's taking you out to the wild, wide sea."

"I thought you said the child was not a danger to me."

"You feel the pull, but you are still not fighting it. You want to to be dragged under. Maybe things be easier if you did."

"No, I don't want to die."

The mambo put her hand out, traced a circle around Max's eyes. "Then what do you want?"

Max exhaled, shook his head. The sea inside him called. He yearned to answer. "I want," he said at last, "the child."

"That not a problem. No one else is having it."

"No," he said, closing his eyes and pushing the mambo's hand away. "I want this thing, no matter what it does to me. It's part of me now. There are bonds . . . I never knew I could feel. Deeper than anything I've ever felt. Deeper than what I feel for the twins. The Beast, it's like a brother to me, sometimes good, sometimes bad. But this child, I made it with my body, my sins. It's the sum of my life so far. The consequence of my acts.

"I don't want to let it go anymore. I don't want it to be born. Do you understand, Legba? I just want to keep the child inside me, where I can protect it from the world. From me. Where I can control it, stop it from coming after me."

"You want the feeling, don't you. Is it like flying

348

through the air for you, or like floating in the sea? Is it a song, or a drumming? Is it like a loa riding you, divine power pouring through you, light exploding in your head, blind joy running you into the ground, to death? Or is it like creation's dawn, soft and gentle, lifting the darkness, tempting you each moment, each day, with more color and radiance, revealing wonders and glories and secrets that make you restless for what's yet to come."

"I'm not . . . is it only that . . ."

"You can't keep children from what they want. The child wants, needs to be born. You got to let it go." The mambo rolled onto her back, closed her eyes. "A choice there is. How much of yourself you give when you let the child go."

The sea broke over Max's thoughts. The mambo sagged, her breath rattled.

"Wait, don't go," Max said, afraid Legba had finally killed his horse, left him forever. Left him to drown in the sea of his desire for his own child.

"Wait, the spirit, you talked of a spirit—what is it? What does it want?"

Silence swallowed him, and he fell asleep to the steady sound of the heart monitors registering the beat of their lives: slow and erratic for the mambo, strong and steady, with a slight echo, for him.

The baby moved like a wrestler twisting out of one hold after another in his belly. Every jab and kick, every shrug and roll, brought Max gasping out of his dream of the sea. Just as quickly, he dove back, eager for the ocean's rocking embrace, for the sense of closeness and purpose he felt in the pull of its currents.

Sometimes the kick he felt was at his feet and legs, as if something under water had snapped a tail or fin against him as it swam past, and he woke startled, sweating, with the primal roar of an enraged land animal ringing in his ears. The fact that it seemed to call his name, seemed to chase him with the same desperate urgency with which he wished to surrender to the water, frightened him more than passing images of mouths brimming with sharp teeth tearing through his body.

Waking, he watched shadows ripple on the wall.

Waking, he glanced over at the mambo, her mouth open, skin pasty.

Waking, he saw Mr. Tung standing at the doorway.

Standing.

Max fought against the sea, forced himself to stay in the waking world.

Mr. Tung, sweat pouring down his contorted face, shoulders shaking, took a step toward Max.

Something gripped his arm. He pulled away, turned. The baby kicked, and he gasped. The mambo, her body shaking, blood trickling from her mouth, cried out, "The angel! It's here—"

Max said, "Angel?"

Mr. Tung looked back over his shoulder at the pod of surveillance equipment, grabbed at the fabric over his heart. "Help me," he croaked. "It's coming for me—"

Max said, "What angel?"

Mr. Tung staggered to the foot of Max's bed, eyes growing wide. A swipe of his hand knocked the candle on the chest down. His face took on the color of flame and shadows, and his knees buckled.

Max crept backward on his back as he watched the

twins' latent command kill Mr. Tung. He did not understand how the man managed to keep moving beyond the first step. He should have died immediately, dropping to the floor as soon as he crossed the boundary drawn for him.

The mambo rolled over, tearing loose wires and IVs, and threw herself partway over Max. Mr. Tung collapsed and tried to save himself by holding on to the bedposts. The frame shook, the night tables tipped, the candle on the mambo's side toppled. Wisps of smoke curled up from the mattress edge. Shadows flickered with frantic abandon on the walls, like a dance of witches. "Enoch," the mambo whispered desperately in Max's face. Her sour breath had the acrid sting of smoke.

Max grabbed her shoulders, pushed her up off of him, shook her. "Who?"

Mr. Tung screamed. Stood up. His face twisted into a mask of horror, as if he had seen the hell to which his soul had been consigned.

Outside, doors opened, smashing against walls. The door to the Box, and to the loft.

Max grunted as the child in his womb delivered a savage kick, as if anticipating a fight for its life.

"Tonton!" Kueur cried out from beyond the doorway.

"Mr. Tung!" shouted the guards rushing into the loft.

Mr. Tung snarled. His eyes darkened into lightless pools of night untouched by Creation.

"Enoch . . ." the mambo said, chest heaving, "an angel . . . of destruction, taking on . . . the Lord's wrath . . . against your sins . . . yours . . . a mad angel, broken heart . . . beware the mad angel—"

A flame crawled up along the sheet, crackling and snapping as it consumed cotton and peeked over the top of the mattress.

Mr. Tung jumped on the bed, crouched. He pulled a thin, black ceramic blade from an ankle strap. Spasms seized the mambo.

Max tried to hold her, protect the fetus, position himself to counter Mr. Tung. He noticed Mr. Tung had stopped breathing.

The twins burst through the bedroom doorway.

The mambo slipped out of Max's hands. One of her convulsive kicks caught Mr. Tung in the chest as he lunged. Max's countering kick was snagged by wires. A medical console flipped over. The mambo cried out as Mr. Tung's knife stabbed her in the back of the neck.

"Farewell," said Legba in the dying light of the mambo's face. "My apologies . . . to her family . . ."

Max threw the mambo aside and grabbed Mr. Tung's head, trying for a head snap. Mr. Tung pulled the knife out of the mambo, stabbed again. Max felt bone break, the blade penetrate his arm. Pain shot straight to his head.

Kueur and Alioune jumped on top of Mr. Tung.

Men in suits piled into the bedroom.

Flames surged up the side of the bed, catching on the mattress. Fire-control foam sprayed down from recessed nozzles.

Mr. Tung pulled out the knife, tried to bring it down again. Alioune held him back, wrapping both her arms around his. Kueur growled as she reached down his pants, ripped at his crotch. The men in suits tackled them from behind, pushed the twins and Mr. Tung toward Max. Hands grabbed, pushed, punched. Bodies piled on top of bodies. Fire pinched flesh. Foam soaked fabric, and a chemical smell filled the air.

A fist landed a glancing blow against Max's belly, despite his frantic efforts to protect himself.

The Beast's roar filled Max's mind. The sound chased off fear and doubt and sickness, shook thought and feeling loose from their moorings in his mind, shot rage like liquid lightning through his body.

It was as if he had never experienced the Beast's appetite before, had not lived with its hunger all his life, had not spent every waking moment satiating the Beast's needs when it was still alive in him. The Beast's voice flowed through him like an instant intoxicant, sparking flashes of hot memory: the flesh, the cries of pain, the spasms of pleasure. For the moment of remembering the Beast was alive, and its power was his.

And the Beast was like a shark breaking through net keeping it from the sea; a leviathan breaking for air through a thick blanket of suffocating kelp.

Max pulled his legs back and under himself, rose up onto his knees, and fended off a pair of men trying to restrain him. He slid out of their attempted locks, struck one in the throat, the other in the solar plexus, sending them both gasping for breath as they scrambled off the bed. Sheets and covers snapped, the mattress rocked, foam flew up even as the rain of fire retardant slowed. Only a pair of candles remained lit, their flames the only fire in the room, but even in the dim light Mr. Tung was easy to spot in the press of bodies. He was at the center, his own men now joining in the twins' effort to contain him. Unlike the twins, they were trying not to hurt him, and interfered with Kueur's and Alioune's attempt to finish him. The conflict allowed Mr. Tung to lash out with his knife every few moments, cutting Alioune on the thigh, stabbing one of the suited men in the eye, scraping Kueur's skull, stabbing himself in the shoulder.

Max, riding the power of the Beast's rage, bullied his way through the crowd, ignoring his belly's cumbersome weight, and locked his fingers around Mr. Tung's throat.

He tore Mr. Tung's flesh with his nails. Forced his fingers through the wounds. Dug into muscle, feeling the artery, the trachea. Confirmed Mr. Tung's heart no longer beat, his lungs no longer drew air.

Mr. Tung suddenly took a breath, shocking Max so that he nearly allowed the ceramic blade to penetrate his ear. But the dead man had only taken air to speak, though Max could not understand his babbling. Max probed with his fingers, tore out the voice box, snapped the windpipe. Dug through blood-soaked tissue, tugged at bone.

The twins, sensing he had a purpose, fought off the men in suits who were bearing down on Max. In a few moments, he succeeded in ripping Mr. Tung's head away from his body. The Beast let loose a triumphant scream that scraped Max's throat raw.

The suited men hesitated, shock on their faces, as Max threw away the head and dug into Mr. Tung's body, which still moved and struggled. The knife point pierced the back of Max's shoulder, but Kueur caught the weapon arm and pulled it away before the blade could penetrate through muscle to bone. Max grimaced, and the Beast tasted its death, remembered, and faltered.

He reached into Mr. Tung's torso, closed his fist around the heart, pulled the organ out. More of the suited men fell back when Max threw the heart after the head. Mr. Tung paused. Kueur reached down his pants again, finished the work she had started and pulled out his genitals. Alioune worked her hand through his back, drew out a liver.

The darkness left Mr. Tung's eyes, where the head lay on the floor. Mr. Tung's body slumped to the floor, the ceramic blade clattering on the wood. The smells of blood and shit and chemical foam and smoke and burnt linen combined to spice the bedroom's night.

The Beast hung on to Max as the sea rolled up to take him, as the baby in Max cried out for attention, for sustenance and nurturing.

Strength left Max, and he melted into the twins' arms. He closed his eyes, clutching his belly with his hands, the Beast with his soul.

A storm shook and tossed the sea. Clouds roiled, dark and wounded, bleeding flashes of lightning. Wind howled with the voice of outrage, keened with the pain of betrayal. Angry waves drove Max back and forth in the rift between the himself and the sea. He no longer felt a part of the ocean. The current that had pulled him to a distant shore still tugged at his legs, but other currents and undertow and waves fought for him, dragging him first in one direction, then another. An invisible boundary, like the idea that he belonged to the living, waking world and the sea was a place of dreams and the not-yet-alive, surrounded him, protected him from the worst of the primal punishment.

Something took hold of Max, dragged him through water. He suddenly found himself clinging to a rocky precipice that might have been the highest peak of a sunken continent peeking above the waves, bracing himself in a crevice as if his life depended on his hanging on to land.

Next to him crouched a shadowy figure, wet and shivering and somehow insubstantial, like a black spirit cut from smoke and shadow. Its talons scraped stone. Its growl echoed thunder.

Man and Beast huddled in the shelter of cold, hard rationality, bonded by death, saved by the life they had just taken in the waking world. Man and Beast, they hung on to the reality of their life together, determined to survive until the storm tides of intimacy with the new life in his body ebbed.

Staccato gunfire ripped through the safety of dreams. Bullets pinged as they bounced off of medical equipment casing, the surveillance pod and armored walls, ricocheting until they embedded themselves or exhausted velocity. Muzzle flash shattered the darkness, burned off images of stormy seas and rocky crags. The roaring echoes of every shot drowned the thunder reverberating in his skull.

Max curled into a ball as he lay on the bed, protecting his belly with legs and arms. By the light of the gun flashes, he knew Kueur and Alioune had seized two nine-millimeter automatics each from some of Mr. Tung's fallen guards and were returning fire coming from the bedroom doorway. He was grateful the twins' fire was keeping incoming to occasional blind shots.

"Cover!" Alioune shouted to Max over the deafening roar of the fire fight. Double clicks and metallic slides signaled her reloading while Kueur kept up her fire.

Bullets whined past Max's ear like angry hornets. Grazed his right hip, punched through thigh meat, stung nerves. He grunted, cursed his stupidity in trying to protect the baby while forgetting the most basic principle of survival: duck for cover. He crawled off the bed as Alioiune leapt over him, guns blazing. Once on the floor, he found Mr. Tung's ceramic knife, grabbed it, went under the bed wishing for a gun. The twins closed in on the doorway from both sides of the room, firing until their guns were empty. Standing at the bedroom entrance, they looked out at the rest of the loft. No one shot at them. They dropped their weapons and rushed to Max.

In the sudden quiet, Max counted the seconds he had lost to dream, the moments the gun battle had taken. The twins helped him out, tried to get him to stand. But he fell back onto the bed soaked with blood and fire extinguishing spray, betrayed again by a body responding not to his will but to the needs of his child. He looked to the ruined surveillance equipment above the doorway and wondered what the observers on the other end had made of what had happened. He threw the knife at the remains of the pod. It clattered uselessly against a lens housing and fell to the floor. Then the accumulated seconds and moments crashed over him and he gave up his concerns to the twins as dream claimed him.

In this dream, the infant was human. It was hot, and though it suckled at his breast Max felt the heat of its body against his thigh. It gnawed at his teat, sucked the milk of life from him. Drained him, left him a shell of brittle skin. Dragged his soul down, down to the sea, the raging sea . . .

Floating in the water, rolling up and down with the steady swell of waves, salt taste in his mouth, Max suddenly panicked, flailed and splashed, sank, blubbering and choking, crying out for the Beast, reaching for the rock island of rationality that had somehow slipped away, until Alioune said, "Stop struggling. We have enough to contend with."

He came out of the dream spitting blood, his wounded thigh throbbing under the field dressing. Kueur and Alioune were carrying him, by the knees and shoulders, out of the ruined bedroom to the wreckage of living room. His belly lay like a mountain across his body. Tremors passed through the baby it sheltered, and in the aftershock blades of pain carved his spine into slivers of agony. He cried out. His voice sounded small and frail in the silence.

The twins brought him out to the couch, laid him out on the cushions, threw blankets over him. Glass crunched underfoot as they walked back and forth, dragging bodies, tossing guns into a pile, clearing broken furniture. He dragged himself up to look out the window. The world was dark beyond the glass, and he wondered how much time had passed since he learned of his pregnancy—a day, a week, a month? Disoriented, he started to ask the twins. Then the darkness flooded through the window and engulfed him.

Storm winds whipped him, walls of water pummeled him, as the storm continued unabated in the world of dream. He turned to the shadow figure and asked, "How long?"

Muscles he never knew existed squeezed, pinched, contracted in his lower abdomen and groin. Soon water seemed to hiss as it shot through gaps and crevices in the rock.

". . . the hell happened—"

"If we needed a critic, we would've called the *Times*, Dr. Plummer."

"I'm surprised the neighbors didn't call in a SWAT team, judging by these bullet holes."

"Our neighbors are discreet. They have done worse. Just check him, Doctor."

"No artery hit, some muscle tissue loss. Good field dressing—Who was it, you or Alioune? Nice job. Although he won't be running anytime . . ."

"The baby?"

"Fine, as far as I can tell. Due, judging by the timing of his moans. Listen . . ."

"There are arrangements to make. . . ."

"And your wounds?"

"We will handle them ourselves."

"I suppose you expect me to deliver—"

"Do not worry, Doctor. Others are coming for that. Just make sure he's stable."

"And who's going to stabilize his surroundings?"

"Not you, Dr. Plummer. . . ."

"The girl? These dead men? The hospital equipment? This is New York City. Don't you think questions are going to be—"

"Let us handle the questions, Dr. Plummer. Vans are on the way to cart out the bodies. There is a . . . market for such things. The mambo knew the risks, and reparations will be made to her people. As for the equipment, you're going to have to bring in whatever's necessary for our Tonton's survival."

"But that's outrageous. . . ."

"No, Doctor. But what we will do to you if you do not cooperate will be."

*   *   *

The air smelled of cordite and burnt plastic and ozone and opened guts and sweat and perfume. Max opened his eyes. Daylight filled the room, though the long shadows told him it was dusk again. He tried to remember the last dawn he had seen, and could not. He tried to recall why his thigh was bandaged, and did not want to.

The shadows moved. Low voices, heavy breathing, the grunts of heavy labor followed the shadows, which in turn lay at the feet of men in coveralls with a moving company's logo and name—Absolute Transport—on their back. A thin, bald man with glasses and an electronic clipboard stood by the loft's entry alcove speaking with Alioune.

"Our blood of killers is honored to perform this service, mistress."

"Did you check the walk-in freezer and pantry?"

"Of course, mis—"

Alioune slapped him, knocking his glasses off and sending him staggering backward a step.

The man fumbled with the clipboard, picked up his glasses, went back to Alioune, got down on his knees, and bowed his head. The movers glanced hungrily in their direction as they wheeled out plastic wardrobe boxes marked "Couture" and bins filled with a jumble of electronics parts and furniture.

A contraction seized Max, and he cried out, putting his hands over his belly in a protective gesture. The baby within kicked. The Beast, still hanging on to the island that was its shared reality with Max, barked a faint protest, then returned its attention to the tableau of Alioune standing over the moving man with her hands on her hips, one brown leg protruding from the slitted white silk and red embroidered dress she wore. IV tubes and wires connecting Max to a new set of monitors stacked beside the couch swung and rattled as he shifted on the couch trying to make himself more comfortable.

"Tonton," Kueur said, descending on the couch, brushing her hand across Max's forehead. "It's almost over. Mrs. Chan and the others are on their way. Dex is ready in the Box. We have him on the brink of releasing his soul, which we've purified and distilled. Hang on, Tonton Bébête. We've worked so hard for you, for the baby. Just a little while longer."

Alioune glanced at Max and her stern expression softened. To Max, they both looked as if they had not rested since his ordeal started. Their wounds were bound with bandages stained by old blood.

"Those look like bad hits," he said, gazing pointedly at their dressings.

"If we were mortal," said Kueur. "They'll heal themselves, though the process will take a little time, and our strength."

"I didn't realize . . ."

Alioune's stern expression returned. "What did you expect? We were taking fire in an armored room. We might as well have been in a tank with a live grenade. Maybe next time you had better rethink your security precautions."

"Thank you, my loves," he said, shame, worry, and joy mixing with an equal measure of anger over their injuries. He traced a line from the corner of Kueur's eye, over her cheek, to her lips, with his thick forefinger while looking to Alioune and smiling. He hoped the touch and the smile were both gentle, and harbored none of the pain or savage rage he was holding inside himself.

"Be careful how you address me," Alioune said, returning her attention to the man kneeling before her.

He whimpered, put his face to the floor, and kissed the brocade on her white satin slippers. "Forgive me, mistress. I was intoxicated by your presence, and the killings, and the honor of performing a service for you and your sister. I forgot myself. Please, on behalf of the blood, I place myself at your mercy."

A pair of movers carrying plastic trash bags paused behind Alioune, tongues rapidly darting over lips, eyes squinting as if to filter out extraneous stimuli and allow only particular details to penetrate and fertilize their imaginations.

"Some other time," Alioune said, crossing her arms. "Be done quickly. We have other matters to attend to."

"Your pleasure," the man said and scrambled away, hissing and snapping at the movers, who flinched and gritted their teeth and picked up their pace with quiet, manic efficiency.

"The angel," Max said, trying to hold on to Kueur's arm as she stood and went to the walk-in closet near the entry alcove. Her cool, soft skin slid against his bloated fingers.

"We know," said Alioune, replacing Kueur by Max's side. "Enoch. We heard the mambo on the Box's surveillance feed."

"The name of Cain's son, the first murderer's child," Kueur said over her shoulder. She laughed. "Do you remember the missionary and the Bible he was so eager to teach to lost little children, sister?"

"The first half of the book; the end of his dying. They were much the same."

"What can we do?" Max asked, waving aside their memories, the irony in his hunter's name. "How do you exorcise an angel?"

"We don't know," said Kueur from inside the closet. She was going through his equipment containers, tossing out weapons and ammo clips, makeup kits and wigs, uniforms, timers, detonators, surveillance equipment, alarm-killing and lock-penetration devices, medical supplies, plastic packets of documentation and identification. "But maybe something else can be done to get rid of it."

"The loa warned me. It's going for the child so it can possess it and kill me," said Max, staring at his belly. "Like it possessed Mr. Johnson, and Mr. Tung. It couldn't enter any of the spirit-walkers and healers, but men with weak souls succumb to its will. A child with no soul is a perfect vehicle."

Alioune put a hand on Max's stomach. "It should have possessed the child by now, if that was its intent."

"That would've given us time to counter its move before birth. And it would have had to fight me, and the Beast, while inside me. No, it will come to the child when I'm most vulnerable. When I'm delivering. It can complicate the procedure, assassinate me as it climbs out of my womb." He winced at the next contraction.

"There'll be help if it tries that," said Kueur. "Healers are on their way. Those with the blood bonds to you, or to us. You're due."

"I can tell. By the way, you won't find anything of any help in there. Those are just the standard kits I keep at every safe house. No magical implements, no tomes. We'd have to go break into the Vatican library to find out the kind of information we need to rid ourselves of this seraphim. And those electronics are useless. Mr. Tung's machines couldn't harness or even detect it. Standard tools of the trade, unless you've changed your mind and decided to gut the baby as it comes out.

Alioune gave him a horrified look. Kueur stepped out of the closet, frowning, shook her finger at him. "How can you talk like that!"

Max closed his eyes. Exhausted, he sank back into drowsy reverie. "Fine."

Two contractions later, the sharp clang of metal on metal brought him up. The traffic of killer movers had thinned. Alioune, sitting with him, looked to the closet as Kueur carried out several pressure bottles and a remote trigger, dumped them on the floor.

"Do you know what you are doing?" she asked.

"I'm no chemist, but I think I can arrange this."

"Without blowing us up?"

"Perhaps we should ask Tonton."

Alioune glanced at Max, who relaxed into the waiting numbness of hanging on to rock, weathering the storm, bracing for the next contraction.

"He has his own problems."

"Then it's up to us. You there, leave that planter where it is."

Gas hissed. A contraction came. The twins dismissed the blood of killers. Another contraction came, sooner than he anticipated. He wanted to ask someone—the twins, the shadow Beast on the rock next to him, Legba, the baby— what exactly was contracting if his plumbing was wrong for the task to come. It felt like new muscle, right behind his genitals and in his belly, rippling with spasms. But another contraction came, and the question fled before the pain.

Then Mrs. Chan came in, hefting her cane as if preparing to defend herself while the mover with the clipboard bowed to her and left. The four Navajo healers followed, flashing turquoise rings and silver buckles, along with the shuwwafat, unveiled but still mysterious, wearing loose, flowing pants and a blouse; the oknirabata in his old suit and a new pair of Air Jordan sneakers; and the sadhu with a freshly trimmed beard and a large, loose white shirt made from an ethereal weave of cotton. They all carried travel bags packed with what Max assumed was sand and stone and herbs, and whatever else was going to be needed in the hours to come. Dr. Pullman buzzed, and through the intercom announced he was bringing up his equipment through the service elevator.

From the Box, Dex moaned.

Max drifted in and out of a haze of pain. The Beast howled for the both of them, and the rock they held on to was cold and gave no comfort. The twins and the healers wandered into and out of focus around him.

"I am his latest sifu," he heard Mrs. Chan tell the sadhu as they both sipped tea over Max. "He has mastered many arts, and came to me several years ago to learn what I had to teach."

"Does he teach you?"

"I am not interested in what he knows. I only agreed to take him on as my student to temper his savage spirit. And you?"

"He's my cousin. A distant cousin, according to my father. We met in India not too long ago. Visiting separately, we became rivals in a temple buried beneath one of the new high-tech centers they're building in Bangalore. We tasted each other's blood as he was about to kill me, and recognized each other. He had never met one of his family before. I was about to meet my next life. He offered me a chance to build karma in this life, and I took it. Together we took what we wanted from the temple, returned here, and since then have done nothing more than have dinner on occasion."

"Are you afraid of him?"

"He walks a path I might have taken. Might yet take. My father has not spoken to me since I've taken up with him."

"So?"

After a moment's hesitation, the sadhu said, "Yes."

"That is wise."

The oknirabata joined them, saying, "The mambo is gone."

Mrs. Chan said, "I know."

"Did you see what the twins did to the crystal healer?" the sadhu asked.

"He was not really one of us," Mrs. Chan answered.

"I wonder how many more will die," said the oknirabata. By his tone, Max understood he did not expect, or want, an answer.

"As many as needed, I suppose," the sadhu said.

"That's always the way with him. Sometimes good comes out of it." The oknirabata lifted his hands, smiled. "He killed the clever-man pointing the bone at me. Not to save me. He was spinning his own web. I just happened to benefit. Still, we belong to the same Dreaming." The oknirabata put his hands down. "Though I think my clan will dance and sing me back to the Dreaming long before he ever moves on."

"You can run," the sadhu said.

"So can you." The oknirabata laughed, dry and low. "You didn't even have to answer the twins' call."

"You can't outrun or ignore death."

"No."

"Better, I think, to carry karma on to the next life."

"Or the Dreaming."

The three fell into silent reverie. Dr. Plummer appeared suddenly over him, flashing a light into his eye. The doctor shook his head, placed a sensor pad on his temple, moved off. Farther away, talk between the Navajos, shuwwafat, and twins penetrated the fog of pain enclosing Max. The rhythm of their speech echoed the crashing waves of contractions washing through him. Max watched the group—four Navajo shamans and three women with the blood of Africa, Asia, and gods running through them—and wondered over the powers watching over him.

"Why do they call them cowboy boots?" the shuwwafat asked, her arms around the twins' waists in a maternal embrace.

The ancient Navajo looked at his boots and frowned. The youngest laughed. One of the middle Navajos tapped the youngest on the shoulder and said, with a smile, "We don't call 'em that on the res."

"Shit-kickers is what we call 'em," the youngest added.

"No," said the other man, who looked like the brother of the first middle Navajo, except for the turquoise in his eyes, ears pointed like a coyote's, and the silver in his hair. "They're called cowboy boots 'cause, first, we get us a cowboy, then we paint him, and then we skin him. Afterward, we make us a boot out of his skin and wear him. Like this." He lifted his foot, brushed off dust, and showed off the leather. The skin shade and pattern was different from that of the other boot the Navajo wore.

The old shaman shook his head and said, "He ain't all Indian, as you can tell. My fault, really. I was a wandering one, a hundred years ago. But we still like the part of him that ain't."

Darkness swallowed the figures, and moments later their laughter faded. For a while he heard the rustle of their clothing as they moved around the loft. Then he heard only the beating of hearts, his and the child's, his breathing, and his gasps of pain. In a moment in which muscles seemed to twist and wrench and squeeze his spine, he believed the twins and all the rest had been snatched away by the scarves, and that he was alone forever with the pain of the spirits of women he had raped and killed throughout the years. He believed, for an empty moment, that the spirits had killed those who tried to help him, and that their deaths had been added to the burden he had created for himself.

"Not their fault," he mumbled. "Not their fault." But no one answered him.

Power gathered in the loft like a wind trapped in a sealed cave, building in intensity with every contraction that seized Max. Candles and lamps distributed throughout the loft released sacred smoke and gave off halos of light. The Navajos stood near him, prayer sticks in hand, solemnly discussing whether to interpret a mad angel as Monster or spirit and debating the use of the Night Chant without proper preparation. The shuwwafat was in the kitchen preparing potions on the stove. Dr. Plummer, wiping sweat from his dark brow and working in shirtsleeves and tie, tinkered with connections between Max's monitoring equipment and a computer workstation set up in front of the Box, muttering "madness" to himself. The sadhu sat on the dining counter, cross-legged in the lotus position, chanting. The oknirabata held a mabanba stone in front of Max's face and said, "Come to take the big one out, this time." He smiled a gap-toothed smile and went to a stool, where he pulled a didgeeridoo out of his long travel bag. "Don't worry about that Djanba spirit," he said with a wink, then blew into the thick, wood instrument, filling the loft with the guttural breath of creation.

Mrs. Chan rolled a cart up to the couch, picked at a tray of shiny surgical instruments as if considering which dumpling to consume next. "Look at what your kind Dr. Plummer let me borrow."

Max glanced at the instruments and said, "Only because he's afraid to use them on me himself."

"A wise man knows his limitations."

The twins emerged from the Box, moving Dex into the main room on a gurney covered beneath a red silk sheet. "The counter or the couch?" Alioune asked Mrs. Chan.

"Leave him on the couch," she answered. "I will get the rest of what I need from his medical supplies." She adjusted the sheets on which he lay, and the blankets and prayer rug covering his nude body.

"There are things we must do; sacrifices to prepare, complications to defend against," Kueur said, holding Mrs. Chan back with a hand on her shoulder.

"There usually are, in these situations," Mrs. Chan replied. "Do not concern yourself. You do what you have to do, dear, and I will follow. As long as we both hold the innocent's life as most important."

"Yes, we do," Max said.

Kueur smiled at him, and Alioune nodded her head.

"Good," said Mrs. Chan, passing her palm over Max. "Now please excuse me while I untangle the child's flow of chi from the mother's. We would not want to make any unnecessary cuts."

The Navajos began singing as the shuwwafat brought a cup of her concoction to Max. After he downed the thick, spiced drink, a chilling numbness crept down from his stomach to his legs. He tensed, afraid the witch had betrayed him, or had been possessed by the angel. But she returned with a warm, greasy substance that she proceeded to spread over his naked belly after drawing back the blankets. "Be calm, boy," she said with a disdainful half-smile. "Just smoothing the way for the child to come. Don't want you jumping around too much when the way gets opened."

A cool sense of remoteness settled over Max as the shuwwafat's mixtures worked their way into his body and spirit. He felt himself floating out of his body until he hovered a few feet over the couch staring down at himself. At the same time, he sank deeper into his flesh, past the rocky crevice that held him and the Beast over the howling sea, the needy embrace of his child, the pain of his tormented flesh, until he was trapped and sealed in a tomb beyond all sensation.

The sadhu brought up a large pot of hot, fragrant water and set it beside Mrs. Chan. While the sadhu chanted prayers, Mrs. Chan dipped cutting tools into the water, cleansing them. The baby moved as if fighting off a gang of robber newborns. The contractions came in fanatical waves, one after the other, but Max felt none of them.

Kueur and Alioune rolled the gurney to the end of the couch and swiveled Dex until the red silk sheet had fallen off and he was nearly erect, facing Max while strapped from head to foot to the gurney bed.

"The sacrifice is ready," Kueur said.

Mrs. Chan glanced at the ruins of Dex, looked away quickly, face wrinkled in an expression of distaste. "Please," she said, then stopped after exchanging looks with the twins.

"His pain is an illusion," the sadhu said in a gentle voice, breaking his chant and patting Mrs. Chan's back.

"Neither truth nor illusion can touch him anymore," said Alioune.

"He is ready," Mrs. Chan said, returning her attention to Max. She took a deep breath, grasped a long, thin instrument, and began to pick at the birth knot of his belly button.

Kueur and Alioune caressed Max as they danced around the couch, slowly at first, like a pair of eels undulating against the current along a riverbed. They glided around the cart full of instruments, Mrs. Chan, the sadhu and the shuwwafat kneeling to either side of her, Dex, the wires and monitor racks and IV stands. The Navajos stood just outside the circle of their dance, and flinched whenever Kueur or Alioune came near them. But the low, driving force of their chanting continued without interruption.

The twins' hands, arms, and legs wove a tapestry of motion in which Max detected ancient sigils that hung in the air like contrails, warping perspective and bending light before evaporating. The twins stared, unblinking, beyond Max and the material reality of the loft. To Max, they

seemed to gaze at bright points of truth veiled in supernatural beauty and terror, peering into the heart of mysteries, which in turn cast the shifting shadows he saw
flicker across their eyes. Max tried to follow their line of
sight and share their vision, but his floating self saw only
the hazy boundary just beyond the circle of his caretakers,
and his buried self saw nothing at all.

The twins danced faster, leaping, darting, spinning, as
they spiraled into Max. The heat of their bodies made the
air shimmer. Their scent was an intoxicant, musky with a
bite like pepper. The hoarse rhythm of their breathing
added a ragged beat to the sounds of singing, chanting,
and blowing. Their dance lured him to places he could not
go, left him unbalanced, between worlds. He became dizzy
watching them and focused instead on Mrs. Chan's work,
until the sight of himself being peeled open unsettled him
and he turned to the hazy border and watched for the mad
angel's intrusion.

Dex's scream brought him back to the operating theater.
The twins had not touched him, but his flayed, broken,
gem-encrusted body writhed under the bonds. His cry reminded Max of a baby's first wail: an innocent confronted
by the corrupting newness of the world.

Instinctively, he looked down at himself, watched Mrs.
Chan clear away blood and fat around a bone-colored,
leathery pod seated atop his organs and entrails, writhing
with the baby's struggle for birth. A cord, pulsing with the
flow of blood, wound around the pod and entered it from
the bottom. Spasms ran through the muscles surrounding
the pod holding it in place.

The shuwwafat passed a surgical saw to Mrs. Chan, who
began to cut open the pod. A feeling of loss washed over

Max, trickling through his mind like the rivulets of blood flowing from the gash Mrs. Chan was making in the pod. He wanted to protect the pod, the child. He did not want to hear the birth cry, its recognition of reality's betrayal.

He felt the baby turn away from him, reach for the light coming through the opening in the pod. The raging storm died away in him as the baby sensed the presence of other people, and their souls. Inside Max, the sea fled, the sky cleared, the storm passed. He found himself and the Beast standing on a mountain peak surveying a dry, dusty expanse of desert wasteland, trying to find the limits of tracks of earth untouched since gods first shaped dirt and rock.

Pain embraced Max. It dragged him down from his floating viewpoint, dug him out of his tomb. He found himself in his body once again, alone with his bond to the Beast, which was roaring in triumph at the severing of ties with the baby.

He reached out to the twins, hungry for their comfort. They danced through his fingers, leaving blood from their reopened wounds on his hand. He tried to rise, to latch on to them and tell them to stop before they killed themselves. But the sadhu held him down with a light touch, and the twins continued their dance though they stumbled and tripped, and the magic they wove showed signs of unraveling.

Mrs. Chan completed her first cut into the pod womb. She and the shuwwafat pried the lips apart. A moist, sucking sound rose briefly above the sacred songs in the air. A tiny, bloody hand pushed out.

Max was blinded by pain. He screamed until his voice was raw, and he thrashed under the shuwwafat's and sadhu's fumbling attempts at restraining him.

"We're losing stability, here," Dr. Plummer shouted. "It's time for the sedatives."

Mrs. Chan shoved a thick slab of wood between Max's teeth, and he bit down hard, moaning, rocking his head back and forth. "No," she yelled back at Dr. Plummer. "We will do this as it was planned." To Max she said, "Hold still. Breathe. Remember your discipline. Unless you want to force him to work on you and your child."

Max focused on his body and its pain, trying to regain the distance the shuwwafat's potions had given him from sensation. The Beast raged, distracting him with its only emotion. He grabbed hold of the couch, locked his body, trembled from the agony. Tears burned his eyes.

"Should I push or something?" he asked between clenched teeth, desperate for something to do.

Mrs. Chan shook her head, scoffed, "Push with what? Through where?" She pulled out a length of crimson cloth from the pod. Max thought she had used it to sop up his blood, until he remembered the scarves, blood red, the symbol of the spirits of his victims. Painfreak. The rape by ghosts. Mrs. Chan glanced at the silk scarf in her hand and then threw it away.

Max wished Kueur and Alioune did not have to dance. He needed their love to balance the pain with pleasure. He wanted the warmth of their bodies to take away the chill in his spine.

Dex relaxed in his bonds. His mouth stayed opened, but he stopped screaming. The crystals in his eye sockets filled with light, one blue, the other green. Light gathered in his mouth, strained from his ears and nose genitals, streamed out, flying up at first, then dipping toward the floor before finally settling into the trail of shimmering air behind the dancing twins.

What was left of Dex's soul flowed along the bridge built by Kueur and Alioune. It spiraled down to the child's emptiness, balanced between heaven and hell on the magic of mortal will and demonic power.

Suddenly, the soul sparked and slipped. A cry split the air, thin and high-pitched, like a distant keening. The stream of light spilling from Dex strained against the path leading to its receptacle, as if tempted by another destination. The air behind Dex wavered like a heat mirage as the outline of a human form appeared, arms spread. Flickering shadows on the wall behind Dex lengthened, curled, shivered with growing frenzy.

Seraphim, Max tried to say through the bit. Enoch. Spreading its wings. Luring the newborn's soul away.

But the twins kept dancing. The shuwwafat and Navajos sang, the sadhu chanted, the oknirabata blew into the didgeeridoo. The power of Kueur and Alioune's primal sorcery kept the soul on the bridge, while the sacred sounds of mortal music drowned the angel's alien song and kept it at bay.

The soul light poured into the hole in the pod. Warmth spread through Max, dampening his pain and fear. A gurgling sound rose from the pod. Max's heart skipped with shock and excitement over the tiny voice.

Mrs. Chan bore down with her instruments on the leathery wall while the soul transfer was completed. Dex's last gasp came with the light leaving his eyes and the extinguishing of the fire coming from his mouth. He sagged against his bindings. The twins fluttered to the floor, gasping for air.

Dex's head snapped back up. The crystals in his eyes turned black. The air behind him lost its mirage of a human figure as the angel took over the empty shell of Dex's body and screamed in a voice Max was certain the twins had never managed to draw from him.

"Ani Enoch!" Dex cried out, the scream dying into hoarse speech made ragged by sporadic breathing, as if the angel was having difficulty playing such a delicate instrument as a deceased human body. *"Achad mayalphi malachi chuurban shel Alohim. Ani haza'am shel Alohim. Ani hanakamah shel Alohim. Ani basi besh'velcham."*

The shuwwafat and sadhu fell silent, and the Navajos' song diminished as the shaman with the turquoise in his eyes and the silver in his hair turned to Max and said, "I am Enoch, one of the Lord's thousand thousand angels of destruction. I am the Lord's wrath, I am the Lord's vengeance. I have come for you."

Max struggled to sit up, but gave way to the shuwwafat's insistent pushing. "What—"

The Navajo said, "It speaks Hebrew. We know the tongues of lost tribes, though this wisdom is one of our secrets. Don't you tell a soul."

The angel spoke again, making the oknirabata lose his breath. *"Bayamim elah shel merivah. Itah'avodah shel Alohim he gadvlah v'norah. Ha'pashaim shelocham tzo'akim le'tagmolim. Aval haim adayin lo maspik gedolim l'hasav es t'shumas ha'lev shel Alohim."* It wrenched an arm out of its restraint and clawed at the other straps holding Dex's corpse.

The sadhu went to the twins, roused them out of their exhaustion. Mrs. Chan worked at removing a part of the pod's shell. The Navajo spoke, his voice quavering as only the oldest of his companions still sang. "In these days of strife, the Lord's work is vast and terrible. Your crimes cry for retribution, but still they are not great enough to command the Lord's attention."

With a triumphant cry, the angel freed its other arm and its legs and slid off the gurney. The twins and the sadhu surrounded him, while the oknirabata hefted the boomerang he had pulled out of his travel bag.

"What the hell is going on over there?" Dr. Plummer yelled from behind his screens and consoles. "These readings aren't making any sense. Did something happen to Max? The baby? Do you need my help?"

Dex's crystal eyes were pools of darkness. He moved toward Max, saying, *"Ha'fachti es atzme l'anayim v'aznayim shel Alohim. Ani hezgarti es atzmme k'tzadik shel Alohim. V'nahafachte l'yad shelo. Ane basee bes'velcham b'shem Alohim."*

The oknirabata threw the boomerang, which struck Dex's corpse in the head and staggered the angel. The twins and the sadhu rushed him, landing bone-shattering blows against Dex's ribs, head, and spine. They forced him down to the ground and tried holding him in limb locks. Crystal fragments embedded in Dex's flesh cut the twins and the sadhu as their bodies ground against each other. The oknirabata approached with a stone knife in one hand, a curved bone in the other. He pointed the bone at Dex, singing of death.

"Shut up," Dr. Chan said to Dr. Plummer as she hunched over Max's belly, plunging her hands, each holding a bright metal instrument, into the pod.

Max reflexively threw his head back, arched his back, and clenched his jaws, trying to fight off the pain. He searched for a thought, an image to shield himself from sensation. For a moment, he distracted himself with concern for Mrs. Chan because she was not wearing surgical gloves, as Dr. Plummer always did when dealing with blood.

The Navajo translating for Max kneeled beside him and whispered, "I have made myself the Lord's eyes and ears. I have surrendered myself to the Lord's justice, and become his hand. I have come for you in the Lord's name."

"Manzer!" Enoch said, grabbing the sadhu's throat and snapping his neck. It threw the sadhu aside. Max's distant cousin crashed to the floor, and his billowing white shirt settled over him like a thin coat of frost.

The twins stood the angel up, trapped his arms, looked to the oknirabata. "To hell with the bone," Alioune said, breathless. "His head. Cut it off."

The angel kicked, breaking the oknirabata's knee. He broke away from Kueur, grabbed the oknirabata's knife hand, forced it back against the shaman. Killed him, with a thrust to the heart. The oknirabata flopped to the floor, one sneaker coming free, bone tapping wood as it came to rest.

Madness, Max wanted to say, agreeing with the doctor, weeping not from the pain but from the death of innocents and allies for his crimes. His sins. He yearned to throw himself at the seraphim, offer himself in exchange for the safety of the twins and the rest. The Beast strained against his control, ravenous for blood and violence. Only the child kept him back, bathing in the pain of birthing, and guilt.

"We're all in the shit now," the eldest Navajo said.

"Time to make us some angel boots," said the Navajo

translator, joining his brother, father, and nephew. They stood in a line between Max and the angel, one shaman for each holy point of the compass they might have taken if they chose to abandon Max, prayer sticks and steel knives in hand.

"Now we pay the price for his help in the old days," the Navajo ancient said, sadly, with resignation, not taking his gaze off Dex.

"Not long now," Mrs. Chan whispered. "Stay strong, for your child."

The shuwwafat whispered prayers in Arabic and glanced at the twins as she took one bloody, sharp-edged instrument from Mrs. Chan and handed her a clamp.

The twins fought with the seraphim. They exchanged a look, moved in perfect synchronization. Sweeping Dex's feet, they picked him up as he fell backward, lifted him, heaved him across the room. They collapsed, tripping over the bodies of the oknirabata and the sadhu, and lay still. With open eyes, fingers curled into fighting claws, and sides rising and falling, they looked like a pair of spent cheetahs watching their prey escape. Foam bubbled from their mouths. Muscles twitched with the memory of battle under their torn skin, the only means left to them of expressing frustration over their helplessness.

After sailing past the Navajos, Dex landed in Dr. Plummer's computer workstation. Monitoring equipment, keyboards, and screens tumbled to the ground. Sparks flew, raw electricity buzzed and hissed. Dex scrambled to his feet, pulling cables and wires. Max cried out as probes and sensors were ripped off of his skin. Dex's flesh crackled under the caress of brief electric arcs. The angel babbled, stopped, pressed hands against the sides of Dex's head.

Mrs. Chan grunted. Max felt his links to the child drop. The constructs of rock and sea dissipated, and the landscape of his mind returned to its familiar bleakness. He was alone with the Beast, which howled its exultation. Max felt a blast of cold air come through his belly.

"The child is free. Time to take the pod out," Mrs. Chan said. She and the shuwwafat deftly sliced connective tissue away the pod. Mixed in with bloody pieces of Max were more scraps of scarlet scarves.

Dr. Plummer emerged from the wreckage, cursing. He froze at the sight of Dex, then dug through his equipment until he found a medical kit. Pulling out gauze and a tube of antiseptic, he approached Dex.

"Sit down, man, and let me look at you," the doctor said, pulling Dex toward an overturned chair. "They wouldn't let me treat you before, but now I can get a—"

The angel shrugged. Dr. Pullman staggered backward, retrieved his balance, reached for Dex again. The angel caught the doctor's arm, and with its free hand grabbed hold of a monitor by its power cord and swung it into Dr. Pullman's skull. The swing's momentum carried the doctor into the Box, where he fell and did not get up.

The seraphim looked at Dex's hands, his feet. "Do not interfere," it said, leaving Dex's mouth open as if surprised by its speech.

"The monster haunts paths the man's soul once walked," the ancient Navajo said.

"Your angel's rummaging in the dead man's head," the Navaho translator said to Max. "Kicked up English, so it don't have to spit that old Hebrew no more. Probably knows how to tango now, too. Not so easy as taking a living man, is it, angel? Nobody in that meat to help you run the show? Like the white man coming here without us showing him how to hold his dick in the woods. Maybe he get it, maybe he don't. Maybe I get me a new pair of boots, one in angel hide, the other in dead man's skin. What's left of him, anyhow." The Navajo flourished his knife and let out a belligerent growl. The tip of his prayer stick trembled as if the spirit it confronted was too vast for it to contain with a single point.

"Good thing you can understand your angel now," said the youngest to Max, " 'cause it looks like we won't be around to translate much longer."

"No," said Max.

"Stand aside," Enoch commanded.

Again Max said, "No."

"Help me lift the pod," Mrs. Chan said. The shuwwafat reached into Max with Mrs. Chan, and together they interlocked their fingers under the pod and pulled it out.

Max convulsed, feeling as if all his internal organs were being removed. The two women placed the pod between him and the sofa back. The pod's walls moved, and something splashed inside. The leathery flesh was warm against Max's hip.

"Give the baby a moment to adjust to the separation," Mrs. Chan said. "We need to close him up."

"I will trim the skin growth," the shuwwafat said. "You sew and tie."

Max turned his head away from their work, the sound of cutting and the sensation of cool metal slicing and puncturing him, and thread stitching him together.

The seraphim walked. Dex's crystalline genitals clinked and shimmered like filled champagne glasses in the candlelight.

With the baby gone, Max saw no reason for more death beyond his own. The Beast filled the void within him with its hungry roar.

"Let it take me," he said to the Navajos. "Save yourselves, take the baby and the twins out of here."

Kueur stirred. "*Non,* Tonton."

Alioune tried to rise on one shaky arm. "Never."

Three Navajos exchanged glances. The other, tainted with blood from another realm, smiled. "Fuck it," he said, and leapt at the angel.

He rammed his prayer stick through Dex's right eye before the angel caught his wrists, crushed them, pushed the Navajo to the ground. A sharp knee to the shaman's jaw snapped his head back. Cracked bone. The Navajo slumped to the floor.

The other three Navajos jumped forward, slashing air and flesh. Four bodies converged, wrestled. Silver and turquoise flashed, along with steel. Wet, sucking sounds and harsh breathing were punctuated by occasional curses and cries of pain.

"Is this what you call vengeance?" Max shouted. "Taking innocent lives?"

The oldest Navajo was thrown aside, knife planted in Dex's other eye. The remaining two forced their blade hands toward Dex's throat as the twins encouraged them to sever the head. Suddenly, the seraphim leaned back, giving way to mortal strength for a moment. With a slight tap of their arms, the angel redirected the Navajos' desperate lunges. They stabbed each other in the shoulder and went to the floor in each other's arms, coming to rest atop broken prayer sticks and a pool of blood.

"If they served you, they were not so innocent," Enoch said.

The shuwwafat sobbed, picked up the oknirabata's stone knife, stood between Max and the angel. Mrs. Chan spared a moment from her furious stitching to slide her cane closer to her foot. Dex's left arm hung by threads of sinew to his shoulder. A deep gash had been carved into the base of his neck. The jewels of his eyes were gone, but living darkness swirled in the pits that had housed them. Gaps showed in the lines of multicolored gem teeth embedded in his shredded gums. Skin flapped loose, exposing ribs, broken bone, glistening organs, a still heart. His genitals glowed bright with the blessed light of angels. When he began walking toward Max, tiny gem fragments rained from his tattered flesh.

"They served me no more than you serve the one you call your Lord," Max said, pushing through Mrs. Chan's attempts to keep him down. "They served honor, and loyalty, and the bonds of blood and justice."

The angel stopped short, raised its good arm high, managed to haul the left arm partway. "Don't dare speak of justice. I will not hear it, not from your mouth. Killer! Rapist!"

"My victims did not send you," said Max, as Mrs. Chan tied off the last thread. He felt the warmth of trickling blood between his legs, running down his thighs.

"No, they could not. They have not yet come to rest."

"Your Lord did not send you."

"He . . . no."

"Then who are you to judge me? Who are you to sacrifice mortal souls to your desire for my death? How are you different from what I was, from what you condemn?"

"I am Enoch! I am an angel of destruction! I am vengeance, I am punishment. I am the consequence which cannot be escaped, the truth from which there is no escape!"

"And what is the consequence that you flee, seraphim? What is the truth that drives you to me, through the blood of so many living men? What is your sin, Enoch?"

The Beast's rage drove Max to his feet. He knocked Mrs. Chan back and upset the pod on the sofa so that some of the bloody fluid it contained spilled. A faint cry came from the pod.

The angel came forward, and the shuwwafat intercepted it. She cut fingers from the hand reaching for her, but could do nothing to stop the elbow that came around to smash the side of her face in. But even on the floor, she hacked at one of Dex's feet, until the seraphim stomped her head and neck and back to make her stop.

Mourning ululation erupted from Kueur and Alioune. Max leaned forward to take a step, but his body betrayed him. The world dropped away from him. Mrs. Chan gave him a push as he lost his balance and fell. He landed on the sofa inches away from the pod.

The Beast's rage was stoked higher by its failure to engage the angel. Max blinked back tears, sweat, blood. "What did Mr. Johnson do? Or Mr. Tung? Neither of them would have given their lives defending me. Yet you possessed them, led them to their deaths."

"Their souls were weighted with enough sin to warrant my attention. Doing the Lord's work granted them a measure of grace." The angel took a step toward Max. Dex's knee snapped from the punishment it had absorbed, gave out. On all fours, the seraphim continued to make its way toward the couch.

Max shielded Mrs. Chan with his body while she probed the pod's depths.

"He is ready to come out," she whispered.

Pride sparked in Max. He had a son. And his son was free from the sins of his father, the pain of his mothers. His son was an innocent. From all the hurt and death and terror of his life, he had brought out something that was its antithesis.

His pride shrank to nothing as he watched the angel's relentless progress. "Take him, train him," he told Mrs. Chan. "Show him the paths I never took."

"Do not flee your work so quickly, student," Mrs. Chan replied. "I cannot do it for you."

Max stared at the angel. "Pride," he said.

The seraphim looked up. The pools of blackness tugged at Max's soul.

"Pride is your sin, Enoch. You think to do the Lord's work. You take on the pain of wronged souls. But what are you? An angel. An instrument of your Lord's will, nothing more. How can you make yourself your Lord's eyes and ears? How can you take on your Lord's power of judgment? Would you take on your Lord's power of creation next? Would you make new worlds, new life? Do you dare usurp your Lord's place in his Heaven?"

The angel rocked from side to side, as if staggered by Max's words. "What do you know of my Lord? His burdens, His trials? He is Lord of all Creation, the Maker of Life. He made me, and you, and all the women you killed."

"He made the men and women you killed, as well."

"Do not presume to judge me, murderer. My Lord is my only judge."

"Then he should have been the one to judge me."

"He has turned his Might on the Chaos that assaults His Order. He battles the Other, and cannot spare—"

"Your Lord has abandoned you."

"You do not understand, sinner. You cannot understand."

Max shook his head. Out of the corner of his eye, he saw Kueur crawling toward the end of the couch. "You upset the order you claim to protect," he said. He held up his hand. "This is my instrument. It does not act on its own. You did not judge this piece of flesh and bone. You chose the soul that empowered the flesh to receive your punishment. That is the order of things in your Creation, is it not? The mind, the will, the soul, drives the flesh. Your Lord would never punish the instruments of mortal sin. He would never destroy a gun, or a knife, or a bomb, in place of their users. The instruments do not act on their own. And yet you do. You, an angel of destruction, one of your Lord's tools for punishment, presumes to act. Will I judge your Maker by what you have done? Will your Maker punish himself because of your reckless killing, the pain and suffering you have caused?"

"What do you know of Heaven? What do you know of the duties and responsibilities of its tenants?"

"I know there are no other angels of destruction seeking me out. I know angels of destruction are not rampaging across the world punishing all the other evil men and women who live with me next to all the weak and the innocent. I know your Lord has not judged me, for whatever reason he has deemed fit. And so I know that you have taken on more than your Lord intended. You are the evil one here, Enoch. You are the one who presumes to change the Order your Lord has created."

The seraphim reared, one arm flailing wildly, the other reaching for Max. "Abomination," Enoch screeched.

A hissing sound came from behind Max, and he turned. Kueur was draped over the end of the couch. She met his gaze, and he saw the dull flickering of life in her eyes. She pressed a button on the remote triggering device in her hand.

A bomb, he thought. No. What have they done? Destroy us all, that is not the way, not what I wanted—

A tower of flame rose up from the planter next to the couch, next to the angel. The planter's ficus tree was a black skeleton sheathed in fiery flesh.

The angel rolled away, shielded its eyes. "My Lord," it said in a hushed voice. "You have returned."

Fire crackled.

"My Lord, have you come to bear witness to my work? Have you come to bless my labor?" Fire whipped through the air, almost touching Dex's ravaged body.

"My Lord, speak to me. What is Your Will? Do you wish to pass Your Judgment on this soul beyond redemption?"

Fire receded, smokeless, until it was a thin rod of flame hugging its wooden frame.

"My Lord, please, I cannot bear this silence. Speak to me. Let me hear Your Voice once again. Let me feel the touch of Your Glory. Let my faith be renewed by Holy Presence."

The fire burned evenly, silently.

"I think your Lord has come to judge you, Enoch," Max said.

"No, He has come for you!"

"I've been here for quite some time, Enoch. You're the newcomer."

"No, my Lord! Tell him. Let him see the Truth of Your Divinity. Show him, my Lord."

The fire did not flicker.

"No, my Lord! Do not forsake me!"

"He hasn't forsaken you, Enoch. He's come to take you away."

"No! Please, my Lord! Do not protect this abomination! The souls of those he murdered cry out for his punishment. I hear them. Their agony fills the emptiness where once You dwelled, my Lord. They wait for him. They wait for You to send him to them. I only seek to help, to do what You shou—must do to satisfy the desire for vengeance that troubles those wronged souls, so they may one day come into Your Light!"

The seraphim threw himself at the couch, but his hand only managed to brush Max's foot. Max drew his leg back. He turned to catch a glimpse of his son before the angel closed with him, knowing even if he managed to destroy Dex's body, Enoch had many more to choose from. The Beast filled him, willing, eager to surrender itself to a final orgy of killing.

A cry split the air. Mrs. Chan held up a squirming, bawling lump of bloody flesh. She put herself between Max and the angel, leaning on her cane while cradling the infant in her other arm.

"Would you kill this one to render your judgement?" she asked.

Chubby legs kicking, the baby wailed.

The angel drew his good arm back as if it had been touched by hellfire. "My Lord, you have come again!" The darkness in Dex's eye sockets thinned, as if its essence were draining through a secret hole at the back of Dex's skull. "No, my Lord. Not from this one! How could You have chosen this, this thing through which to manifest yourself?"

Mrs. Chan took the boy in both her hands and thrust him toward the angel. Max wanted to haul her back, but could not reach her.

"Now you come? Now you answer my prayers? Now you break what is left of my heart?" Tears of starless night dripped from the Dex's angel-filled eyes. It balled its hand into a fist. Stared at the baby. Turned away. "I am not Judas, or even Peter. I am not one of the Pharisees. I cannot bring harm to the Lord again!"

Dex's body settled as the seraphim withdrew from its material house. The black pools vanished, revealing the two raw holes in bone. Silence smothered the loft.

Mrs. Chan prodded Dex's body with the cane, then offered the baby to Max. He took the child, stared in wonder at the pinched face, the blind eyes and round, open mouth. Holding the baby awkwardly against his chest, he offered one of his thick fingers to the baby's clutching hands. He looked over at Kueur, who smiled as she fingered the remote device. The fire in the planter went out.

The flicker of candlelight stroked Max's weariness. He closed his eyes, and when he opened them again the candles had burned out. He was lying on his back on the couch, his head in Alioune's lap, his feet in Kueur's lap. Mrs. Chan walked back and forth in front of him, nursing the baby. He closed his eyes again, opening them moments later, and found himself holding the baby. Mrs. Chan was framed in the doorway to the loft, absently spinning her cane. At last he gave himself to sleep, where he found no dreams or pain.

"So how did you know fire would be the key?" Max asked Kueur as they watched Alioune sitting between them on the couch, humming to the baby.

"We didn't," Kueur said, playing with the baby's hands. "But when we heard the demon pursuing you was an angel, we remembered the missionary's lessons, the Old Book's burning bushes. Of course, we've seen the desert's flaming gas vents during our traveling days. So we took some of your supplies, pieced together a device that would give us a decent flame, put it in the planter. We hoped for a moment's diversion during a fight, something to give us the room for a death blow."

"But if Enoch fled," Alioune said, "where can it hide?"

"Where all angels go when they've fallen," answered Max.

The blood of killers moved the last of the black plastic body bags out of the loft. The killer carrying the clipboard stopped in front of Max. "Busy night, sir?" he said with a smile.

Max waved him away, but the killer sank into a crouch.

"A van is waiting for your party downstairs, sir. I understand there were parties killed here connected to forces who will hold you responsible for their deaths. Arrangements have been made for your safety, until you can negotiate a settlement."

"Mr. Tung's and Mr. Johnson's—" Alioune began.

"I understand," said Max. "Your idea saved our lives." He reached over to the ficus, rubbed one of its a waxy leaves between his fingers. "Did your people replace this tree?" he asked the supervisor.

"No. We only have time for wet cleaning."

"I see." The gentle hands of the blood of killers helped him to stand and supported him as he walked toward the door. In a crevice between thought and action, the Beast sulked, worrying at the invisible feathers of escaped prey.

Alioiune gave Max the baby, then sagged into the arms of her helpers. "We must stop at a few stores in China-town," she said. "Before she left, Mrs. Chan told us what we needed to get for the baby."

"Not a problem," said the man with the clipboard. "And may I say what an honor it is to perform this service for you and your family. May I ask the name of your latest addition?"

Kueur stopped short. "Tonton?"

Max exchanged a look of despair and horror with the twins. In all that had happened, none of them had given a thought to naming the child.

Max resisted the pull of his handlers. He searched the ruined loft for a clue, something to offer the blood. He had a terrible premonition that if the child left his birthplace unnamed, he would not survive his first night. Then he relaxed and gave the twins a forlorn smile.

"We've named him in honor of those we've lost," he said. "Wulumu Bearpaw Chaudhri Mad Owl Pullman Ashes Blowing Shenara Child of Thunder."

"But we'll call him—" Kueur began.

"Not Dex," Max said.

"Max?" Kueur finished.

Gerard Houarner

"Feu?" asked Alioune.

"No, not fire," Max said. "Angel."

The twins nodded their heads and smiled, and all three were carried away, surrounded by the reverent murmuring of the blood of killers.

MOUNTAIN
KING RICK
HAUTALA

The mountain stands proud and alone, shrouded in mist and snow, and surrounded by legends and fear. Some say a demon resides on the rocky slopes, an unholy thing that periodically emerges from the mist to claim a life. Mark Newman has hiked the trails to the mountain's peak many times. He's heard the tales, but he doesn't believe them.

Mark learns to believe the tales on the terrible day his friend disappears in a sudden, blinding snowstorm while the two of them are on the mountain. On that day Mark witnesses something he knows can't be real, something hideous lurking near the summit . . . something that will kill again and again.

___4887-6 $5.99 US/$6.99 CAN

The
LOST
Jack Ketchum

It was the summer of 1965. Ray, Tim and Jennifer were just three teenage friends hanging out in the campgrounds, drinking a little. But Tim and Jennifer didn't know what their friend Ray had in mind. And if they'd known they wouldn't have thought he was serious. Then they saw what he did to the two girls at the neighboring campsite—and knew he was dead serious.

Four years later, the Sixties are drawing to a close. No one ever charged Ray with the murders in the campgrounds, but there is one cop determined to make him pay. Ray figures he is in the clear. Tim and Jennifer think the worst is behind them, that the horrors are all in the past. They are wrong. The worst is yet to come.

___4876-0 $5.99 US/$6.99 CAN

Elizabeth Massie

Wire Mesh Mothers

It all starts with the best of intentions. Kate McDolen, an elementary school teacher, knows she has to protect little eight-year-old Mistie from parents who are making her life a living hell. So Kate packs her bags, quietly picks up Mistie after school one day and sets off with her toward what she thinks will be a new life. How can she know she is driving headlong into a nightmare?

The nightmare begins when Tony jumps into the passenger seat of Kate's car, waving a gun. Tony is a dangerous girl, more dangerous than anyone could dream. She doesn't admire anything except violence and cruelty, and she has very different plans in mind for Kate and little Mistie. The cross-country trip that follows will turn into a one-way journey to fear, desperation . . . and madness.

___4869-8 $5.99 US/$6.99 CAN

DOUGLAS CLEGG

NAOMI

The subways of Manhattan are only the first stage of Jake Richmond's descent into the vast subterranean passageways beneath the city—and the discovery of a mystery and a terror greater than any human being could imagine. Naomi went into the tunnels to destroy herself . . . but found an even more terrible fate awaiting her in the twisting corridors. And now the man who loves Naomi must find her . . . and bring her back to the world of the living, a world where a New York brownstone holds a burial ground of those accused of witchcraft, where the secrets of the living may be found within the ancient diary of a witch, and where a creature known only as the Serpent has escaped its bounds at last.

___4857-4 $5.99 US/$6.99 CAN

Dorchester Publishing Co., Inc.
P.O. Box 6640
Wayne, PA 19087-8640

Please add $2.50 for shipping and handling for the first book and $.75 for each book thereafter. NY, NYC, and PA residents, please add appropriate sales tax. No cash, stamps, or C.O.D.s. All orders shipped within 6 weeks via postal service book rate. Canadian orders require $2.50 extra postage and must be paid in U.S. dollars through a U.S. banking facility.

Name_____
Address_____
City_____State_____Zip_____
I have enclosed $ _____ in payment for the checked book(s).
Payment <u>must</u> accompany all orders. ❏ Please send a free catalog.
CHECK OUT OUR WEBSITE! www.dorchesterpub.com

T. M. WRIGHT
Sleepeasy

Harry Briggs led a fairly normal life. He had a good job, a nice house, and a beautiful wife named Barbara, with whom he was very much in love. Then he died. That's when Harry's story really begins. That's when he finds himself in a strange little town called Silver Lake. In Silver Lake nothing is normal. In Silver Lake Harry has become a detective, tough and silent, hot on the trail of a missing woman and a violent madman. But the town itself is an enigma. It's a shadowy twilight town, filled with ghostly figures that seem to be playing according to someone else's rules. Harry has unwittingly brought other things with him to this eerie realm. Things like uncertainty, fear . . . and death.

___4864-7 $5.99 US/$6.99 CAN